Justice!

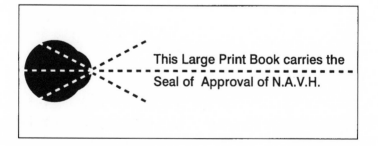

Wagons West:

The Empire Trilogy
Book 3

Justice!

Dana Fuller Ross

Thorndike Press • Waterville, Maine

Published in 2001 by arrangement with Book Creations, Inc.

Thorndike Press Large Print Western Series.

The tree indicium is a trademark of Thorndike Press.

The text of this Large Print edition is unabridged.
Other aspects of the book may vary from the original edition.

Set in 16 pt. Plantin.

Printed in the United States on permanent paper.

Library of Congress Cataloging-in-Publication Data

Ross, Dana Fuller.
    Justice! / Dana Fuller Ross.
      p.   cm. — (The empire trilogy ; bk. 3)
    ISBN 0-7862-3117-3 (lg. print : hc : alk. paper)
    1. Holt family (Fictitious characters) — Fiction. 2. Large
type books. I. Title.
PS3513.E8679 J87 2001
813′.54—dc21   00-053225

NORTH AMERICA

CHICHAGOFF IS.

BARANOFF IS.

Sitka

Alexander Archipelago (Alaska)

Pacific Ocean

TLINGIT VILLAGE

R. TOELKE '99

LIST OF CHARACTERS

JEFF HOLT — A peacemaker by nature, he prefers to settle his fights without violence. But sometimes a man has no choice . . . and now, pursued by enemies old and new, his only way out may be on the right side of a gun.

MELISSA MERRIVALE HOLT — Separated from her husband, Jeff, by fate and her father's intrigues, this dark-haired beauty has had to learn to fend for herself. Yet nothing could prepare her for what awaits in the wilderness . . . far from the man she still loves.

CLAY HOLT — Lethal with knife, gun, and fist, this brave and resourceful man is the nation's best hope of defeating a treacherous enemy from another land. He will need all of his skills and more to succeed as he must infiltrate the enemy camp . . . and get out alive.

LIEUTENANT JOHN MARKHAM — Young and eager to measure up to his heroic father's legacy, he joins Clay on his perilous mission. Now he must be ready to prove himself in the wilds of a beautiful frontier that can turn savage in an instant.

COUNT GREGORI ORLOV — A Russian diplomat posted to the remote wilderness of the Alaskan territory, he is bitter, disillusioned, and consumed with one thought: to kill by any means necessary Jeff Holt — the man he suspects of having an affair with his wife.

PROUD WOLF—When he came east to be educated in the white man's ways, Clay's brother-in-law never imagined he'd end up running for his life . . . or finding his only hope in the kindness of strangers and the woman he loves.

AUDREY STODDARD — Flame-haired and flirtatious, she never knew what it meant to really love a man until she met Proud Wolf. Yet theirs was a love destined to end in tragedy . . . unless they can escape a man driven by hatred and bent on revenge.

NED HOLT — Cousin to Clay and Jeff, he is a master sailor, a man who lives for adventure and the chance to wander the world. He has always depended on his luck, his skill, and his instinct for survival. He will need all three and more when he finds himself lost in a raging ocean where his troubles have just begun.

INDIA ST. CLAIR — The dangerous, tantalizing woman who has won Ned Holt's heart, India is a woman of rare beauty and extraordinary talents. Yet her life is a mystery she has kept hidden from everyone — even from the one man she loves — and the secrets she keeps can be fatal to any who get too close or dare to cross her.

CHAPTER ONE

The steamboat *New Orleans* veered toward the bank of the Mississippi River, where an empty wharf awaited it. Beyond the wharf lay the teeming streets of the steamboat's namesake city.

New Orleans! The bustling, colorful town, established originally by the French, was sometimes called the Crescent City because of the great bend the Mississippi made as it flowed through on its way to the delta. Scores of flatboats and keelboats traveled up and down the mighty river, carrying goods to and from the city. Tall-masted sailing ships glided up to the docks and then left again, laden with cargoes bound for ports around the globe.

But the *New Orleans* was the first steamboat to have made the trip down the Mississippi from Pittsburgh, a feat most rivermen had insisted could never be accomplished. Not only had the steamboat navigated over a thousand miles of often treacherous river, it had also encountered unforeseen troubles and delays as a series of powerful, terrifying earthquakes sundered the land and caused the mighty river to flow backward for a time.

Even in the face of nature's destructive rampage, the *New Orleans* and her captain, the man who had designed the boat, Nicholas Roosevelt, had persevered. And now the goal had been reached — the journey was over.

For some.

For others, such as the tall, dark-haired, powerfully built man standing at the railing of the *New Orleans*, another journey was just beginning.

Clay Holt's hands tightened on the rail. Below him, the giant paddlewheel churned the muddy waters of the Mississippi. That paddlewheel had almost claimed the life of Clay's Sioux wife, Shining Moon, when she was knocked overboard by the turncoat Senator Morgan Ralston, the man Clay had pursued all the way down the river from Pittsburgh. As Clay remembered bleakly how close Shining Moon had come to dying, his thoughts turned to the event that had led to this dangerous mission. Months earlier, a message from beyond the grave — a letter written by Clay's old commander, Meriwether Lewis

— had summoned Clay and his brother Jeff to Washington City. There the two of them, at the behest of former president Thomas Jefferson, had helped uncover a grandiose, complicated scheme that would have placed much of the western half of the continent in the hands of a group of conspirators hostile to the interests of the United States.

Morgan Ralston was dead now, but his death had not ended the planned takeover of the west. As far as Clay knew, Ralston's partner was still very much alive and had every intention of carrying on.

That was one reason Clay was glad to see New Orleans. He hoped that he and John Markham, the young army lieutenant who was working with him, could finally write an ending to the treacherous plot of Comte Jacques de La Carde.

Shining Moon, Clay's wife, stepped up to the rail beside him. She was tall and slender for a woman of her people, with long, raven-black hair and intense dark eyes. She wore the clothing of a white woman, a blue dress with a white shawl around her shoulders, although like her husband she much preferred buckskins.

Shining Moon rested a hand on the rail and looked at the city sprawled on the banks of the river. "It seems bigger even than St. Louis," she said in awe. "Never have I seen such a village."

Clay nodded. "It's big, all right. Makes me a mite edgy just to look at it. All those people."

To be sure, the streets were full of pedestrians and men on horseback and wagons. Clay wondered how anyone ever got where they were going. He rubbed the back of his hand across his mouth, feeling the bristles of his closely trimmed mustache and beard. He was a man who liked wide open spaces and plenty of elbow room. New Orleans offered neither.

"Look at all the boats!" cried Matthew Garwood, the sturdy, dark-haired, nine-year-old ward of Clay and Shining Moon. He and Lieutenant Markham were coming along the deck toward them.

"I'll wager there are more boats here than you've ever seen in one place before," Markham said, smiling. The lieutenant was dressed in civilian clothes, since he was on detached duty for the duration of this special assignment, and his beaver hat was pushed back on close-cropped sandy hair. He carried his left arm in a black sling; he had suffered a deep knife slash while trying to capture Senator Ralston. The wound was healing nicely, but he still had to be careful with the arm.

"I want to have my own boat someday," said Matthew. "I'll sail it all over the world."

"I don't doubt that for a moment."

Matthew pointed to the empty wharf. "Is that the dock where we're going?"

"I imagine so. I'm not a sailor myself, so I don't really know."

"That's where we're bound, all right," said Clay. He turned away from the railing. "We'd better get our gear together."

That would not take long; the party had traveled fairly lightly. There were only a handful of passengers on the *New Orleans* for the steamboat's inaugural voyage downriver. Two other politicians, Senator Charles Emory and Senator Louis Haines, had made the trip, along with several journalists who were on board to chronicle the historic voyage. Other than those individuals, Clay and his companions were the only passengers, and they were on board only because Captain Roosevelt knew of the special mission Clay and Markham were undertaking.

Clay, Shining Moon, and Matthew were on the way to the cabin they shared when they met Roosevelt on the deck. The captain grinned expansively. "Well, we've succeeded! I suppose this will show all those naysayers who claimed it couldn't be done."

"We haven't docked yet," Clay pointed out dryly.

Roosevelt waved a dismissive hand. "I have the best pilot on the river, and the helmsman with the steadiest hand. Have no fear, Mr. Holt. Soon we shall be safely docked, and you and your party can go ashore."

"It won't be too soon for me," said Clay. "You've got a fine boat here, Captain, and I reckon it'll do everything you said it would. But I'm ready to have dry land under my feet again for a while."

And ready to see the mountains again, too, he thought. The mountains were his home and always would be.

But first he had a job to finish.

That was it, thought Ned Holt. The last crate had been loaded in the cargo hold of the *Lydia Marie.* He turned and called up to Captain Canfield, who stood on the ship's bridge, "That's all of them, Captain!"

"Excellent, Mr. Holt," Canfield called back. "Batten down the hatches!"

"Aye, aye, Captain!"

Ned relayed the order to the seamen standing ready to comply. In an hour, perhaps less, the *Lydia Marie* would set sail from the Chinese port city of Whampoa, bound for America and home.

A tall, brawny man with blond hair under his sailor's cap, Ned had spent twenty-odd years as a landlubber before discovering the pleasures of life at sea. The first time he had set foot on the deck of a ship, it had felt like coming home. That had been a short voyage, from New York City down the eastern coast of the United States to Wilmington, North Carolina, but it was enough to convince Ned he had found his true calling.

On that voyage he had also met and fallen in love with the young woman called India St. Clair. A damned shame that cold-blooded murder had come between them.

With a shake of his shaggy head, Ned forced that thought from his mind. He had no proof that India was a murderess. True, the sailor called Donnelly had gone overboard during a storm when India was nearby. The sea was in such an uproar that it would have been a simple matter for her to send him into its hungry maw with a

single push. And true, too, that Donnelly had given both of them no end of trouble during the voyage across the Pacific. Donnelly's discovery of the fact that India was a woman had been a threat to her continued ability to function as a crewman on the *Lydia Marie*. India had been masquerading for years as a young man, at first to protect herself from harm and later so that she could continue her life as a sailor. So she had reason enough to wish the scoundrel Donnelly dead.

But had she actually taken the next step and ensured Donnelly's death? Ned had been asking himself that question for weeks now, and he was no closer to an answer.

One of the sailors, a wizened little Englishman called Yancy, stepped up to Ned and rubbed his hands together in anticipation. "Glad I'll be to be out o' this stinking 'ole," he said. "I always worried that them Chinee 'ad treachery in their yellow 'earts."

Ned shook his head. "The Chinese want to establish trade across the Pacific as much as we do," he said. "But they want to do it on their own terms."

The idea of opening up trade routes to China, Russian Alaska, and the Hawaiian

Islands had been proposed by Melissa Holt, the wife of Ned's cousin Jeff, and Lemuel March, another Holt cousin who owned the *Lydia Marie* and several other ships. The partnership of the March Shipping Line and the Holt-Merrivale Company, a burgeoning mercantile enterprise, had been profitable for all concerned, but the Pacific held even greater promise.

Ned didn't have much of a head for business. That didn't bother him; he had never wanted to be stuck in an office all day. He was content to act as Holt-Merrivale's unofficial representative on this voyage. Captain Canfield was in charge, and he was doing a good job. By the time the *Lydia Marie* got back to North Carolina, Holt-Merrivale and March Shipping would have a profit of upwards of thirty thousand dollars to split. That was ample proof the risks of a Pacific voyage had been well worth it.

"Well, I don't trust the slant-eyed bastards anyway," continued Yancy.

"We'll be done with them soon enough," Ned said, clapping a hand on the smaller man's shoulder for a second. Then he moved on along the deck, making certain all the preparations for sailing were going smoothly.

With his back turned to Yancy, Ned didn't see the murderous hatred that flared for a moment in the little Englishman's eyes as he watched him walk away.

India St. Clair scrambled deftly up the rigging. Climbing among the towering sails of the *Lydia Marie* came as naturally to her as if she had been doing it all her life.

She paused in her climb, holding the line that would start the topsail unfurling with a simple tug. As she looked down at the deck far below, she felt no dizziness or fear. A sailor couldn't afford to. She was cautious, of course; she was a long way up, and the wooden deck of a ship would be hard and unforgiving to anything that might fall from high in the rigging. But at the moment her attention was focused on the tall, muscular form of Ned Holt as he strode toward the bow of the ship.

Her life would have been infinitely simpler, India reflected, had she never encountered Ned in that filthy New York City alley with a dead man at her feet. She had never had a chance to try her masquerade on him and his cousin Jeff. They had known from the start that she was a woman, since she had foolishly revealed as much in her boasting to the doomed ruffian who had attacked her. If Ned had truly believed that she was Max St. Clair, a British seaman, he never would have pursued her.

And they never would have fallen in love.

Now there was no turning back. India could not simply snap her fingers and stop caring for Ned. They had shared too much, been through too many good times and bad, for the bond to be broken that easily — even by suspicion.

Ned had been on deck during that awful storm when Donnelly had gone overboard. In fact, India had seen him just a few moments before Donnelly was lost to the sea. There had been bad blood between the two men; they had beaten each other half senseless in more than one clash. Worst of all, Ned had known that Donnelly was a threat to the woman he loved. Would he have killed Donnelly in cold blood if the opportunity presented itself?

India couldn't answer that question. She was no longer sure she *wanted* to answer it.

A shouted command from the first mate floated up through the rigging. India tugged on the line she held, and the topsail began to unroll. All along the masts, the other sails unfurled and billowed as they caught the wind. The *Lydia Marie* began to move, cutting gracefully through the water as it slid away from the dock. Whampoa and its teeming streets fell away behind the ship. India turned her head to cast a last look at the mainland. Unlike the Hawaiian Islands, which were a paradise, China held little appeal for India. She was glad they were setting sail.

She went back down the rigging, hand over hand, and dropped lightly the last few feet to the deck. As she landed, a figure appeared at her side and reached out a hand to grasp her arm and steady her. Without thinking, she jerked her arm free of the man's grasp, then turned and saw Ned standing there, a surprised frown on his face.

"Don't help me!" she hissed at him. "You ought to know that by now."

"I was just giving you a hand —"

"I don't need it," she said. "I don't want it."

His jaw grew taut with anger. "All right," he said. "If that's the way you feel, that's fine." He turned and walked away.

A part of India wanted to cry out for him to wait. She wanted to explain. He couldn't give in to his protective impulses where she was concerned. In truth, she seldom needed protecting; she was quite capable of taking care of herself. But more importantly, Ned's protectiveness jeopardized her continued disguise as a man.

So she stood watching stonily as he stalked off. He would get over it, she told herself.

Still, between her suspicions and the growing friction between them, India was afraid the return voyage to America would be long and unpleasant.

The trip had been long and hard already . . . and they had barely gotten started, Melissa Holt told herself as she stood in the doorway of the keelboat cabin.

A sudden popping noise made her turn around. A man said angrily, "Damn it, boy, be careful with that thing! Ye like to put me eye out!"

Melissa's son, Michael, was standing on top of the cabin, the plaited length of a bullwhip dangling from his right hand. "I'm sorry, Mr. McCollum," he said. "I was just practicing. I didn't mean to hurt nobody."

"*Any*body, Michael," Melissa corrected him out of habit as she went up the steps that led to the roof of the low-slung cabin. "You didn't mean to hurt *any*body."

"If I were you, lady," said the man who had complained a moment earlier, "I'd worry less about the younker's grammar and more about where he pops that damned whip."

A tall, dark-haired, rawboned man came up behind McCollum and dropped a heavy hand on his shoulder. "And if I was ye, I'd worry more about gettin' me pole back in the river where it belongs," he advised in a gravelly voice.

McCollum shrugged and dipped the long pole he carried into the muddy water of the Mississippi. In rhythm with the other men lined up along both sides of the keelboat, he planted the pole against the bottom of the river and began walking forward. The poles pushed the boat steadily forward against the sluggish current.

A keelboat was a slow way to travel upriver, Melissa reflected, but there was no viable alternative for reaching St. Louis. She and Michael and Terence O'Shay could have gone overland, but that would have required hiring wagons and drivers and exposing themselves and their goods to the dangers of the road, which were considerably greater than those one normally encountered on the river. It was true that river pirates sometimes attacked boats, but the highwaymen who haunted the roads were more numerous — and more bloodthirsty, according to O'Shay.

Melissa trusted the big Irishman. She would have to; she had placed her life, and the life of her son, in his hands.

Terence O'Shay had been a friend of the Holt family's for several years. He had first met Jeff Holt when both of them were locked up in the jail in Wilmington, O'Shay for smuggling and Jeff for a murder he hadn't committed. More than once since then Jeff and Melissa had turned to O'Shay for help, and he had always come through for them.

Now, faced with problems she couldn't begin to solve herself, Melissa had turned to O'Shay again after they had chanced to meet a couple of weeks earlier in New Orleans. She might not be able to get her husband back, but she could keep herself busy in other ways. She needed a challenge to get her mind off what had happened in Alaska.

And what bigger challenge could she have found than starting a fur trading business in the Rocky Mountains with Terence O'Shay?

"Why don't you put the whip away now?" she said to Michael. "It would be better if you practiced while we're ashore. You'll have more room that way."

"I have to practice all the time," Michael protested. "I want to be really good when Papa gets back next spring."

Melissa's lips tightened into a thin line. She couldn't very well explain to Michael that his father might not return from Alaska in the spring. Jeff might prefer to stay right where he was — with Irina Orlov.

Unbidden images appeared in Melissa's mind. Images of Jeff and the countess, her full breasts brazenly bare as Jeff fondled them. Jeff hadn't even had the decency to defend his actions. He was lucky that Irina's husband, Count Gregori Orlov, hadn't had him killed outright. With all the Russian soldiers at his command, Orlov could easily have done that. He could have had everyone on the *Beaumont* killed, for that matter, and burned the American ship that had dared to visit Russian Alaska in search of a trade pact. Jeff had put not only his own life in danger with his wanton behavior, but the lives of all the other Americans as well, including his wife and child.

So what was she doing now? she asked herself. Heading off into a rugged, perilous wilderness with Michael in tow, all because she hadn't wanted to return to Wilmington and face the pitying stares of her mother and everyone else who would know that Jeff had stayed behind in Alaska with his Russian trollop.

This was different, Melissa told herself stubbornly. This was a business venture, that was all. She had no interest in O'Shay other than as a friend and business partner, and she knew that O'Shay's sense of honor would never allow him to think of her in any other way. Not only that, but they were on their way to a real settlement, the settlement that Jeff and his brother Clay had helped establish in a lush mountain valley and named New Hope.

That was what she needed more than anything else: a new hope. Terence O'Shay had said much the same thing when she met him in New Orleans.

He climbed onto the cabin roof and came forward to join Melissa and Michael. "Best do as your ma says, Whip," he told Michael, using the nickname that Melissa was coming to tolerate, though she was still not fond of it.

"All right." Michael began to coil the bullwhip. Melissa felt a prickle of resentment that he had accepted O'Shay's suggestion without complaint. But that was typical, she supposed. Little boys the world over probably whined no matter what their mothers told them to do.

O'Shay put his hands on his hips and looked upriver, eyes narrowed as if he could see all the way to their destination. "With any luck, we'll reach St. Louis tomorrow," he said.

"Is there still time to get to New Hope before winter sets in?" asked Melissa.

O'Shay scraped a thumbnail along his rugged, beard-blued jaw. "I'm hoping so," he said. "I'd like to settle in and be ready to start trading for furs come spring."

Under their feet inside the cabin was a large load of trade goods that Melissa had purchased in New Orleans. While she and O'Shay had been preparing for this expedition there, the *Beaumont*, which had brought her and Michael from Alaska, had set sail for Wilmington. Captain Vickery had been dubious about leaving her and Michael behind, especially when she told him she was planning to make the treacherous journey to New Hope, but Melissa had insisted, and the captain had had no choice but to go along with her wishes. More than once since then, Melissa had wished that she could be there to watch when Vickery reported to Lemuel March and her mother, Hermione, that Melissa and Michael were on their way to the Rocky Mountains. She could imagine what their reaction would be. They would think she was insane.

Well, maybe she was, she thought. But it was better to be busy and insane than to allow the crushing pain and loneliness of her husband's desertion to ruin her life.

"We'll find a guide as soon as we reach St. Louis," she said decisively. "A frontiersman who can tell us whether or not we can reach New Hope in time."

Proud Wolf lay back on the bunk in the enclosed, darkened wagon. He was breathing heavily, and a fine sheen of sweat covered his body despite the coolness of the night. He needed time, time to catch his breath and recover.

But Audrey seemed determined not to give him that opportunity. She was already snuggling against his right side, her hands boldly exploring his body.

Proud Wolf stifled a groan and rolled toward her, pulling her nude body tighter against his. The fingers of his left hand delved into her lush red hair and cupped her head as he brought his mouth to hers.

His right arm went under her, his hand gliding down the smooth length of her back until he reached the swell of her hips. Holding her against him, he rolled onto his back once again and brought her with him so that she was lying atop him. Her tongue slid between his open lips and explored hotly. Her hips lifted briefly from his body and then sank as she slowly, maddeningly sheathed his heated flesh within her.

He would have thought himself well beyond the intense reaction he was experiencing now. They had already made love twice tonight. But Audrey Stoddard was an expert at arousing him. From the first time he had seen her, on the grounds of the Stoddard Academy for Young Men in Cambridge, Massachusetts, Proud Wolf had wanted her. The fact that she was a well-bred young white woman and Proud Wolf was a warrior of the Teton Sioux, son of the great chief Bear Tooth, brother to Shining Moon, made their courtship more difficult, of course; nor did it help that her father was the headmaster of the academy. In the great scheme of things, Proud Wolf and Audrey Stoddard would normally never have met.

But meet they had, and everything had changed for both of them.

At the moment, as he and Audrey panted and thrust and clutched each other, there was no room in his head for thoughts of the past. As their coupling became more urgent, Proud Wolf arched his back off the bunk and emptied himself into her yet again as she cried out softly in her own culmination. Audrey's body went slack, finally sated. Proud Wolf tipped his head back and tried not to gasp as if he had just run from sunup to sundown, which was how he felt. As it often did at such times, his spirit turned and turned, and images of what had led them to this place unfolded in his mind like paintings on the lodges of his people.

His life as a young man in Bear Tooth's band had been anything but simple. Blessed with a keen mind and swift feet — but not the other requisite skills of a Sioux warrior — Proud Wolf had learned to speak both English and French from the black-robed missionaries who were the first white men to visit his home in the Shining Mountains. Then had come the fur trappers, among them Clay and Jeff Holt, who had befriended Proud Wolf and his people. Shining Moon, Proud Wolf's sister, had married Clay Holt, and Proud Wolf had shared in many of their adventures.

However, when the time had come to embark on what would become his greatest adventure, Proud Wolf had been alone — save for his spirit guide, a shimmering vision of a great mountain cat. Professor Abner Hilliard, a scientist and educator from one of the white men's schools in the East, had come to the mountains in search of a Sioux youth willing to return with him, receive the same education a young white man of privilege might receive, and disprove the prevailing notion that the red man was savage and uneducable. The proposal had immediately captured Proud Wolf's interest, and he had accompanied the garrulous, white-haired Dr. Hilliard back to Massachusetts and been enrolled at the Stoddard Academy. There he had met and fallen in love with Audrey. There, too, he had first encountered his greatest enemy.

Will Brackett, another student at Stoddard and the scion of a wealthy, influential Boston family, had been outraged that Audrey preferred Proud Wolf — a *savage* — to him. Will's hatred of them both had grown to the point that Proud Wolf had been forced to flee from the academy, and Audrey had come with him. Will was somewhere behind them, pursuing them, and Proud Wolf knew that the vengeful young man wanted him dead.

But it had been an innocent storekeeper who had wounded Proud Wolf during a late-night robbery, not Will Brackett. Doubtless Will would have been incensed had he known how close the storekeeper's musket ball had come to robbing him of his chance for vengeance. Proud Wolf might have died from the wound had he and Audrey not been taken in by a traveling troupe of actors. Ulysses Xavier Dowd and his band of players had offered refuge, a temporary home, for the two fugitives, and Proud Wolf and Audrey had accepted, becoming part of the group for the time being.

The twists and turns of fate were strange indeed, Proud Wolf thought now as he caressed Audrey's flank and kissed her hair while she pillowed her head on his chest. From his homeland in the Shining Mountains — the Rockies, as the white men called them — to this troupe of actors slowly making its way down the eastern seaboard, it had been an amazing journey, of a kind no one among his people had ever embarked upon, with the possible exception of his sister. Shining Moon had also visited the white man's world.

Proud Wolf wondered where she was at this moment. He hoped she was happy.

"So good . . ." Audrey murmured against his chest. "That was so good."

Proud Wolf stroked her damp, tangled hair. "You make me happy, Audrey," he said quietly.

They shared this wagon, which had once been used by Walter Berryhill, the elderly former leading man of the troupe. Berryhill had moved in with Frederick and Theodore Zachary, twins in their early twenties.

Audrey rolled off Proud Wolf and lay down beside him. She laughed softly and said, "Theodore and Frederick were flirting with me today. They probably think I'm a terribly wanton woman."

Proud Wolf raised himself on an elbow. "This is not good. I will speak with them."

"Oh, no." Audrey sat halfway up. "That's not necessary."

"They must not disrespect you."

"They didn't mean anything by it," she said. "It's just that all actresses have a bit of a . . . a reputation, simply because they're actresses."

Proud Wolf cocked his head. "Mrs. Dowd is an actress, and she is a virtuous woman."

"Yes, but she's married."

"Ah." Proud Wolf understood now. "Then we should be married, too."

"But we can't do that," Audrey began.

"Do you not love me?"

"Of course I do!"

"And I love you. So we should be married. That way, Frederick and Theodore and all other men will know that you are my woman."

"That would be wonderful, Proud Wolf, but we have to be practical. If we show up at a minister's house, or a justice of the peace, and ask him to marry us, don't you think he'll be liable to remember us?"

She had a point, he knew. A beautiful young white woman with fiery red hair and a Teton Sioux only a few months removed from the wilderness of the frontier . . . yes, such a couple would likely be remembered. And that would be one more thing that might lead Will Brackett to them and bring his vengeance down on their heads.

Proud Wolf nodded slowly. "You are right," he admitted. "Still, I will think on this. There must be something we can do."

"I'll tell you what we can do," Audrey said, her voice husky with renewed desire. "Better yet, I'll show you."

"Audrey," he said despairingly, "I cannot —"

But then her mouth began to roam down the lean, muscular lines of his body, and he discovered to his astonishment that indeed he could.

Life with Audrey Stoddard, Proud Wolf reflected, contained no end of surprises.

Jefferson Holt bit back the groan that welled up his throat. During the previous two days the constant cold had seeped into his bones, becoming a deep, gnawing ache despite the fur robes in which he was wrapped.

His Tlingit Indian companions did not seem to feel the frigid air. But they were accustomed to it. Jeff himself had endured cold weather before; he had spent a winter at Fort Lisa on the Yellowstone River, when he and his brother Clay had been part of the first fur-trapping expedition to venture up the Missouri River into the western wilderness. But the cold in Russian Alaska was different. Here every breath scoured a man's lungs and left ice behind.

Jeff leaned awkwardly against the skins piled atop the sled on which he rode. In front of him, a team of heavily furred dogs pulled against their harness and hauled the sled easily across the frozen ground. Behind Jeff, perched on runners at the back of the sled, rode the Tlingit Indian who had been dubbed Vassily by the Russians in the coastal settlement of Sitka. Vassily's true name was too difficult for even the Russians to wrap their tongues around. He had worked as a guide for Count Gregori Orlov, and on one of the hunting expeditions that the count had mounted into the interior, Vassily's life had been threatened by a monstrous grizzly bear. Luckily, Jeff Holt had been a member of the hunting party, and he had downed the bear with a superb shot, saving Vassily's life.

And saving his own life in the process, Jeff now knew, because when Count Orlov later decided to have him killed and his body disposed of by the Indians, Vassily had intervened. Orlov, back in Sitka, no doubt believed Jeff to be dead. Orlov's lust for vengeance, prompted by the mistaken belief that his wife Irina had had an affair with the visiting American, had been satisfied.

But Jeff was still very much alive — which was more than could be said for Irina.

Jeff could not help but shudder as he remembered the awful moment when Vassily had brought out the canvas bag Orlov had ordered him to dispose of along with Jeff's body. Grinning, Vassily had opened the pouch and dumped out its grisly contents: Irina Orlov's head, brutally severed from her body. Jeff wondered if Count Orlov himself had murdered his wife or if that task had been entrusted to his aide, the sycophant Piotr. Jeff suspected that Piotr himself had carried on an affair with the hot-blooded, amoral Irina. Piotr was more afraid of Count Orlov than he was enamored of Irina, however, and Jeff did not doubt for a moment that he would have carried out such an order from the Russian nobleman.

Nobleman, Jeff thought bleakly. That was a deceptive word for Gregori Orlov. The man was about as ignoble a human specimen as Jeff had ever encountered.

But now Orlov, and the rest of the Russian garrison at Sitka, were far behind him. Jeff had no idea where Vassily and the other Tlingit were taking him, but he hoped they would reach their destination soon.

Irina's remains had been left behind. At Jeff's insistence, Vassily had used an ax to chop a shallow hole in the frozen ground, then placed the severed head in it and covered it with a mound of rocks. It had been clear from his expression that he thought Jeff was insane to request such a pointless gesture, and his patience was further tried when Jeff stood over the cairn and muttered a prayer, but Jeff would not leave until he had done at least that much for her.

Now, two days later, the sled was still sliding along over endless stretches of rock, snow, and ice. Thick gray clouds scudded so low to the ground that it seemed to Jeff he could reach up and drag his fingers through them. The light was dim, a kind of perpetual dusk that barely distinguished the short hours of daylight from the long, black nights.

At the moment there was enough light for Jeff to see the densely wooded slope that rose ahead of the sleds. The dogs floundered a little as they labored up the incline, but their masters pulled them to a stop and let them rest when they reached the top.

Jeff looked down the far side of the slope and saw a narrow valley. On the opposite side a taller hill rose, and beyond it a succession of peaks climbed toward the clouds to form a rugged range of mountains. The valley formed a pocket of protection from the frigid winds. Along the near side of a rushing stream were at least a dozen large structures that looked like houses. Jeff knew without asking that the group had reached its destination.

Vassily stepped up beside the sled and pointed. "My home." He looked down at Jeff. "Your home now."

Jeff fought back the feeling of panic that rose inside him. Vassily had saved his life, and for that Jeff was grateful. But the Tlingit had also made it clear that Jeff had no choice but to go with him and his companions, wherever they were bound. During the past two days Jeff had speculated that the Indians were returning to their village, and now he knew that to be true.

But what did they expect of him? That he would become one of them?

For now, Jeff told himself, he had no choice but to go along with whatever Vassily and the others wanted. Once he learned more about their plans, perhaps he could turn them to his advantage. One thing was certain: he had no intention of remaining with the Tlingit permanently. Sooner or later he would return to Sitka and avenge Irina Orlov's murder. Although the countess had caused him no end of trouble and had perhaps even destroyed his marriage, she had not deserved such a gruesome fate.

Thoughts of his marriage sent Jeff's mind spinning back to Melissa. By now the *Beaumont* would be well on its way home, and Jeff prayed that Melissa and Michael were all right. True, Melissa's stiff-necked pride had prevented her from listening to his explanation when she learned about Irina, but someday they would put that behind them, Jeff hoped. Melissa would realize that they still loved each other, and she would forgive him for a moment of weakness.

"We go now," Vassily said, moving behind the sled and stepping up again on the runners. At his shouted command, the dog team began moving again. The other teams fell in behind.

The slope was steeper on this side of the hill, but a zigzag trail led down into the valley. The dogs followed it expertly, as if they had trod the path many times before. As they neared the village they began barking, and the barking of other dogs rose in reply. People emerged from the houses, their attention caught by the commotion, and hailed the approaching party.

The ground gradually leveled out, and the dogs raced toward the village, eager now to be home. When the sleds came to a stop, the Tlingit leaped down and embraced their welcoming friends and relatives, laughing and slapping backs.

Vassily hugged a heavily clad figure for a moment, then stepped back and pointed to one of the houses, speaking in his native tongue. The person he was addressing, whose face was partially hidden by a tall, woven hat of some kind, nodded and turned to hurry into the hut. Vassily walked back to the sled and extended a hand to Jeff. "Come, my friend," he said in English. "I have place for you."

Jeff grasped Vassily's hand and stood up on legs stiff with cold. He had no idea what the inside of a Tlingit home might be like, but as long as there was a fire at which he could warm himself, that was all that mattered. Stamping his feet, he gingerly followed Vassily.

Jeff looked in some wonder at the structure they were approaching. It was unlike any he had ever seen. The walls were built of planks — probably cedar from the surrounding forest — and the roof was peaked; what made the building unusual was the tall carved and decorated wooden post set into the front wall and towering above it. Jeff, peering upward in the fading light, could make out the likenesses of birds and beasts, imaginatively wrought and painted in shades of black and red.

The entrance to the dwelling was the open maw of one such carved creature. Even as short as he was, Vassily had to stoop to enter. Jeff, much taller, was forced to bend almost double. Inside, as his eyes grew accustomed to the dim light, he saw numerous low bunks along one wall and guessed that this was a communal habitation. The bunks were elevated a few inches above the ground on stout poles made from the trunks of saplings and were piled high with bear and seal pelts. On rafters overhead Jeff could see what looked like hunting and fishing gear, baskets, and paddles. The smoke from a stone hearth rose through a hole in the roof.

Jeff spread his numb, stiff hands toward the fire in the hearth. Vassily grinned and said, "Soon you forget how cold it is, my friend. The fire will warm you." He gestured toward the Tlingit who had preceded them into the house. "And so will she."

Jeff's head snapped up.

The Tlingit turned toward him, pulling

back the hat. A round-faced, dark-eyed woman with glossy, straight black hair smiled broadly, welcomingly, at Jeff.

"My sister," Vassily went on. "The Russians call her Nadia. She is your woman now, Jefferson Holt."

CHAPTER TWO

Clay left Markham and Shining Moon on board the *New Orleans* to see to their bags and went ashore in the company of Captain Nicholas Roosevelt. The captain pointed out a small building made of weathered planks that sat at the edge of the docks.

"That's the harbormaster's office," Roosevelt said. "Come along, Mr. Holt. I'll introduce you."

Clay had asked that favor of the captain. Roosevelt did not know all the details of the mission that had brought Clay and Markham to New Orleans, but he was aware of their status as special agents of former president Thomas Jefferson.

The inside of the harbormaster's office was as plain and functional as the outside. Seated at a desk was a burly, barrel-chested man with a graying black beard that thrust forward almost belligerently. He glanced up from the documents on his desk as the two visitors entered the office, then looked again sharply as he recognized one of them.

"Nicholas Roosevelt?" he rumbled. He came to his feet, a man as tall as he was broad, and thrust out a blunt-fingered hand that seemed almost as large as a keg of nails. "I heard about your voyage," he said as his hand enveloped Roosevelt's. "I have to admit, I didn't expect to see you here."

"The *New Orleans* came through with flying colors, Peter," Roosevelt said. He waved Clay forward. "Clay, this is the harbormaster of New Orleans, Peter Gentry. Peter, meet Clay Holt."

Gentry's grip was firm but not crushing. "Holt, eh?" he said as he eyed Clay. "The frontiersman?"

As always, Clay was taken aback by the fact that a stranger should have heard of him. He did not consider himself famous, certainly not in the way his old captains, William Clark and the late Meriwether Lewis, or John Colter, a fellow member of the Corps of Discovery, were. He nodded to the harbormaster. "I reckon I'm him, all right."

"I've heard a great deal about you from the rivermen who make the trip between here and St. Louis," Gentry said as he released Clay's hand. "The fur traders have carried stories about your exploits back from the wilderness." He waved a hand at a couple of cane-bottom chairs in front of the desk. "Sit down, sit down, gentlemen. What can I do for you?"

Clay sat down as Roosevelt settled himself in the other chair. Across Clay's lap was his long-barreled Kentucky rifle, and the North & Cheney flintlock pistol he had carried for years was tucked behind his belt, as well as a hunting knife with a long, heavy blade. If Gentry was surprised to see a man armed for bear in his office, he gave no sign of it. From what Clay had heard about New Orleans, he knew it could be a pretty rough town. No doubt Gentry was accustomed to rugged men and their weapons and their plain-spoken ways.

Clay hesitated only a second before saying bluntly, "I'm looking for a man. Before I tell you who he is, I want your word that none of what I say here will ever be repeated outside this office."

Gentry's bushy eyebrows drew together. "Are you implying that I can't be trusted, Mr. Holt?"

"I'm saying I never met you until just now," Clay replied honestly. "Captain Roosevelt vouches for you, so that's worth something. But I'm here on a mighty important job, so I can't take any chances."

Gentry pursed his lips under his drooping mustache for a moment before saying, "You have my word, Mr. Holt. Now, what's all this about?"

"Do you know a man named Jacques de La Carde? He's some sort of French nobleman."

"The Comte de La Carde?" said Gentry. "Sure, I know him. Know of him, anyway. I don't think I ever met the man, but the boat that brought him to America docked here about a month ago."

Clay leaned forward slightly, trying to rein in his excitement. "Do you know where I can find him?" It seemed too good to be true that Gentry could direct him straight to La Carde, too much to hope that Clay might be able to bring this sordid affair to a conclusion this very day.

And so it was. Gentry spread the fingers of his big hands and said, "Somewhere upriver. He stayed here less than a week before he and his companions took passage on a keelboat bound for St. Louis."

Clay bit back a groan of bitter disappointment. One of the countless vessels the *New Orleans* had met on its trip downriver had been carrying the very man Clay

46

sought, the madman behind the scheme to carve out a new French empire in the western part of America. La Carde had spun his plan like a spider spinning a web, casting strands all the way to Washington City that had dragged men like the crooked financier Gideon Maxwell and the corrupt politician Morgan Ralston into the scheme. With the help of his brother Jeff and then Lieutenant Markham, Clay had severed those strands, but La Carde was still on the loose, still free to keep spinning.

Gentry must have seen the frustration on Clay's face, because he asked, "Did you have business with the Comte de La Carde, Mr. Holt?"

"You could say that," Clay replied with a curt nod. "Did he say when he expected to be back from St. Louis?"

Gentry looked surprised. "Why, not for a long time. His party wasn't coming back this way, I don't believe. They were traveling west."

"West?" Clay echoed. And Gentry had said something else that puzzled him. "What sort of party was La Carde traveling with?"

"A group of French noblemen. They were accompanied by two officials from the government in Washington City. They're on a hunting expedition."

Clay pounded his knee in frustration. Testily he said, "It's very important that I find La Carde as soon as possible, Mr. Gentry. This isn't a business deal. I'm down here working for the government."

Gentry glanced at Captain Roosevelt, who nodded silently in confirmation of Clay's statement. Gentry sat back in his chair and rubbed his bearded jaw. "Well, now," he said. "I suppose I'd better tell you everything I know."

"I'd be much obliged," Clay said.

Gentry launched into his tale, explaining that a French military cutter had cruised up the river to New Orleans a month earlier. The presence of the French naval vessel had caused no alarm — no one had mistaken it for the start of an invasion — because the details of its arrival had been worked out ahead of time between Gentry and several government officials. The French ship had carried not only the Comte de La Carde but half a dozen other young French noblemen as well. They had been accompanied by the two government men, who explained to Gentry that the foreign visitors had come to the United States for a tour of the western regions.

"It was my impression those Frenchmen were representatives of that Bonaparte fellow himself," Gentry said. "Some people in France aren't too happy with him for selling the Louisiana Territory to us in the first place. I think La Carde and the others are hoping that they find a real wilderness that'll never do anybody much good, so they can go back to France and report that to the people. Our government's cooperating because while Bonaparte may have his hands full right now fighting the British and the Russians and everyone else in Europe, one of these days he's liable to look back in this direction again. We want to keep him happy with us, especially since we've been having our own problems with the British lately."

Clay nodded. He had no stomach for politics and the double-dealing schemers who practiced that not-so-fine art. Everything Gentry had said about the motives of the French noblemen and of the American government seemed to make sense.

Which didn't mean the whole thing wasn't a pack of lies.

Clay would have been willing to bet that La Carde and the other Frenchmen had *not* been sent to America by Napoleon Bonaparte. They were more likely part of the little emperor's opposition, the group that had violently opposed the sale of the Louisiana Territory, the loss of France's foothold in North America. The way Clay understood things from what he had been told by Senator Morgan Ralston, La Carde's plan was to rectify that mistake by establishing his own empire in the west.

As for the two officials of the United States government who had accompanied the party of Frenchmen, La Carde had bribed American officials before; that was how the whole land grab scheme had been set into motion. Even if the two Americans really were in the employ of the government, Clay thought it likely their superiors in Washington City knew nothing of what had brought them to New Orleans.

"So you see, it may be quite a while before the comte and his companions return to New Orleans," Gentry concluded. "Their journey should take several months at the very least."

Clay couldn't stop himself from sighing. He had hoped this chore was almost over, but the end was not even in sight.

On the other hand, if he continued his pursuit of La Carde — and what else could he do? — that would take him back toward the mountains, and that was where he wanted to go. It was simple enough, he told himself. All he had to do was catch up with La Carde's party, put a stop somehow to the Frenchman's plan, and then send Markham back to Washington City with a report for Thomas Jefferson. Clay himself could stay in the mountains with Shining Moon, where he belonged.

"What about the French ship?" Clay asked. "You say it sailed after La Carde got off?"

"Well, it was docked here for several days," Gentry replied. "But then, yes, it sailed."

"Returning to France?"

Gentry shrugged. "I'm afraid I don't know where she was bound, Mr. Holt."

He could worry about that later, Clay told himself. The most important thing was to get started on La Carde's trail once more. He got to his feet and looked at Nicholas Roosevelt. "You're taking the *New Orleans* back upriver, aren't you, Captain?"

"The voyage downstream was only part of the test," Roosevelt said. "If my boat can't go back upstream, I will have failed."

"It will succeed," Clay said confidently. "And it looks as if you're going to have some passengers again, at least part of the way."

All the way to St. Louis, Clay thought.

And from there, who knew where the trail would lead?

Jeff started to shake his head, and the eyes of the Tlingit woman called Nadia grew wider and even darker, if that was possible. As they glittered in the firelight, he realized that she was about to cry.

Quickly, hoping to soften any insult he might have given, he said, "Your sister is lovely, Vassily, but I . . . I don't need a woman."

"All man need woman," Vassily said, and Jeff could not argue with the logic or the truth of that statement. Vassily went on, "She cook for you, skin animals you kill, make you cedar cape."

That might not be so bad, Jeff thought. Maybe Nadia would be more like a servant for him.

"And warm your bed at night or whenever you desire her," Vassily went on.

Well, that put it plainly enough. Nadia was here to be a wife to him.

To tell the truth, many men would have been pleased at that prospect. Nadia's face was attractive, and although he could tell little about her body under her clothing, he was sure it was pleasant enough. The

American fur trappers who wintered in the Rockies often took an Indian woman as a wife until spring came again. Sometimes it was a different woman every year. The arrangement seemed to work out fine, at least for the men. And the women didn't seem to mind, either. They and their families usually considered it a mark of honor that a visitor should want to keep them in his lodge. Perhaps Tlingit women had something in common with their cousins to the south.

But Jeff had never taken an Indian wife. By the time he had gone west, he knew there was only one woman in the world for him: Melissa.

He wiped the back of his hand across his mouth. Melissa was long gone now, sailing back to Wilmington on the *Beaumont*, taking their son with her. For that much, at least, he was grateful. They hadn't had to suffer Orlov's vengeance. He shuddered at the thought of what might have happened to them had they fallen into the Russian's hands.

Nadia and Vassily saw his reaction, and once again Nadia's eyes glittered with tears. She spoke to her brother, a torrent of incomprehensible words. Vassily scowled and slitted his eyes at Jeff, as if he were wondering if he had made a mistake by saving the white man's life.

Hastily Jeff said, "I would be honored to stay in this house with you and Nadia, Vassily, for as long as I'm here."

"This your home now," Vassily said, bobbing his head. "And Nadia your woman."

Later, Jeff told himself. *Deal with this later.* For now, he was just glad to be alive . . . and to be out of the cold wind. Other villagers were coming inside now, taking off their capes and staring curiously at Jeff. They clearly lived here, too; there were enough sleeping bunks for at least a dozen people. Jeff pushed back the hood of his coat. Nadia, eyes widening at the sight of his sandy hair, stepped closer and lifted her hand to touch him. He stood still as her fingers brushed over his hair. Her touch was gentle, and she was close enough that Jeff could feel the warmth from her body. He could smell the bear grease on her hair — an odor that to some might have been offensive, but he was accustomed to it.

"Does your sister speak any English?" he asked Vassily in a husky voice.

"No. Some Russian, that is all. She worked at Sitka one time. But she will understand your gestures."

Jeff had no doubt that she would. He summoned up a smile, and instantly she smiled back at him, beaming broadly. The others, watching them closely, smiled as well.

Vassily grunted in satisfaction. "Good. You will be happy here, Jefferson Holt."

Jeff doubted that, but he kept smiling. For now, that was all he could do.

The goods belonging to Clay, Shining Moon, and Matthew fit into two carpetbags, and Shining Moon had them packed and ready, sitting on the floor of their cabin, when Lieutenant Markham knocked on the open door and called out cheerfully, "Ready to go?"

"Yes, I am ready." Shining Moon knew that Clay and Markham planned to find the man called La Carde, but not what their first steps would be now that they were in New Orleans.

Wherever Clay went, she would follow. It was that simple. She was his wife.

But that was not the only reason she did not want to be separated from Clay Holt again. She glanced at Matthew, who had left the cabin and was now standing on the deck outside, leaning on the railing.

So much had happened since she and Clay had taken Matthew to raise. The boy was a Garwood, and there was a long history of bad blood between his family and the Holts. The enmity between the Holts and the Garwoods was as deep and instinctive as that between the Crow and the Blackfoot. In recent years hopeful signs had appeared, signs that perhaps the long-standing feud was finally ending. Aaron Garwood, Matthew's uncle, had become a good friend to Clay and Jeff Holt and was now living in New Hope, the settlement in the mountains. Matthew himself had been taken in by Clay and Shining Moon when he was orphaned, taken to raise as if he were their own child.

Unfortunately, not everything had gone smoothly where Matthew was concerned. He and Shining Moon had remained at the Holt farm in Ohio while Clay and Jeff went to Washington City, and while they were there, Shining Moon suspected that Matthew had had something to do with the death of an elderly woman who had befriended her. Not only that, but she feared that he had even tried to kill her on one occasion.

During the voyage down the Mississippi River Matthew seemed to have changed, in part because of the new environment. He loved boats and thoroughly enjoyed the trip. But he had been drawn into Senator Ralston's schemes, although Shining Moon was uncertain to what extent the boy was involved. Still, she reminded herself, when Ralston had knocked her over the railing and she had almost plunged to certain death under the churning paddlewheel, Matthew had helped save her. Shining Moon could not forget that.

But she still could not decipher what was going on behind those dark eyes, and she did not want Clay to leave her behind with the boy again. The family would stay together, she vowed.

Markham picked up one of the carpetbags with his good arm and carried it out onto the deck. Shining Moon followed. She saw several men walking along the deck toward the gangplank that connected the *New Orleans* to the dock. They saw her as well, and one of the men lifted a hand in greeting.

"Ah, good morning, Mrs. Holt," Senator Charles Emory said. He was tall and distinguished-looking in his top hat and cutaway coat, every inch the politician.

Shining Moon knew nothing about politics and had even less interest in understanding that world than her husband. But she nodded solemnly. "Good morning, Senator Emory."

"And young Mr. Markham," Emory went on. "How are you on this fine day?"

"Quite well, Senator, thank you," Markham replied as he set down the carpetbag.

"That arm is healing properly?"

Markham moved his left arm slightly in its sling. "It seems to be."

"Good." Emory shook his head sadly. "I still have a hard time comprehending that Morgan was behind all those attempts on your life. *All* your lives," he added with a nod toward Shining Moon.

"*I* don't believe it," declared the man standing beside Emory. Senator Louis Haines was a small, sour-faced figure who had disliked Clay and Markham ever since he had met them in Washington. "There's been a terrible misunderstanding somewhere," Haines went on, "and when I get back to Washington City I'm going to get to the bottom of it. Then we'll see who's really to blame for all the trouble." He looked pointedly at Markham and Shining Moon.

"I hope you *will* investigate, Senator," Markham told him. "I wish you luck."

Haines snorted, clearly not believing a word Markham said. And he was right not to believe, Shining Moon knew. Haines and Emory, although they had been good friends of Ralston's, had had no idea what the renegade senator had secretly been planning. Nor had Clay or Markham explained it to them after Ralston's death, since Thomas Jefferson had insisted on discretion. The United States was still young enough, still raw enough, that news of an attempt to wrest away a portion of the new land might cause a dangerous panic and weaken the country in the eyes of its foes. It might be best if the truth *never* came out.

"I see that you gentlemen are disembarking," Markham went on, gesturing toward the crewmen who were following Emory and Haines, carrying traveling bags.

"We'll be catching a sailing ship here in New Orleans that will take us back to Washington," Emory said. He asked Shining Moon, "What about you and your party, Mrs. Holt? Are you making the voyage back upriver?"

"I do not know —" Shining Moon began.

A new voice said, "Yes, we will be."

Shining Moon looked down toward the dock. Clay was striding up the gangplank, carrying his rifle. Captain Roosevelt, who had left the steamboat in Clay's company earlier, was not with him.

"Good day to you, Mr. Holt," Emory said. "You've already been ashore, I see."

Clay stepped onto the deck. "That's right. I had some business to take care of." He looked at Shining Moon and Markham. "We're staying on board."

Markham looked surprised. "You're sure?"

"I'm certain."

Matthew let out an excited whoop. "We're going back upriver!" he said. "I hope there's another earthquake!"

Shining Moon put a hand on his shoulder. "Do not say such things," she told him. "It was bad when the land shook."

"No, it was exciting," Matthew insisted. "I liked it!"

Shining Moon could not understand how anyone could have enjoyed the cataclysm that had ripped the earth apart. The devastation had been widespread, and hundreds, perhaps thousands, of people had died in the earthquakes, which had lasted several days.

"I reckon the earthquakes are over," Clay said. "There hasn't been a tremor for quite a while now. And good riddance to them."

Senator Haines looked as if he wanted to say good riddance to all of them. He strode down the gangplank without a word of farewell, never looking back. Senator Emory paused long enough to shake hands with Clay and Markham and even Matthew, then tipped his hat to Shining Moon. "Good-bye, madam," he said, then followed Haines ashore, the crewmen close behind with their bags.

Markham stepped closer to Clay and asked in a low voice, "What's all this about going back upriver? I thought we were going to find La Carde here in New Orleans."

"He's not *in* New Orleans anymore," Clay said. "I found out from the harbormaster that La Carde and some other Frenchmen landed here a month ago on a French military ship, then headed for St. Louis."

"St. Louis?"

"They're on their way west," Clay said. "So are we. And the quickest way there is to stay on Captain Roosevelt's boat for the return trip."

Markham looked skeptically at him. "You're sure about this information?"

"Roosevelt says the harbormaster is as honest as the day is long, and that's good enough for me."

Markham nodded grudgingly and sighed. "I suppose you're right. It's just that we've been looking forward to getting here and finding some way to bring this assignment to a successful close."

"We'll just have to wait a while longer."

Shining Moon had been following the low-voiced conversation with great interest, and so had Matthew. Shining Moon said, "From St. Louis, we will go to the mountains?"

"I don't know," Clay replied, "but it seems likely to me."

That was all Shining Moon had to hear. She wanted Clay and Markham to be successful in their mission, of course. She did not understand all the intricacies, but she knew it was important to them that they stop this man La Carde from whatever it was he planned to do. For her, though, the most important thing was that they were on their way back to her homeland. She had been afraid that they would have to stay in this city by the river for weeks before they could journey on to the mountains.

And New Orleans, judging by what she had seen of it from the boat, was crowded and dirty, and it smelled bad. The sooner they left it behind for the clean, sweet air of her home, the better.

Clay looked at her and asked softly, "You're not disappointed, are you?"

Men could be so blind sometimes. She wished she could throw herself in his arms and kiss him in gratitude. Instead, she said with dignity, "No, Clay Holt. I am not disappointed."

How could she be, when she was going home to the Shining Mountains?

CHAPTER THREE

With its hold full of silk, spices, and tea, the *Lydia Marie* ran before the wind on its voyage back across the Pacific. The ship would make port again in Hawaii to replenish its stores of food and fresh water, but this time there would be only minimal trading. On the outbound stop, the *Lydia Marie* had taken on a cargo of sandalwood after some shrewd bargaining by Ned, India, and Captain Canfield.

Ned was standing night watch on the bridge, several days after the ship had left China, when he heard someone approaching. The sea around the ship glittered with reflected starlight and shone with its own natural phosphorescence, so as Ned glanced around, he could see fairly well the man coming up the ladder to the bridge.

"Evening, Mr. Holt," the man greeted him. Ned recognized him as a sailor named Syme, a normally taciturn New Englander.

"Beautiful night, isn't it?" Ned commented. Though the time of year was approaching for storms to begin raging through the South Pacific, for now the steady breeze was warm and peaceful.

"Aye, 'tis," Syme replied. He rubbed the callused, leathery palm of one hand over a jutting shelf of jaw. Something was clearly bothering him. He would not have come up on the bridge simply to make conversation.

Ned let the silence drag on for a moment, then prodded, "What is it, Syme?"

"Well, sir, I was thinkin' . . . ye know Captain Canfield pretty well, don't ye?"

Ned nodded. "This isn't the first time I've sailed with him. He's a good captain."

"What do ye reckon 'e'd do, if some of the crew was to . . . well, turn against 'im?"

Ned stiffened. "You mean mutiny?"

"Aye."

A frown creased Ned's forehead. He had never given the subject of mutiny much thought, because Lemuel March paid his sailors a fair wage and provided better provisions than did many of his competitors. As far as he knew, the crews on all the March ships were relatively satisfied with their lot.

"I don't know," he answered honestly. "I suppose the captain might hang any mutineers. The law of the sea would give him that right."

"Aye. And 'e's a hard enough man to do it, too."

"Syme . . . what have you heard? Do we have mutineers on board?" Ned spoke quietly, aware that voices traveled well at night on the sea.

"Now, that's not what I said, Mr. Holt. I was just talkin'."

"You must have had a reason for bringing up mutiny," Ned pressed him.

Syme shook his head. "I shouldn't have said nothin'. Ye should just forget all about it, Mr. 'olt."

Syme started to turn away, but Ned's hand shot out and closed over his arm. "You've been a loyal member of this crew for a long time, Syme," Ned said. "If you know something, you owe it to the captain and to Mr. March to tell me about it."

Again Syme shook his head, then cast a worried glance over his shoulder. "I shouldn't've said nothin'," he said again and jerked his arm loose from Ned's grip. "I ain't on watch. I'm goin' below."

Frustration boiled up in Ned. He wanted to grab Syme again and beat the truth out of him. There had been a time when he would have done exactly that, heedless of any possible consequences. But these days he was trying to be less reckless in his behavior. Having India St. Clair around had already stopped him from chasing married women whenever the ship was in port. Ned was trying to temper his propensity for brawling, too. So he opened the hands that had automatically clenched into fists and forced himself to say in a reasonable tone, "All right, Syme. But if there's ever anything you want to tell me, you know where to find me."

"Aye." Syme moved off quickly in the darkness, clattering down the ladder from the bridge and heading for the hatch that led belowdecks to the crew's quarters.

Puzzled, Ned watched the sailor go. What in blazes had that been about? Was there really the chance of a mutiny aboard the *Lydia Marie*? That was always possible, Ned supposed. Should he tell Captain Canfield about the hints Syme had dropped?

"What was that all about?"

The unexpected question echoing his own thoughts made Ned jump, but he knew immediately who had spoken. There was only one person aboard the ship who could have gotten so close to him without his being aware of it.

He turned and saw India standing on the bridge. The only way she could have gotten there was to drop down from the rigging above.

Ned ignored her question for a moment and asked one of his own. "What are you doing skulking about like that?"

"I wasn't skulking," India replied. "I didn't like the way the foresail was flapping earlier, so I went aloft to tighten up the lines."

"Not too tight, I hope."

She laughed quietly. "I sailed every one of the seven seas while you were still a drylander, mate."

Ned had to admit she was right about that. When it came to practical experience at sea, India possessed more than he ever would. Her masquerade as a male had begun when she was an adolescent; she had signed on as a cabin boy at the age of twelve. Or so she had told him. He no longer knew what to believe.

"That was Syme I saw up here with you a moment ago, wasn't it?" India went on. "What did he want?"

"I'm not sure," Ned replied honestly. "Something was bothering him, right enough. He wanted to know about Captain Canfield."

"What about Captain Canfield?"

Ned was holding the wheel now, and his hands tightened on the smooth wood. "He wanted to know what the captain would do if there was a mutiny."

"A mutiny?" India exclaimed.

"Well, not in so many words. Not at first, anyway. But that's what he was getting at, I'm sure of it."

"Do you think he overheard some of the men plotting to take over the ship?" India asked anxiously. She thought for a moment, then added, "Or do you think he's one of the plotters himself? He could have been feeling you out, seeing if you might be willing to join them."

"That's insane! I'd never join a band of mutineers."

"Perhaps not everyone knows that."

She might be right, Ned thought. Most, if not all, of the crew members were aware that he was related to Lemuel March, the owner of the ship. But blood relatives had turned on each other in the past, and if there were mutineers on board the *Lydia Marie*, they might believe they would have an easier time of it if they could get the cousin of the owner on their side. If Ned was to turn against the captain, the mutineers might be able to use him to persuade more of the crew, perhaps even some of the officers, to join their cause.

That was not going to happen, of course, because Ned would never turn against Captain Canfield.

"Should we tell the captain about this?" Ned asked India.

"I wouldn't, not yet. Perhaps Syme just overheard something that he misunderstood. There might not be any mutineers at all."

"But if there are . . ." Ned pressed.

"Let's both keep our eyes and ears open, see if we can find out any more," India suggested. "I'll work on Syme."

"Be careful," Ned told her. "If there *is* a plot afoot, these boys would probably be willing to kill in order to keep it from being exposed before they're ready to strike."

India laughed softly, and Ned remembered how, on the night he had first met her, she had killed a man so coolly and calmly. "I'm not afraid of this lot," she said.

No, Ned thought, she wasn't.

They probably had reason to be afraid of *her*.

★ ★ ★

Proud Wolf sat beside Audrey on the high seat of the wagon as she handled the reins of the team. Though Proud Wolf had long shown an interest in acquiring some of the skills of white men, driving a wagon was not one of them. Nor had Audrey, given her pampered background at the academy, known how to handle a team at first, but she had learned quickly. She could curse the plodding horses every bit as sharply as anyone else in the acting troupe, but since she was a lady, she muttered the imprecations under her breath rather than roaring them out as Professor Dowd did.

The convoy of wagons was entering the outskirts of Providence, Rhode Island. Dowd's plan called for the troupe to follow the coastline from city to city until they reached Virginia, where the group would swing inland and turn north again.

Providence was the capital of the state and a good-sized city. Dowd was expecting a good turnout for the troupe's performances and a profitable stay. Driving the first wagon, which was emblazoned on the sides with the name of the troupe, Dowd led the convoy toward a large square in the center of the town. As the wagons rolled over the cobblestoned streets, they began to attract attention. Children ran alongside, shouting questions, and barking dogs followed the children. Men and women on the street turned to watch the colorful procession.

Vanessa Dowd sat beside her husband, waving gaily at the citizens of Providence. Her honey-blond hair and mature beauty attracted many admiring glances from the men, as did the occupants of the wagon following, Elaine and Portia Yardley, mother and daughter, graceful brunettes who looked enough alike to portray sisters in the troupe's performances. On the next wagon were Kenneth and Phillippa Thurston. The dark-haired Phillippa was also a beauty, and her husband, Kenneth, was handsome enough to have taken over the leading-man roles Walter Berryhill had grown too old to play. Proud Wolf and Audrey came next, followed by the final wagon in the group, driven by Theodore Zachary. His twin brother, Frederick, sat beside him, while Walter Berryhill rode inside the vehicle. Standing on the roof of the Zachary brothers' wagon, balancing easily on his short legs, was Oliver Johnson. He drew the most attention from the children by making faces at them and capering back and forth. Several times it looked as if he might fall off the wagon, and Oliver exaggerated the effect by pinwheeling his arms and balancing on one leg while kicking frantically at the air with the other. Then he would retreat to the center of the wagon and draw more whoops of laughter by pretending to trip, sitting down hard and looking startled.

Proud Wolf turned to watch Oliver's antics. He felt a vague discomfort at the sight of the crowd laughing and hooting at the little man. That was Oliver's intention, of course — to draw laughter — but somehow the reaction of the bystanders bothered him. Among his people, those who were different were not laughed at. They were accepted as they were, as Wakan-Tanka, the Creator, had made them, and all knew that Wakan-Tanka did nothing without a purpose.

Audrey nudged him and said quietly, "Wave at the people, Proud Wolf." She was holding the reins in one hand and waving with the other at the people along the roadside.

"Why do you wave at them?" Proud Wolf asked. "You do not know any of them, do you?"

"No," she hissed, "but they've got

money in their purses, and we want them to bring it to the performance tonight, don't we?"

Audrey clearly grasped the significance of some things more quickly than he, Proud Wolf thought. It would never have occurred to him to smile and wave at someone simply so they would spend money. During his time at the Stoddard Academy he had learned much of mathematics and natural sciences and classical literature, but there were some things white men did not have to study to learn. They simply *knew*.

The wagons reached the park and came to a stop. Professor Dowd clambered in an ungainly fashion atop the seat of his wagon and lifted his hands, sweeping the top hat off his balding head and holding it aloft. "Good citizens of Providence!" he bellowed, his voice carrying well to the back of the crowd that had followed the wagons. "I am Professor Ulysses Xavier Dowd, the leader of this merry band of minstrels, gadabouts, and thespians! On this very evening, we will stage the first in a series of performances in your fair city. Come one, come all! Laugh at the pranks and tricks, shed a tear at the songs of yore, and be moved by the dramatic interpretations of classic scenes from the plays of the Bard of Avon, Mr. William Shakespeare! Ladies and gentlemen, you have never seen the like! So come, come and be entertained!" Dowd bent low in an elaborate bow, sweeping his hat before him. "I thank you!"

People applauded and laughed, and Dowd wore a grin on his ugly, bulbous-nosed face as he straightened. With Vanessa giving him a hand, he climbed down off the wagon seat.

Proud Wolf hopped to the ground, then turned back to help Audrey down from the wagon. A man standing nearby asked in a loud voice, "Hey there, boy, are you an Indian?"

Proud Wolf ignored the man and reached up to take Audrey's hand. A hard shove sent him staggering sideways and drew a gasp of surprise from Audrey, who nearly lost her balance when Proud Wolf's hand was suddenly no longer where she expected it to be. She was forced to grab the wagon seat to keep from toppling off.

Turning quickly, Proud Wolf saw that the man who had pushed him was the same one who had asked him if he was an Indian. "I asked you a question," the man said angrily. "Are you an Indian?"

"I am of the Teton Sioux," Proud Wolf said, tight-lipped.

"That so? I thought maybe you was a Huron or a Delaware or one of them tribes." The man gave an ugly laugh. "It don't matter. That's a white woman, and you keep your dirty red hands off her."

"Please, sir," Audrey said, "we don't want any trouble —"

"Then you should stay away from redskins, missy," the man said, leering up at her. Leaning over as she was, the low-cut gown she wore exposed the upper half of her creamy breasts, and the way the man's eyes were raking over them, he might as well have been pawing her.

"Leave us," Proud Wolf grated, trying to control his temper. His natural pride more than justified his name, and it was difficult for him to swallow the insults of this lout.

"Go on about your business, redskin," the man said, not even looking at him. He was still grinning lecherously at Audrey.

Proud Wolf glanced around. Several other men stood nearby, friends of the man who now held his hands up to Audrey and said, "Let *me* help you down from there, missy." The other men called out encouragement, peppered with ribald comments at Audrey's expense.

Proud Wolf understood now what she had meant about actresses and their reputation. To these men she was little better than a prostitute. Proud Wolf's hands closed into fists. He would have to show them how wrong they were about Audrey — and about him.

"Hey, mister!" a high-pitched voice piped up.

The troublemaker looked down. Without anyone noticing, Oliver Johnson had come up beside him. Oliver tugged on the man's coattails and said again in an urgent voice, "Hey, mister!"

Clearly annoyed, the man snapped, "What?"

"Bet you can't catch me," Oliver said.

"Why would I want to catch you?" the man asked, his lip curling in a sneer.

"Oh, you'll want to." Suddenly Oliver grabbed the man's leg, lunged forward, and sank his teeth into the man's thigh.

The man howled in pain and surprise, Proud Wolf and Audrey totally forgotten now, and staggered backward a couple of steps with Oliver hanging on to his leg. He swiped a big fist at Oliver's head, but in the twinkling of an eye Oliver had released him and darted back out of reach. "Told you you can't catch me!" he cried.

The troublemaker's friends were howling, too, but in laughter. "Go get 'im, Macy," one of them shouted.

Macy lunged at Oliver, reaching out with both hands. Again Oliver danced back, easily staying just out of Macy's reach as the man chased him. Suddenly Oliver stopped, lowered his head, and raced forward, bending over to dart between Macy's legs. He spun around and kicked Macy in the rear end, sending him stumbling forward.

Macy tripped, lost his balance, and went down hard, falling on his face in a puddle of mud. He tried to get up, but Oliver was not done with him. As Macy pushed himself to his hands and knees, Oliver bounded forward, grinning devilishly. One foot landed between Macy's shoulder blades, driving his face back into the muck. Oliver leaped past him, then turned and made faces as he struggled to get up. Macy, howling his rage, managed to get to his feet and lumber after Oliver, but by this time the little man was disappearing around one of the wagons. Macy followed, trailed by his laughing companions.

Proud Wolf started after them, but Audrey stopped him by saying, "Help me down from here, Proud Wolf."

"But Oliver —"

"Oliver knows exactly what he's doing. He stepped in to keep you from killing somebody or getting killed yourself. So help me down, and don't worry about Oliver."

Proud Wolf reached up and took Audrey's hands, then clasped her waist to steady her as she climbed down to the ground. He could track the progress of Oliver and his pursuers up the far side of the wagons by the sounds of cursing and laughter. Proud Wolf and Audrey hurried toward the lead wagon in time to see Ulysses Dowd stepping between Oliver and Macy.

Dowd was a formidable figure in his own right, and his booming voice made him seem even bigger. "Here, now!" he said. "What's all this uproar?"

Oliver hid behind Dowd, leaning out to make faces at Macy and lure him on. Macy, breathing heavily, planted himself in front of Dowd and wiped mud off his face. "That little bastard tried to kill me!" he accused, leveling a finger at Oliver. A look of embarrassment suddenly came over his face as he realized how that must have sounded to his friends.

"Right, Macy," one of them jeered. "The

midget tried to kill you."

Macy whirled around, scowling. "Damn you, he did!"

Dowd threw his head back and laughed, then stepped forward and clapped the surprised Macy on the back. "Now I understand, sir," he said, still chuckling. "You want to join our humble troupe, so you've been demonstrating what a fine comedian you are. Tell me, sir, can you play tragedy as well? Have you ever trod the boards?"

"Trod the — what?" Macy shook his head. "I don't know what you're talking about."

"Why, surely a sprite such as Oliver here could not possibly present a true challenge to a man of your worthy physical attributes. You were only *acting*, sir."

Macy looked around warily and wiped the back of his hand across his mouth, succeeding only in smearing more mud on his cheeks. He sniffed, shuffled his feet, and then finally said, "Uh, yes, that's what I was doing, all right. Just having some fun with the little fellow."

"Of course!" Dowd slapped him on the back again. "And quite a jolly dance it was, too!" He slid his arm around Macy's shoulders. "Tell me, sir, do you plan to attend tonight's performance?"

"Well, I, no, I haven't given it much thought —"

"I want you to come. You'll be my personal guest. And when we pass the hat, I don't want you to put anything in it, not even one slim copper. You've already contributed so much with your wit and graciousness."

"Well, I . . . all right," Macy said.

"Very good, sir. We shall see you anon!" Gently, Dowd steered Macy back toward his friends, who closed in around him and led him off toward a nearby tavern.

As soon as they were gone, Dowd swung around and said ominously, "Oliver . . ."

Oliver had retreated under the Dowds' wagon. He poked his head out cautiously and said, "I had to do it, Ulysses. That big oaf was going to start a fight with Proud Wolf."

Audrey stepped forward. "It's true, Professor Dowd. The man was very rude. He would have turned violent."

Dowd leveled his gaze at Proud Wolf. "And you would have been violent right back, wouldn't you have, lad?"

Proud Wolf lifted his chin. "He insulted me and was disrespectful to Audrey. My honor demanded —"

"Your honor demanded damn near

81

enough trouble to land the whole lot of us in the local jail," Dowd cut in sourly. "Best ye learn now, lad. There are a lot of ignorant people in the world, and you can't educate all of them with your fists, or even with a knife or a gun. You should thank Oliver for stepping in when he did."

Proud Wolf nodded stiffly to the little man, who had emerged from under the wagon. Oliver grinned.

"Oliver, have a talk with the boy," Dowd said.

"Be glad to. Come along, Proud Wolf. Let's walk back to your wagon."

Proud Wolf hesitated, then fell in step beside him. Audrey started to go with them, but Vanessa Dowd reached out and put a hand on her arm. "Audrey, dear," she said, "Portia and Elaine and I need some help with the costumes."

Audrey hesitated, then shrugged at Proud Wolf and went with Vanessa. Proud Wolf knew Mrs. Dowd was simply trying to give the two men some privacy. Out of courtesy, he would listen to what the little man had to say.

"Well, that was a close call, wasn't it?" Oliver said after a moment.

"I do not flee from a fight," Proud Wolf said.

"That gent was twice your size. You'd have had to kill him to beat him, and where would that get you?"

"If he was twice my size, he is four times the size of you," Proud Wolf pointed out.

"You can cipher. Pretty smart for a dumb Indian, aren't you?"

Proud Wolf stopped short and looked down at Oliver, stunned.

"What's the matter?" Oliver asked. "Never been called a dumb Indian before? How about a filthy redskin? A dirty savage?"

"I am a warrior of the Teton Sioux —" Proud Wolf began.

"And I'm an actor. Before that I wanted to be a professor of classical literature at Harvard. That doesn't stop people from calling me 'Shorty' and 'Half-Pint' and 'Sawed-off Little Runt' and 'Freak.' I've had children look at me and run away crying. That's really not fair, because if there's anyone in this troupe who ought to make children cry, it's Ulysses. He's much uglier than I am."

Proud Wolf cocked his head. "What do you mean by saying these things?"

"What do I mean?" Oliver reached up as high as he could and prodded a finger into Proud Wolf's chest. "I mean that you're who you are in here, no matter what people call you. Just as I am." He poked Proud Wolf again. "And the sooner you learn to listen to yourself, rather than a bunch of ignorant bumpkins, the better off you'll be."

"You mean I should ignore people when they insult me?"

"They don't know you as well as *you* do, now, do they?" Oliver waved a hand. "Ignore them? You can't always. But don't give them any more importance than they deserve." He hooked his thumbs under his suspenders. "Me, I make them laugh. They don't know it, but sometimes when they're laughing at me, I'm really laughing at them."

Proud Wolf shook his head. "I do not understand."

"That's all right. Just remember what I told you, whether you understand it now or not. Someday you will." Oliver grinned. "Listen to me. I know what I'm talking about. And someday, if I'm ever in your part of the world, I'll listen to you when you tell me how things are."

Proud Wolf nodded slowly. "All right." As he and Oliver started walking again, he went on, "I would like to show you the land of my people someday."

"I'd like to see it," Oliver said wistfully. Then he added with a laugh, "But I'll bet you don't have any squaws my size."

CHAPTER FOUR

After visiting Philadelphia, New York, and New Orleans, St. Louis looked like a rude frontier village to Melissa Holt. The keelboat on which she, Michael, and Terence O'Shay had traveled was tied at a wharf on the west bank of the great river. The docks were bustling and noisy, with men loading and unloading keelboats, flatboats, and other, nondescript vessels. Heavily armed men in buckskins and coonskin caps, undoubtedly fur trappers from the mountains, mingled among the rivermen, having come to the settlement to sell their loads of plews.

"Those men look like Uncle Clay!" Michael said excitedly from his place by Melissa's side. "Is he here?"

"I don't know, Michael." Melissa smiled faintly. "It's always difficult to tell where Clay Holt will turn up next."

The last she had heard of Clay, he had been in Washington City, still working on the assignment for Thomas Jefferson.

Where that mission might have led him, she had no idea. Jeff had chosen to come home to Wilmington rather than remain with Clay, and he had walked right into the plan Melissa and Lemuel March had hatched for opening new trade routes across the Pacific. Jeff had taken to the idea immediately; from a business standpoint it had been a sound one.

As for its effect on their marriage, however . . .

With a small sigh, Melissa put those thoughts out of her head. She had other things with which to concern herself at the moment, more pressing matters than those of the heart. She turned to Terence O'Shay. "Do you think you'll be able to find a guide for us?"

O'Shay waved a knobby-knuckled hand at the settlement before them. "With all these gents around, I'll be findin' who we need, I'm thinkin'."

Melissa nodded. "All right." She cast a dubious glance at the narrow, dirty streets that led away from the docks. "Perhaps it might be better if Michael and I stayed aboard the boat."

"I want to see the town!" Michael protested.

" 'Old on a minute," O'Shay told them.

He bounded ashore easily, approached one of the men lounging on the dock, and spoke briefly with him. When he returned to the boat, he said to Melissa, "Accordin' to that fellow, there's a decent hotel only a couple of blocks from 'ere. I'll walk you and Whip down there, see that ye're settled in, and then go lookin' for a guide."

"The goods will be safe here?"

"Aye." O'Shay's fingers lightly touched the butt of the flintlock pistol tucked behind his broad belt. "The crew'll spread the word that nothin's to be disturbed."

At moments like this, Melissa was reminded of the threat of violence that lay just beneath the surface of the man. In Wilmington Terence O'Shay had been feared and respected throughout the criminal community. But he had always been a good friend to the Holt family, she reminded herself, and anyway, where they were going, it was a good thing indeed to have a man along who was handy with gun and knife and fists.

She took Michael's hand to help him up onto the dock. O'Shay reached down, grasped Michael's arms, and lifted him easily. Then he extended his hand to Melissa, and she was grateful for his strength as she stepped up. She was aware of the admiring glances of the men on the docks as she and Michael and O'Shay walked off the wharf and started down the street, but no one leered too boldly. Terence's presence probably accounted for that, too.

The hotel was a two-story building, the first she had seen in St. Louis. It was made of heavy, unpainted beams and had a covered porch along the front. A roughly lettered sign saying only HOTEL hung from the roof over the porch.

Half a dozen men were sitting on the porch, smoking pipes in the shade. They nodded pleasantly to Melissa, and one of them commented, "That's a fine-looking boy you and your husband have there, ma'am."

Melissa felt herself flushing in embarrassment. "Oh, we're not —" she began, then thought better of it. If she told these men that she and Terence weren't married, they might jump to the wrong conclusion. Instead she smiled and said, "Thank you."

Once they were inside the hotel, O'Shay said, "I'm sorry about what 'appened out there, Melissa."

"It's not your fault," she assured him. She laughed softly. "It's certainly not your fault that my life has gotten so . . . complicated."

"No, but with us travelin' together, folks might misunderstand."

"Don't concern yourself, Terence," she said. "I'm accustomed to letting people think what they will. Most people thought it quite odd when I decided to run Holt-Merrivale myself while Jeff was . . . gone."

And now he was gone again, she added to herself. For two people who supposedly loved each other, they had wound up apart a great deal of the time. During their marriage they had been separated more than they had been together, Melissa mused.

But there was no point in dwelling on a situation that couldn't be helped. Holding Michael's hand, she walked up to the hotel desk, a counter roughly hewn from raw lumber. The man behind it wore a suit with a tight collar and a limp cravat, but he looked as if he would have been more at home in buckskins, like the men outside. "Something I can do for you folks?" he asked.

"The lady and the boy need a room," Terence said. "Somethin' clean, and quiet."

"We keep the place swept out pretty

good. Don't know that we can do much 'bout the quiet, though. That depends on the folks staying here."

"I don't want 'em bothered."

"Won't be any shootings or knifings, if I have anything to say 'bout it." The clerk shrugged. "That's about all I can promise."

And this was the *good* hotel in St. Louis, Melissa thought wryly. She was getting a rapid education in what life on the frontier was like. And it would only get more primitive the farther behind they left St. Louis.

"This will be sufficient," she said to Terence. "We just need a place to rest for a day or two while you find a guide for us."

"A guide?" the hotel clerk said. "Where might you be headed? Perhaps I can point you in the right direction."

"Do you mean you know someone who'd hire on to guide us?"

"Hell, I'd do it myself! Begging your pardon, ma'am. It's just that I'd be happy to take any job that would get me out from behind this desk."

Melissa looked more closely at the man. He was in his early thirties, she judged, and balding, with a close-cropped brown beard. His eyes were a washed-out blue and had an apparently permanent squint to them that told her he had spent a great deal of time outdoors.

"Are you familiar with the frontier?" she asked, ignoring the warning glance Terence shot her.

"Yes, ma'am. Made four trips up the Missouri to trap beaver."

Terence asked, "Then why aren't ye still doin' that, instead of clerkin' in a hotel?"

A pained expression crossed the clerk's face. "Well, sir, that's a long story. What happened is, I ran afoul of a fellow who couldn't be trusted, and I made the mistake of trusting him. It's an old story, I know, but it's true. I got swindled out of the money I had coming to me for a load of plews, so I couldn't put together another outfit. Been clerking here for nigh onto a month, trying to save enough coin to buy some more traps and powder and ball." He sighed and shook his head. "Rate I'm going, I ought to have enough in five years or so. Course, by then all the beaver'll be gone."

"Is that right?" Terence asked with a frown.

The clerk guffawed. "Aw, hell, no! They won't ever run out of beaver out yonder in the mountains. Folks can trap them from now 'til doomsday, and there'll still be plenty of the critters to go around!" He leaned forward eagerly. "What do you say?" he prodded. "I'd be glad to sign on with you folks if you're heading west."

"That's where we're going," Melissa said. "Mr. — ?"

"Oh. Pardon me." The man spit in the palm of his hand, wiped it on the seat of his pants, then stuck his hand out to Terence. "Name's Casebolt, Pinkney Casebolt. Folks generally call me Pink."

Terence shook his hand. "Terence O'Shay. This is Mrs. Holt and 'er son, Michael."

Pink Casebolt frowned. "That so? I figured that you two were —"

"Mr. O'Shay and I are business associates," Melissa said coolly.

"Oh. Well, that's fine by me, ma'am." Casebolt gave her a polite nod. "I'm pleased to meet you." He reached over the counter to shake hands with Michael. "And you, too, son."

"Are you a mountain man?" Michael asked.

"Some would call me that," Casebolt said.

"Where's your coonskin cap? Do you have a rifle?"

Casebolt grinned. "Yes, sir, the finest

Kentucky rifle you ever saw. Why, I can hit a playing card turned sideways at five hundred yards with that gun. And I got a coonskin cap, too." He looked up slyly at Melissa and Terence. "If your ma and Mr. O'Shay hire me as a guide, I reckon you'll get to see the cap *and* the rifle, too. Might even let you wear the cap."

Michael's face lit up, and Melissa was gratified that Terence didn't hire Casebolt on the spot just so Michael could wear a coonskin cap. "We'll let you know," Terence said.

Casebolt nodded. "Certainly, sir. Take your time. Ask around about me if you like. Anybody who's been in St. Louis a while will tell you that Pink Casebolt knows the lay of the land, yes, sir."

"We'll see. What about that room?"

"Yes, sir. Number seven, at the top of the stairs. Best room in the house."

"Thank you," Melissa said.

"That will be a dime a night."

Terence dropped a coin on the counter, which Casebolt raked off into a box. "Much obliged," he said, bobbing his head.

Melissa, Michael, and Terence turned toward the stairs. Casebolt leaned on the counter and called after them, "Enjoy your stay. Hope you don't take too long deciding about hiring me."

The three travelers went up the stairs and into room seven, which had an unplaned wooden door with a simple latch and no lock. That would be all right, Melissa told herself. The citizens of St. Louis might be rough around the edges, but none of them would dare bother a respectable woman and her child. She was confident of that.

"I'll 'ave a look around the town, maybe ask a few questions about that character downstairs," Terence said. "I'll sleep on the boat tonight, just to be sure nobody comes aboard that shouldn't be there, but I'll be back before then to 'elp you find a place to eat supper."

"Thank you. Thank you for everything, Terence." Melissa felt a warm surge of affection as she looked at him. She smiled. "What do you think of Mr. Casebolt?"

"A bit of a braggart." Terence chuckled. "But 'ow can an Irishman fault a man for 'avin' the gift of gab? 'E 'as no more of the blarney about 'im than many I've seen."

He left the room and clattered back down the stairs. Melissa looked around the room. It was very simply furnished, with a single bunk topped by a crude straw mattress, one chair, and a chamber pot. It would do for sleeping, but that was all. Of course, that was all she and Michael needed it for, Melissa reminded herself. It was no worse than the cabin of the keelboat in which they had spent the past week.

"What do you think, Mama?" Michael asked.

"It'll do," Melissa said practically.

"I like Mr. Casebolt. He's funny."

"Well, what's important is not that he's funny. If we hire him, he has to be able to lead us to where we're going."

"To New Hope?"

"That's right," Melissa said.

That was where they were bound — New Hope, that tiny outpost in the mountains that Clay Holt and Shining Moon called home. It was a particularly appropriate name for her destination, she thought. New hope, a beginning, a new life for her and her son. She wondered briefly if Jeff would ever be a part of her life again, then resolutely shut him out of her mind.

Jeff woke up shivering, his teeth chattering violently. The fire in the hearth had died down and gave off only a faint heat and a feeble glow. He sat up, trying not to groan at the movement of muscles grown stiff overnight. He wrapped the thick fur robe more tightly around himself.

It was dim inside the Tlingit hut, but he could see the gray circle that marked the smoke hole in the roof. The morning was well advanced.

Nadia lay under a pile of robes on the far side of the hearth. There was no one else in the room. The night before, Jeff had insisted with his gestures that she sleep there instead of sharing a bunk with him as she had wanted. Her mouth had turned down, but there were no tears this time. Instead she had curled up in the robes and turned her back on him, as if she were angry.

That was fine with Jeff. He could deal with her anger and resentment more easily than he could with a determination to act like his wife.

Sitting here like this was not going to make him any warmer, Jeff told himself. Keeping the furs wrapped around himself, he put a hand on the ground to balance himself as he stood up. He picked up a few twigs from the pile near one wall and stumbled toward the hearth. Fingers working awkwardly in the cold, he peeled off the bark to use as tinder, then blew on the embers until they glowed. He held one of the strips of bark against a red-hot coal until it abruptly curled into flame. Quickly but carefully Jeff fed the other shreds into the coals until he had a tiny blaze going. He laid the rest of the twigs in the fire, arranging them so that they would burn efficiently.

Jeff held out his hands toward the dancing flames and sighed gratefully as the warmth seeped into his joints. At moments like this he wondered what had ever possessed him to come to Alaska in the first place. Greed? He had never thought of himself as an avaricious man, although it was important to him that the Holt-Merrivale Company succeed. Like any man, he wanted to do his best for his family. But he didn't think that instinct had ever translated into naked money-grubbing.

Ambition? Pride? The knowledge that his enterprise would be one of the first to open up Pacific trade routes? No one would deny that all the Holts had their share of pride, but no, that was not his motivation either.

Jeff stared into the flames and let his mind wander. He recalled the journey of discovery his brother Clay had undertaken with Lewis and Clark seven years earlier. Clay had the wanderlust in his blood, no doubt about that, and that had contributed greatly to his decision to go west. So had the trouble that was brewing between the Holts and the Garwoods over Josie Garwood's claim that Clay was the father of her young son, Matthew. But Jeff remembered something else Clay had told him back then.

"We may be the first, but we won't be the last," Clay had said the night before he left the family farm in Ohio to join Lewis and Clark. "Other folks will come after us and follow the trails we've made." Then he'd grinned that reckless, lopsided grin. "Unless, of course, we all get killed and nobody ever sees us again."

They hadn't gotten killed, although in the more than two years that the Corps of Discovery was gone, many people assumed that the wilderness had claimed them. Lewis and Clark and Clay and the others had returned, and as Clay had predicted, others had gone west. Clay himself had returned to the frontier, taking his younger brother with him. By now hundreds, perhaps thousands, of white men had journeyed to the mountains. "Gone to see the elephant," they called it. There were even a few settlements out there, far beyond what had been thought to be the limits of civilization.

That was what it was all about, Jeff suddenly realized: building things. Someday, from the seed planted by a small group of men trudging across the wilderness, infinitesimal against their vast surroundings, would come roads and homes and bustling enterprises, spreading all the way across the continent from sea to sea. Some people might not think that was necessarily a good thing; Jeff knew that Clay had his doubts about so-called civilization. But it was coming, no doubt about that.

And that was why he had come to Alaska, Jeff thought, why he had sent Ned to Hawaii and China: so that others could come after them. It was as simple as that.

Lost in his musing, he had not heard the change in Nadia's breathing as she awoke, nor the soft rustle of the furs as she sat up. But he heard the padding of her feet and turned to see her standing beside him.

She spoke in the Tlingit tongue and gestured toward the fire. Jeff heard the repentance in her voice and guessed that she was apologizing for letting the fire burn down so low. If she was going to take care of him, as Vassily had said, it was her duty to share the communal duty of keeping the fire going at all times.

"It's all right," Jeff told her, keeping his voice gentle since he knew she would not understand the words themselves. "I don't mind building up the fire."

"Fy . . . urr," Nadia said, pointing at the flames.

Jeff grinned up at her. So she did know at least one word of English. "That's right," he said. He pointed at the flames, as she had done, and repeated, "Fire."

"Fire," she said, more confidently this time.

Jeff pointed at her and said, "Nadia." If she had worked in the Russian settlement, she probably knew the name by which the foreigners had called her.

She nodded and easily said, "Nadia." She poked at the robes wrapped around her with a forefinger.

Jeff indicated himself. "Jeff."

"Juh . . . Juh . . ." Nadia frowned in concentration. "Juh . . . eff."

He laughed. "That's right!"

"Jeff. Jeff." Pride glowed on her face.

A second later, firelight glowed on her body as she dropped the robes and stood before him, nude except for the fur boots she had pulled on when she arose.

Jeff swallowed hard. The house had warmed a little since he had built up the fire, but he certainly had not expected Nadia to discard her sleeping robes. He was also surprised to discover that she had removed her clothing sometime during the night. He had slept in his trousers, shirt, and heavy wool socks.

Nadia stood there, completely at ease. Jeff knew he should not be looking at her, but he was compelled to. Her dark, shining hair was braided and decorated with bits of painted bark and fell on smooth shoulders. Her skin was a dusky red. Large, rounded breasts crowned with dark nipples rode high on her chest, and at the moment those nipples were pebbled and erect, whether from the cold or from arousal, Jeff did not know. Below her breasts, her belly was slightly rounded, and it flowed down to flaring hips and muscular thighs. The triangle of hair between her legs was large and dark.

A faint, knowing smile tugged at her lips as she watched him studying her. Like all women since the dawn of history, she was well aware of her power over the male of the species.

Tearing his eyes away from her, Jeff grabbed the robes she had dropped and held them up between them. "You'd better put these back around you," he said hastily. "You'll catch your death of cold."

That was unlikely, since she had lived her entire life in this frigid climate, and at any rate she could not understand what he was saying, but he babbled the words anyway. For a split second as he had looked up at her, the image of the blond, fair-skinned Irina Orlov had appeared, superimposed over Nadia's darker, earthier figure, and Jeff remembered all too well what had happened the last time he had almost given in to temptation. Melissa had left him, and he had almost been killed, narrowly escaping death only to wind up a prisoner in a Tlingit village. He would not allow himself to be tempted again.

Nadia shoved the robes away as he tried to wrap them around her. "Jeff," she said, clutching at his arm. "Jeff, Nadia. Jeff, Nadia." She gestured at the bunk where he had slept.

Stubbornly, Jeff shook his head. "No. I'm sorry, but I can't do that."

She caught his hand and brought it to her breast, filling it with the soft, warm flesh. He felt the hard nipple against his palm and groaned.

Nadia must have taken his reaction as an

encouraging sign, because suddenly she was pressing herself against him, nuzzling her face against the beard stubble on his jaw. His other arm instinctively went around her waist. His hand was trapped between them, the fingers digging into her breast.

Jeff fought down the physical need that surged inside him. With a gasp, he pushed Nadia away. As soon as he was free of her, he stumbled around the fire, putting the flames between them.

He shook his head again and said, "No, Nadia. This isn't right. I . . . I'm a married man."

The sheer absurdity of the statement struck him as soon as the words were out of his mouth. Of course he was married, but his wife was thousands of miles away and wanted nothing to do with him. And it was ludicrous to dole out such a platitude to Nadia under these circumstances and expect her to have even the foggiest notion of what he was talking about.

What she did understand was that he had rejected her. Anger and sorrow warred on her face, and sorrow won out. She reached up and caught hold of her braids, tugging hard until she grimaced in pain. Then she began clawing at her bare breasts and wailing like a woman tormented.

Jeff's eyes widened in horror. He had seen Indian women behave this way before. She was grieving, grieving because he had turned her away. She might do physical harm to herself. He sprang back around the fire and grabbed her wrists, pulling her hands away from her breasts, now streaked with angry red lines where she had scratched them.

"Don't do that!" he told her sharply. "This has nothing to do with you, Nadia. I . . . I cannot allow you to be a wife to me. You have to understand —"

But how could she do that? he asked himself. He could ask Vassily to explain things to her, he supposed, but that would be awkward and embarrassing; besides, Vassily might be angered that Jeff had rejected his sister.

She said in a whimper, "Jeff, Nadia?"

Jeff took a deep breath and shook his head. There was no other answer he could give her.

She jerked out of his grip and turned away. This time she was angry, there was no mistaking that. She gathered up her robes and hastily wrapped them around her. Throwing Jeff a glare over her shoulder, she stalked to the door, threw it open, and stomped out across the thin layer of snow that covered the ground. Gray dawn light washed in through the door she had left open behind her.

Jeff sank down on his bunk without bothering to close the door. Maybe he would be lucky and freeze to death, he thought miserably.

Several minutes later, something blocked the light in the doorway, and Jeff looked up to see Vassily standing there. He was holding a short spear in his hand, and for a second Jeff thought he had come to kill him for offending Nadia.

But a grin stretched across Vassily's round face, and he said, "Good morning, Jeff Holt. Come with me." He held up the spear and shook it slightly. "We catch our morning food in the stream."

Vassily wanted him to go fishing, Jeff realized. He came to his feet and nodded. "All right. Do you have another spear?"

"No. But I let you use mine. Teach you Tlingit ways, since you one of us now."

There it was again, Vassily's assumption that Jeff would remain in the village and become one of them. Jeff felt a prickle of irritation and restlessness. He wanted to be out of here. He wanted to go back to Sitka and settle the score with Count Gregori Orlov.

But it was not time yet to be contemplating matters of revenge. He said, "All right. I'll see if I can spear a fish."

Vassily chuckled. "You do better with fish than you do with Tlingit woman."

Jeff tensed. "You saw Nadia . . . ?"

"Come. We catch fish. Worry about woman later."

Jeff left out a long breath. Hugely relieved, he followed Vassily from the house and walked beside him toward the creek.

CHAPTER FIVE

Captain Nicholas Roosevelt wasted no time in New Orleans. Now that he had proven against all odds that the steamboat he had designed, built, and captained could indeed make the voyage down the Ohio and Mississippi Rivers, he was ready for the second, more difficult part of the adventure: returning upstream to Pittsburgh.

That suited Clay perfectly. The sooner he and Shining Moon and Markham reached St. Louis, the sooner they could get on the trail of Comte Jacques de La Carde. The bigger La Carde's lead, the longer it would take to catch him.

During the trip up the Mississippi to St. Louis, Clay was racked again with doubt about the wisdom of taking Shining Moon and Matthew along on the chase. And yet, what else could he do with them? The *New Orleans* would be stopping at Marietta on its return trip, and Clay supposed he could send them back to the family farm. But Shining Moon had suffered so much at the farm that she never wanted to go back there. Nor could he blame her.

What she longed for was her home in the mountains. Clay understood. He felt the same way himself.

If La Carde's trail took them anywhere near the village of Bear Tooth's band of Teton Sioux and the settlement of New Hope, Clay would leave Shining Moon and Matthew there, he decided. She would be back among her people, and Matthew would have a blood relative there, his uncle Aaron Garwood. That would be the best solution.

Winter was settling over the countryside. Clay thought about the blizzards that roared through the mountains and the northern plains, making travel difficult, if not downright impossible sometimes. La Carde would likely hole up somewhere and wait a few weeks for the worst of the storms to pass. If the party had competent guides, they could probably find a friendly Indian village in which to spend that time.

That would give Clay and Markham a chance to cut into La Carde's lead, because Clay was determined to keep moving except in the worst weather. He knew it was a risky plan, the more so because Shining Moon and Matthew were with them. But it was the only way to catch up to the Frenchman in time.

The Mississippi was peaceful as the *New Orleans* steamed upriver against its slow-moving but powerful current. Fighting the current, of course, the steamboat did not make as good time as it had coming downriver. Several days after the boat had left New Orleans, Clay was standing at the railing, watching the countryside roll slowly past and wishing there was some way to speed up the journey.

At least the earthquakes had stopped. Looking out at the peaceful land now, it was hard to believe that only a few weeks earlier the earth had moved before his very eyes, ripping itself apart.

Lieutenant Markham came up beside Clay and rested his hands on the railing. "Thinking about La Carde?" he asked quietly.

Clay grunted. "Not really. Wishing I could get him in the sights of my rifle, maybe."

"He must be a madman. What can he truly accomplish? He can't possibly take over the entire western half of the continent. For God's sake, he'd be taking on the whole nation. He'd have to raise an army!"

Clay looked at him, eyes narrowed in

thought. "What if he figures to find one out there, ready-made for him?"

"How could he do that?"

Clay turned his gaze back to the riverbank. "Nobody knows how many Indians there are beyond the mountains," he mused.

Markham's breath hissed between his teeth. "Good Lord! You mean you think La Carde might somehow unite the tribes and raise them against the United States?"

"It's not as if the French haven't done anything like that before," Clay pointed out. "I recollect my papa talking about how, when the states were still English colonies, the French got some Indians together and fought a war against the British and the colonists. That's where George Washington got his start."

"Indeed," Markham muttered. "The French and Indian War. I remember. But the French government was behind that. La Carde is one man."

Clay shook his head. "He may be the leader, but he's got some other folks with him. I reckon they feel the same way he does about Bonaparte selling the Louisiana Territory to us."

"Still, you're only talking about a handful of disgruntled people —"

"I've been thinking about that French military cutter the harbormaster in New Orleans told me about," Clay said. "What if its hold is full of guns? What if it's on its way around South America and plans to meet La Carde when he reaches the west coast?"

"Now, Clay, that's rather far-fetched, don't you think?"

"It could happen."

Markham could not argue with that. "All right," he said, "I'll concede that perhaps La Carde and his people could gain a foothold on the frontier. But how much actual harm could they do?"

"I've seen some big fires start from a single spark. Besides, even though he went about it underhandedly, he managed to get his hands on legal title to a lot of land out there. He might fight the United States in the courts as well as with gun and knife."

Markham shook his head. "Never! Our judicial system is a bastion of honesty and fairness."

Clay looked at him, smiled wryly, and shook his head. "Anything run by human folks can be corrupted. And chances are it will be, sooner or later."

"I'd hate to think that you're right to be so cynical, Clay."

"I reckon we'll see." Clay looked upriver, wishing he could see St. Louis on the bank ahead of them. "Time's going to tell us, whether we want to listen or not."

The *New Orleans* tied up every evening, although on some occasions the moonlight was so bright that Captain Roosevelt was tempted to proceed. But the upheavals that had shaken the earth a few weeks earlier had been so powerful that new sandbars and snags had formed in the river, and even the best pilot on the Mississippi no longer had any hope of knowing where all the hazards lay. It would take keen eyes and good light to get the steamboat through safely.

The *New Orleans* was moored a day's voyage north of the settlement of Natchez. Sturdy ropes ran from the boat to a pair of good-sized trees on the riverbank. The deck was quiet; with no passengers on this trip but Clay and his companions, Captain Roosevelt had had the vessel loaded heavily with cargo. The hold was full of goods bound for the ports upriver. The empty passenger cabins, as well as areas of the deck, were being used for storage as well.

Without the politicians and journalists

aboard, the salon was generally empty. When Clay wandered into the room tonight, there was no one behind the bar, no one at the tables scattered around the room. He thought about helping himself to a drink, then decided not to. As he looked around, he reflected that he never would have believed he could miss Senators Emory and Haines, but at this moment it might have been nice to have them there to spar with. Especially Haines. The senator from New York was adamantly opposed to the development of the western half of the continent, considering it a waste of money. Clay agreed with him about the folly of expansion, but for completely different reasons. He hated the thought of towns setting down roots all over the frontier, so that a man had no elbow room anymore.

Clay shook his head ruefully and turned toward the doors of the salon. He was ready to head back to the cabin he shared with Shining Moon and Matthew and turn in for the night.

As he turned, he heard the scuff of boot leather on the hardwood floor and smelled the sharp tang of dirt and sweat. Warning bells went off in Clay's brain, and he twisted around to see who had sneaked up behind him.

He didn't get the chance. Something slammed into the side of his head and sent him staggering against the bar. He caught the edge of the bar and stopped himself from falling, but he could not see anything. A red haze had descended over his vision, with explosions of a darker red blooming within it.

He heard a grunt and instinctively threw an arm up to block a second blow. The move didn't keep the blow from landing, but it softened the impact enough to keep his skull from being crushed. He sagged to his knees, then sprawled in front of the bar as darkness slid over the crimson haze.

Clay was not aware of when the blackness overwhelmed him and he passed out. Nor did he know how long he had been unconscious when, finally, his senses began to function again. As awareness seeped into his stunned brain, he felt a pounding ache in his head. Waves of heat were beating against him, and a thick, choking smoke filled his nose and mouth. A racking cough seized him, setting off fresh explosions of pain inside his head.

Clay forced his eyes open and pushed himself up on his hands and knees. His body moved sluggishly, but he gritted his teeth and willed it into action. He blinked and looked around and saw a wall of flame only a few feet away. The fire seemed to have started behind the bar, and now it was consuming the bar itself, feeding off the liquor stored behind it.

As he staggered to his feet, Clay looked desperately around the room. Fire was one of the most feared disasters on any boat. If a blaze got out of control, the largely wooden vessel could burn to the waterline in a matter of minutes. And this one was very nearly out of control already, Clay saw.

Still unsteady, he lumbered to the doors of the salon and tried to push them open so that he could rush out on deck and raise the alarm. The doors would not open. Clay threw his weight against them. Still they would not budge. Whoever had knocked him unconscious and started the fire had also locked the doors on the way out.

A bucket of sand sat beside one door. Other buckets stood at each end of the bar. They were a safety measure for putting out fires, Clay realized. He snatched up the bucket by the door, stumbled across the room, and flung the sand into the flames.

A small area of the fire subsided, but not by much. Clay dropped the empty bucket and ran to fetch another. The second bucketful of sand knocked down another pocket of flames, but Clay knew he would never be able to put out the fire in time. Already the flames were spreading to the wall behind the bar.

He was suddenly aware that someone was pounding on the doors. "Clay! Clay, are you in there?"

It was John Markham's voice. Clay turned toward the doors and bellowed, "Fire! Fire in here!"

"Stand back!"

A second later something crashed against the doors. A pause, then another crash, and this time the doors sprang open as the wood around the lock splintered. As air rushed into the salon, the fire roared even brighter, but several crewmen ran into the room carrying more buckets of sand. They dumped them on the flames, then passed the buckets back to other crewmen, who dipped them into the Mississippi and passed them forward again. The river water soon put out the fire. A couple of soot-stained sailors stomped out the last lingering flames.

Clay stumbled over to join Markham just inside the entrance. "What happened?" the lieutenant asked anxiously.

"Somebody fetched me a couple of clouts on the head when I stepped in here a while ago," Clay explained. "Knocked me out, and when I came to, the place was on fire."

"I can see that. I smelled it, too," Markham added. "Smoke was seeping out around the doors and I noticed it as I passed by on the deck. If I hadn't . . ."

Markham's voice trailed off into grim silence. Clay nodded. "The whole boat might've gone up in flames. I would have, for sure."

"But . . . who would have done this?"

Clay shook his head. "I don't know, but I intend to find out."

The fire was out now. The bar and the area behind it were heavily damaged, but the wall was charred only in a narrow strip along the bottom.

Captain Roosevelt rushed in and looked around in horror, exclaiming, "My God! What happened?"

Clay decided it was best to keep quiet about the attack. "I don't know for certain," he said, hoping Markham would follow his lead. "A fire started somehow and almost got out of control. Your crew put it out in time, though."

"But . . . but how could that happen?"

Roosevelt sputtered. "Were you in here when the fire started, Mr. Holt?"

Clay glanced at Markham and said, "No, Mr. Markham and I were strolling along the deck and smelled the smoke. We raised the alarm." In the confusion, it was possible that the crewmen who had answered Markham's yells for help had not noticed that Clay was already in the room.

"That's right," Markham said. "I'd say we were all fortunate it wasn't worse."

"Indeed," Roosevelt said emphatically. He shuddered. "There's nothing a riverman fears more than fire."

"With good reason," Clay said. He put a hand on Markham's arm and inclined his head toward the deck. "We're going back to our cabins."

"By all means," Roosevelt agreed. "Thank you, Mr. Holt, and you, Mr. Markham. We all owe you a debt of gratitude."

Clay led Markham out on the deck. As they walked toward their cabins, leaving Roosevelt and his crewmen behind to clean up the sooty mess in the salon, Markham said quietly, "Why didn't you tell the captain what really happened?"

"Because I want the fellow who jumped me to think that maybe my brain was addled by getting walloped. Maybe he'll think I don't actually know what happened."

"So that he'll feel safe enough to try again?"

Clay shrugged. "It's a possibility."

"A dangerous one."

"How did you manage to break those doors open?" Clay asked, changing the subject.

"I picked up a keg of nails that was sitting nearby and hit the lock with it a few times. Luckily the lock gave way before the keg did."

"I reckon you saved my life."

Markham smiled. "Just returning the favor. You've saved mine several times, I recall." He peered intently at his companion. "Clay, what's going on here? Who would want to kill you?"

Clay stopped and stared out into the night. "There's one fellow who's got reason to want us both dead."

"You mean the Comte de La Carde?" Markham asked in astonishment. "But how could he be behind this? He's probably hundreds of miles away."

"Maybe he has someone covering his back trail."

"How could that be possible?"

"I'll have to think on it," Clay said. "In

the meantime, watch your back . . . because I have a feeling somebody else already is."

If the island had a name, Ned had never heard it nor seen it marked on any maps. But there was a settlement there, a huddle of buildings around a cove. Some thirty years earlier, the story went, the British ship *Boylston* had ripped out its hull on a coral reef about half a mile offshore. Fifty members of its crew had made it to the sandy beach along the cove by clinging to debris from the wreckage. It had been pure luck that the sharks that usually frequented the waters around the reef were not about that day.

As it was, the survivors not only reached land but found friendly natives waiting for them. Instead of roasting over a cannibal's fire, as might have happened to them had they landed on some other southern Pacific island, they were made welcome, even given wives and adopted into the tribe. By the time another ship had come along, three years later, none of the sailors wanted to leave. They had found an idyllic home in which to spend the rest of their years.

Not many ships passed the island, but

those that did usually made port there, lured partly by tales of an unusually potent liquor the native islanders brewed from the milk of coconuts. The settlement became known as Boylston, after the sunken ship that had brought the sailors there, and it offered a few amenities that made the crews of visiting ships feel almost as if they were home.

Ned had heard the stories of Boylston but had never been there, of course. The *Lydia Marie* had followed a slightly different course on its way to China. Now, on the return voyage, the ship passed close enough that Captain Canfield had decided to stop overnight. "The lads will be sick in the morning," he told Ned with a grin as they stood at the rail and looked out at the village, "but not so sick that they cannot do their work."

"We hope," Ned added dryly.

"Indeed. That's why I'm counting on you to keep the men in line."

Ned looked surprised, and India, who was standing nearby, let out a quiet laugh at Canfield's words. "That's rather like setting a fox to guard a henhouse, don't you think, Captain?" she asked.

Ned flushed. "Never you mind," he said. "I'll see that things don't get out of hand,

Captain." He glared at India, who only shrugged.

The helmsman skillfully took the *Lydia Marie* around the reef that guarded the cove. The ship dropped anchor about a hundred yards offshore; the men would go ashore in small boats.

Ned was in the first boat, along with India and several other seamen. Captain Canfield planned to stay aboard the ship with a skeleton crew. The oarsmen rowed up to the beach, and Ned and a couple of others hopped out into the shallow water to haul the boat up onto the sand. A delegation from Boylston was already on its way down to greet them.

"Hallo!" one of the men called, lifting a hand in a friendly wave. Around fifty years of age and clearly one of the original castaways from the sunken ship, he was burned as dark by the sun as any native islander, and his hair was as light as straw. He grinned as he shook hands with Ned. "I'm Winston Fitch, the mayor of Boylston."

"Ned Holt, from the ship *Lydia Marie*."

"American, aren't you?" Fitch asked.

"That's right," Ned said. He suddenly realized that when the *Boylston* had gone down, the War for Independence had been over for only a year or so. These Englishmen might still harbor ill feelings toward Americans.

If that was the case, Winston Fitch didn't show it. His smile was friendly and welcoming. He said, "I take it your lads want to sample some of our famous hospitality?"

"Aye," Ned replied. "If that's all right."

"Always glad to have visitors," Fitch said heartily. "You're the first ones we've had from America. Usually 'tis Dutchmen or Spaniards who come calling. Occasionally we get a ship from England, so we keep up on the news from home."

Ned wondered exactly how current the citizens of this tiny outpost were. Fitch and the others might be aware of the increasing tension between the United States and England over maritime rights. Some said the growing friction might even lead to war. But here, thousands of miles from both America and England, it was clear the islanders had no interest in such disputes.

Fitch and his welcoming committee led Ned and the others into the village. The buildings were solidly constructed of logs and had thatched roofs made from palm fronds. Ned saw native islanders around the settlement and could not help but notice that men and women alike wore only a length of colorful cloth wrapped around their loins. The bare-breasted women were undeniably attractive, with long black hair and smooth skin the color of honey. Ned did his best not to stare, but it was difficult. He could well understand why the crew of the *Boylston* had chosen to remain on the island.

The largest building in the village was a tavern. Ned, India, and their companions were offered drinks. The coconut-milk brew packed as much power as Ned had heard tell; it slid smoothly down his throat and set off white-hot explosions in his belly. Several of the sailors downed their drinks in one gulp, then clenched their fists and pounded them on the split-palm logs that formed the bar. Ned knew exactly how they felt.

India, on the other hand, tossed back her drink, then licked her lips and nodded in satisfaction to Winston Fitch, who had gone behind the bar to serve the visitors. "Excellent," she said in the husky voice that was part of her masquerade.

Fitch grinned. "For a lad who probably doesn't shave more than once a week, you've got a right smart taste for liquor."

"I'm older than I look." India held out

her cup, a hollowed-out coconut shell, for Fitch to refill.

Ned frowned and drained his own cup. He'd be damned if he was going to allow India to outdrink him. For a fleeting second he thought about the responsibility Captain Canfield had placed on his shoulders. He would take only a few drinks, he told himself. That would be more than enough to put India under the table.

Instead, after a couple more cups, he found himself clutching the bar with his free hand to keep himself upright. His head was spinning, and all he wanted to do was find someplace to lie down.

"— that you leave our women alone."

Ned heard only the last part of that sentence. He stared bleary-eyed at Winston Fitch. "Wha' was that?" he asked.

"I said, all we ask is that you leave our women alone," Fitch repeated. "Some sailors, Mr. Holt, carry diseases, and we don't want them spread to our population. You and your men are welcome to drink all you like, however."

Ned felt some of his old belligerence rearing up inside him. "So we're good 'nough to buy your liquor but not your women, is that it?"

"In a nutshell, yes," Fitch said affably.

India took Ned's arm and turned him toward the tables that were scattered around the tavern. "Come," she said. "You need to sit down." She still seemed none the worse for the drinks she had consumed.

Ned thought about jerking away from her, but in the end he allowed her to steer him over to a table in the corner. He sat down gratefully, then grabbed the table edge to steady himself as the whole world spun wickedly for a moment. When things settled again, he leaned back with a sigh. His eyelids were suddenly unbearably heavy.

"Wait a . . . a minute," he said as India started to move away from the table. "Aren't you gonna . . . gonna sit down wi' me?"

"Rest, Ned," she said quietly. "That's what you need, not my company."

"But I want . . ."

Ned didn't finish his sentence. He slumped forward on the table, barely managing to pillow his head on his forearms before senselessness overwhelmed him. A moment later, a ragged snore came from his slack, open mouth. Ned Holt was dead to the world.

It was about time, India thought as she

left Ned sleeping at the table. She had worried that it would take another cup or two of liquor to put him out, and she was not certain her own exceptional tolerance for liquor would have held up. She already had a bit of a headache. But the coconut brew had not muddled her thinking. She was still very clear about what she wanted to do.

She returned to the bar and took another full cup from Winston Fitch, sipping from it as she turned and strolled across the room. This drink could be nursed for a while, now that she was no longer competing with Ned. Her destination was a table in the corner across from where Ned was snoring. Four men were seated there. One of them was Yancy, the little Cockney sailor, and another was Syme. The other two men were cronies of Yancy's, one an Englishman and the other an Italian who had wound up working on an American ship. Citizens of the world, they never saw their homelands except when their ships happened to dock there.

Without waiting for an invitation, India picked up an empty chair at another table, swung it around, and gave the men a pleasant nod as she lowered herself into the chair. She took another sip of the coconut liquor.

"Evenin' to ye, St. Clair," Yancy said. "What brings ye over 'ere?"

India inclined her head toward the other side of the room. "Holt's passed out, the sot," she said harshly. "The captain was a fool to put him in charge."

"His cousin owns the ship," Syme pointed out, "and another cousin owns the cargo we're carrying. Canfield has to kowtow to him."

"Aye, but we don't," India said.

Yancy looked at her shrewdly. "I thought ye and Holt were friends."

"We were, until he got too big for his britches. Always telling me what to do and how to do it — as if I don't know more about the sea than he ever will. All the bloody officers are like that."

" 'Tis their job to command," Yancy said, watching her.

India downed another slug. "Perhaps." She licked her lips, looked around the room, and went on, "A place like this island, now, this would be heaven on earth for a sailor. Warm breezes and pretty girls and plenty to drink. Best of all, no bastard giving you orders all the time."

"I'm surprised to hear you talking like that, St. Clair," Syme said. "You've always been loyal to the line."

"I'm not saying I'm not loyal," India snapped. "I'm just saying that I've been doing a lot of thinking."

Yancy leaned forward. "Thinkin's a dangerous thing for a poor seaman to be doin'. *I* think maybe ye'd best be on yer way, St. Clair."

India glowered at him. "You don't like my company?"

"It ain't that. Mebbe ye've had too much to drink. Ye're not thinkin' straight."

"I'm thinking better than I ever have before," India said ominously. She shoved back her chair and stood up. "What I'm thinking is that it would pay certain people to know who their real friends are."

With that, she turned and stalked back to the bar.

She kept her eyes straight ahead, fighting the impulse to look behind her and see if the men were discussing what had just happened. She hoped that in their brief conversation she had planted a seed, a seed that would grow and flower and convince them that she had turned against Ned and Captain Canfield. If she could overcome the natural suspicion with which they obviously regarded her, as a friend of Ned's, she might be able to uncover what they were planning — and, more importantly, when they were planning to do it.

Her strategy had entailed playing on Ned's pride and getting him drunk tonight, because if he had stayed sober he never would have allowed her to play such a dangerous game with men who might well be mutineers. Her efforts would cost him a bad headache when he woke up.

But that was better than losing the ship and all their lives later on. Because one thing was certain: If mutineers took over the *Lydia Marie*, they would leave no loyal members of the crew alive to testify against them.

CHAPTER SIX

The wagons of the Dowd acting troupe were pulled off the road and stopped in a field beside a tree-lined stream in Maryland. The actors deserved a few days of rest after two weeks of performing in a different town each night, Ulysses Dowd had declared. No one in the group had argued with him.

The life of a traveling actor had its trials, Proud Wolf had discovered. True, it was less arduous physically than the life of a Sioux warrior; an actor did not have to run all day, fight, run again, then fight again. And the audiences, though occasionally intimidating, did not carry scalping knives as did the Crow and the Blackfoot. But the routine of driving from town to town, village to village, stopping to put up the proscenium and then dressing in costume and staging a performance, was wearying. Proud Wolf was grateful that Professor Dowd had called a brief halt to their travels.

Setting up camp near a brook gave the

performers a chance to wash their clothes. The women saw to that task, while the Zachary brothers, Kenneth Thurston, Walter Berryhill, and Oliver Johnson got up a game of cards. Proud Wolf rummaged among the trunks of props until he found the spear he carried in his role as a Roman soldier during the scenes from a play called *Julius Caesar*. He had noticed that the edge of the spearhead was rather dull, and without telling Dowd why he wanted it, he had borrowed a whetstone to sharpen it.

Proud Wolf lowered the steps from the rear door of the covered wagon he shared with Audrey and sat on them while he sharpened the spear. He ran the whetstone back and forth across the edge several times, then tested it with the ball of his thumb. Not satisfied, he resumed his work with the whetstone.

"My goodness, Proud Wolf, what are you doing?" a woman's voice asked.

He looked up and saw Portia Yardley standing in front of him with a wicker basket full of laundry. "Sharpening this spear," he told her.

"Why in the world would you want to do that?"

"A dull weapon does no one any good."

"But it doesn't have to be sharp. It's just a prop."

Proud Wolf shook his head. "A weapon not properly cared for is an offense to the spirits."

"Perhaps you're right. I wouldn't know about any spirits . . . except that I like a jot of rum in my milk every now and then." She laughed. "Come with me."

Proud Wolf glanced up, surprised. "What?"

"Come with me down to the stream. Please? I didn't mean to make it sound like an order."

"You require . . . assistance of some sort?"

"Yes, that's it," Portia answered quickly. She hefted the wicker basket. "This laundry is heavy, and it'll be even heavier when I'm through washing it, because it will be wet. You can help me, can't you, Proud Wolf?"

He frowned. "I can." But did he want to?

This was the longest conversation he had ever had with Portia Yardley. She and her mother, Elaine, were generally rather reserved around Audrey and him. Portia was in her late teens, about the same age as Proud Wolf. Like her mother, she had glossy dark hair that fell in wings around her face and over her shoulders. Her face was lovely; her cheeks dimpled prettily when she smiled. She was slender yet womanly. Proud Wolf thought she was very pretty, though not as pretty as Audrey, of course.

"Well?" Portia said. "Are you going to help me, or are you going to sit there all day fooling with that old spear?"

Proud Wolf set the spear aside. "I will help you." He stood and took the basket from her.

"Thank you. It's nice to know that *someone* around here is a gentleman." She glanced toward the table where the men were playing cards. "Theodore and Frederick saw me lugging this basket around, and neither of them offered to help me." Portia sniffed. "They'd rather play cards."

Proud Wolf understood now. Portia was angry with the Zachary brothers, so she made sure that she led him toward the stream along a path that would take them within view of the twins. Perhaps she wished to make them jealous.

He walked beside her, and after a moment he became aware that the trail they were following did not lead to the same part of the brook where the other women were washing clothes. "Where are we going?" he asked.

"I found a spot over here that will be perfect," she replied. "And we won't have to listen to Mother and Mrs. Dowd and Phillippa gossiping."

Proud Wolf noticed that Portia had not mentioned Audrey. He wondered if that was deliberate, because he knew that Audrey was with the other women.

The path led through the trees and down a short slope to the bank of the creek. "Here we are," Portia said. "Isn't this a beautiful spot?"

Proud Wolf looked around. The scene was indeed tranquil and lovely. With the coming of autumn the trees had lost many of their leaves, but some still clung to the branches, painting the landscape with patches of red, gold, and brown. The broad, slow-moving stream twisted between high banks; the trees and a shoulder of land that jutted out into the water hid the other women from Proud Wolf's view. He could hear their voices faintly, but other than that he and Portia might have been completely alone.

"Set the basket on that rock by the water," Portia told him. When he had done that, she took one of the garments from the basket and knelt at the edge of the stream. She dipped it into the water and began scrubbing it.

"I will return to the wagon now," Proud Wolf announced.

Portia stood up quickly and turned toward him. The wet gown she held splashed water on the front of her dress. "You can't," she said. "I'll need you to carry the basket back."

"Leave it here when you are finished. I will return for it."

She shook her head stubbornly. "No, it will be better if you stay here with me." She clutched the wet clothing against her, soaking her dress.

"You have no need of me."

Portia dropped the sodden garment on the rock beside the basket. "You're wrong," she said softly. "I have great need of you, Proud Wolf."

Then, before he could do anything to stop her, she stepped forward and wrapped her arms around his neck, holding him tightly as she brought her mouth to his and kissed him hard.

Had she been an attacking Crow warrior lunging at him, Proud Wolf could have easily avoided her and struck back in deadly fashion. But Portia was a young woman, and he could only stand dumbstruck as she kissed him. He was only vaguely aware of what he was doing as he lifted his arms and slid them around her waist. Portia responded by pressing herself more tightly against him, molding her body to his. Her lips parted, inviting him to plunder the warm, wet cavern of her mouth with his tongue.

His people seldom kissed, but Proud Wolf had learned from Audrey how pleasant it could be. That thought went through his head, and immediately after it came a surge of guilt. He was embracing Portia Yardley and kissing her as if she were his woman. That was wrong, and as he pulled his lips away from hers, he moved his hands to her shoulders and tried gently to put some space between them.

Portia let out a low moan of disappointment. "Proud Wolf . . . ," she said huskily.

"We cannot." His words were emphatic, leaving no room for argument. "This is not right."

"There's nothing wrong with it," she argued. "You're a man and I'm a woman —"

"I am in love with Audrey."

Portia's eyes glittered with anger. "How do you think Audrey would feel if I told her that you brought me down here and grabbed me?"

"You must not. That is not true."

"I will!" she threatened. "Unless you —"

Proud Wolf's head lifted at the sudden sound of rapid hoofbeats in the distance. His hand shot up and clamped over Portia's mouth. She started to struggle, so he hissed at her, "Be still!" He was trying not to hurt her, but every instinct in his body was telling him that something was about to happen.

Portia stopped trying to pull out of his grip. Proud Wolf said, "If I take my hand away, will you be quiet?"

She nodded, and he carefully lifted his hand, holding it poised near her mouth in case she was trying to trick him. Evidently his urgency had communicated itself to her, because she asked in a half-whisper, "What's wrong?"

"Someone comes," he said. The hoofbeats were closer now. Holding Portia's hand, he turned toward the slope and started up toward the band of trees that lined the stream. He did not follow the path, and she gasped with effort as she tried to keep up with him. He pushed through some undergrowth and came out among the trees, then dropped into a crouch behind a bush. From here, through gaps in the foliage, he could see the road as it approached the spot where the wagons had turned off into the field.

Riders appeared. Proud Wolf counted eight men on horseback. They were still a couple of hundred yards away, but as he looked at the two men leading the group, something about them struck him as familiar. His eyes, made keen by life in the mountains of the frontier, studied the pair of riders for a moment.

Then recognition struck him like a blow to the belly.

He must have gasped without being aware of it, because Portia asked, "What is it?"

"Go back to the wagons," he told her. "But if anyone asks you, you have never seen me, or Audrey."

"What —"

Proud Wolf did not wait to hear the rest of the question. Instead, he slid back down the slope to the stream and splashed out into it. He would make better time following the creek than he could by staying on the path.

The water was shallow. He ran through it, around the jutting shoulder of ground. Audrey, Phillippa Thurston, Elaine Yardley, and Vanessa Dowd were still on the bank, wringing out wet laundry. They gaped in surprise as Proud Wolf dashed up to them, water flying around his feet.

He came out of the creek only far enough to grab Audrey's wrist. "Come!" he told her, jerking her toward the water.

"Proud Wolf, what —"

"Brackett is coming!"

That was all he had to say. Audrey's eyes widened in confusion and fear, but she came willingly as he tugged her into the creek.

Vanessa took a step toward the water. "Proud Wolf, what is this about?"

Though he chafed at the delay, Proud Wolf knew he had to tell her. "Men will come," he said quickly. "They will ask about us. Please, Mrs. Dowd, tell them you have not seen us."

"I don't understand —" Vanessa began.

"Please, Mrs. Dowd," Audrey said. "You have to."

Vanessa exchanged a glance with Phillippa and Elaine. Up at the wagons, the men had noticed the commotion and were looking curiously down toward the creek. Finally, after another long moment, Vanessa nodded. "Go," she told them. "I'll tell the others what to say."

Proud Wolf did not take the time to thank the woman now. With Audrey's wrist still gripped tightly in his hand, he led her downstream, opposite the direction he and Portia had taken earlier.

The creek flowed around another bend, and as soon as Proud Wolf had led Audrey around it, he veered toward the bank. There was an overhang there, with roots from the bushes and saplings on the bank above growing down through the dirt. Audrey grimaced as Proud Wolf pushed her under the overhang and then huddled underneath with her. Someone would have to wade out into the creek to see them as long as they remained here.

But Will Brackett might do that, Proud Wolf thought.

After all, he had already come back from the grave.

Vanessa led the other women toward the wagons as a group of men on horseback came into sight on the road. The riders slowed when they noticed the wagons parked in the field. For a moment Vanessa thought they might go on, but then the two men in the lead veered their mounts off the road, the other riders following suit. There were eight of them, Vanessa counted as they approached.

Ulysses came up to her. "What's this all

about, Vanessa?" he asked her. "I saw our young Indian friend come running up the creek and grab Miss Stoddard —"

"Hush," Vanessa said. "We're not to mention that we've ever seen them. Tell the others."

Noting the urgency in his wife's voice, Ulysses nodded immediately. She would not have asked such a thing without good reason. Ulysses turned toward the table where the men had been playing cards and in a low voice cautioned them to say nothing about Proud Wolf and Audrey.

The riders were almost within earshot now, but the sound of their horses' hooves drowned out the hurried words. Vanessa moved over to stand beside Ulysses. Phillippa Thurston stepped up behind her husband, Kenneth, and rested a hand on his shoulder. Elaine Yardley glanced around, concern growing on her face. She asked Vanessa, "Where's Portia?"

Spotting movement along the creek, Vanessa glanced in that direction and saw Portia coming toward them from the trees. "There," she told Elaine with a nod. Elaine sighed with relief.

The strangers reined their horses to a halt. The two in the lead were both young men, around twenty years of age, Vanessa guessed. They were also well dressed, though their expensive garments were covered with a layer of dust. They had clearly come a long way.

The other six men were older, more coarsely featured and roughly dressed. They reminded Vanessa of highwaymen — certainly not the sorts with whom two young gentlemen would normally associate.

Ulysses held up a hand in greeting. "Good day to you, sirs," he said in his booming voice.

The shorter of the two young men, who had blond hair curling out from under his hat and was rather handsome in an arrogant way, looked around at the wagons and asked, "What sort of outfit is this?"

"The world-famous Dowd acting troupe," Ulysses announced. "And I am Professor Ulysses Xavier Dowd himself. No doubt you've heard of me?"

The young man shook his head impatiently. "No, I haven't. Have you seen an Indian and a young woman?"

A startled expression came over Ulysses's ugly face. "An Indian and a young woman?" he repeated. "Do you speak of a savage, sir? I was under the impression that there were no more of them in this part of the country."

"Damn right he's a savage," said the second young man. "He almost beat Will and me to death."

The one called Will shot him a glance, as if telling him to keep his mouth shut, then turned back to the actors. Portia had joined Elaine now, and the older woman had her arm around her daughter.

"The Indian is a Sioux, or some such," Will said. "From the wilderness beyond the Great American Desert."

"Then what's he doing here in the east?" Walter Berryhill asked.

"Some fool of a university professor brought him here." Impatiently Will went on, "But that's not important. He's a wanted criminal, and we're hunting him down."

"Wanted for what?" Ulysses asked mildly. "Other than handing the two of you a whipping, that is."

Will flushed angrily. Vanessa squeezed her husband's arm, glad that Ulysses had taken the youngster down a peg. She felt an instinctive dislike for this young man called Will.

"He kidnapped a young lady," Will said. "Carried her off from the Stoddard Academy in Massachusetts. Not to be indelicate about it, but I'm sure that by now he's had his way with her more than once. That's a hanging offense, right there."

Oliver Johnson crowed, "He sounds like a monster, all right. How big is he? Seven feet tall? Must be rather large if he bested the two of you."

Both Will and his companion flushed with indignation. "Hold your tongue, you little runt," snapped the second young man. "This is none of your business."

"Take it easy, Frank," Will said, controlling his own temper with a visible effort. He managed to force a smile on his lips. "We don't want to argue with these good people. We just want to find out if they've seen those two fugitives."

"Two?" Ulysses repeated. "I thought you said the young lady was kidnapped. Is *she* a fugitive, too?"

"I just meant that she'd be with the Indian. Have you seen them, or heard anything about them?"

Ulysses shook his head. "I can only speak for myself, but I haven't seen hide nor hair of anyone such as you describe, sir." He turned and looked at the other members of the troupe. "What about the rest of you?"

Almost as one, they shook their heads.

"Haven't seen them," Frederick Zachary said.

"Or heard of them until now," his brother Theodore added.

In his sonorous voice, Walter Berryhill asked, "Are you certain that you're not on a wild-goose chase, gentlemen?"

Will muttered a curse under his breath. "Are you all sure?"

"We're sure," Ulysses replied, and for the first time he allowed some steel to creep into his voice. "Now, if you're through questioning us, sir, perhaps you'll leave us to our rest."

For a moment Will looked as if he wanted to argue, but then he jerked his head toward the road and turned his horse around. "Let's go," he said curtly to the others. They trotted away from the wagons and resumed their trek to the south when they reached the road.

When the riders were out of sight, Ulysses turned toward the creek. His face was dark as a thundercloud as he rumbled, "Where are they?"

"You . . . you're sure it was Will?" Audrey panted in their hiding place under the creek bank.

Proud Wolf nodded. "I saw him, and I

saw his friend Kirkland. They rode at the head of six other men."

"Looking for us." Audrey's words were a statement, not a question.

Again Proud Wolf nodded. "They must be."

"I thought he was dead!"

Proud Wolf's mind went back to the fateful night at the Stoddard Academy, the night he had thought he'd beaten Will Brackett to death, the night he and Audrey had fled Cambridge. Jealous to the point of insanity, enraged by the knowledge that Audrey preferred Proud Wolf to him, Brackett had made life a living hell for the Sioux youth who was so far from home. Proud Wolf might have been able to withstand the torment for himself, but when Brackett had threatened Audrey — that he would not tolerate. Proud Wolf had done what his honor demanded: He had killed his enemy.

Or so he had believed. Today he had learned differently. Will Brackett was still alive, and apparently bent on vengeance. Otherwise, why would he be in Maryland, hundreds of miles south of Massachusetts?

"He must have recovered from the beating," Proud Wolf said slowly, keeping his voice pitched low. "I left him for dead, but it is obvious he survived."

"You said Frank Kirkland was with him?"

Proud Wolf nodded. "And six other men. He probably paid them to come with him while he looks for us."

"What are we going to do?" Audrey moaned.

"Mrs. Dowd promised not to tell that we are here. If the others will lie, too . . ."

Proud Wolf's voice trailed off. He had asked Portia not to reveal the truth, but would she cooperate? Or would her anger with him prod her into telling Will Brackett where they were? Proud Wolf could not answer that question. The only one who could was Portia.

"They'll help us," Audrey said, seizing on the only shred of hope left to them. "I just know they will. They've known all along that we're running from something. You were wounded when they found us. And yet they took us in and cared for us. They won't betray us now." Her voice cracked. "They can't."

She was about to say something else, but Proud Wolf stopped her with a finger on her lips. He tightened his arm around her shoulders. He heard footsteps along the creek bank, but from down here, there was no way to tell who was approaching. The only thing he knew for certain was that if it came down to a battle, he would fight with his last breath to protect Audrey from Will Brackett.

The footsteps stopped, and the familiar bellow of Ulysses Xavier Dowd rolled out over the creek. "I know you're here somewhere, Proud Wolf," Dowd said. "You'd better come out, lad. I think you've got some explaining to do."

CHAPTER SEVEN

Vassily did not seem upset or offended because his sister was angry, for which Jeff was thankful. The Tlingit might have been beaten down by their Russian conquerors, but Jeff recalled hearing stories of their fierce valor in earlier times. It had been Tlingit warriors, in fact, who had wiped out some of the first Russian landing parties nearly seventy-five years earlier.

But Vassily was more interested in catching fish than in avenging Nadia's hurt feelings. He took Jeff down to the stream and led him out onto the ice. Jeff hesitated as the ice groaned and creaked under his feet; the stream was not yet completely frozen over. Vassily noted his concern and chuckled. "Ice is safe, Jeff Holt. This I know."

Jeff relaxed. A Tlingit could be trusted to know when the ice was safe and when it wasn't.

Vassily knelt at the edge of the ice and lifted his spear, poising it for the thrust.

Jeff waited and watched a few feet behind him. "Look for flash in water," Vassily grunted, and then, a moment later, the spear suddenly shot downward, driven hard by Vassily's arm. When he lifted it out of the water, a squirming fish was impaled on the iron head. Vassily pulled the fish off the spear and tossed it onto the snow at the edge of the creek. It flopped around for a moment, then lay still. Vassily held the spear out to Jeff.

"You try now," he said.

Jeff took the spear and stepped cautiously to the edge of the ice. He wasn't completely convinced it would hold his weight. He was taller than Vassily, though Vassily was stockier and probably weighed almost as much. Still, Jeff did not want to seem a coward in the eyes of his newfound friend and protector, so he knelt at the edge of the ice the way Vassily had done. He lifted the spear and peered down into the frigid flow.

The water was almost crystal clear. He could see the rounded shapes of stones at the bottom, polished smooth after years of being tumbled by the river. Suddenly he saw a flicker of movement, a flash of bright scales, and, letting his instincts take over, plunged the spear down into the water.

Jeff yelled as he realized that he had overbalanced and was about to topple into the stream. He waved an arm, trying to catch his balance again, but before he could fall, a strong hand gripped the back of his coat and tugged him upright.

"Must be more careful," Vassily said. "Must strike quicker, too. Look, no fish."

Jeff looked at the spear. Indeed, there was no fish on the end of it. "I saw one down there," he said.

"Take much practice," Vassily told him. "Try again."

Jeff took a deep breath and knelt once more. All the fish would have been spooked by his plunging spear; he would have to wait for them to return.

That was all right, he told himself. Waiting was something he could do. Many was the time he had gone hunting with Clay and been forced to wait out a deer or an antelope or a moose. There was always one precise, right moment to make a shot, and Jeff had learned to be patient until that moment arrived. He waited now, watching with his eyes but allowing his mind to drift.

How long was Vassily going to insist that he stay here? And why? The Tlingit were not a poor, starving people, from what he had seen of their village, but why would they want an extra mouth to feed? It couldn't be because of Nadia. Vassily could not be so desperate to find her a husband that he would keep Jeff here solely for that reason. Nadia was comely and sweet-tempered; surely she would have her pick of the young men in the village. The image of her standing nude before him suddenly slid uninvited into his mind.

His eyes warned him, and his nerves and muscles reacted automatically. He thrust the spear back into the water, and this time he planted his other hand on the ice to steady himself. The spearhead hit something, then grated on the rocks at the bottom. Jeff tightened his grip on the wooden shaft and lifted it out of the water, feeling extra weight on the end. Sure enough, a good-sized fish was impaled on the spearhead. Behind Jeff, Vassily exclaimed in his native tongue. Jeff did not understand the words, but they sounded like a shout of congratulations.

Jeff stood up and turned around. He grasped the tail of the fish firmly in his gloved hand and pulled it off the spear, then flung it onto the bank next to the one Vassily had caught earlier.

"Good, Jeff Holt," Vassily said. "You catch fish second time. *Very* good."

Jeff grinned, accepting the praise. He did not have long to enjoy it, however, because more movement caught his eye, this time from the direction of the village. Several figures were approaching, bundled in the peculiar capes Jeff had learned were woven of cedar bark. Vassily saw them, too, then glanced back at Jeff, an anxious frown on his round face. "You be quiet," he said. "I will speak to them."

That was good, Jeff thought, because there was no way he could talk to these men anyway. They came close enough that he could see their faces, and none of them looked particularly happy.

One of the men stepped forward and spoke quickly to Vassily. The words sounded angry. Vassily responded in similar fashion. The other man made a curt gesture with his hand and then turned to stalk off.

Vassily glanced over his shoulder at Jeff again. "Yuri does not think you should be here. He says we should have killed you, as the Russians wanted."

"Yuri?" Jeff said.

"That is the name the Russians call him when he takes furs to trade. It is easier to speak of him this way."

"Why doesn't he want me here? Why should it matter to him?"

Vassily shook his head and turned back to the other men, speaking quickly. A couple of them replied, and for several moments the conversation went back and forth at a furious pace.

Finally Vassily turned to Jeff again. "The leaders of my people say you will be allowed to stay. Yuri is wrong; you do not wish to harm us."

"That's right. I don't," Jeff said emphatically. He looked at the other men and hoped they would understand at least the tone of his voice as he went on, "The Tlingit are my friends. I owe you my life."

Vassily nodded. "They know this. Yuri is the only one opposed, and that is because of Nadia."

"Nadia? What does she have to do with this?" Even as Jeff asked the question, he had the sick feeling that he already knew the answer.

"He wishes to have her for his own," Vassily replied, confirming Jeff's hunch. "He does not want her given as wife to you."

"Then why doesn't he take her?" Jeff asked. "I'm not going to stop him."

Vassily frowned. "Nadia will not have him, nor do I wish her to wed him. Yuri is not a good man. If the Russians had told him to kill you, he would have done that. He always does what the Russians tell him."

And that was a source of irritation for Vassily, Jeff guessed.

One of the other men said something to Vassily, who hesitated before responding. Evidently his answer was satisfactory, because the men turned and walked back toward the huts. Vassily sighed.

"What were they asking?" asked Jeff.

"They want to know if you and Nadia are mated." Vassily looked intently at Jeff. "I told them that you are. Is this true, Jeff Holt?"

Jeff swallowed hard. "She wanted to, but I . . . well, I'm already married . . . it just wasn't right."

"Nadia will not speak of this unless Yuri asks her. But she does not lie. If he wants to know what happened, she will tell him." Vassily shook his head and sighed again. "Tonight must be different."

"You mean I have no choice in the matter?" Jeff demanded.

Vassily looked at him solemnly. "You lose choice when Count Orlov decide you must die . . . and I decide you must live."

Terence O'Shay lowered the empty mug to the bar and wiped the beer foam from his lips with the back of his hand. He nodded to the bald, mustachioed, bullet-headed man behind the bar. "Good," O'Shay admitted. "Just as you said."

"Best beer you'll find west of the Mississippi," the tavern keeper said.

"I'll not be doubting it."

The tavern keeper mopped the bar with a rag. "What did you say your name is?"

"O'Shay."

"Well, Mr. O'Shay, since you asked me about Pink Casebolt, I don't mind telling you: The man owes me money. I've staked him to more'n one drink since he got back from the mountains this last time."

"Then he *has* been to the mountains?"

"Oh, yes, several times, I reckon. He worked for the North American Fur Company for a spell, and he's been a free trapper as well. If he says he knows the ground, I'd believe him." He stopped cleaning for a moment and scowled. "But as I said, he still owes me money."

"Is he an honest man, would you be thinking?"

The barman shrugged. "Couldn't say. I

don't know anything about him before he came to St. Louis. And I got to admit, he didn't promise to pay me and then try to run out on his debt. He's still here in town, and he still comes in from time to time and tells me he's going to settle up with me as soon as he can." He looked shrewdly at O'Shay. "Are you considering giving him work?"

"If I was, now, you'd be a fool not to recommend that I hire him, wouldn't you, friend?"

"How do you figure that?"

"If I hire him, I'm liable to give him some money in advance, and then he can pay you what he owes."

For a moment the bald-headed man didn't say anything. Then he shrugged. "You're right," he admitted. "But I didn't tell you to hire Casebolt. I just told you the truth of what I know about him."

"And I'm appreciating it." O'Shay dropped a coin on the bar to pay for his beer and nodded farewell to the tavern keeper.

This was the third place he had asked about Pinkney Casebolt, and he had received essentially the same answer each time: Casebolt had been to the frontier; he was honest, as far as anybody knew; and he was definitely in need of a job, because he had cadged drinks in all three taverns.

Night had fallen by the time O'Shay got back to the hotel. He found Melissa and Michael waiting for him in the parlor, sitting on rough-hewn chairs. He would have preferred that they stay in their room, but he supposed Michael had persuaded his mother to come downstairs. That boy always had to know everything that was going on, and he didn't like to sit still for any longer than he had to.

"I noticed a hash house a few doors down the street," O'Shay told Melissa as she stood to greet him. "Food probably won't be much, but likely the best we'll find around here."

"All right." She glanced at the counter, where Casebolt was trying to look busy. O'Shay figured the man was trying to overhear what they were saying without being obvious about it. Melissa went on, "Did you find out anything about —"

"We can talk about it while we eat," O'Shay said. He linked one arm with Melissa's and took Michael's hand.

He supposed they *did* look like a family, O'Shay thought as they walked down the street. He would have been honored to be married to such a fine woman and to have

160

such a strapping lad for a son. But the thought made him uncomfortable. Jeff Holt was his best friend in the world, and he knew he had no right to be thinking such things about Melissa.

She *was* a fine-looking woman, though, and smart as could be. It was more than enough of an honor, he told himself, for a bruiser such as himself to have her as a friend.

The tavern offered nothing but boiled beef, biscuits, potatoes, and tea. The fare was not particularly appetizing, but it was certainly filling. Besides, both O'Shay and Melissa were more concerned with discussing their next move.

"I think we should go ahead and hire Casebolt," O'Shay told her. "I asked around about him, and everyone told me that he knows the frontier. And he's honest, as far as anyone can say."

"He struck me as being honest, too," Melissa said. "All right, we'll hire him." She took a sip of her tea, a strong, bitter brew. "Now then, how do we proceed? How do we travel to New Hope?"

"We take the keelboat up the Missouri as far as we can," O'Shay said. "Once the Yellowstone splits off, we may have to build canoes and carry the goods in them, since the river probably won't accommodate the keelboat. The Yellowstone will take us nearly all the way to New Hope. Jeff told me all about it whilst we were in the jail in Wilmington."

No sooner were the words out of his mouth than O'Shay regretted them. Though Melissa had been quite close-mouthed about the matter, O'Shay knew there was some sort of trouble between her and Jeff. Any fool could see that. And to make things worse, he had reminded her of that terrible time when Jeff had been charged with the murder of her father and locked up.

There was a short, awkward silence. O'Shay coughed, then gamely forged ahead. "When we get to New Hope," he said, "we'll build a warehouse for all the furs we'll be trading for. Then we'll have to hire men to bring them downriver to St. Louis."

Melissa nodded, and O'Shay could tell she was glad to be discussing business matters again. "There's already a trading post there, I understand, so we'll have some competition."

"Nothing wrong with that."

"As long as it stays peaceful."

He grinned and pressed a hand to his

chest. "These days I'm about the peacefulest lad ye'll ever hope to see. I want to leave all me troubles far behind me."

"Yes," Melissa said, her tone a bit wistful. "That would be nice, wouldn't it?"

O'Shay didn't know what to say to that, so he said nothing. When they had finished their meal, the three of them returned to the hotel. Pinkney Casebolt was waiting for them. He tried not to look too eager as he asked, "Well, did you folks enjoy your dinner?"

"It was fine," Melissa said. "Mr. Casebolt, we've reached a decision. We wish to hire you."

A broad grin broke out on Casebolt's face, and he thumped a clenched fist against the counter as he exclaimed, "Hot damn! I mean, thank you, ma'am. You won't regret it, I can promise you that."

"We had better not," O'Shay said.

"I'm just glad to be heading back to the mountains at last." Casebolt paused and stroked his chin. "This ain't the best time of year to be heading in that direction, though. Weather's liable to be pretty bad some of the time."

"I know. We'll push on as best we can," Melissa said. "And when spring comes . . ."

"We'll be in business," said O'Shay.

Jeff spent the day with Vassily, who showed him around the village. The Tlingit were excellent workers in wood. Nowhere was that more apparent than in the posts, fashioned from huge cedar logs, that stood in front of many houses. Each post was decorated from base to top with animals carved in the same elaborate style Jeff had noticed when he had first arrived.

"This tells the story of the *ketchuke,*" Vassily explained as they stopped to admire one of the poles. He pointed to the large figure of a hawk at the very top. "That is the spirit that protects the clan that lives here."

Jeff stepped closer to study the carvings that ran all the way around the pole, ascending to the hawk with its fierce beak and outspread wings. "Magnificent," he muttered. "I've never seen anything like it."

They walked over to a building larger than the others but with no doors. Inside were more than a dozen canoes. They were a far cry from the small, lightweight, birch-bark vessels with which Jeff was familiar. These canoes had been hollowed out of massive cedar trunks. Some of them were five feet wide, so that two men could sit beside each other on the benches inside; others were long enough to hold upwards of fifty men, Jeff estimated.

"We take them down creek to river and down river to sea," Vassily said. "Row far out, hunt the big fish."

"You mean whales?"

Vassily nodded. "Catch one, have enough meat and fat and bone to last all winter."

"How in the world do you catch them?"

"Big spears," Vassily said. "We tie ropes to them, throw at big fish until many hit him. When he dies, tie all umiaks together and row. Pull big fish back to land."

"It sounds difficult. And dangerous."

"Sometimes tail of big fish hits boat and knocks it under water. Sometimes those men come back up." He shrugged. "Not often."

Jeff could only imagine what it was like. These canoes, large and impressive though they might be here, would seem smaller and more fragile out on the vast open sea. On the voyage to Alaska on the *Beaumont*, Captain Vickery had pointed out a pod of whales sounding in the distance, and the thought of pursuing those huge creatures armed only with spears was almost more than Jeff could comprehend. Some of the whales weighed seventy-five to eighty tons, he recalled Vickery telling him. Jeff was finding new reasons to respect the Tlingit all the time. Bravery was one of them.

"What else do you hunt?" he asked Vassily as they strolled back through the village.

"Bear and deer. Mostly catch fish in sea, in stream, you saw." Vassily smiled and waved his arms to take in all their surroundings. "Food all around. Wood and fat to burn, furs to keep warm, cedar tree for house and boat. It is a good life, Jeff Holt. You will be happy here."

Jeff took a deep breath, wondering whether it was too early to broach the subject of his departure. After all, he had been in the Tlingit village less than twenty-four hours. He decided it might be wise to plant the seed that he might not remain here permanently.

"Your people are good people, Vassily," he said. "But they are not my people."

"Yes," Vassily said with an emphatic nod. "You will be one of us."

"How can I be?" Jeff stroked the stubble on his jaw. "I can never be the same as the Tlingit. I come from a different place, a different people."

Vassily shook his head. "It does not matter how you look or where you come from." His voice hardened. "Tlingit give you back your life, Jeff Holt, when Russians want to take it from you."

Jeff lowered his head and grimaced. He could not argue with that. "As you say, Vassily," he conceded. "But someday —"

Vassily took Jeff's arm, ignoring what he was trying to say. "Come. We have potlatch. You say . . ." He paused, searching for the right word. "Feast. In bighouse. To welcome you among us."

He tugged Jeff toward the largest building in the village. It was lavishly designed, with animal motifs in the familiar red, black, and white tints decorating all four sides. Vassily led Jeff inside, where they found many of the village's inhabitants gathered. Two tables were being loaded with food by Tlingit women — wooden platters piled high with salmon and halibut and thick slabs of roasted meat that Jeff could not identify. Vassily told him it was seal meat. The air was filled with inviting aromas, Jeff noted with some surprise. He had eaten sparsely since he was taken from Sitka, and he suddenly realized that he was very hungry.

He recognized several men in the room

as members of the group that had come down earlier to the creek. Vassily had referred to them as the *hitsaati;* each one spoke for the house he shared with others of his clan. They nodded gravely to Jeff. He returned the nod, then looked around the room at the other people there. He was struck by how openly affectionate the families were. They clearly loved a celebration, and laughter and happy chatter filled the air.

Jeff did not see Yuri, but as Vassily led him to a place at one of the tables, he noticed that Nadia was already there. At Vassily's insistence he sat down awkwardly next to her. She did not look at him but kept her eyes straight ahead.

Then Vassily spoke to her in their native tongue, and she turned and looked at Jeff with eyes that were suddenly shining with expectation. Jeff wished he knew what Vassily had told her, but another part of him warned that he might be better off not knowing. Besides, he could make a pretty good guess.

The hall quieted down when the *hitsaati* began to speak. They talked for what seemed like a long time, and although Jeff had no idea what they were saying, he got the impression that much of it concerned him. Two or three of them gestured animatedly toward him as they spoke. Jeff tried to keep a pleasant, neutral expression on his face. He was going to have to learn at least the rudiments of the Tlingit language, he told himself.

Then the feasting began. Jeff ate ravenously, tearing chunks from the succulent fish that was placed in front of him and washing it down with deep drafts from a cup made of some kind of bone, whale perhaps. He did not know what he was drinking, but from the way it warmed his belly, he guessed it was some sort of native whiskey. It was good, that was all he knew, and so was the food, although he politely declined the big chunks of bear fat that the Tlingit seemed to regard as a delicacy.

His cup never ran dry and his plate never emptied. Finally, when he could eat and drink no more, he pushed away the plate and cup and motioned that he was full. Everyone else stopped eating, too, and Jeff felt a stab of guilt. He had not meant to bring the party to a halt.

Vassily stood up and motioned for Jeff to follow him. They went outside, trailed by Nadia. Night had fallen. The clouds of the past several days had moved off, leaving the sky clear, and Jeff looked up in awe at the shifting bands of brilliantly colored light that played across the heavens. This was only the second time he had ever witnessed them. Their glow made the night almost as bright as day.

"Come," Vassily said. "It is time."

Jeff was about to ask, "Time for what?" when he remembered the discussion earlier. He and Nadia were to be wed, and he realized with a shock that the feast he had just attended was probably a wedding celebration. He looked at Nadia. She was smiling shyly, and he could not deny that in the coruscating glow of the northern lights she was lovely, luminous.

Almost before Jeff realized what was happening, he found himself standing in front of the house in which he had spent the previous night. Vassily opened the door and stepped back, an expectant look on his broad face. Jeff took a deep breath. There was nothing he could do, no way to make things different. He owed Vassily his life, and it was only through the forbearance of the Tlingit band that he was still alive.

Jeff held out a gloved hand, and Nadia took it. Together they entered the house, and Vassily quietly closed the door behind them.

CHAPTER EIGHT

As the *New Orleans* made its way back upriver, the signs of destruction from the earthquakes were still plainly visible. Raw scars had been gouged along the riverbank where massive sections of earth had sheared off and plunged into the Mississippi. Trees that had stood on the banks for hundreds of years had toppled into the river, caught on sandbars, and now formed jagged hazards that could rip out the bottom of any vessel steered by an unwary pilot. Smoke curled upward from huge piles of debris that had been heaped up and set afire. Entire towns were now little more than rubble, and as the *New Orleans* steamed past, Clay and the others could see figures moving through those destroyed settlements, tattered figures walking stiffly and painfully, staring in numb disbelief at the shambles, all that was left of their lives.

But not every community had suffered so terribly. The *New Orleans* put in at one small river town a few days south of St.

Louis and found it much the same as it had been on the journey downriver. Captain Roosevelt wanted to take on more wood for the great furnace in the bowels of the boat.

A fine mist was falling, interspersed with sleet, and a cold wind blew out of the northwest. Clay walked along the deck, studying the gray clouds scudding through the sky, then returned to his cabin, where Shining Moon and Matthew were waiting for him.

"Well?" Matthew asked impatiently. "Can we go ashore?"

"It's mighty poor weather for that," Clay replied. "We'd be better off staying here where it's warm and dry."

Matthew looked disappointed. Shining Moon nodded and said, "That is wise."

A knock sounded on the door, and Clay went to open it. Lieutenant Markham stood there, his hat tugged down low on his forehead and his coat collar turned up. "May I speak with you, Clay?" he asked.

Clay was still wearing his own hat and jacket. "Certainly," he said as he stepped out onto the deck.

The two men walked along the deck to where an overhang shielded them from the mist. The wind was still blowing, cutting through their coats with icy fingers.

"What is it?" asked Clay.

Markham pulled his coat open far enough for Clay to see the paper-wrapped package he was shielding. "I've prepared a report for President Jefferson," he said. "I'd like to mail it to him while I've got the chance."

Clay frowned. "Do you think that's a good idea?"

"Mr. Jefferson knew we left Washington City and that we were going downriver on this boat. But other than that he has no idea what we're doing or if we're even still alive. I suppose that when Senator Emory and Senator Haines get back to Washington, they'll report the death of Senator Ralston."

"The accidental death," Clay grunted. "He died in the earthquake."

That much was true, although no one but Clay, Markham, and Shining Moon knew that Ralston had met his grisly end just as he was about to shoot Clay.

"Of course," Markham went on. "Mr. Jefferson has eyes and ears all over the capital, so he'll probably hear that you and I are still alive. But if we pursue La Carde up the Missouri to the mountains, Clay, it's liable to be months before we return to civilization. Mr. Jefferson needs to be aware of the plot we've uncovered. That way, if we're unsuccessful, perhaps he can still take steps to foil La Carde's plans."

Clay nodded slowly as he thought about what Markham was saying. He had made a good point. If anything happened to the two of them, La Carde's scheme might go unchallenged until it was too late to put a stop to it.

"All right," Clay said. "Mail your report. I reckon there's a post office here?"

"I've already checked with Captain Roosevelt. He says there is one."

Clay clapped a hand on Markham's shoulder. "This is a good idea, John."

Markham flushed. "I'll go ashore right now and take care of it," he said.

Clay smiled. "Go right ahead. I'm going back to my cabin where it's warm." He glanced out at the gloomy, frigid day. "Never did care much for weather like this."

Markham left the *New Orleans*, walking swiftly along the street with his head lowered to block the cold wind from his face. Few people were out and about; it was too tempting on a day like this to sit around a warm fire and wait for better days. But there were a handful of pedestrians on the streets, and Markham stopped the first man he met to ask, "Excuse me, sir, but could you tell me where to find the post office?"

The man jerked his head in the direction Markham had been heading. "Four blocks down, on the left," the man said. "You'll find it in Edson's Emporium. Edson's the postmaster, too."

Markham tugged at his hat. "Much obliged."

He started walking again, repressing a shiver as a chilly blast of wind roared down the street. He was just reaching for his hat to hold it down when the wind caught it and plucked it off his head.

"Damn and blast!" Markham exclaimed. He hurried after the hat, feeling pinpricks of sleet against his face. The hat rolled and bounded over the cobblestones, carried along by the wind, and before Markham could reach it, it vanished into the mouth of an alley.

Muttering another oath, he hurried into the alley, which was narrow and filthy. On this dark, overcast day, it was cloaked in shadows, and stepping into it was almost like stepping into the darkness of night. At least, Markham noted, the buildings on each side blocked the wind.

After a moment Markham spotted his hat lying on the ground about ten feet in front of him. He started toward it, saying under his breath, "There you are." He had gone only a couple of steps when something hit him hard from behind. He staggered forward, past the hat, and was hit again. This time he went down, his feet slipping in the mud as he landed heavily. The impact knocked the breath out of his lungs, and he had fallen on something that gouged his side painfully. He tried to roll over, but a booted foot slammed into his back, driving him back down. His mouth and nose filled with mud as he tried to gasp for air.

"Don't move, damn you," a rough voice hissed. "I've got a pistol, and I'll put a ball in the back o' yer head if you give me any trouble."

Markham was too breathless even to speak, but his mind had recovered and was racing now. He had a fairly good idea what was going on. Some ruffian had seen him venture into the alley and had decided on the spur of the moment to follow him and rob him. Markham decided to cooperate if he could. He had very little money in his purse, and losing it would not matter. The report inside his coat was much more important, and he was glad now that he had secured it in an oilcloth pouch and then wrapped the pouch in paper and twine. Even if the outside covering got wet, the document inside should be safe.

The foot was still grinding down on his back. He could barely drag enough air into his body and was beginning to feel dizzy. Then, unexpectedly, the foot was lifted and a hand grasped his shoulder. Strong fingers dug in and hauled Markham around on his back.

He saw a tall figure looming over him, and even in the faint light in the alley he could make out the pistol the man was holding. The man was wearing a cap, and there was something familiar about it.

"Let's have it," the man said as he pointed the pistol at Markham's face.

"My . . . my purse?" Markham said. He wasn't quite as breathless now, and the dizziness had receded.

"Aye, that, too, I suppose, just to make it look right."

What did *that* mean? Markham wondered. To make what look right?

"T'was pure luck that hat o' yours blew off and rolled in here," the man went on. "Gave me a chance to get rid of you and get my hands on those papers at the same time. Now hand them over, or I'll be searching your dead body in a minute."

A realization even colder than the wind washed over Markham's mind. His eyes had adjusted to the dim light, and he could discern some of the hard planes and angles of his attacker's ugly face. The man was a crewman on the *New Orleans*, one of a handful of men who had signed on with Captain Roosevelt to replace crewmen who had chosen not to make the return voyage up the Mississippi and Ohio Rivers. He apparently had another reason for being on the steamboat, however.

"You're one of La Carde's men!" Markham gasped.

The man snorted. "I figured on killing you anyway, but that makes it certain. You're too smart for your own damned good."

Markham spoke quickly. "You attacked Clay Holt and set the salon on fire. You must have overheard what I told him about mailing the report I wrote for President Jefferson."

"Stealing it from you will be easier than getting it back from the post office," the man said. "I'm getting tired of waiting, too."

"La Carde left you in New Orleans to watch for anyone who might be following him," Markham hurried on, stalling for time, looking for a chance, any chance, to turn the tables on his captor. "You were probably supposed to meet Senator Ralston and tell him that La Carde had gone on upriver, and when you found out Ralston was dead, you asked around and found out that Clay and I had had trouble with him. That led you to believe that we were working against La Carde."

His attacker grinned evilly. "So I signed on with Roosevelt, and I've been keeping an eye on you two ever since. You didn't really think you had a chance to stop the Frenchman, did you?" He thrust the gun closer to Markham's face. "Now give me those papers!"

Markham felt a sudden surge of confidence. "You won't risk a shot," he said. "That would draw too much attention."

For a frightening moment he thought he had made a fatal guess. Then, abruptly, the man tipped up the pistol and said, "You're right." He reached under his coat with his other hand and brought out a short, thick club. "It'll be a lot quieter beating your head in."

Markham tensed as the man lifted the

club. The only thing he could do now was try to grab the man's wrist as the first blow fell and wrestle the club away from him.

Markham never got the chance. He heard a soft thudding sound, and the man suddenly staggered. His mouth opened but emitted only a strangled sound of pain and surprise. The club and the pistol slipped from his fingers, falling to the muddy ground. Gasping, the man straightened and tried to reach around behind him with first one hand, then the other. Feebly he clawed at his back. Then he pivoted and plunged forward on his face.

Markham saw the handle of a knife sticking up from the middle of the man's back.

As he pushed himself to his feet, Clay Holt came striding into the alley. He stopped beside La Carde's man and dug a booted toe into the man's ribs. "Dead, is he?"

"I . . . I think so," Markham said raggedly. He wiped the back of his hand across his mouth. "Clay . . . how . . . where did you come from? I thought you were back on the boat."

Instead of answering, Clay bent over, grasped the handle of the long-bladed hunting knife, and pulled it free of the man's body. He wiped the blood from the blade on the man's coat, then rolled him over and checked for a pulse in his throat. "Dead, all right," he confirmed as he straightened. "And good riddance."

Markham shook his head. "I don't understand. How did you know I was in trouble?"

Clay sheathed his knife and jerked a thumb at the corpse. "This fellow followed you off the *New Orleans*. I followed him. Figured he was up to no good. He could've been planning just to rob you, but there was a chance he was working for La Carde. If that was the case, it seemed to me he might try to keep you from posting that report to Jefferson, assuming he knew about it."

"He's been spying on us since we left New Orleans," Markham said.

"Yep, I heard." Clay glanced down at the body and grimaced. "Reckon he's the one who tried to burn me up in the salon, too."

"He admitted as much." Markham frowned. "You stood and listened to what he was telling me?"

"Most of it. I didn't get here until after he'd jumped you."

"Why did you wait? He could have shot me!"

Clay grinned and slapped Markham on the back. "It's mighty hard to keep your powder dry in weather like this. That's why I used my knife. I figured even if he pulled the trigger, the gun would probably misfire."

"You . . . figured," Markham said hollowly. "When the gun was pointing at *me*."

"Well, he *didn't* shoot you, did he? And we found out what we needed to know." Clay stepped over to Markham's hat and picked it up. "Here," he said, handing it to the young officer. "Let's go post that report."

Markham took the hat and brushed it off. "What about him?" he asked, inclining his head toward the corpse.

"We'll leave him here for the scavengers," Clay said.

Markham opened his mouth to protest, then shrugged and put on his hat. He reached under his coat, which was wet and muddy, and groped for the package containing the report to Thomas Jefferson. It was dry and still intact.

As he and Clay reached the street and turned toward the post office, Markham asked, "Do you think he was the only agent La Carde left behind to cover his trail?"

"I can't say," Clay answered. "But sooner or later I reckon we'll find out."

For an entire day after the *Lydia Marie* sailed from the unnamed island and the settlement called Boylston, Ned Holt's head pounded unmercifully. Not only that, but he'd had to endure withering glares from Captain Canfield after the captain had witnessed the spectacle of three crewmen dragging Ned back on board the night before. Ned knew he had let the captain down. Canfield had made him responsible for the men's behavior, and what had he done once he was ashore? Promptly gotten into a stupid rivalry with India and allowed himself to become dead drunk. It was probably the most foolish thing he had done since his wild, reckless younger days, before he'd met his cousin Jeff and started growing up a little.

Fortunately, the crewmen of the *Lydia Marie* had behaved themselves. No serious fights had broken out during the visit, nor island women assaulted. Ned considered himself lucky that there had been no trouble.

But he was still angry with India for goading him on. Angry . . . and puzzled. India was acting more strangely all the time. What was wrong with her?

The afternoon of the next day, he found himself working next to her as they reefed the mainsail to take better advantage of the wind. Ned hauled on one of the lines and held it in place. He glanced over at her as she held another line and asked, "What was that all about?"

She threw him a curious look. "What was what all about?"

"Last night. In Winston Fitch's tavern."

"You mean where you had too much to drink."

Ned's hands tightened on the line. "You've never been one to boast," he said. "Why did you challenge me that way?"

Instead of answering the question, India gave one back. "Why take up the challenge? What do you have to prove, Ned?"

"Prove? Why, nothing!" He went on hotly, "I'm as good a man as any on this boat —"

"Aye," India broke in, surprising him, "that you are. That was never in doubt."

Now Ned was more confused than ever. She sounded as if she respected him, when the night before she had been nothing less than disdainful. Women! They were a damned puzzle, a puzzle that no man could ever hope to solve —

"Hush!" India hissed.

"What?" Had he spoken aloud?

Syme was coming along the deck. "St. Clair," he said with a nod to India, which she returned. He ignored Ned.

"Since when is he so friendly?" Ned asked when Syme had gone on.

"My friends are none of your business," India replied, her voice pitched a bit louder than was necessary. "I'll associate with whomever I like."

"That's your right," Ned bit off curtly. At a shouted order from the first mate, he released the line as the wind freshened and filled the sail towering over his head. India let go of her line as well.

Without looking at her, Ned went to the rail and grasped it tightly. He wished he could understand her, that he could make some sense of all the undercurrents of emotion that were tugging both of them in every direction.

And above all, at this moment he wished his head would stop hurting.

"Sail ho!"

The cry floated down from the crow's nest. Several days had passed, and the *Lydia Marie* was still cutting easily through the waters of the southern Pacific.

Ned heard the shout from the lookout and hurried up to the bridge, joining Captain Canfield. Canfield seemed to have forgotten about the debacle at Boylston, for which Ned was grateful. At the moment the captain had a spyglass pressed to his eye.

India came up to the bridge and stepped beside Ned. "What is it?" she asked in a low voice.

"Another ship." Ned pointed. A tiny white triangle of a sail was barely visible on the horizon.

"I see it," India said.

Captain Canfield lowered the spyglass. "I can't tell for certain, but I believe she's flying the Union Jack."

Ned and India exchanged a glance. Not many ships traveled these sea lanes; in the voyage to China and back, they had seen only a handful. All save one, a Spanish ship, had been sailing under the Dutch flag. If that ship on the horizon was indeed flying the Union Jack, she was the first English ship they had spotted since leaving Wilmington.

"All right, there's no cause for alarm," Captain Canfield said tautly. "She doesn't seem to be coming in this direction, and I saw no indication that she's changing course."

"If we can see them, they can see us," Ned pointed out.

"True. But if that's a trading vessel, her crew won't wish any trouble with us."

"But if it's a warship . . ." India's voice trailed off.

"That's still not necessarily a problem," Canfield insisted, but his words had a hollow ring to them.

Any American sailor knew the dangers inherent in encountering a British warship at sea. England and France had been at war for years, and the various embargoes and blockades the two powers had directed at each other had wreaked havoc on the shipping of other countries, notably the United States. Most American ships tried to circumvent the trouble between England and France by trading with neutral countries, but the so-called paper blockades still aroused a great deal of resentment.

England had made matters worse in recent months by asserting that its navy had the right to stop neutral ships and search them for British deserters. If found, those deserters were impressed back into service.

Ned was no politician. He had no opinion on whether or not England could

187

indeed claim the right to reclaim deserters from its navy. But he and the other sailors on the *Lydia Marie* knew that wasn't the only reason British warships stopped American vessels. Always short of seamen because of the harsh conditions on their ships, the British navy was not satisfied with reclaiming only British seamen. American sailors, too, were taken off their ships, often at sword's point while the cannons of the British vessel were trained on the American ship. Those luckless Americans, called the press gang because they had been impressed into service, were even worse off than their British counterparts. From everything Ned had heard, life for an American prisoner on a British ship was a truly hellish existence.

So, as word of the sighting spread like wildfire among the crew of the *Lydia Marie*, the men had good reason to line up along the starboard rail and stare anxiously at the ship passing to the south. As Ned looked along the railing, he saw several Englishmen, including the little Cockney called Yancy. Yancy always claimed that he had been mustered honorably out of the British navy, but Ned doubted that. More than likely the man was a deserter. There were probably others like him among the crew.

"Maybe we should turn north," Ned suggested to Captain Canfield. A change of course would take them out of the view of the British ship.

Canfield shook his head immediately. "Hold steady," he told the helmsman. "I'll not turn and run. Besides, if that is a warship, trying to get away would only give them more reason to pursue us."

Ned supposed the captain was right. He looked worriedly at India. There had been reports that British ships not only kidnapped American sailors but also looted trade ships they encountered. "Reparations," they called the cargoes they stole — punishment for Americans harboring British deserters. It was all very legal and tidy, at least in the eyes of the British navy. To Ned's way of thinking, it was nothing more than piracy.

The *Lydia Marie* was armed with two small cannons — hardly sufficient to hold off a British warship for more than a few minutes. If there was a confrontation, Captain Canfield would have no choice but to surrender and let the British do whatever they wanted. If he put up a fight, his ship would be blown out of the water.

As everyone watched intently, Canfield studied the distant ship once more through his spyglass. "Still no sign of her changing course," he announced after several anxious minutes. He lowered the glass and unashamedly heaved a sigh of relief. "It's either a trading vessel or they decided not to bother with us."

"Either way is fine with me," Ned said. He wiped away the beads of sweat on his forehead.

The British ship dwindled into the distance and finally disappeared altogether. The crew returned to their duties, but Ned and India lingered on the bridge with the captain. Ned said, "It might be a good idea, Captain, if we armed ourselves a bit more heavily."

Canfield looked at him sharply. "This is not a warship," he said. "We're on a mission of peaceful trade."

"Aye," Ned agreed, "but it never hurts to be prepared for trouble. The British aren't the only threat on the seas. There are pirates and hostile islanders and God knows what else out there."

"And you don't want to lose the cargo we're carrying."

"Of course not. But I don't want to wind up in a British press gang, either."

"I'll consider your suggestion, Mr. Holt," Canfield said with a thin smile. He gave a nod that Ned took to be one of dismissal.

As he left the bridge, India fell in alongside him. "You'd fight the whole blasted British navy, wouldn't you?" she asked with a laugh.

Ned chuckled ruefully. "You've got to admit, it'd be a pretty good scrap." He peered into the distance, over the now empty expanse of ocean. "But maybe if we're lucky, it won't ever come to that."

He hoped he was right.

CHAPTER NINE

"I never meant to bring trouble down on any of you," Proud Wolf said miserably as he sat on the rear steps of his wagon. Audrey huddled beside him, still shaky from the close call they'd had with Brackett and his cohorts.

Ulysses Dowd and the others stood around them in a half-circle. Dowd was pacing back and forth, glowering.

" 'Tis our own fault, I suppose," he rumbled. "We knew the two of you had been in some sort of trouble. You didn't get that musket ball in your side by accident, now, did you, lad?"

"No, but that had nothing to do with Brackett."

"The fellow who was here earlier?"

Proud Wolf nodded. "His name is William Brackett. He hates me and wants to see me dead."

"Oh, no!" Portia exclaimed.

Oliver Johnson sidled closer and said gently, "Maybe you'd better start at the beginning and tell us the whole story, Proud Wolf."

Proud Wolf and Audrey exchanged a glance. She gave a tiny nod, and he took a deep breath as he turned back to the others. "All right," he said. "I will tell you."

He started with Professor Hilliard's trip west to seek a suitable subject for his experiment, even though the troupe knew some of this already. He described his days at the Stoddard Academy for Young Men and the enmity that sprang up almost instantly between himself and Will Brackett. He did not mention that Audrey had flirted with him from the beginning, playing him against Will. Audrey had long since gotten over that adolescent mischief and now regretted it, because she knew that her actions had contributed to Brackett's hatred of Proud Wolf. Proud Wolf felt no resentment toward her; Audrey had admitted her mistake and had stood by him faithfully ever since.

When he reached the point in the story at which he had been lured into Boston and then attacked and severely beaten by Brackett, Frank Kirkland, and some of their cronies, Portia gasped and brought her hand to her mouth. Oliver clenched his hands into fists and said, "I'm glad I didn't know about this while that scoundrel was here. I would have been tempted to give him what he deserves."

Some might have laughed at that bold declaration from such a small, seemingly powerless individual, but Proud Wolf knew that Oliver meant it. He said solemnly, "If I had had such friends in Cambridge, matters might not have gotten so bad."

"Go on with your story," Dowd told him, but now he did not sound quite so gruff.

Quickly Proud Wolf sketched in the rest of the tale, omitting the more personal aspects of his relationship with Audrey. He concluded by saying, "I believed that I had killed Brackett after he attacked Audrey. I was wrong."

"Obviously," Theodore Zachary said.

Kenneth Thurston spoke up. "Those men riding with Brackett and Kirkland today looked like hard lads. Do you suppose he hired them to help find the two of you, Proud Wolf?"

Proud Wolf nodded. "And to help kill me when he does find us," he added.

Vanessa stepped over to Audrey and placed a hand on her shoulder. "What about you, dear?" she asked. "Are you in danger from this man Brackett, too?"

Audrey nodded. "I think so. I don't believe he would kill me . . . but he would force me to watch while his . . . his henchmen murdered Proud Wolf. And I'm sure he would . . . molest me." Her voice dropped to a frightened whisper.

"Over the dead bodies of every man here," Dowd said.

Audrey looked up. "Do you mean that? You'll protect us?"

Dowd looked severely at both of them. "You're telling us the truth, now?"

"We have spoken the truth," Proud Wolf said.

"Then you're safe as long as you're with us." Dowd looked around at the others and received a chorus of agreement and support from everyone. "We'll not allow any harm to come to either of you if there is anything we can do to prevent it."

Proud Wolf felt some of the tension leave his body. The troupe would continue to be a safe haven for him and Audrey. Brackett and his band of ruffians had continued southward, so now they were ahead of the troupe. It was entirely possible that Proud Wolf, Audrey, and their companions could avoid further trouble.

"You have my thanks, all of you," he said

as he looked around at them. "I am in your debt."

Dowd chuckled. "Don't concern yourself any further, lad. I'm not about to let anything happen to you. You're the best spear-carrier we've ever had."

Pinkney Casebolt told Melissa that he would take care of gathering the supplies for the trip up the Missouri, and he was as good as his word. The afternoon after Melissa and O'Shay had hired him, Casebolt went down to the river and enlisted some of the crewmen from the keelboat to help him load several kegs of powder and shot as well as more bags and barrels of staples to augment what was already on board.

"Can't have too many provisions when you're traveling up the Big Muddy," Casebolt assured O'Shay after the captain of the keelboat, a man named Tompkins, had complained that Casebolt was exceeding his authority. Casebolt and O'Shay were standing on the dock overseeing the loading. Casebolt had traded his dusty suit of the night before for dark brown buckskins, high-topped moccasins, and a broad-brimmed brown felt hat with an eagle feather tucked behind the band at the back. He continued, "And as for all that powder and shot, well, you'll be mighty glad to have it if we run into a bunch of unfriendly Crow or Ree."

"I'll admit, I know little about the savages who populate the area," O'Shay said.

Casebolt grinned. "That's why you've hired me, because I know all about those red heathens. Most of them are friendly, or at least willing to tolerate white men, but those that aren't — they'll gut you as soon as look at you."

O'Shay was glad Melissa and Michael were in the hotel where they could not hear this gruesome talk. Worriedly, he asked, "What do you think the chances are that we'll encounter hostiles?"

"Hard to say," Casebolt replied, tugging thoughtfully at his earlobe. "Most of the touchy tribes are north and west of where we're headed. But with Indians you never know. They can be friendly as can be one day and howling to lift your hair the next. All depends on what kind of mood they're in."

O'Shay did not find that too reassuring, but he told Casebolt, "Well, carry on." To Captain Tompkins, who was standing on the deck of the keelboat, he called, "Mr. Casebolt is in charge of all decisions regardin' supplies."

Tompkins, a rawboned man with a red beard, shrugged. "If that's the way you want it, Mr. O'Shay," he said.

"That's the way I want it," O'Shay affirmed. He left Casebolt at the dock to supervise the preparations and went back to the hotel, where he found Melissa and Michael waiting for him in the parlor. Casebolt's place behind the counter had been taken by a tall, cadaverously thin young man with a bad cough.

Michael ran forward to meet O'Shay. "When can we leave for the mountains?" he asked eagerly.

"Don't be gettin' too impatient to leave, lad." O'Shay patted his head. "Once we've started, you're liable to wish you were back here in civilization again."

Michael shook his head vehemently. "No. Civ'zation can get along without me just fine. I want to see the elephant!"

Melissa laughed. "Goodness gracious. What elephant are you talking about, Michael?"

The boy turned toward her. "I don't know. But I heard Mr. Casebolt saying something about it, so I thought there must be an elephant in the mountains where we're going."

"That's just a saying the frontiersmen have," Melissa explained. "I've heard your uncle Clay say it, too. Even your father —" She stopped short, her smile disappearing.

O'Shay noticed the reaction, but thankfully Michael did not. He had already turned back to the big Irishman. "Do you think we'll see Indians, like Shining Moon and Proud Wolf?"

"Mr. Casebolt seems to think it's pretty likely we'll encounter Indians," O'Shay replied. He glanced at Melissa and saw her lips tighten. Encountering Indians might not be the grand adventure Michael anticipated.

But they had both known from the start that this venture had its dangers. Under better circumstances Melissa would never have put Michael's life at risk by taking him to the untamed frontier. But the boy had accompanied his parents to Russian Alaska, a voyage fraught with peril; the boy had come through with flying colors. O'Shay was confident the boy would do just fine on this trip to the mountains. He was such an adventurous lad — once they got him in the Rockies, he might never want to leave.

"Come on, Whip," he said. "I'll take you down to the river so you can watch the men loadin' the boat. We'll give your mother a chance to rest a bit."

"I'm not tired," Melissa said, "but I wouldn't mind a chance to take care of a few things. Thank you for looking after Michael, Terence."

" 'Tis my pleasure," O'Shay assured her. "Come along."

Michael took his hand and went with him eagerly, while Melissa turned toward a small writing desk in the parlor. A pen and an inkwell sat on the desk, and she had already checked in its drawer and found several sheets of paper.

Sitting down, Melissa withdrew one of the sheets and carefully placed it in front of her. She went through the familiar ritual of checking the nib on the pen. She knew she was simply postponing the inevitable, however, so she took a deep breath, dipped the pen in the inkwell, and wrote at the top of the paper, *My dearest Mother.*

She paused, already at a loss for words. How should she tell her mother that she was not coming home? Hermione would already be aware of that fact by the time this letter reached her, of course; Captain Vickery would bring the news to her when the *Beaumont* reached port. But Melissa felt the need to explain for herself why she had decided to go through with the impulsive idea that had occurred to her on the dock at New Orleans.

There was also the matter of her separation from Jeff. Melissa hoped that in putting the situation into words for her mother, she might come to understand it better herself. For weeks now, ever since leaving Alaska, she had alternated between missing her husband terribly and being furious with him. Sometimes the two emotions came and went so quickly she did not know herself what she was feeling at any given moment.

With a sigh, Melissa dipped the pen in the inkwell again and forced herself to write.

By now I trust you will have been informed by Captain Vickery that I am not returning to Wilmington at the present time. I write these words to you from St. Louis, not far from the confluence of the Mississippi and Missouri Rivers, and I beg you to understand, Mother, why the steps I have taken are necessary at this moment in our lives . . .

Delaying served no purpose. The keelboat was fully loaded with supplies and trade goods, the crew had had a short time to rest after the voyage upriver from New Orleans, and everyone was ready to depart. The morning after Melissa had written the letter to her mother and entrusted it to the consumptive hotel clerk to mail, she and Michael walked with Terence O'Shay down to the dock and boarded the boat. Their belongings had already been taken from the hotel and loaded aboard.

Pinkney Casebolt stood on the deck and rubbed his hands together in anticipation. He had brought his own gear, carried in what he called his possibles bag, and piled it atop the boat's cabin along with some of the other personal belongings. Several beaver traps were lying with Casebolt's bag, and Michael eyed them curiously, intrigued by the bright metal jaws of the traps. To Melissa they looked more dangerous than interesting.

"Morning, ma'am," Casebolt called to her as O'Shay helped her aboard the boat. "Mighty fine day for starting on a trip, wouldn't you say?"

As a matter of fact, considering the season, it *was* a beautiful day. The sky was clear except for a few fluffy white clouds, and the air, while chilly, was not frigid.

"How long do you think the weather will

remain clear like this, Mr. Casebolt?" Melissa asked the guide.

Casebolt tipped back his head and looked up at the sky, squinting in thought. "Hard to tell," he finally said, "but I reckon we're in for a week or more of good weather. That'll get us a ways up the Missouri. If it turns bad on us, there are some Mandan villages where we can lay up for a while."

"Indian villages?" Michael asked excitedly.

Casebolt grinned at him. "That's right, boy. The Mandan are friendly, though, so you don't have to worry about them. Lewis and Clark took one of the chiefs back to Washington City with them to visit President Jefferson, or so I heard tell."

"My uncle was with Lewis and Clark," Michael said. "His name is Clay Holt."

"Do tell. Seems I've heard the name, all right."

Melissa was certain that Casebolt had heard of Clay. Most of the mountain men had. Next to John Colter, Clay Holt was probably the best-known explorer of the wilderness.

When everyone was on board, the lines holding the boat to the dock were untied, and the crewmen hefted their long poles and moved into position along each side of the boat. Captain Tompkins stood at the tiller and shouted, "All right, lads! Pole!"

The men poled off, pushing the boat away from the dock. Tompkins maneuvered the tiller to turn the vessel so that it faced north, and then the crew got down to the serious work of propelling the boat against the river current. It would be slow going, but Melissa was confident they would eventually reach their destination.

She wished she could feel as confident that she was doing the right thing.

Casebolt settled down cross-legged on the roof of the cabin, facing forward. Michael came up and stood beside him. "Hello, Mr. Casebolt," he said.

"Howdy. Call me Pink, all right?"

"Are you sure?"

"You bet. What's your name again?"

"Michael. But you can call me Whip," he added proudly.

"Whip, eh?" Casebolt grinned. "Where'd you get a name like that?"

"It's because I can use a bullwhip. My papa taught me."

"A little fella like you can crack a bullwhip?"

"I'm not so little," Michael said. "And I can pop a fly right off a cow's arse."

"Michael," Melissa said warningly. "Don't boast, and don't use vulgar language."

Michael turned and looked at her. "What's vulgar about a cow's arse?"

Casebolt chuckled. "Never you mind, son. You'll have to show me how you use a whip one of these days."

"I'd like that." Michael pointed. "The banks of the river are getting higher."

"Yep. Those bluffs keep rising until we get to the Missouri. They call it the Big Muddy. You know why?"

Michael shook his head.

"Because it's a big river," Casebolt said, "and it's darned muddy."

"Oh," Michael said. "Does it go all the way to the mountains?"

Casebolt nodded. "Yep, all the way to the mountains." He turned his head and gazed off toward the west, adding quietly, "And then some."

The acting troupe reached Baltimore, Maryland, bypassing Washington City. Like Boston and the other cities they had visited along the coast, the air in Baltimore was pungent with the scent of the sea. Accustomed to the clean air of the high country, Proud Wolf had never gotten used

205

to the damp in the eastern part of the country. The air felt heavy, and it smelled strongly of fish. But he could tolerate anything as long as he was with Audrey.

And as long as they were not found by Will Brackett.

Professor Dowd decided that they would not give a performance on their first night in town. "I want to introduce some new scenes," he told the group. They had parked their wagons and set up camp on a small hill overlooking the city and the wide expanse of bay beyond the settlement. "We'll rehearse them tomorrow and be ready to present them tomorrow night."

In his sonorous voice Walter Berryhill said, "Thankfully, I am a quick study. What role shall I play this time, Ulysses?"

"We'll be doing *Hamlet*," Dowd replied. "You'll be Polonius, Walter."

The elderly actor struck a pose. " 'To thine own self be true,' " he quoted.

That sounded like good advice to Proud Wolf. He had learned to read English fairly well by now, so he decided that he would ask Dowd if he could borrow a volume of the writings of this man Shakespeare. Proud Wolf doubted that Shakespeare could tell a tale as well as Otter's Haunch, an old man of Bear Tooth's band who knew all the stories of the People and the Creator, but Proud Wolf was willing to give the Englishman's work a chance.

That evening after supper, when everyone had returned to their wagons, Proud Wolf told Audrey he would be back shortly and headed for the brightly painted vehicle that served as the Dowds' home. He planned to ask Dowd about borrowing the book, but before he reached the wagon, someone stepped out of the shadows to stop him.

"Hello, Proud Wolf," a woman's voice said. Only starlight washed down over the camp; the moon had not yet risen. But the light was bright enough for Proud Wolf to recognize Phillippa Thurston.

He halted and nodded politely to her. "Good evening, Mrs. Thurston," he said.

"My, don't you have the most wonderful manners," she said. She had been born in one of the southern states, Proud Wolf knew, and although generally she spoke without an accent, tonight her words had a hint of soft drawl.

He did not think her question required an answer, so he started to step past her. She stopped him again. "I was talking to Portia about you."

Proud Wolf tensed. All too well he

recalled the incident several days earlier when Portia Yardley had kissed him and brazenly offered herself to him. Could that be what Mrs. Thurston meant? Would Portia have spoken about such a private matter?

Any doubt about what Portia might have done was erased when Phillippa said, "That was certainly a bold thing you did, grabbing her and kissing her like that. And you with that pretty little redheaded girl who adores you."

Anger surged inside him. Portia had lied to Phillippa about what had happened between them. Phillippa's words could be taken as a rebuke, but she did not sound as if she were scolding him. Indeed, she seemed amused. "You're lucky she didn't slap your face and raise a commotion," she went on. "You can't treat a girl like that, Proud Wolf." She moved closer and reached out of the shadows to put a hand on his arm. "But an experienced woman, now that's different. If you were to kiss me . . ."

She left the rest of the sentence unsaid, but Proud Wolf knew what she meant. Stiffly, he said, "You are married, Mrs. Thurston."

She gave a brittle laugh. "You needn't

worry about that. Kenneth certainly doesn't. Where do you think he is right now?"

Proud Wolf frowned. The question was irrelevant. "I do not know," he said.

"He's been keeping an eye on your wagon, waiting for a chance to catch Audrey alone." Resentment edged into Mrs. Thurston's voice. "He thinks I don't know what he's up to, but I do, of course. He's been panting after that girl ever since the two of you joined us."

Proud Wolf did not wait to hear any more. He wheeled and broke into a run toward the other side of the camp, where he had left Audrey alone in their wagon.

"Proud Wolf, wait!" Mrs. Thurston called after him, suddenly sounding frightened. "I didn't mean to . . . Oh, God, don't hurt him!"

Ignoring her pleas, Proud Wolf raced on, his steps sure despite the darkness. As he approached the wagon, he saw that the door at the rear was open. A man's figure was silhouetted against the glow of lantern light, but there was something odd about the shadow cast on the ground. The shadow's torso was too long for its legs.

Oliver Johnson stood just inside the door, talking to Audrey. He turned and smiled as he heard Proud Wolf's running footsteps. "There you are," he said. "Audrey told me you'd gone over to Ulysses' wagon to borrow a book."

Proud Wolf was confused. He had believed that he would find Kenneth Thurston there, forcing his attentions on Audrey. Instead Audrey was sitting on the bunk, evidently enjoying an innocent conversation with Oliver.

"What sort of book was it you wanted?" Oliver asked when Proud Wolf did not say anything. "I've got quite a few myself."

"Shakespeare," Proud Wolf said.

"You're in luck. I have a copy of the *Complete Works*. I'll run over to my wagon and bring it to you."

"I will come with you." Even though he was now worried about leaving Audrey in the wagon alone, Proud Wolf did not want to be rude to Oliver.

"No, you stay here," Oliver said firmly. "I'll be right back." He hopped down the steps and started across the camp toward his wagon. Proud Wolf watched him go.

Audrey came to the door of the wagon. "My, we've certainly had visitors tonight. First Mr. Thurston came by, then Oliver."

Proud Wolf looked around sharply. "Thurston was here?"

"Yes, but just for a moment."

"What did he want?"

"He just said that he hoped Professor Dowd would let me play the role of Ophelia in these scenes from *Hamlet*. Wasn't that nice of him?"

"That is all he wanted?"

"I suppose so," Audrey said. "He only stayed a moment. He left as soon as Oliver came."

Proud Wolf understood now. Oliver's timely arrival had saved Audrey from perhaps more than good wishes on the part of Kenneth Thurston.

Proud Wolf heard a step, glanced around, and saw a figure moving away in the darkness. It was Mrs. Thurston, he knew. She had followed him, hoping to keep him from harming her husband, but when she saw that Thurston was not at the wagon, she had hung back in the shadows. Proud Wolf was relieved. The events of the evening were complicated enough as it was.

"Well, I'm going to bed," Audrey said.

"I will wait out here for Oliver," he said.

"Don't be too long."

Audrey closed the door against the chill of night. A moment or two later, Oliver appeared, carrying a large book. He

211

grinned up at Proud Wolf as he held out the leather-bound volume. "Are you sure you want to wade into Shakespeare?"

Proud Wolf took the book, feeling the considerable weight of it. "This man had much to say," he commented.

"And most of it said quite well." Oliver looked around, then said in a low voice, "Kenneth Thurston was here earlier."

"Audrey told me."

"I saw him on his way here to your wagon, so I thought I'd better pay a visit, too. I'd seen you leave earlier."

"Then you know the sort of man Thurston is," Proud Wolf said grimly.

"The question is, do you?"

"I encountered his wife on my way to Professor Dowd's wagon. She told me."

"Ah," said Oliver, "the lovely Phillippa. The two of them are well matched."

"She is very bold."

Oliver laughed softly. "That's putting it politely. I'll be honest with you, Proud Wolf. Actors have a reputation for not caring very much about things like marriage vows. The women especially are considered not much better than trollops."

"I know," Proud Wolf said, thinking of Portia Yardley.

"But most of us aren't really bad sorts.

We're honest, generally, and when it comes to affairs of the heart, we tend to prey on each other, instead of on innocents."

"Such as Audrey and myself."

Oliver shrugged. "You threw your lot in with ours, so I suppose there are some among us who would consider both of you fair game. I'd watch out for Portia and her mother both, if I were you, and, well, you've already seen for yourself what Phillippa can be like. I'm just saying that you should keep an eye on Audrey, and don't think too badly of us."

"I will not think badly of *you*," Proud Wolf said. "I owe you a debt of honor for what you have done tonight."

"What, loaning you a volume of Shakespeare?" Oliver asked mockingly. "Save your thanks until you've read some of it."

"I *will* read the book," Proud Wolf pledged.

"You know, I think you will. You strike me as the sort to do whatever you set your mind to." Oliver lifted a hand and waved. "Well, I'll be saying good night."

"I must go in. Thank you for the book."

"Don't read it *all* night," Oliver advised as he started to walk away. "There are more things in life than books."

Proud Wolf smiled. He suddenly remembered that Audrey was waiting up for him. He went into the wagon quickly and closed the door behind him.

CHAPTER TEN

It would have been easy, Jeff thought more than once during the first few weeks of his stay in the Tlingit village, to let the time drift by and never even notice its passing.

True, the weather became harsher. Snow fell nearly every day, and the wind sometimes blew so hard that the flakes flew in straight, horizontal lines. The brilliant bands of light in the northern sky disappeared behind impenetrable layers of cloud that never lifted. Darkness hung over the land much of the time, relieved only in the middle of the day by a graying that was more like twilight than noon.

Despite the cold and the darkness outside, the house Jeff shared with Nadia and the rest of her clan was always warm and bright inside. The fire was never allowed to die down. And late into the night, when the others were alseep, Nadia and Jeff were wrapped in their sleeping robes together.

215

At first Jeff was uncomfortable about the public nature of their lovemaking, but he soon grew accustomed to it. Nadia had been a virgin, but she had come to him eagerly and showed no pain or regret when he took her. Their first coupling was brief; because of the intensity with which she heaved and thrust beneath him, he could not hold back. But the second time had been long and slow and sweet.

But he had felt little true joy. In the back of his mind was the stubborn knowledge that he was married, that he was being unfaithful to Melissa. But what else could he do under the circumstances? Vassily had saved his life, and Jeff tried to tell himself that he was simply returning the favor by saving Nadia from an unwanted match with the man called Yuri.

Still, that was nothing but a rationalization. Jeff could not justify what he had done . . . but neither could he change things now. So he did the best he could and gave himself over to the pleasures of the flesh.

And with Nadia, they were pleasant indeed.

There was more to life than lovemaking, of course. During the day, as he helped her with her various tasks, Jeff taught English to Nadia, and she helped him learn Tlingit words and phrases. In a matter of weeks the two could communicate reasonably well in a mixture of both tongues. Vassily visited often and taught Jeff much about the Tlingit way of life. Under Vassily's tutelage Jeff quickly became an expert fisherman.

They were on the frozen creek one day, crouched next to a hole that Vassily had chopped in the ice with a short-handled ax much like the Sioux tomahawk. The creek was completely frozen over now, and the ice was much thicker than it had been the first time Jeff had ventured out upon it. But under the ice the water was still flowing, and Vassily's keen eyes could make out the flitting forms of fish below. Jeff saw them, too, so he was not surprised when Vassily's spear suddenly flashed down and skewered one. Vassily brought it up through the hole in the ice, removed it from the spear, and tossed it in the snow nearby.

"Won't the Russians in Sitka wonder what happened to you and your friends after you left there with me?" Jeff asked idly as Vassily handed him the spear. It was his turn.

Vassily shook his head. "Orlov knew we

were coming back to our village for the winter," he said. His English had improved in the weeks he had spent conversing with Jeff. "I think that is why he chose us to kill you and get rid of your body."

Jeff smiled thinly. "He'll be mighty surprised when he finds out I'm still alive."

He heard Vassily's sharply indrawn breath and glanced up. Vassily was frowning at him.

"You can never go back to Sitka, my brother," the Tlingit said. "You are one of us now."

"But won't you and the others go back in the spring to work for the Russians again?"

"Perhaps. But if Count Orlov sees you, he will know we failed him. He will take revenge on us."

Jeff had not considered that possibility. His thoughts had all been focused on settling his own score with the murderous Russian nobleman. But Vassily was right: Orlov was obsessed with vengeance. If he blamed the Tlingit for cheating him out of his revenge on Jeff, he might well descend on the village with his soldiers and wipe out everyone who lived there, including Nadia.

Jeff could not allow that to happen.

"We will talk about this later," he said. He would have to think about the problem and resolve it in a way that would allow him to settle matters with Orlov, return to the United States, and yet not endanger Vassily and his people.

Vassily was still watching him worriedly, but Jeff turned his attention back to the hole in the ice. He crouched motionless in his heavy, hooded coat, the spear gripped in a gloved hand. His breath fogged and hung in the air in front of his face, and it was so cold he could have sworn he saw ice crystals forming in the vapor.

Abruptly, he drove the spear downward, impaling a fish that had been unwise or unlucky enough to swim directly under the hole. He threw it on the bank next to the one Vassily had caught, then handed the spear back. They passed an hour or so taking turns with the spear, until their muscles were too cramped from the cold to do the job. Six fish lay in the snow. They would eat well tonight.

Vassily had no woman of his own. He had been married, but his wife had died a couple of winters earlier, Nadia had told Jeff. They had had no children, and Vassily was so devastated by her death that he had not courted another woman. Jeff felt sorry for his friend. Vassily had no one, while Jeff had not only Nadia but Melissa as well, back in America.

That subject was open to debate, of course, Jeff reminded himself as he walked beside Vassily back to the village. He was confident that one day he would see Melissa again, but when he did, would she still want him?

What would she think if she were to see him and Nadia together now?

Shuddering a little, Jeff tried to put that thought out of his head. He had never been in the habit of lying to his wife, but the less Melissa learned about Nadia, the better.

"Tomorrow we will hunt a bear," Vassily said, breaking into Jeff's gloomy musing.

"What?"

"A bear," Vassily repeated. "One has been seen near the village."

"This is the first I've heard of it," Jeff said. "I thought bears hibernated in the winter."

Vassily nodded. "Yes, that is what they are supposed to do. But something must have disturbed this one. It is dangerous for him to be around the village. He will be maddened by hunger."

Jeff could understand that. Bears stored up fat in the autumn and lived off it during the winter, but only while they were sleeping. Whenever one of the huge creatures woke up and started moving around again, it had to eat. At this time of year there was little food available to bears. All the berries and plants they ate in the summer were gone, and a bear could not chop a hole in a frozen stream in order to fish. That left only one option for a starving bear.

Hunting humans.

Vassily grinned. "Soon we will have fresh bear steaks for the whole village. You and I met during a hunt for a bear, Jeff Holt. Will you come with us tomorrow and help hunt another?"

"Yes," Jeff said without hesitation.

Early the next morning the men of the village gathered in front of the big structure in which the potlatch had been held. The sky was still dark and overcast, but no snow was falling. One of the men sniffed the air and declared that there would be no more snow for three days. Jeff had no idea how the man could make such a prediction, nor how accurate it might be. But the other men in the hunting party nodded and seemed to agree.

They were armed with spears longer than the ones they used to fish in the stream. Vassily had an extra spear that he gave to Jeff, who hefted it and studied its balance. He wished he had his flint-lock rifle. With it he could bring down the rogue bear from a safe distance, and the men of the village would not have to risk their lives. But the flintlock he had carried all the way to the Rocky Moun-tains and back again, through the Cumber-land Gap into Tennessee, even to the dangerous back alleys of Washington City, was thousands of miles away in Wilming-ton. Jeff wondered if he would ever see it again.

As the group prepared to leave the vil-lage, Jeff glanced around and noticed the Tlingit called Yuri among them. Yuri glared coldly at him, then deliberately turned away.

It would do no good to explain to Yuri that the match with Nadia had not been his idea, Jeff knew. Yuri was too blinded by jealousy. Jeff resolved to keep an eye on him. Yuri might well be more dangerous than the bear they were seeking.

The men left the village, heading north,

where the bear had been spotted. They would make a big circle around the village looking for tracks.

Jeff walked beside Vassily, toward the front of the group. "Has this bear harmed anyone?" he asked in the Tlingit language.

Vassily shook his head. "No. The first ones to see it were women who were out gathering firewood. It roared at them but did not pursue them."

"Then it's probably not starving . . . yet."

"There are ptarmigan and rabbits, but it would take many of them to satisfy a bear. Perhaps it has killed a deer or an elk. It could feed off a large carcass for several days."

"Who else has seen it?" Jeff asked.

"Some of our hunters. But each of them was alone when he saw the bear and could not attack it. That was why it was decided that many of us would seek out the bear together and kill it. It is the only way."

"What could have put him on a rampage?"

Vassily shook his head. "I do not know. In all my years I have never seen a bear at this time of year."

One of the other men, listening to the conversation, spoke up. "The spirits are angry with us," he said. "We have allowed the Russians to come to our land, take our settlement, and make us their slaves. The spirits have sent this great bear to punish us!"

Jeff put little stock in such talk, but he was intrigued by the resentment the Tlingit expressed toward the Russians. Of course not all of them felt that way; judging by what Vassily had said, Yuri and some of the others had cooperated fully with the Russian interlopers.

Yuri spoke up now. "The Russians have many guns, and we have only spears. If we fought them, they would kill us all."

"Such was not the way when the Russians first came," said another man. "Then we fought, and we defeated them. We killed them all."

"That was a much smaller party," Vassily said. "Now there are many soldiers at Sitka."

"Not as many as there are Tlingit warriors."

"The guns make the difference," Yuri insisted.

Jeff followed what he could of the conversation with great interest. Feelings against the Russians apparently ran quite strong, and those who hated the invaders outnumbered those who wanted only to cooperate with them. Perhaps, come spring, Jeff could put that resentment to his own use. If the Tlingit could be organized, and if they could get their hands on some rifles . . . it was a possibility worth serious consideration.

In the meantime, they had a rogue bear to catch. The sky overhead had lightened to its usual pale, midday gray. The hunters trudged through powdery snow that had been disturbed only by smaller animals. When Vassily judged that they had gone far enough north, he gestured and sent the party veering to the east.

It was only a few moments later that they crossed the trail of the bear.

The tracks were unmistakable, and recent to boot. They led northeast, away from the village. The men could not assume that the bear would no longer haunt the area, however. In its wandering it could easily double back to menace the village again. They began following the line of tracks in the snow.

The landscape gradually grew more rugged. Jagged, densely treed hills thrust up toward the sky. The bear's trail meandered between the hills, following frozen streams where the bear had pawed at the ice in a futile attempt to get at the fish in the stream.

At one point they found a smear of blood on the snow, standing out stark and red against the white. One small, furry, mangled paw lay on the snow near the blood. Vassily picked it up and grunted. "Rabbit," he said. "The bear ate the rest. But that will not fill its belly for long."

The hunters moved on. The trail led up a long slope toward a ridgeline dotted with rocks. Halfway up the hill was a dense clump of pines. The bear tracks led into the trees but did not emerge anywhere. Vassily held up a hand to bring the group to a halt.

"There," he said quietly, pointing with his spear. "The bear is in those trees."

Jeff checked the wind. It was sweeping down the hill toward them, away from the pines. He knew from his experiences with grizzlies in the Rocky Mountains that most bears had limited vision but an excellent sense of smell. At the moment, the wind favored the hunters.

"He won't know we're here," Jeff said to Vassily.

"Then we can take him before he knows he is under attack."

"Maybe." An idea occurred to Jeff. "But

if you really want to surprise him, send a couple of men around the trees and get above him."

Vassily shook his head. "If we do that, the bear will smell them."

Jeff nodded. "Yes, but when he comes out of the trees and turns in that direction to challenge them, the rest of you can attack him from behind."

Vassily considered, then slowly nodded. "It is a good idea," he said. "Who will go to draw the wrath of the bear?"

A grin spread across Jeff's face. "It was my idea. I reckon I ought to be one of them."

Vassily nodded again. "And I will be the other." Somehow that didn't surprise Jeff at all.

Quickly, Vassily explained the plan to the others. Some of the hunters looked dubious, but in the end all agreed to try it. After making sure that they understood to wait until he and Jeff were in position, Vassily signaled to the American that they were ready.

Tightly gripping their spears, Jeff and Vassily left the main party and walked as quickly as they could through the deep snow. They circled wide around the trees and slogged up the slope toward the ridge.

When they were even with the upper edge of the growth, they turned and looked back down the hill. The other hunters were visible at a distance Jeff estimated to be two hundred yards. The ridge was a hundred and fifty yards or so above them.

Vassily lifted his spear over his head and waved it back and forth in the prearranged signal to the others. Then he and Jeff exchanged a look and a grim nod and began angling across the face of the hill in a path that would take them a short distance above the trees.

Moments later, the relative quiet was broken by sounds Jeff had not heard in a long time: the snuffling grumble of a curious bear, followed by a furious roar as it caught their scent. Jeff and Vassily looked at each other again but kept moving. Something crashed within the stand of trees, and Jeff saw the top of a slender evergreen sway and then topple. The enraged bear had knocked it down.

Jeff and Vassily were directly between the trees and the crest of the ridge now. They stopped and turned, facing down the slope, spears lowered.

In a sudden flurry of motion, the bear burst out of the trees. The massive creature was on all fours, but it stopped short and reared up on its hind legs, waving its huge forepaws in the air and bellowing another challenge.

Jeff and Vassily both noticed an ugly gash on the bear's left shoulder. Something had ripped the flesh open and left long, bloody slashes around the wound. Jeff had seen similar injuries before.

"That bear's been attacked by a cougar," he said in a low voice to Vassily, who shook his head.

"We rarely see cougars."

"Well, one of them must have wandered up here and tried to den up in the cave the bear was using to winter over," Jeff said. "That's what disturbed the bear. It probably killed the cougar, but the damage was already done. Injured like that, the bear couldn't just go back to sleep."

"You may be right," Vassily said as he began backing slowly up the hill. "What is important is that we have drawn the beast into the open."

"And the rest of our group will be ready in a minute to jump him from behind," Jeff said. Like Vassily, he was backing up the hill now, luring the bear on.

Jeff glanced at the pines. He saw shapes flitting through them and knew the hunting party was coming. He hoped they wouldn't make too much noise. The bear's sense of hearing was not as highly developed as its sense of smell, but it was better than its eyesight. When the bear let out another deep roar, Jeff bellowed back, to add to the distraction. Vassily glanced at him in surprise.

"Shout at it," Jeff said. "Keep its attention focused on us."

Vassily faced the bear and let out a roar of his own. The bear waved its forepaws in the air again, its rage growing. It was going to charge them at any second, Jeff sensed.

The hunters came out of the trees behind the bear, spears drawn back and ready to throw. Two or three of them launched the missiles, putting all their strength behind the throws. Jeff saw the spears arch through the air, then descend to strike the bear from behind. The sharp stone spearheads thudded into the thick layers of fat and muscle on the bear's back. The animal gave a startled, angry roar.

The rest of the hunters ran forward now, their weapons thrust out in front of them. At the same time, Jeff and Vassily bounded down the slope. The bear swung around, searching for the enemies that had attacked from behind. Two of the Tlingit were there to meet it, ramming their spears into its belly and then throwing themselves back, out of reach of its curved, slashing claws.

The hunters' best chance was to bait the bear from all sides and keep it confused. Vassily stopped and threw his spear, which lodged in the creature's right side. The bear turned again, still roaring. More spears flew through the air from downslope. Two struck it on the left side and penetrated; another lodged in the side of its neck. Blood streamed out around the shaft, soaking the thick brown fur. The bear stumbled, weakening.

As it turned away from him, Jeff leaped forward. He thrust up and out with his spear, bringing the point under the bear's right foreleg. He felt the tip of the weapon penetrate through fat and muscle, then grate off bone. He shoved as hard as he could, driving the spear deeper into the bear's body. The bear bellowed and swung toward him.

Jeff flung himself backward but could not completely avoid the massive paw that slashed at him. Luckily, only the back of the paw hit him. Had the long, wickedly sharp claws found him, they might have ripped his head from his body. As it was, the blow sent him flying through the air, his head ringing from the impact. Although the snow cushioned his fall, the breath was knocked from his lungs.

He pushed himself up on an elbow and watched as the men who had not yet used their spears rushed in to finish off the wounded bear. The huge creature doggedly fought back, but it was staggering, weak from loss of blood, and its paws were moving so slowly that the hunters had no trouble avoiding them. The bear swayed and stumbled, and the men dashed back, out of its reach. It lifted its head for one last, defiant roar, then fell forward, landing with such force that Jeff felt the ground shake beneath him.

The hunters shouted their jubilation. Jeff grinned as he picked himself up from the snow.

"We have killed the beast!" Vassily said triumphantly, extending a hand to Jeff. "This bear will trouble us no more."

"And as you said, the whole village will have bear steaks."

Vassily reached under his heavy coat and pulled out a knife. "We will skin and gut the carcass, then pack it with snow. The rest of you, fell some small trees so that we may make a sled on which to drag it back to the village."

The hunters, still laughing and slapping each other on the back, retrieved their spears from the bear's body and started down the slope toward the trees. Several of them had brought small axes in the hope that they would need them for just such a task. They set to work, as did Jeff and Vassily. Skinning and cleaning the bear would be as big a job as chopping down trees.

They went about their grisly task quietly and efficiently. Jeff made long cuts in the bear's hide so that it could be peeled away from the flesh underneath, while Vassily slit open the belly to clean out the entrails. Fetid steam rose into the frigid air as bear guts spilled out onto the snow.

Jeff had never cared for this part of the hunter's work, but it had to be done. In his intense concentration he almost did not notice the soft grinding sound that came to him on the wind. But then his instincts took over, sounding an alarm in his mind and making him look up from what he was doing.

He turned his eyes toward the ridge just in time to see one of the large rocks that dotted the upper part of the slope begin to roll.

Jeff grabbed Vassily's arm and yelled,

"Look out! Avalanche!"

One falling rock was all it took. The first rock hit another, which hit another, which started two more tumbling down the slope . . . and in less time than Jeff would have thought possible, a wall of rock and snow forty feet wide and five feet high was sliding down the hill toward Jeff, Vassily, and the bear carcass.

"The trees!" Jeff shouted as he broke into a run and yanked Vassily into motion with him. "Head for the trees!"

They left the partially skinned bear where it had fallen and ran hard toward the stand of cedar. They had a better chance of reaching the trees, Jeff knew, than they did of outflanking the rockslide. The other hunters, alerted by Jeff's shouts and the rumble of rolling rocks, emerged from the trees long enough to shout encouragement to the two men, then retreated at a dead run.

In the deep snow, running was slow and difficult. And with each lunging step, each breath of frigid air, Jeff felt as if he was breathing in a cloud of tiny knives. But he kept moving, Vassily close beside him.

Jeff glanced back over his shoulder and saw the rushing wall of rocks and snow engulf the bear. One instant the bear's gory carcass stood out starkly against the white snow; the next it had vanished so completely it might as well have never been there.

And Jeff and Vassily were barely halfway to the trees.

Redoubling his efforts, Jeff pulled ahead of Vassily. Even over the rumble of the avalanche, he heard Vassily's harsh panting as he struggled to keep up. Jeff slowed and reached back, grasping the sleeve of Vassily's coat. "Hurry!" he urged.

"I . . . I cannot . . . ," Vassily gasped.

"We're almost there!" Jeff shouted. Then he had no more breath to waste on words.

The ground shook under his feet as the avalanche gathered speed and power with every passing second. But the trees were close now. Jeff tugged again on Vassily's arm, and then they were there, stumbling into the cedars.

Jeff grabbed a tree, putting the trunk between himself and the approaching mass of snow. A few feet away, Vassily did the same. That was all they had time to do before the avalanche slammed into them.

The trees broke the brunt of the rockslide's power, as Jeff hoped they would. He held on to the trunk for dear life as he and it were pummeled by snow and flying rocks. He could not breathe; the snow had swallowed the trees like a wave washing over a beach. It was all he could do to keep his head down and hold his breath.

He felt the tree shifting under the awesome weight of the avalanche. If it was uprooted and swept away, he was as good as dead. But the roots held, and after several terrifying seconds that seemed like an eternity, the worst was over. The rumble died away. Sliding snow had cascaded deeply around the trees, and branches snapped off by the tumbling rocks were scattered everywhere. But the avalanche, which had been relatively small except to the two men trapped in its path, had lost its destructive power.

Jeff found himself completely encased in white, powdery snow, one arm still wrapped around the tree. He pulled himself closer to it, got the other arm around the trunk, and began pulling himself up. He broke the surface of the snowdrift and saw hands reaching for him as he flailed with one arm. He half fell, half stumbled out of the drift and collapsed on the ground.

The Tlingit hunters surrounded him. One asked anxiously, "Where Vassily?"

Jeff looked around, trying to get his bearings. He could see the top of the tree that had protected him, and he believed the one Vassily had stood behind was to the right of it. He waved toward the deep drift at its base and said, "There! Dig there!"

The Tlingit did, throwing aside the snow with their hands. A minute later, they uncovered a motionless lump of fur and elk hide. Jeff recognized it: Vassily's coat. He climbed unsteadily to his feet, but before he could go to help, the other men had grasped Vassily and pulled him clear of the drift.

They rolled Vassily onto his back, and Jeff saw an ugly purple lump on his forehead. He had probably been struck by a falling rock and knocked senseless. "Vassily!" Jeff cried, slogging through the snow to his friend.

The hunters lifted Vassily into a sitting position and pounded on his back. With a racking gasp, Vassily drew air into his body. Jeff felt a surge of relief — Vassily was alive.

Vassily got to his feet, rubbing gingerly at the lump on his head. "I feel as if that bear has jumped up and down on me," he said wryly.

"Maybe we can dig the carcass out of the snow," Jeff said. "If we can find it, that is."

In the Tlingit tongue, one of the men said vehemently, "We must leave it where it is. It is a demon bear. I told you the spirits sent it to punish us."

"We killed it," Jeff pointed out.

"And you and Vassily nearly died, even though the bear was already dead." The man folded his arms across his chest. "What else could have caused that avalanche unless it was vengeful spirits? There was no reason for the rocks to fall."

Unless one of them fell because somebody pushed it.

The thought flashed unbidden through Jeff's brain. He glanced at Yuri. The man looked back at him defiantly.

He had no way of proving anything, Jeff thought. He and Vassily had been concentrating on the bear's carcass, and the other men had been busy in the woods. Someone could have slipped away from the group, circled up to the top of the ridge, and started the slide. The avalanche itself would have wiped out any tracks. Then, in the confusion, the assailant could have easily rejoined the others without anyone being the wiser.

"Maybe it *was* a demon bear," Jeff said,

"but it won't ever hurt anyone else. It's gone. I reckon we should leave it that way."

Vassily shook his head regretfully. "So much bear meat," he said. "But you are right, my brother. Come. Let us return to the village, where we will tell the story of the mighty battle against the demon bear."

It would make a good yarn, all right, Jeff thought. But as he glanced again at Yuri and met the man's hate-filled gaze, he realized that the ending to at least one story had yet to be told.

CHAPTER ELEVEN

Once again, the steamboat *New Orleans* made port at St. Louis, much to the consternation of some of the grizzled old men who spent their days loitering around the docks. One of them called up to Captain Nicholas Roosevelt, "Didn't figure to ever see you again, Captain! Figured the river'd get you and that fancy boat of yours."

"The *New Orleans* came through splendidly, just as I knew she would," Roosevelt replied as he leaned on the railing and watched his crewmen tying stout hawsers to the dock. "We even rode out those earthquakes!"

Shining Moon was standing nearby on the deck with Clay, Matthew, and Lieutenant Markham. She hoped that she would never again have to endure anything like the earthquakes the captain had just mentioned.

Their bags were packed and ready at their feet. They would be leaving the steamboat here and arranging to travel up the Missouri on another boat. Shining Moon glanced apprehensively at the leaden sky. The dead of winter was a bad time to be traveling on the frontier. There had been no more snow or sleet the past few days, but the threat was always present.

Clay must have been thinking the same thing, because she heard him mutter to Markham, "La Carde's going to have to lay up somewhere for a few weeks, maybe a month or two."

"That'll give us a better chance to catch up to him, won't it?" Markham asked.

Clay looked dubious. "If the weather's too bad for La Carde to travel, chances are it's going to be too bad for us. Like it or not, winter's here, and we'll have to contend with it."

Matthew was watching the other boats moving along the river and seemed to be paying little attention to what Clay and Markham were saying. Every so often he glanced up at them, and Shining Moon wondered what the boy was thinking and how much he understood of grown-up matters. With Matthew, one could never tell.

Once the *New Orleans* had been made fast, Clay and Markham gathered up the bags, and the group said their farewells to Captain Roosevelt. "It's been an honor to travel with you, Captain," Clay said, gripping Roosevelt's hand.

"And I've enjoyed your company as well, Mr. Holt," Roosevelt replied. He lowered his voice to add, "I hope the rest of your mission, whatever it may be, goes well for you."

"Amen to that, Captain," Clay said wholeheartedly.

"Godspeed, Mr. Markham," Roosevelt told the young officer.

"Thank you, sir," Markham replied.

Roosevelt turned to Shining Moon and tipped his cap. "May your journey be safe, madam." Then he extended his hand to Matthew and said, "I hope you travel again with me someday, Master Garwood."

"I'll have my own boat someday," Matthew declared, not for the first time. "And it'll be bigger and faster than this one."

"Matthew," Shining Moon scolded. "Do not be disrespectful to the captain."

Matthew looked up at her. "But my boat *will* be bigger and faster!"

Roosevelt laughed. "It's all right, madam. That's exactly the kind of thinking the country needs. What's the point of building a boat — unless someone can come along and build one that's better?"

Clay heartily voiced his agreement. Of course he would feel that way, Shining Moon thought. The Holts were always thinking of ways to do things bigger and better.

Clay and Markham picked up the bags, and the group disembarked. They would have to make arrangements for the next leg of their journey, and that entailed at least a short stay in St. Louis.

Clay queried a man they passed on the street and was directed to what was supposed to be the best hotel in St. Louis. As they approached the place, Markham muttered, "If this is the best, I'd hate to see the worst."

"Looks mighty fancy to me," Clay said.

"I suppose, compared to a lodge made of buffalo hide, it would be." Markham looked quickly at Shining Moon and had the good grace to flush in embarrassment. "Begging your pardon, Mrs. Holt, I meant no disrespect —"

"All people live in the ways they know, Mr. Markham," Shining Moon said.

They entered the log building and were met by a tall, thin young man on duty behind a counter. He barely stifled a racking cough as he checked them in and gave them two rooms.

"I'd like to talk to someone about putting together a party to go up the Missouri," Clay told the clerk. "If you've got any suggestions —"

The young man doubled over coughing, and when he straightened, he wiped the back of his hand across his mouth and said, "Why in blazes are so many people starting upriver at this time of year? Don't you people know it's winter?"

Shining Moon saw Clay stiffen and knew his reaction was a mixture of anger at the clerk's tone and keen interest at what the young man had just said. "So we're not the only ones, eh?" he asked.

"You're the third group in the last month. I wouldn't be working so hard here if the last bunch hadn't taken the fellow who was clerking."

"Took him to do what?" asked Markham.

"To be their guide." The young man shrugged. "Oh, well, Pink Casebolt was always pretty lazy and no-account, anyway."

"What about the first group?" Clay asked casually. "They already have a guide?"

"Yes, and a much larger party. Some sort of foreigners, I reckon. They talked mighty strange, I know that."

Comte de La Carde and his group, Shining Moon thought. She was suddenly curious about something else.

So was Clay. "What about the second group? Who were they?"

Again the clerk shrugged. "I don't really know. A man, a woman, and a little boy. They had a keelboat and a crew, and they hired Pink Casebolt as their guide."

"They say where they were going?"

"Not to me. All I know is they were headed up the Missouri, like you folks." The clerk paused, then added, "You don't need a guide, do you?"

Clay grunted. "Not hardly." He dug some coins from his purse to pay for the two rooms. "Don't know how long we'll be here. This should cover the bill for a while."

"Yes, sir, it sure will." The clerk raked the coins off the counter into a wooden box. "Rooms are at the top of the stairs."

They went up, carrying their own bags, of course. Markham took the room closest to the stairs, while Clay, Shining Moon, and Matthew carried their belongings into the other room. Both chambers were small and functional, at best. Despite Markham's earlier comment, Shining Moon thought, she would have been much more comfortable in one of the lodges of her people.

Markham knocked lightly on the door. Clay let him in, and they discussed their next move.

"We'll have to find some canoes," Clay said. "That'll be the fastest way to travel. I thought about trying to hire a keelboat, but we can make better time than that."

Markham looked dubious. "Paddle canoes all the way to the mountains? Can we actually do that?"

Clay said dryly, "It's been done before."

"What about supplies? Will there be room to pack enough provisions?"

"As long as we travel light, there will be. We'll just take a few staples. Game won't be as plentiful now as it is the rest of the year, but as long as I've got my rifle, we won't go hungry, I can promise you that."

"I've been wondering . . . from what I've heard, the frontier is huge. Once we're out there, how are we going to find La Carde?"

"It's true there's plenty of room, but not that many people," Clay said. "You'd be surprised how fast word gets around. If there's a bunch of Frenchmen somewhere between here and the divide, we're liable to hear about them from any Indians or trappers we meet, even if the ones we're talking to haven't seen them for themselves. Besides, there are some main trails, and I reckon La Carde and his men are going to stick to them."

"Well, we can certainly hope so." Markham paused. "I didn't notice anyone suspicious lurking about downstairs. It seems likely that man who attacked me downriver was the only agent La Carde left behind watching for pursuers."

"As you said, we can hope so," Clay replied.

Nothing else unusual had happened after the incident Clay and Markham had told Shining Moon about, so she believed Markham was right. The Frenchman La Carde would not expect anyone to be coming after him. That could work in their favor later on.

"What about that second group?" Markham asked thoughtfully. "Do you think they could have anything to do with La Carde?"

"I don't see how," Clay said. "A man, a woman, and a boy, the clerk said. And they took a keelboat upriver. Sounds to me like settlers, maybe. Could be they're figuring on doing some fur trading." He shrugged. "If we catch up to them, I reckon we'll find out."

A sudden gust of wind howled outside. Shining Moon glanced toward the small, shuttered window. The room was already chilly, and the sound of the wind made her feel even colder.

She would be warm, she thought, if she were in her own lodge, wrapped in sleeping furs with her husband. Soon, soon . . .

If Wakan-Tanka willed it so.

"And may God have mercy on your soul," Captain Canfield intoned. The plank on which the canvas-shrouded body of third mate Thaddeus Kirby lay was tilted up over the railing, and the corpse slid down and plummeted into the sea below.

The *Lydia Marie* had not struck her sails and stopped for this solemn occasion; it was still cutting through the waters of the southern Pacific, bound for Cape Horn at the tip of South America. Save for the helmsman and the lookout, however, all the crewmen had gathered for the funeral service, caps off and heads lowered. Thad Kirby had not been a particularly well-liked officer, but a death at sea always had a sobering effect. Everyone on board the ship knew that such an end could be waiting for him — or her.

Ned stole a glance at India. Her head was bent, and the wind was plucking at her short brown hair. As Captain Canfield concluded the service, she whispered "Amen" along with the rest of the crew.

Kirby's body had splashed into the water and disappeared. When the fish were through with him, Ned mused, he would be nothing but a few bones scattered over the ocean floor. Ned shuddered. As much as he had come to love the sea, he did not want to be buried there.

Now Captain Canfield addressed the crew. "We'll be needing a new third mate." He glanced at Ned, who gave a tiny shake of the head. He didn't want the job, certainly not at the expense of another man's death. Canfield went on, "I've chosen Edmund Syme."

Ned was not surprised. Syme was a good sailor and a veteran of several years with the Marsh Shipping Line. He would make a decent officer, perhaps even better than Kirby had been, because he was closer to the rest of the crew. Kirby had been a taciturn, standoffish sort and a firm believer in the cat-o'-nine-tails for any offense.

Syme's shipmates clapped him on the back in congratulations. He shook hands with Captain Canfield, who promptly assigned him his first duty. "You have the bridge, Mr. Syme."

"Aye, sir." Syme went quickly up the ladder to join the helmsman.

"Mr. Holt, Mr. St. Clair, please come with me," Canfield went on. Ned exchanged a puzzled glance with India as they followed Canfield to his cabin.

When the door was shut behind them in the captain's cabin, Canfield tossed his plumed hat on the table and sighed. He gestured for Ned and India to take the two chairs as he sank tiredly onto his bunk, then leaned forward, his clasped hands held between his widespread knees.

"What do you think happened to Kirby?" he asked.

The question took Ned by surprise. "He fell ill and died," he said. "From the way he acted, I wouldn't be surprised if something ruptured inside him."

"The appendix, perhaps," India said. Ned didn't know what an appendix was, but India sounded as if she knew what she was talking about.

"Aye, perhaps," Canfield said. "But perhaps something else."

India asked bluntly, "What are you saying, Captain?"

Canfield's face and voice were grim as

he replied, "I'm saying that I think Kirby may have been murdered."

"Murdered!" Ned stared at the captain. "But . . . how? Why?"

Canfield shook his head. "I don't know the how or the why of it, Mr. Holt, but I nevertheless have a feeling in my bones that it's true."

Ned's thoughts went back to the previous night. Kirby had been standing watch on the bridge, not long after the sun had gone down. The sailors who were not on duty, Ned and India among them, had eaten supper but had not yet turned in for the night. As he stood on the deck at the railing, talking idly with India, Ned had heard Kirby's terrible cry. So had India, and she had started immediately for the bridge. Ned was right behind her.

Captain Canfield had reached Kirby's side first. By that time Kirby was lying on the deck, the helmsman standing by at the ship's wheel, uncertain what to do. As Ned and India reached the top of the ladder leading to the bridge, they saw Canfield kneeling beside Kirby. The third mate's legs were thrashing, but before Ned and India could reach him, he gave a final kick, uttered another wrenching cry, and lay still.

Captain Canfield, looking up as Ned and India approached, had announced, "Kirby's dead."

That was shocking news in itself, but even more shocking was the suddenness of the death. As Ned thought back on it now, sitting in Canfield's cabin, he understood why the captain was suspicious.

"Kirby showed no signs of illness earlier in the evening, did he?" Ned asked.

Canfield shook his head. "No. We had supper together at the usual time with the other officers, and he seemed fine then."

"Poison," India said.

"Exactly," Canfield agreed. "When I bent over Kirby as he was dying, I thought I caught a whiff of something odd on his breath."

Ned grimaced. The thought of a poisoner loose on the *Lydia Marie* made *him* feel ill.

"Why would anyone want to poison Kirby?" he asked.

"To get him out of the way?" Canfield said. "Kirby was a good officer. A bit harsh perhaps, but a staunch defender of discipline on board. Without him around, anyone who has it in mind to make trouble will have an easier time of it."

Ned's jaw tightened. "Trouble?" he

repeated. "You're talking about mutiny, Captain?"

Canfield sighed. "I wish to heaven I wasn't, Mr. Holt. But every officer on every ship at sea always has to be alert to that possibility."

Ned looked at India. They, too, had considered the potential for a mutiny on board the ship, but so far they had said nothing to Canfield. It seemed the time had come to do so.

"Captain," Ned said slowly, "maybe you shouldn't have appointed Syme to take Kirby's place."

Canfield stared at Ned. "What do you mean by that?" he demanded. "Mr. Syme is an excellent seaman, and he's been a member of the crew ever since the *Lydia Marie* first sailed."

"He's also asked several questions that made me think he was trying to assess what my reaction would be if there was a mutiny," Ned said. "I thought at first that he had overheard some grumbling among the crew and was trying to warn me there might be trouble, but now I don't think so. I think he's part of whatever is going on and was trying to judge if I might be persuaded to join the conspirators."

"That's outrageous!" Canfield exploded.

"I'll have the man flogged!"

"No," India said sharply. "That would only warn the plotters that you're aware of what they're doing. If you leave Syme as third mate, at least you can keep an eye on him."

Canfield considered the suggestion, rubbing his chin, then finally nodded slowly. "What you say makes sense. But I still don't like it. We have to find out for certain if a mutiny is in the offing."

"That's what I've been trying to do," India said.

Ned looked quickly at her, and understanding dawned on him. "That's why you got me drunk back at Boylston!" he exclaimed. "And why you've been acting so strangely. You're trying to get close to the mutineers!"

"*Possible* mutineers," India said. "We don't know anything for certain yet."

"We know that's too dangerous a game to be playing," Ned snapped. "You have to stop it, India. If they suspect you, they'll murder you, too."

"Not easily," she said. "Kirby probably never suspected anything. The three of us know to be watchful."

Canfield leaned forward, his hands still clasped between his knees. "Whom else do you suspect?" he asked.

"Yancy," Ned and India said at the same time.

"Aye," Canfield agreed. "The Cockney skulks around and seems harmless enough, but he's always about when trouble's brewing. Who else?"

"Cupp and Siros," Ned answered without hesitation.

"McHaney," India added. "And Osman, Teeple, and Flanagan. Cutthroats all."

"Anyone else?"

Ned considered, then shook his head. So did India. "That's more than enough, though," she said.

"Aye," Canfield answered somberly. He put his hands on his knees and pushed himself to his feet. "We'd best not stay in here any longer. We don't want that bunch getting suspicious of the two of you."

Ned and India stood as well, and Ned said, "I don't want you trying to win their confidence anymore."

"It's a bit late for that," India said. "If we're to have a chance of heading off disaster, we need all the advance warning we can get."

"The lad's right, Mr. Holt," Canfield said. The captain knew that India was a woman, but at times he succumbed to the illusion of her masquerade along with everyone else.

"But —" Ned began.

India stepped to the door and jerked it open. "Go to hell, Holt," she growled loudly, then stalked out.

Although he understood why she had said that, the words pierced Ned's heart. He had known better than to try to talk her out of her plan. Once she had settled on a course of action, nothing deterred India St. Clair. It was always full speed ahead.

Ned looked at Captain Canfield and shook his head. A dull ache had settled behind his eyes. Between worrying about the British and the mutineers and India, it was going to be a long voyage home.

A long voyage indeed.

Clay bought two sturdy canoes from a pair of trappers who intended to spend the rest of the winter in St. Louis. One of them warned him, "You'll freeze your ballocks off if you start up the Big Muddy at this time of year."

"Reckon you could be right," Clay said wryly.

As it turned out, no one was going anywhere. Before the small group could leave

St. Louis, a fierce blizzard roared down out of the north and raced south over the Great Plains, dropping six or seven feet of snow. For several days the wind blew so hard and the snow fell so heavily that anyone foolish enough to venture outside was in peril of losing his way before he'd gone ten yards.

The only thing Clay and his companions could do was hole up in the hotel, huddled around the stove with everyone else in a largely futile attempt to stay warm. Clay tried to stay calm, but inside he was seething. Any chance they'd had of gaining ground on La Carde had blown away with the wind. His only consolation was that with a storm this intense, La Carde's party had no doubt been forced to halt, too.

The storm lasted a week, and it was another week before temperatures climbed high enough to start melting the snow. Word came to St. Louis that the Missouri River was frozen over almost all the way down to its junction with the Mississippi. The year 1812 had gotten off to a hellacious start with the massive earth-quakes a couple of months earlier; now, after what had been an unusually mild winter, the weather was finally showing its fangs.

As the great piles of snow began to diminish, Clay realized that these developments might be turned to their advantage. He and Markham walked outside one day and stood on the hotel porch looking out at the street, which had been turned into a sea of mud. "I've been thinking that we might want to go ahead and pull out in another few days, when things have had a chance to dry out a little."

The clouds had departed and the sky was a clear, brilliant blue. The wind was still cold, but it was a far cry from the numbing blasts of the past weeks.

"How can we leave?" Markham asked. "I thought you said the Missouri would probably stay frozen for several weeks yet."

Clay nodded. "So it will. But that won't stop us from going overland."

Markham's eyebrows lifted as he began to understand what Clay was suggesting. "La Carde and his group are traveling by keelboat," the young officer said quietly. "Wherever they are, they're stuck until the river thaws."

"That's right. But if we can get our hands on some horses, the frozen river won't stop us at all."

"Horses?" Markham repeated. "Oh, dear. I remember our trip to Gideon

Maxwell's estate in Virginia. My arse still hurts."

Markham's light tone concealed some painful memories, Clay knew — more than just sore muscles from riding. Markham had fallen in love with Gideon Maxwell's daughter, Diana, and had refused to believe that she had had a role in the land grab scheme with her father. He had held stubbornly to that conviction — until the showdown came and Diana Maxwell shot him.

Markham had recovered from the bullet wound, and his broken heart seemed to have healed, too. But Clay knew he had not forgotten Diana.

"You'll get used to riding again," Clay assured him. "And I know some shortcuts that will cut the gap between us and La Carde."

"What about Mrs. Holt and the boy?"

Clay chuckled. "Don't worry about Shining Moon. Her people haven't always been good at riding, but they're learning. I wouldn't mind having some Sioux ponies for the trip. I reckon we'll have to make do with whatever we can find here in St. Louis, though." He snorted. "Plow horses, more than likely. I don't really care, as long as they get us to the mountains."

"And to La Carde," Markham added.

Clay's mouth set in a grim line. "And to La Carde."

Markham looked out at the street. Melting snow was dripping from every roof, but in the shadows between the buildings, the drifts were still several feet deep. "I can't help but wonder," he said, "about that second group of pilgrims who were on their way up the river . . ."

Chapter Twelve

Melissa Holt pulled the buffalo robe more tightly around herself and tried to stop shivering. The robe smelled faintly of dead animal and mildew, but it kept her warm, and that was all that mattered. She wondered, not for the first time in recent weeks, just what madness had possessed her to suggest they start west at this time of year.

It had not been madness at all, she knew. Pride was what had gotten her into this predicament — foolish, stubborn pride. She should have believed Jeff and forgiven him for what was surely a moment of weakness and nothing more. If she had, they would all be back in Wilmington now, safe and warm, not nearly freezing to death in some godforsaken Indian village.

At least Michael, bless his heart, had seemed utterly unperturbed by their sojourn with the Mandans. He was somewhere outside now with Terence O'Shay and Pink Casebolt, while his mother huddled in a lodge next to a small fire made of dried buffalo droppings. On the other side of the fire, an elderly Mandan woman, round-faced and nearly toothless, mended buckskins and chanted some sort of song to herself. *She* seemed perfectly happy.

Melissa took a deep breath and immediately wished she hadn't as the stench of the buffalo robe assaulted her. She exhaled quickly, rubbed her nose, and said to the Mandan woman, "Is there anything I can do to help you?"

The woman looked up in surprise. She said something in her native tongue. Melissa could only shake her head and say, "I don't understand you. I want to help you with what you're doing, if I can." She gestured at the garment in the woman's hand and the other buckskins piled beside her, then made sewing motions with both hands. "I would be glad to help you, if I can."

The woman smiled a gap-toothed smile and nodded. She picked up a beaded dress and handed it across the fire to Melissa. Then she gave her a curved needle made out of a sliver of bone and a ball of thread — not cotton thread, as Melissa knew, but animal gut stretched thin and fine. The dress had a long rip in it, and Melissa set to work mending it. She had never been a particularly good seamstress under the best of circumstances. Her hands, clad in thin gloves, were half frozen, and she was not accustomed to working with such primitive tools as a bone needle and gut thread. But she persevered — stubbornness was sometimes a good thing, she told herself — and slowly closed up the rip in the dress.

It felt good to be doing something useful again, Melissa realized. Ever since the ice had grown too thick on the river for the keelboat to proceed and the party had been forced to stop at this village, she had done little but sit in various lodges and feel sorry for herself as she tried to keep warm.

"I hope I'm doing this right," she said aloud. "It's a bit more ragged than your work. I wonder if whoever this dress belongs to will wear it knowing that it was mended by a crazy white woman?"

The Mandan woman smiled and nodded.

"I hope Michael is all right," Melissa went on. "He and Terence and Pink have been gone for quite a while. I'm certainly glad that Pink knew the chief of your tribe so that we had a place to stay when that terrible storm struck. If we hadn't gotten off the river, I'm sure we would all have frozen to death." She added under her breath, "We may anyway, in these drafty lodges."

The Mandan woman said something and smiled again.

"First Alaska, and now this place. It seems I cannot escape the cold this winter. In my home in Wilmington we have a fireplace, and when the wind blows, we build a roaring fire in it, and the whole house stays warm. Of course, we rarely have snow there. It's too warm for snow, there on the coast."

The flap of hide that hung over the lodge's entrance was suddenly thrust back, and Michael scurried in. He was wrapped in a heavy coat and wore a fur cap. He held up something and said proudly, "Look what I have, Mama!"

He was holding the bloody carcass of a rabbit. "My Lord!" she exclaimed. "Where did you get that?"

"I killed it! With an arrow!"

Terence and Pink came into the lodge behind the boy. Pink said, "Howdy, ma'am. Reckon your boy has the makings of an Indian warrior. He knocked down that rabbit with his first arrow."

Melissa knew that Michael had been practicing for several days with the small bows and arrows that the Mandan children used. She smiled weakly and said, "That's very good, Michael. You should be proud."

"Will you cook it so we can eat it?" Michael asked eagerly.

Melissa was struggling for an answer when Pink said, "Got to clean the critter before we can roast it, boy. Take it back outside, and I'll be there in a minute to show you how." He pulled a knife from a sheath on his belt. "Here's my skinning knife. You wait for me, now, and don't go trying anything by yourself."

"All right." Michael hurried back out, carrying the knife and the dead rabbit.

Melissa wasn't sure it was wise to hand over a sharp knife to a small boy, but she could see that Pink didn't mean to leave him alone for long. Pink spoke quickly in Mandan to the woman, who nodded and answered him. He turned to Melissa and said, "Wah-nee-wa says she'll cook up that rabbit for the boy."

"Thank you, Mr. Casebolt. I'm not very . . . experienced . . . at roasting rabbits over a buffalo chip fire."

Pink chuckled and left the lodge. Melissa said to Terence, "I didn't know you were going hunting."

Terence settled down cross-legged on a

robe near the fire. "Michael wanted to show me how good he's gotten with the bow, and I didn't see any harm in it."

"Oh, no, that's quite all right," Melissa assured him. "It's just that you were gone longer than I expected."

Terence grinned. "The lad's become quite a hunter, as Pink said. If he stays out here on the frontier very long, you'll be mistaking him for half Indian before you know it."

"I'm not sure I *want* to mistake him for that. I want him to stay my sweet little boy."

"Maybe for a while," Terence said. "But that youngster's got the love of far places in him, Melissa. When he's a man full grown, nobody will be able to stop him from roaming."

Melissa sighed as she set aside the dress she had mended and reached for a pair of buckskin leggings with a seam that needed repairing. "I know," she said. "He has too much of the Holt blood in him."

"Too much of the Holt blood," Terence O'Shay mused. "I'm not sure that's something a fellow can be having . . ."

"All right," Pink Casebolt told Michael. "Now you want to hang the carcass up so the blood can drain out of it. The meat'll keep a heap longer that way."

"Hang it where?" Michael asked as he lifted the skinned and gutted rabbit.

Pink pointed to a nearby evergreen. "I reckon one of those branches will do. Take some strips of rawhide and use them to tie the rabbit's hind feet to the branch."

Michael did as he'd been instructed, then stepped back to observe his handiwork. Pride shone on the boy's face.

For a little fellow, Michael had a way about him, Pink thought. He seemed to pick things up quickly, and he was always on the lookout for something new to see or to learn. With a little bit of luck, he'd go far in the world.

Probably a hell of a lot farther than a loser like Pinkney Casebolt.

Pink rubbed his bearded jaw and looked around at the Mandan village, a sprawl of bark-and-hide lodges along the bank of the Missouri. The blizzard that had come howling down out of the north weeks earlier had frozen the river solid. A thick blanket of snow lay over the gently rolling hills on both sides of the river. Little was moving on that broad expanse of white. A hunter might run across an occasional rabbit, such as the one Michael had killed, or a small herd of moose. Everything that could migrate to warmer climates in the south had already done so.

Pink wondered what it would be like to be warm in the winter. One of these days, he told himself, he was going to meander down to those southern lands that were held by the Spanish. He'd known a few Spaniards in his time and knew they liked the weather — and their women — hot.

Thinking about women turned his mind to Mrs. Holt. *Melissa.* A mighty pretty name for a mighty pretty woman. He wasn't sure how hot-blooded she was, though. It had been his experience that women without much meat on their bones, like Mrs. Holt, tended to be a mite on the cool side.

"Well, you won't never get to find out, will you, Pink?" he muttered to himself.

"What did you say, Mr. Casebolt?"

Michael's question made Pink jump. He looked down at the boy, glad that he hadn't voiced some of his other thoughts out loud. "I was just talking to myself," he muttered.

"About what?"

"If I knew that, I'd know how to answer myself, now wouldn't I?"

Michael looked confused, which was just

what Pink wanted. "I guess you would," Michael said after a moment.

"Come on. We'll come back later and get that rabbit. You hung it up high enough none of the dogs can get at it, didn't you?"

"I think so."

"How's about giving me my knife back?"

"Oh." Michael had cleaned the blood off the knife and then stuck it behind his belt. He took it out and handed it back to Pink, bone handle first. "I forgot."

"I reckon it won't be long until you've got a knife of your own."

"I don't know," Michael said dubiously. "I asked my mama about it, and she said I was too little. That's what she said when I told her I wanted a pistol and a rifle, too."

"Can you shoot a gun?"

"Some. My papa and my uncle Clay taught me."

Pink nodded. "That's good to know. If we run into bad trouble somewhere along the way, we're liable to need every man we've got."

"Bad trouble?" Michael repeated. "You mean like unfriendly Indians?"

"Yep. Or a pack of hungry wolves, say."

Michael's eyes widened. "Wolves? There are wolves out here?"

"Why, of course there're wolves," Pink

said. "And at this time of year, they're liable to be starving. You see, a wolf won't normally attack a man, but when he gets hungry enough . . ."

"Wolves," Michael said again, softly.

Pink put a hand on the boy's shoulder. "Don't you worry none. I won't let wolves get you, and I reckon neither will your ma or Mr. O'Shay. If your pa was here, neither would he."

"Papa's in Alaska."

"You don't say. Where's that?"

"I don't know exactly. But it's a long way off. We rode on a ship for a long time to get there, and a long time to get back."

Pink nodded slowly. "Do tell. That's mighty interesting."

And it was. He had wondered where Mrs. Holt's husband was. Now that he knew, he wondered why the damn fool wasn't with her. If *he* was married to a woman like that, he sure as hell wouldn't ever let anything come between them.

Pink grimaced. He knew already that he would not sleep well tonight. He was going to be too busy thinking about what it would be like to be married to Melissa Holt.

After a successful run in Baltimore, the

Dowd acting troupe moved on into Virginia. Richmond was their ultimate destination, the southernmost stop on their circuit. From there they would swing over into Tennessee and then back up through Pennsylvania, New York, and New England.

Before that time came, Proud Wolf and Audrey would have to decide what to do. They were loath to return to Massachusetts. Although Will Brackett was still alive — and therefore no murder charge hung over Proud Wolf's head — other charges had probably been filed against him. The authorities were more likely to take Brackett's side in any dispute, too. Then there was Audrey's father. Jeremiah Stoddard would almost certainly press a kidnapping charge against Proud Wolf, and Audrey's testimony that she had accompanied him willingly would likely be ignored by the law.

But an idea had begun to form in Proud Wolf's mind. If he was willing to give up the idea of obtaining a white man's education — and under the present circumstances that seemed an impossible goal — then he would be free to return to the mountains and prairies of his homeland. Surely Will Brackett, as strong as his hatred was — and as influential as he and his family were — would not pursue him that far. And Audrey could go with Proud Wolf, far beyond the reach of her father. *If* she would go . . . and he had not yet asked her what she thought of the idea.

In the meantime there were miles to travel and performances to be staged, and the troupe stopped at a string of small communities between Baltimore and Richmond. No settlement was too small to ignore, Dowd said; they were in the business of spreading entertainment and good will wherever people were to be found.

They were camped one evening on the edge of a town so small that it had only one street and no village green or square. Professor Dowd thought it sufficient that they present an abbreviated version of their usual performance: a song and dance from Portia, a dramatic reading by Walter Berryhill, and two scenes from Shakespeare's plays. Attendance would probably be light, so Dowd warned the players that they might not bring in much money from this stop.

"Just think of it as getting paid to rehearse a bit," he told them as he assembled them that evening. He looked around at the group. "Where's Walter?"

Proud Wolf glanced around the camp but saw no sign of the tall, spare Walter Berryhill. None of the others seemed to know where he was either, but after a moment, Oliver Johnson cleared his throat and spoke.

"Walter said something a little while ago about finding a place to have a, ah, small libation. Priming the creative pump, he called it."

Dowd muttered a curse, and beside him, Vanessa shook her head. "You're supposed to keep an eye on him, Oliver," Dowd said.

"I try," Oliver said, "but once he's got it in his head to go, how do I stop him, short of knocking him down and hog-tying him? Do you really want me to humiliate him that way, Ulysses?"

Dowd grimaced and shook his head. He put his hands on his hips and glared down the street toward the other end of the settlement.

"There can't be too many taverns in a town this small," Dowd said. "I'll go haul him out of whichever one he's visiting."

"Hold on, Ulysses," Oliver said quickly. "Let me go. After all, I'm the one who was supposed to be watching him. It's my responsibility."

"And if he's so far in his cups that he won't come?"

"I'll appeal to his sense of duty. The show must go on, and all that."

Dowd shrugged his massive shoulders. "All right," he said. "But take someone with you, in case there's trouble." His gaze fell on Proud Wolf. "You, lad. Go with Oliver and help him bring Walter back to us."

The request took Proud Wolf by surprise. He glanced at Audrey, who nodded. "Go ahead," she urged him. "I'll be busy getting ready for tonight's performance, anyway."

Proud Wolf hesitated. As far as he knew, Audrey was unaware of what Kenneth Thurston had had in mind for her on the night he paid a visit to their wagon. But Thurston would be busy preparing for the night's performance as well, too busy for romantic intrigues.

"All right," Proud Wolf said. He turned to his diminutive friend. "I will go with you, Oliver."

"Good," Oliver said. "Come along, then. There's not much time."

They left the camp and started down the street, the slender young man, of less than medium height, and his companion, a decade and a half older but only half his size. They had gone only a short distance when they came to a tavern. The sign hanging over the door, burned into a plank with a hot iron, read HIGGINS ALE HOUSE. Lantern light shone golden through the windows. Proud Wolf opened the door halfway, and Oliver leaned in to look around.

"Hey!" a man called from behind the bar. "No young 'uns in here!"

Oliver replied in a mock falsetto voice, "But, sir, I'm just looking for my pa. Are you him?"

The barman lifted a bungstarter as if he were about to throw it at the door. "Go on, you little scamp! Get out of here!"

Oliver backed out and jerked his head at Proud Wolf. "Come," he said in his normal voice. "I didn't see Walter in there." He glanced back at the door as it swung shut and muttered an obscenity in the barman's direction.

The only other tavern in the settlement was at the far end of the street. It was called the Golden Dragon and had a fanciful picture of the mythical beast painted on its sign. Proud Wolf looked up at the dragon in approval. Any artist so skilled would have been welcome to paint on

Sioux lodge skins.

Oliver opened the door and looked inside, then glanced back over his shoulder at Proud Wolf and rolled his eyes. "Walter's here, all right."

Even standing outside, Proud Wolf could hear Walter Berryhill proclaiming loudly, " 'Now is the winter of our discontent.' "

Oliver pushed his way inside the tavern and motioned for Proud Wolf to follow. As he stepped into the smoky, low-ceilinged room, Proud Wolf had no trouble locating Berryhill. The actor was standing at the end of the bar, clasping the lapel of his coat with one hand and gesturing grandiosely with the other. He continued to quote Shakespeare but grew confused as he went along, switching from *Richard III* to *Hamlet* and gravely intoning, " 'That is the question. Whether 'tis nobler to take up arms —' "

"Take up a cup of ale is more like it," one of the men gathered around Berryhill called, and that gibe brought a laugh from the crowd. "He's drunk as a lord!"

Indeed, Walter Berryhill was very drunk. The old man was swaying, and as the patrons laughed, he suddenly lost his balance and would have fallen had he not grabbed the bar.

"Give him another tankard!"

"Aye! I want to see what the old sot will do next!"

Listening to the crowd's jeers, Proud Wolf seethed with anger. Walter had been an actor for decades, had performed all over the United States and Europe. He deserved better than to be made sport of by louts such as these.

Proud Wolf started forward, but Oliver put a hand on his arm to stop him. "Let me take care of this," he said quietly.

Oliver moved forward, maneuvering skillfully between the legs of the customers gathered around Walter. He disappeared, cut off from Proud Wolf's view by the crowd, but a moment later Proud Wolf heard one of the men exclaim, "Here now! Who's this? The old man's grandson?"

"Come along, Walter," Proud Wolf heard Oliver say. "We have a performance this evening —"

"I am . . . I am putting on a performance right here, my little . . . little friend," Walter said. "Perhaps you could do something as well."

"Later, Walter," Oliver insisted. "I need you to come with me —"

One of the men interrupted. "What if we're not ready for him to go? The old man's damned amusing."

"And three sheets to the wind," added another man with a laugh.

"Leave him be, little man." Someone grabbed Oliver's shoulder and shoved him out of the circle. Oliver stumbled toward Proud Wolf but caught himself before he fell.

Proud Wolf reached for the knife at his belt. There was only one way to deal with these men.

Before he could draw the weapon from its sheath, someone shouted from across the room, "Hey, you there! Indian!"

Proud Wolf tensed. His raven-black hair was pulled back and tied at the nape, a not uncommon fashion, and he wore white man's clothing. Only his dark skin and hawkish countenance suggested he was different from anyone in the crowd. Evidently that had been enough to catch the eye of someone in the Golden Dragon.

He turned and saw two men standing up from a table in the corner. Both were roughly dressed and bearded. Proud Wolf thought they looked familiar, but it took him a moment to remember where he had seen them before.

Oliver recognized them first. "Those are a couple of Brackett's men!" he hissed.

Brackett's men! Proud Wolf yanked his knife out. They would not take him alive back to Brackett, he vowed silently. As the blade glinted in the lantern light, one of the men grabbed for the pistol tucked behind his belt. He fired hastily as the weapon came free.

The ball whipped past Proud Wolf's head and thudded into the wall behind him. He was about to draw back his arm and throw the knife, but someone grabbed his arm.

"No!" Oliver said. "Out the back!"

Running from his enemies did not sit well with Proud Wolf, but as he glanced around he saw he had a chance to escape. The tavern was in a state of chaos now, primed by the unexpected gunshot. Men were shouting questions and angry curses and shoving each other aside. The crowd suddenly surged between Proud Wolf and Brackett's men, separating them for a moment, and once again Oliver tugged urgently on Proud Wolf's arm.

"Go! And take Walter with you!"

Proud Wolf turned and lunged toward the elderly actor, who still stood leaning against the bar, clearly befuddled by the sudden outbreak of violence around him. Proud Wolf slid his knife back in its sheath and grabbed Walter's arm. Walter stumbled, but Proud Wolf managed to keep him upright as they ducked toward a door at the end of the bar.

"Get out of the way, damn it!" That furious shout came from one of Brackett's men. Proud Wolf glanced back as he and Walter reached the door. He saw Oliver suddenly spring up onto the bar.

"Call me little, will you!" he shouted at one of the customers. He launched himself into space, tackling the man from behind and grabbing him around the neck, at the same time wrapping his legs around the man's torso.

Oliver's weight drove the man forward, and both of them fell to the floor, sprawling in the path of Brackett's men as they charged forward. That was all Proud Wolf had time to see, because a second later he and Walter Berryhill were out the rear door of the tavern.

"Get back to the camp!" Proud Wolf told Walter as they hurried around the building. "Go!"

The old man pawed at him. "What . . . what was all that trouble in there?"

Walter was too drunk to know what was happening, let alone to find his way back to the wagons now that night was falling. Proud Wolf's breath hissed between clenched teeth as he half led, half shoved the actor toward where the Dowd troupe was camped. They were halfway there, hurrying along the street, when a voice called behind them, "Hey! Wait for me!"

Proud Wolf paused and looked behind them, and a second later a small figure came running out of the gathering gloom. At the other end of the street, shouts and crashes were ample testimony that the brawl in the tavern was going full force, but Oliver had slipped out somehow.

He ran up to them as fast as his short legs could carry him. "Keep going," he panted.

The three of them ran back to the camp, where they found an anxious group waiting for them. "We heard a shot," Dowd said.

"We'd better hitch up the teams and pull out, Ulysses," Oliver advised him. "These folks will be busy busting each other over the head for a while, but sooner or later they're going to come looking for us."

"Damn and blast!" Dowd exploded. "All I did was send you after Walter —"

"It is not Oliver's fault, nor Walter's," Proud Wolf said. "Two of Brackett's men

281

were in the tavern. They saw me and recognized me."

He heard Audrey gasp in dismay and wished there was something he could say to reassure her. But in truth there was nothing that could be said. Tonight's developments could only lead to more trouble.

But perhaps it could be put off for a while longer. Ulysses Dowd was already snapping orders, and the Zachary brothers started hitching the teams to the wagons. Proud Wolf went to help them. Audrey put a hand out to him as he passed her, but he only grasped it for a second, squeezing hard, then hurried on.

In less than ten minutes the troupe was ready to move. The wagons rolled out onto the road and headed south. With any luck Brackett's men might not connect Proud Wolf with Oliver and Walter. They might not even think to pursue the troupe but concentrate their search in the village instead. That would give the troupe a little more time to build up a lead.

But sooner or later they would figure it out, Proud Wolf knew. Sooner or later Will Brackett would come for him, and he would bring trouble for Proud Wolf's friends.

He could not allow that to happen, he thought as he drove the wagon, Audrey sitting beside him and clutching his arm in fear. As soon as he got the chance, he would tell her about his idea of heading west, back to his home, and taking her with him.

But they had to stay out of Brackett's way until then.

Horses pounded to a halt outside the tavern, and Will Brackett strode in a moment later, followed by Frank Kirkland and the rest of his band of hired ruffians. He spotted his men at a table in the corner and noticed immediately that their faces were bruised and scraped. "What happened here?" he snapped as he walked over to them.

"There was a fight," one of the men growled. "Look around you. Everyone in here has taken a drubbing."

That was true, Brackett saw as he looked at the other men in the tavern. Chairs and tables were overturned, and a surly bartender was sweeping up what was left of several jugs of whiskey.

"You're supposed to be looking for that damned Indian," Brackett said coldly, "not getting into tavern brawls."

"He was here."

Brackett stiffened as he drew in a sharp breath. "You're sure?"

"An Indian, not too big, wearing white man's clothes. Who in blazes else could it have been?"

Frank Kirkland leaned forward. "Where did he go?"

"He slipped out during the fighting. We were just about to start asking questions around town —"

"You'd be wasting your time." Brackett turned on his heel and stalked back toward the door, never looking back to see if Kirkland and the other men were following him. He knew they would be. "Proud Wolf is already a long way from here, and he's probably putting more distance between us even as we speak. Did you see the girl?"

The two men hurried up alongside him. "He didn't have a girl with him," one of them said.

Brackett nodded curtly. "It doesn't matter. She'll be with him now." He slapped the door aside and strode out into the night. "They're out there. I can feel them. I can almost hear them, still laughing at me. But they won't be laughing much longer."

No, soon they would both be screaming,

Proud Wolf in agony and Audrey in horror at what was happening to her redskin lover before her very eyes.

And Will Brackett would be laughing as they screamed.

CHAPTER THIRTEEN

The story of the battle between the hunters and the demon bear became a Tlingit legend almost overnight, and Jeff was assured of his place in the tale as the Tlingit's white brother from a faraway land. Vassily told him that the story would be carved into house posts all over the village.

In the story, the avalanche that had swallowed the bear and almost killed Jeff and Vassily became the evil spirits reclaiming the body of their vessel. Jeff was perfectly willing to let the Tlingit believe that if they wished, but he knew better. He was convinced the rockslide had been purposely started, and he had a good idea who was responsible. The seething resentment he had seen in Yuri's eyes that day was enough proof for him.

Nadia made a great fuss over him when the band of hunters returned to the village. Jeff was given credit for thinking up the plan by which the bear had been destroyed, and the story of his brush with death was told over and over. That night, when he and Nadia were wrapped in their sleeping robes, she clutched him especially tightly. "I almost lost you," she said breathlessly as he made love to her. "Never will I let you go again."

Jeff was not so caught up in the throes of passion that he did not hear those words and mull them over later. Like Vassily and the others, Nadia assumed he would remain there with them for the rest of his life. He would have to start laying the groundwork soon for his eventual departure.

Otherwise he would never be allowed to go home, would never see his family again.

Winter was slow in passing, and the nights were long and cold. But as the weeks went by, the heavy cloud cover thinned, the midday sun grew brighter, and the ice on the stream near the village began to melt where the water ran shallow. Jeff accompanied Vassily and a handful of other men on a trip to the bay between the mainland and the island on which the Russian settlement of Sitka stood, and the ice in the bay had thinned as well.

From where he stood, Jeff could not see Sitka; it was on the other side of the island. But he knew it was there, and thinking about the settlement gave him the glimmerings of an idea.

After they had returned to the village, he sought out Vassily and asked, "The Russians came here to trade with your people, didn't they?"

Vassily nodded gravely as he sat beside the fire in his hut. "And to make us their slaves and steal the bounty of our land."

"Well, yes," Jeff agreed. "But their original goal was trade."

"That is so."

"And when *I* came to Alaska, my goal was trade also. But I intended to trade with the Russians."

Vassily frowned. Jeff was explaining things to him that he already knew. "Who else could you trade with?" he asked.

"The same people the Russians came to trade with." Jeff pointed a finger at Vassily. "You."

"Me?" Vassily's eyebrows lifted.

"Your people. The Tlingit. Why can't American ships trade directly with you?"

"The Russians would never allow that. They would come with their soldiers and destroy us."

"Not if you were protected by the United States."

Vassily regarded Jeff across the fire.

"What you are talking about might lead to a war between your people and the Russians. The Tlingit know of war. We have fought other tribes and have always defeated them." He stared into the fire. "But in this war, the Tlingit would be caught between those who make the war."

Vassily had quickly grasped the possible implications of Jeff's proposal. Jeff said, "It doesn't have to be that way. In fact, there's no reason for the Russians to know about what we'd be doing, at least not at first. There are plenty of small bays along the coast where a trading post could be established."

"Russian ships sail in those waters. They would see any American ships that might come."

"Well, then," Jeff said with a shrug, "your other choice is to continue serving the Russians."

He felt a twinge of guilt. He was using the Tlingit, and he knew it. But at the same time he had serious doubts that the Russians would choose to go to war over a harsh, mountainous chunk of land that was icebound much of the year. It was possible, of course — but an American presence in Alaska might lead instead to negotiations between the two countries and a compromise of some kind.

Vassily, deep in thought, did not respond. After a moment Jeff said, "The ship that brought me here will be returning to Sitka in two or three months, when the weather has improved. We can paddle out in one of your canoes and meet the *Beaumont* before it reaches Sitka. If we had a trading post ready, somewhere down the coast, the ship wouldn't have to come anywhere near the settlement. The Russians wouldn't know anything about it."

"You are a persuasive man, Jeff Holt," Vassily said. "What you suggest might be very good for my people. But it might also be very bad."

"Everything in life has its risks," Jeff said.

"True." Vassily nodded abruptly. "We will talk about this again. I cannot make a decision now."

"All right, that's fair enough." Jeff got to his feet and bid Vassily good night. He left the hut and headed back toward his own lodge, keeping a careful watch for any sign of danger. Yuri had not made any further attempts on his life since the avalanche, but several times Jeff had caught the man glaring at him. It was only a matter of time, Jeff believed, before Yuri tried to kill him again.

Perhaps by that time, though, Vassily would have agreed to the idea of the trading post, and Jeff would be taking the first steps toward returning to his own home.

But if that happened, he asked himself, what would become of Nadia?

Clay sold the canoes he had bought earlier and, with some of the money he and Markham had left from what the government had advanced them, he bought a string of eight horses, four on which to ride and four to carry their supplies. By alternating between the animals, Clay hoped the party could make better time. They had a lot of ground to cover.

"I'm going to ride my own horse?" Matthew asked excitedly when Clay explained the plan.

"That's right," Clay told him. "Reckon you can manage it?"

"I've ridden horses before," Matthew replied, a hint of disdain creeping into his voice. "I'm a good rider."

"Good, because we'll be pressing on pretty hard."

The threat of winter storms had not passed, but Clay knew they had to risk it if they were going to catch up to La Carde.

He spent a couple of days buying supplies and packs, then told Markham to be ready to ride early the next morning. "We'll be pulling out of here about dawn," Clay said.

Markham nodded. "I can't say I'm looking forward to riding halfway across the continent," he admitted. "But it does seem to be the best way to find La Carde before he has time to establish himself."

The next morning, Clay was up well before the sun. For the first time in almost a year, he unpacked the soft buckskin shirt and trousers that had been his everyday garb until he'd gone east for the reunion at the Holt family farm in Ohio. It was at that reunion he had received the letter from Meriwether Lewis, two years after it had originally been mailed. The letter had sent him to Washington City in search of a reward he hadn't known existed, and that journey had embroiled him in the mass of avarice and pride that was the Comte de La Carde's scheme.

Things would have been very different if he and Shining Moon and Matthew hadn't gone to that family reunion, he thought as he pulled on the buckskins and buckled a broad belt around his waist. A part of him wished they had stayed in the mountains;

life was often harsh and perilous there, but at least the dangers were out in the open where a man could see them.

But if La Carde's empire got a foothold in the American West, sooner or later there would be a war, and that war would likely be fought in the land that Clay called home. He could not allow that to happen.

"My husband," Shining Moon said softly from the bed Clay had slipped out of a few minutes earlier. He turned and saw her watching him. A single candle burned on the table in the hotel room, casting a warm glow over the bed. Matthew was still asleep in a small bed in the corner.

"Didn't mean to wake you just yet," Clay said quietly.

Shining Moon sat up, wrapping herself in the covers. "You could not wait to clothe yourself in the garments of the mountains," she said.

Clay grinned. "I'm ready to go home, that's for sure."

"As am I."

She opened her arms to him, and he went to the bed and leaned down. Her arms went around his neck. His mouth found hers.

When he broke the kiss and drew back slightly, a long moment later, he whispered, "I just put these buckskins on."

Shining Moon leaned over and blew out the candle, then reached for him again.

"Of course, I reckon it wouldn't be that much trouble to put them on again in a little while."

A lumpy hotel bed ran a poor second to a pile of warm buffalo robes in a Sioux lodge . . . but for now it would do.

They tried to be quiet, stifling their moans and cries and moving slowly so that the bed wouldn't squeak, but Matthew heard them anyway. He lay with his face to the wall, eyes open and staring unseeing into the darkness, his breathing deep and regular so they wouldn't know he was awake.

It wasn't as if this was the first time he had heard these sounds. His mama had had a lot of men in her life, and Matthew had heard what they did with her. He had seen some of it, too, when they lived in Marietta and fellows would come to the farm to see Josie Garwood. She would always send him away, but he knew how to sneak back. The loft where he slept had a small window at one end, and he could climb up the log wall and slip in through it. He would push aside his straw-tick mattress, remove a piece of chinking between the puncheons that made up the floor, and look right down at his mama's bed. For a while he had tried to count how many different pale, hairy buttocks he'd watched pumping up and down between his mama's widespread thighs, but eventually he gave up. There were just too many.

So he knew all about what men and women did together, and when he thought about it too much, he started to feel hollow inside, as if he'd lost something and would never get it back. The feeling was strange and he didn't like it, but it was there all the same.

But he didn't care what Clay Holt and that red-skinned woman did with each other. Matthew Garwood had bigger and better things in mind. Clay wanted to find the Comte de La Carde, and Matthew hoped he would. For a while, when they were all on the *New Orleans* on its journey downriver, Matthew had joined forces with Senator Ralston. But then the senator had decided to double-cross him, because he was only a child.

Well, Ralston was dead now, wasn't he? And Matthew was very much alive. Things hadn't worked out with Ralston, but maybe they would with La Carde.

Matthew smiled into the darkness.

The *Lydia Marie*'s stopover in the Hawaiian Islands was a short but productive one. Captain Canfield, accompanied by Ned, visited the royal palace of King Kamehameha once again, but this time no trade pacts were discussed, only a simple item of business.

On behalf of the March Shipping Line, Canfield bought four cannons from the Hawaiian king. They were older models that Kamehameha had obtained from the English during the years when he was fighting his wars to unite the islands into one nation. Since then he had replaced them with more powerful cannons.

"These will not be used against my people one day, I trust," Kamehameha said gravely as negotiations were concluded.

"You have my word on that," Canfield assured him. "They are for our protection at sea only."

Kamehameha grunted. "Protection from the English?"

Ned grinned. Apparently the Hawaiian king managed to keep abreast of what was going on in the rest of the world. "Rather fitting, wouldn't you say? If an English warship tries to stop us so they can take half our crew for their press gang, they'll get a hotter welcome than they bargained for."

Still, even with these cannons added to the ship's armament, the *Lydia Marie* would be outgunned in any confrontation with a warship. Despite his bravado, Ned hoped they would never have to use the weapons.

The cannons were loaded onto wagons provided by the king and hauled down to the docks. With ropes and sheer muscle, they were pulled up planks onto the deck and then rolled into position and lashed into place.

India had not gone with Ned and Captain Canfield to the palace. In fact, she had gone out of her way to avoid Ned since the meeting in the captain's cabin following the death of Thaddeus Kirby. She had grumbled to anyone who would listen about how Ned and Canfield had questioned her concerning the death of the former third mate, as if they thought she might have been involved in it somehow. The resentment she displayed toward them, and toward all the officers, came across as genuine. At least Ned hoped so. India was playing a hazardous game.

So far there had been no sign of trouble

from Yancy or Syme or any of the other sailors Ned suspected. They were either biding their time, waiting for the proper moment to strike, or else the suspicions of Ned, India, and Captain Canfield had been misplaced.

The *Lydia Marie* spent only one night docked at Honolulu before setting sail again. The course was ever more southerly now, and it became something of a race as well. Winter would soon be settling all through the southern climes, and the always stormy passage around Cape Horn would become even more treacherous. Captain Canfield hoped to slip around the cape and start north before the worst of the weather arrived.

So far, Edmund Syme had proven to be a capable officer. He could be counted upon to keep a cool head while on duty on the bridge, and he got along well with the men. Maybe too well, Ned thought one day as he came along the deck and saw Syme talking to a small group of seamen, including Yancy and a heavyset man called Cupp, whom Ned suspected of being one of the potential mutineers.

Abruptly, Syme broke off the conversation when he saw Ned approaching. With a curt nod to the men, he turned toward

Ned. "Good afternoon, Mr. Holt," he said.

As an officer who technically outranked Ned, Syme did not have to call him Mr. Holt. But like everyone else on board, Syme was aware of the relationship between Ned and Jeff Holt and Lemuel March. "Afternoon, Mr. Syme," Ned replied. "A fair wind, isn't it?"

Syme grinned. "A chilly wind, that's for certain."

Indeed, it was a blustery day, with thick clouds overhead. The sea was gray and choppy. Ned estimated that in less than a week they would reach Cape Horn and slide through the Strait of Magellan between the mainland and the rocky, desolate island known as Tierra del Fuego, the land of fire. The islanders who lived there were a hardy breed — they had to be to survive in such rugged country — but at this time of year the fires they burned night and day would be larger than usual, to ward off the chill of approaching winter.

"We're making good time," Ned said. "It won't be long before we're headed north again, into better weather."

"Aye. Can't be too soon for me."

Syme started to turn away, but he was stopped by the cry "Sail ho!" from the crow's nest. Both Ned and Syme stiffened and looked up. The man on lookout duty was pointing toward the southeast.

That was the course on which the *Lydia Marie* was heading. Ned could not see the distant sail; it was probably still below the horizon from where he stood. But he didn't doubt it was there, and he said, "I'll fetch the captain —"

Syme was already giving the order. "Go tell Captain Canfield!" he told Ned, then turned and ran toward the bridge.

Ned went the other way, toward the captain's cabin. He didn't like Syme, didn't particularly trust the man, but under the circumstances he was willing to carry out his orders. If the other ship proved to be trouble, any thoughts of mutiny among the crew would vanish, at least temporarily, and everyone would work together. It was a matter of survival.

Ned reached Canfield's cabin and rapped sharply on the door. "Captain!" he called. "The lookout's spotted a sail!"

Canfield jerked the door open. He was coatless but otherwise dressed. "Where away?" he demanded.

"Southeast."

"Who has the bridge?"

"Mr. Syme, sir."

Canfield nodded. "Tell him to order the helmsman hard to the northeast. Did you see the sail?"

"No, sir," Ned replied.

"Well, perhaps they haven't seen ours."

That was a slim hope, Ned thought, but the possibility could not be ruled out. Sometimes a man on lookout duty might curl up in the crow's nest and go to sleep. On a British warship such behavior led to flogging or worse, but sailors sometimes took that chance.

Ned turned and ran toward the bridge, taking the steps of the ladder two at a time. "Captain says to turn the wheel hard to the nor'east!" he called to Syme.

"You heard the man, helmsman," Syme rapped to the sailor at the huge wheel, who spun it quickly in response to the order. Ned felt the deck shift under his feet as the *Lydia Marie* began to heel over.

A minute later, Captain Canfield climbed onto the bridge, his coat on and his plumed hat in place now. He strode over to join Ned, Syme, and the helmsman.

"Any sign of the sail?" he asked as he lifted his spyglass and extended it.

"I haven't seen it, sir," Ned answered.

"Nor I, Captain," Syme added.

Canfield put the glass to his eye and scanned the gray, unruly sea. After a moment he muttered, "I can't — no, wait, there it is!"

Ned still could not see the other ship's sail. The gray of the sea and the gray of the sky blended together at the horizon into a haze that swallowed everything when viewed with the naked eye.

"Still too far away to make out a flag," Canfield said as he continued to peer through the spyglass.

"Can you tell if they've seen us?" Ned asked.

"No, I . . . Wait a moment." Canfield's jaw tightened. "Damn it all! She's changing course. She's turning toward us."

Ned knew what that meant, and so did Syme. A Dutch or Spanish trader would not have changed course to intercept the *Lydia Marie*.

But a British ship of the line would.

"Well, gentlemen," Canfield said slowly as he lowered the spyglass, "I hope you're ready for a game of cat and mouse." He added grimly, "And I don't believe I have to tell you which one of us is the mouse."

Aaron Garwood walked carefully toward Malachi Fisher's trading post in the settlement of New Hope. It was a glorious morning, a harbinger of the spring that would arrive in a few more weeks. Already the snow was beginning to melt, and the path was slippery and a little muddy. With his pegleg, Aaron had to pick his way slowly across the soft ground.

Fisher stood on the porch of the trading post, pipe clenched between his teeth. He raised a hand in greeting. "Morning," he called. "How are you, Aaron?"

"I'm fine." Aaron clumped up the steps to the porch and took the chair Fisher offered. The trader settled himself in another chair. The two men were good friends who enjoyed sitting together in companionable silence, savoring the morning.

Snow-covered prairie stretched out for miles in front of the trading post, which faced east. Far in the distance, a range of mountains reared up along the river called the Bighorn. Behind the trading post the mountains were closer, looming over the valley in which the settlement of New Hope and the village of Bear Tooth's people lay.

Despite the proximity of the white settlement to the Sioux village, there had been little contact between the two groups over the winter. Aaron wasn't sure what had caused the friction between them; in the past, Bear Tooth and his people had been good friends to the inhabitants of New Hope. In fact, Clay Holt, who had been among those who founded New Hope, was married to Bear Tooth's daughter, Shining Moon.

But nothing was immune to change, Aaron thought with a sigh. He was living proof of that. His right leg was gone from below the knee down, crushed in a rockslide so badly that Father Thomas, the priest who also served as the settlement's doctor, had been forced to amputate it. His left arm was thinner and weaker than the right from being broken and never healing correctly.

The man who had broken that arm was none other than Clay Holt, once a mortal enemy of anyone whose last name was Garwood, now Aaron's best friend. In Aaron's mind the Holt-Garwood feud had long since been laid to rest.

Father Brennan was coming up the path toward the trading post. "Good morning to you, gentlemen," he called.

"Good morning, Father," Aaron said. "Where are you off to? I reckon I can guess."

"I should hope so," Father Thomas replied with a smile as he hefted the fishing pole he was carrying. "I thought I might try to hook a trout. I have an appetite for fried trout for breakfast."

"Need some company?" Aaron asked.

"Certainly. I'd be glad to have you come along."

Aaron glanced at Fisher. "May I borrow your fishing pole, Malachi? That is, unless you want to come along, too."

Fisher took the pipe out of his mouth. "I've got a business to run, unlike some folks." He grinned to take any sting from the words and jerked his head toward the door of the big log building. "It's leaning in the back corner. Help yourself, Aaron."

"Much obliged." Aaron stood up and clumped into the trading post, then came back a moment later carrying a fishing pole. He went down the steps and fell in alongside Father Thomas as the priest headed for the creek near the settlement.

Father Thomas had brought a tomahawk with him, and he used it to chop a couple of holes in the ice. "It's thinner now," he commented to Aaron. "In a few weeks all the ice will begin to break up."

"Yes, spring's on the way, all right."

The two men baited their hooks with

small pieces of rotten meat Father Thomas had brought wrapped in oilcloth. They stood on the bank and settled down to wait for a bite, and Aaron found his gaze following the course of the creek. This was the same stream that ran past the village of Bear Tooth's band, about a mile to the south of New Hope.

"You know," he mused, "I've been thinking about paying a visit to Grass Song again."

Father Thomas frowned. The previous autumn, Aaron had been infatuated with the Sioux maiden called Grass Song, but Father Thomas had hoped that the young man's interest would fade over the winter. "From what I hear, the Sioux aren't very partial to white visitors right now. When Proud Wolf and Professor Hilliard were here last year, they told us that animosity was running high among Bear Tooth's people."

Aaron shrugged. "They've surely had time to get over that. To tell you the truth, I got a mite annoyed at the professor myself. Never did see such a man for talking so much and saying so little."

"Well, if you go down there, you'd better be careful," Father Thomas said.

Aaron chuckled. "Are you worried about

my immortal soul, Father?"

"Of course. That's my job," Father Thomas replied with a smile. He felt a jerk on his line and jerked back to set the hook. A second later, a trout broke the surface of the creek, its scales sparkling brilliantly in the morning light. Skillfully Father Thomas landed the fish, and as he worked his hook loose from its mouth, he added gravely, "But I'm worried about your hair, too."

"My hair?"

The priest was kneeling on the bank of the creek. He looked up at Aaron and said, "About the Sioux lifting it."

CHAPTER FOURTEEN

After quickly packing the wagons and stealing out of the small Virginia village, the Dowd acting troupe traveled southward long into the night, following the road by the light of the moon and stars. Proud Wolf was sick at heart over what had happened. As soon as he'd discovered that Will Brackett was still alive, he thought, he should have faced his tormentor. Better to have done with it, so that his new friends would not have to risk their lives and livelihood for him. Besides, running and hiding was not the way of a Sioux warrior. Never had it been so; never would it be so.

Ulysses Dowd finally called a halt in the wee hours of the morning, after leading the caravan off the road and into a clearing in the middle of a grove of trees. "No fires," he told the others. "If Brackett and his lads come along the road, perhaps they'll just keep going and not spot us back here."

"I will stand guard," Proud Wolf said.

"They will not take us unaware."

"Good idea," Dowd said. "I was just about to suggest the same thing."

Sitting beside Proud Wolf on the seat of their wagon, Audrey said, "You need to rest. You've been driving all night."

"I am no more tired than anyone else. And besides, this trouble is of my making. It is my responsibility to guard you and the others from it."

"I had something to do with it, if you recall. Will wouldn't be chasing us if I had just ignored you when you came to the academy."

There might be a grain of truth in that statement, Proud Wolf thought, but overall, he doubted Audrey's assertion. True, Audrey's flirtatious manner with him at the academy had roused Brackett's jealous wrath, but he had been hostile from the very start — because Proud Wolf was an Indian, because he was *different.*

As the teams were unhitched, the horses hobbled, and preparations made for the troupe to catch at least a couple of hours' sleep, Oliver Johnson mused, "I wonder exactly where we are."

"On some sort of plantation would be my guess," Dowd rumbled. "We've passed one cultivated field after another."

"What do they grow here?" Proud Wolf asked.

Walter Berryhill stumbled out of his wagon in time to hear the question. "Cotton, tobacco, various grains," he answered. He rubbed his forehead and moaned. "At this moment I could most assuredly make good use of the wonderful nectar distilled from certain of those grains."

"A little hair of the dog, eh, Walter?" asked Dowd. "I imagine you're already a mite hung over."

"More than a mite, old friend," Berryhill muttered. "I feel a veritable Greek chorus of demons performing inside my cranium."

"Well, it serves you right," Dowd snapped, dropping his affable pretense. "If you'd not been drunk in that tavern back yonder, we wouldn't have had to skulk away from there like a band of gypsies!"

Berryhill winced and looked properly ashamed.

Vanessa stepped up beside her husband and put a hand on his arm. "That's not fair, Ulysses. If Brackett's men hadn't spotted Proud Wolf in the tavern, they might have attended our performance and seen him and Audrey there. That would have been even worse. At least this way we had a chance to get away."

"And I hope they do not realize I was with Oliver and Walter," Proud Wolf said. "Truly, it is not my wish to cause distress for any of you." He hesitated, then decided to seize the moment. "That is why I think Audrey and I should leave the troupe."

"Leave?" Audrey said. "But where would we go?"

Proud Wolf turned toward her and rested his hands on her shoulders. "We could go to my homeland," he said. "My people would welcome me back among them, and as my woman, they would welcome you, too."

Audrey stared at him in the moonlight. "You . . . you mean go all the way out to the mountains?" Her voice had a faint squeak of disbelief to it. "To the wilderness?"

"It is a beautiful land," Proud Wolf told her. "The prairie is full of game. Great herds of buffalo wander there. And in the mountains there are moose and antelope, and more fish in the streams than a man could ever catch and eat. Everything we need is there."

"But . . . but what about civilization?" Audrey asked. "What about . . . newspapers and . . . and thread and candle wax and butter churns — ?"

"Everything we need is there," Proud Wolf said again.

"Everything *you* need, perhaps! You're —" She stopped short and took a step backward, her hand going to her mouth.

Proud Wolf felt something inside him emptying, like a vessel of water that had been kicked over. He said softly, "I am a savage. That is what you mean to say."

"No!" Audrey cried. "Not a savage. You could never be that. But you *are* an Indian. You're accustomed to a different way of life."

"I have tried to become accustomed to the white man's ways. You could learn to live as my people do."

Even as he made the argument, Proud Wolf wished miserably that he had never brought the subject up. Audrey was exhausted and upset, like everyone else in the troupe. She could not see that his idea was the perfect solution to their problems.

The others had moved away, he noted, going on about the business of setting up a rough camp. They were trying to give him and Audrey at least a semblance of privacy, he supposed, and he was grateful.

Audrey shook her head. "I can't discuss this now, Proud Wolf. I can't. We'll have to talk about it later, after we've had a chance to get some rest."

He nodded. "That is fine. But think about what I have said."

"Oh, I'll think about it. You can be sure of that."

Somehow her response did not make him feel better. She went into the wagon and shut the door behind her, and he sat down on the lowered steps to stand guard, as he had volunteered to do.

A few minutes later, Oliver ambled over and said quietly, "She didn't take to the idea very well, did she?"

"She does not understand," Proud Wolf said with a rueful smile. "I wish only for us to live a life of peace, and I do not think that is possible anywhere except in the mountains and prairies of my home." He looked off into the darkness. "At least, not as long as Will Brackett is still alive."

Oliver gripped his shoulder. "You'd better not do too much thinking along those lines, my friend. You can't just go around killing people. It's not done here in the east. That's why we have laws."

Proud Wolf turned his head to look at Oliver. "Your white man's laws have done nothing to help me," he said bitterly.

"Well, I suppose that's true," Oliver

admitted. "But still . . . I think I'll sit up with you tonight, just so you don't decide to slip off and do a little . . . hunting."

For a moment Proud Wolf was about to tell Oliver to go away. Then he decided that he could wait a little longer before taking action. Perhaps Audrey would come around to his way of thinking. He had to give her that chance.

But if she would not come with him to the frontier, then he would have no choice but to make things safe for them here in the east.

No matter whose blood had to be shed.

Aaron was glad it was his right leg he'd lost, because he could still mount a horse, putting his left foot in the crude stirrup and swinging the pegleg up and over the animal's back.

He didn't have a horse of his own, but he occasionally borrowed one from Malachi Fisher. Today he was riding along the creek, enjoying the warm sunshine. The ice had begun breaking up earlier than he had expected. A few days before, a dry wind had swept down out of the mountains and across the plains, the kind of wind the Indians called a *chinook*. Now much of the snow was gone, and large brown patches showed through the white. The creek was bubbling and leaping, deeper and faster from the snowmelt.

The time had come, Aaron had decided, and nothing Father Thomas or Malachi could say would change his mind. He was going to the Sioux village to pay a visit to Grass Song. Malachi had threatened not to let him borrow the horse, but Aaron had said, "All right. I'll just walk." Malachi had relented then.

A man needed a woman, Aaron told himself, even a cripple like him. And it wasn't as if he was helpless. He could still hunt; he was a good shot with a flintlock rifle. And he could run a trapline, too. With Grass Song to help him, he would manage perfectly well. It would be a good life for the two of them, and when the children started coming, it would get even better.

The conical lodges of the Sioux village came into view. Aaron heard dogs barking and knew they were announcing his arrival. He saw women and children moving around the village, and smoke from cooking fires rose into the clear blue sky.

As he reached the edge of the village, several young men emerged from a lodge and strode toward him. Their faces were expressionless; they didn't look welcoming, but they didn't seem bent on attacking him, either, Aaron decided. He reined the horse to a stop and nodded to the delegation, a friendly smile on his face. "Howdy," he said.

"What do you want?" one of the men asked. Like his face, his voice held not even a hint of emotion.

"I thought I'd pay a neighborly visit," Aaron said. He wasn't quite ready to announce that he'd come a-courting, not until he got a better feel for the response he was likely to get. He inclined his head toward the settlement behind him. New Hope was not visible from here, but the smoke from the chimney in the trading post was. "I'm from New Hope. You all know me. My name is Aaron Garwood."

"We know you," the Sioux spokesman agreed. "You are a friend to Clay Holt." There was a grudging acceptance in his tone now.

"That's right," Aaron said quickly. "And a friend to the people of Bear Tooth's band." He looked around the village. "Where *is* Bear Tooth? I figured he'd come out to say hello."

"Bear Tooth has gone to be with the

spirits of his ancestors."

Aaron stiffened in shock. Bear Tooth was dead? This was the first he'd heard of it. Immediately he felt a surge of sympathy for Shining Moon and Proud Wolf, the children of the old chief. Both of them were back east somewhere, and Aaron realized that neither could be aware that their father had passed away.

"I'm sorry to hear that," he murmured. "Bear Tooth was a good friend to everyone."

"All but his enemies. To them he was a warrior of the Sioux!" The other men nodded proudly.

Suddenly Aaron felt uneasy. Proud Wolf had warned him the previous autumn that sentiment against the whites was growing among the Sioux. Too many trappers had come to the mountains, and the Sioux might be feeling a mite crowded, especially with the settlement of New Hope only a mile or so up the creek. Without the pacifying influence of Bear Tooth to keep the younger men in line, there was no telling what might happen.

"Who is your chief now?" Aaron asked. If Proud Wolf had been here, that duty would probably have fallen to him as Bear Tooth's son, although leadership of the band was not always a hereditary position.

The warrior who had been doing the talking crossed his arms across his chest. "I am called Falling Sky in your tongue," he said. "I lead the Sioux."

"Well, I'm pleased to meet you, Falling Sky," Aaron said. He could at least try a little diplomacy, he decided, and see where it got him. "I hope you'll be as good a friend to the white men as Bear Tooth always was."

"Bear Tooth was old. His vision was clouded. But mine is keen, and I see the truth."

That didn't sound too promising. Still, Aaron hadn't ridden all the way here just to pass the time of day. He wanted to see Grass Song. He was casting around for some way to phrase the request politely when he saw the buffalo-hide entrance flap on one of the lodges pushed back. A woman stepped out of the lodge. She turned so that Aaron could see her face . . .

Grass Song. He knew her right away. Then he saw something else: the large, rounded belly under the buckskin dress.

Grass Song was in the family way, Aaron realized with a shock. She was the woman of one of these Sioux warriors — perhaps Falling Sky himself. Aaron was not going to ask.

He took a deep breath, telling himself that he shouldn't be surprised. He had visited Grass Song a few times, and she had seemed to return his interest. But clearly she had found someone more to her liking among her own people, and although Aaron wanted to be angry with her, he found that he couldn't really blame her.

After all, what woman wouldn't want a strapping Sioux warrior rather than a one-legged white man? A sour taste rose in his throat.

"I reckon I'd better be going," he said. "Just thought I'd ride down and say howdy, now that spring's on the way."

"Who knows what the summer will bring?" Falling Sky asked. The question seemed ominous somehow.

"Yes," Aaron grunted. "Who knows?"

He hauled on the horse's reins and turned it around. Part of him wanted to kick it into a trot, but he kept the animal moving at a walk. He would not run from the Sioux like a dog with its tail between its legs. He might have lost Grass Song — not that he'd ever really had her, he told himself — but he had not lost his dignity.

Still, his back had an almighty itch in the middle of it as he rode away from the Sioux village, as if it was expecting an arrow to strike at any second. The sensation did not ease until Aaron was halfway back to New Hope, and even then he cast a nervous glance or two over his shoulder.

Things change, he thought again. *And rarely for the better,* he added now.

Proud Wolf jolted awake with the sound of hoofbeats in his ears. Sunlight slanted through the trees around the clearing and shone painfully in his eyes. He sprang to his feet, startling Oliver out of the slumber that had claimed him also. Both men must have dozed off before dawn, Proud Wolf realized.

And that was a mistake that might prove fatal.

Men on horseback were crashing through the underbrush nearby. Proud Wolf heard a man's voice shout, "Over here!" The voice was familiar. It belonged to Frank Kirkland, Will Brackett's friend and sycophant. Where Kirkland was, Brackett was sure to be, too.

Proud Wolf whirled to the door of the wagon and jerked it open. "Audrey!" he called in a soft but urgent tone. He could not leave her here for Brackett to find.

She sat up on the bunk, still dressed except for her shoes. Blinking sleepily, she said, "What . . . Proud Wolf, what is it — ?"

He sprang into the wagon and grabbed her wrist, pulling her up from the bunk. The covers tangled around her, and she cried in fright as he ripped them away.

"Brackett comes." As he spoke the name of his enemy, the idea he had had the night before came flooding back into his mind. He should have sought out Brackett and killed him long before this moment, he realized. Now he might never have the chance.

This was what came of trying to behave as a white man would, he told himself. Running from one's enemies was the white man's way. A Sioux warrior would have faced up to trouble and met it head on.

Now even his spirit guide had deserted him, no doubt disgusted by what he had become. The great white mountain lion had appeared to him in the past at times of danger, warning him. Today there had been no warning . . . only a fool sleeping as death crept upon him.

Those thoughts flashed through his head in the blink of an eye. He tugged Audrey to the door of the wagon and almost threw her down the steps. They would have to run again. His degradation was complete.

He leaped to the ground and caught her hand. "Come *now!*" he hissed.

"We'll slow them down," Oliver promised. "Run, you two!"

Hand in hand they raced toward the woods, away from the sound of the approaching horses. But as they reached the trees, several large forms loomed up, blocking their path. A horse whinnied. Their way was blocked by men on horseback. One of them was Will Brackett.

"I thought that would flush you out, redskin," Brackett gloated. He had taken one foot from the stirrup, and he lashed out with it, aiming a kick straight at Proud Wolf's face.

Proud Wolf shoved Audrey behind him, shielding her with his body, and tried to avoid Brackett's kick at the same time. The heel of Brackett's boot slammed into his shoulder and sent him spinning backward. Audrey screamed, "Will! No!"

Proud Wolf regained his balance before he fell and saw Brackett spurring toward him. Brackett intended to ride him down. Proud Wolf flung himself to the side as the horse thundered past. He landed on his hands and knees and was about to scramble upright when one of the other riders leaned over and slammed the butt of a flintlock pistol against the side of his head. Proud Wolf sprawled on the ground, blackness spinning around him for a moment before he fought it off.

"No!" Brackett shouted. "Don't kill him!"

The order was not prompted by compassion, Proud Wolf knew. Brackett wanted to reserve the pleasure of killing him for himself.

Proud Wolf rolled over and came up with his knife in his hand. They might take his life, but he would sell it dearly. He had tried to live as a white man, and that had been his undoing. But he would die as a Sioux warrior. The words of a death chant came to his lips.

A few yards away, sitting on the back of a skittish horse, Will Brackett raised a pistol. He cocked it with his thumb and pointed it at Proud Wolf, then said, "Drop the knife, Indian, or I'll put this ball in your elbow. You know I can do it. If you're hoping your death will be a quick one, you're going to be disappointed."

His chest heaving, Proud Wolf looked past Brackett into the clearing. He saw that one of Brackett's men had dismounted and was holding Audrey from behind, his hands clamped brutally on her upper arms. She was sobbing. Kirkland and the other men had swarmed into the camp, and they were holding pistols and rifles on the members of the troupe, who had come hurrying out of their wagons when the commotion began. Ulysses Dowd's face was dark with rage, but there was nothing he could do as long as the guns were menacing his wife and friends. Oliver, Walter Berryhill, and the Zachary brothers looked just as angry and just as helpless. The women were frightened, and so was Kenneth Thurston.

"You might as well surrender, Indian," Brackett said. "I don't mind hurting these other people if I have to."

Proud Wolf did not doubt that. Brackett was cruel and ruthless enough to do almost anything, as he had proven on more than one occasion.

Proud Wolf's hand opened. The knife fell to the ground at his feet. The only sound to break the tense silence was Audrey's sobbing.

Brackett swung down from the saddle, keeping his pistol trained on Proud Wolf. "It's long past time I caught up with you. I would have before now" — he cast an angry glance at Dowd and the rest of the troupe — "if these fools hadn't lied to me."

"I didn't think you were worth telling the truth to," Dowd said with a sneer.

"Frank," Brackett said.

Kirkland stepped over to Dowd and backhanded him sharply, knocking him away from Vanessa. She cried out and took a step toward Kirkland, but Dowd caught her arm and held her back.

"All this lot wants is an excuse to kill us all," he warned.

"Oh, we have that already," Brackett said casually. "You've been harboring a fugitive. An Indian, at that. We could say that you fought back when we tried to capture him, and we were forced to defend ourselves. But I'm not really interested in anyone dying except this red-skinned bastard."

"Fight me," Proud Wolf said abruptly.

Brackett glared at him. "What?"

"The hate between us is strong. We should fight, just the two of us. Leave these others out of it."

"You'd like that, wouldn't you?" Brackett asked with a chuckle. "Well, that's not the way it's going to be. What kind of fool do you take me for?" Without looking away from Proud Wolf, he ordered, "Frank, build a fire."

"Yes, Will," Kirkland answered without hesitation.

Brackett smiled. "I've heard stories about how you savages like to torture white men by burning them alive. Now we'll find out how *you* like it."

"No!" Audrey screamed again. "Don't, Will, please don't! Oh, God, I'll do anything you want! I'll go back with you to Cambridge, I'll marry you, you can do anything you want with me —"

Brackett finally turned toward her. "That's exactly what's going to happen, my dear. But *after* the savage is dead, not before. I'll not be cheated of justice."

"Justice?" Oliver Johnson said with a brittle laugh. "Is that what you call this?"

"What you intend to do is barbaric, sir," Walter Berryhill put in. "It is nothing less than pure murder, and no one here will rest until you have paid the penalty for it."

Proud Wolf wished they would stop baiting Brackett. The man was insane and fully capable of killing everyone here except Audrey. She would be spared, Proud Wolf was sure of that — but only so that Brackett would make her life a living hell for years to come.

Brackett did not appear to be upset, however. He was still smiling. "I'd hardly call it murder," he said. "I'm simply carrying out a legal order."

"What sort of legal order?" Dowd demanded in disbelief.

Brackett reached into his pocket and pulled out a folded document that was sealed with wax. "This was signed by a magistrate in Boston, giving me the authority to apprehend a fugitive by any means necessary, said fugitive having been charged with assault, attempted murder, robbery, kidnapping, and assorted other crimes. So you see, I've anticipated your protests. As far as this Indian is concerned, *I* am the law!"

"This . . . this is a farce!" Dowd sputtered. "That document can't be legal!"

It probably was not legal, Proud Wolf thought, but that did not matter. He would soon be dead, and Brackett would use his family's wealth and influence to cover up anything that might cause trouble for him. But at least the others might be safe. Brackett might feel that he had no real reason to kill them after all.

Kirkland and one of the other men had gathered some wood and stacked it in the center of the clearing. Now Kirkland used flint and steel to start a small fire. The flames grew quickly.

Brackett lowered the striker on his pistol and tucked the weapon behind his belt. "Hold his arms," he snapped at two of his hired ruffians. They moved in quickly, grabbing Proud Wolf's arms even as he tried to pull away from them. Brackett strode over to the fire and bent to pick up a burning branch. As he turned back toward Proud Wolf, he said to the man holding Audrey, "Don't let her go. I don't want any interference." He took in the actors with a glance and ordered his other men, "If any of them move, shoot them."

Proud Wolf, panting, struggled against the grip of the men holding him, but they were too strong. He could not break free. Brackett approached, carrying the burning branch in front of him. He was not smiling now. His eyes were wide and his face was transfixed, as if he were undergoing a spiritual experience. Proud Wolf looked into his eyes and saw nothing there but pure evil.

"Now," Brackett said softly as he thrust the branch toward Proud Wolf's face, "I think I'll start with your eyes. I want to listen to them pop."

Proud Wolf felt the heat on his face, the

awful heat of the torch, and squeezed his eyes shut. A loud crash shattered the morning air, the sound of a gunshot. His eyes flew open in time to see the brand spinning out of Brackett's hand. Gasping, he looked up in surprise and saw a stranger, a white man, step out of the cover of the trees. The stranger had a pistol in each hand, and powder smoke curled from the muzzle of the gun in his left.

The stranger pointed the other pistol straight at Will Brackett and said in a powerful voice, "Tell your men to drop their guns or the next ball goes in your brain, you devil's spawn."

CHAPTER FIFTEEN

For almost a week now, huge chunks of ice had floated like a frozen armada past the Mandan village in which Melissa and Michael Holt, Terence O'Shay, and Pink Casebolt had waited out what they hoped would be the last big storm of the winter. From the looks of the river, Pink told the others, the spring thaw was beginning.

"Sometimes the Big Muddy freezes over again after the thaw, but it's not likely," Casebolt said as the four of them stood on the bank and watched the ice drift past.

"When will we be able to use the keelboat again?" Melissa asked.

Casebolt rubbed his bearded jaw. "Give it another day or two," he said after a moment. "You don't want one of those pieces of ice ramming into the boat. That might just sink us."

O'Shay asked, "Once we're on our way again, how long will it take us to get to where we're going?"

"Three weeks, maybe a month," Casebolt replied with a shrug. "Depends on whether or not we run into anything else that slows us down."

"Like Indians?" Michael said.

Casebolt grinned. "No, I was thinking more of another storm."

"But we could see some more Indians?" Michael persisted.

"I think you can count on it."

Melissa bit her lower lip. Hardly a day went by that she did not berate herself for including Michael in her plan. But it was too late to turn back, much too late.

Besides, once they reached New Hope and established their trading post, Michael would be safe enough. Both Jeff and Clay had told her that the Indians in that area were friendly to whites. It was the tribes farther north and west that were dangerous. The Blackfoot were the most hostile, she recalled Clay saying.

And when Jeff finally returned home from Alaska — assuming that he was willing to leave — he would discover that she had gone to New Hope to start a fur trading business, and he would know where to find her.

If he wanted to.

The next couple of days went by slowly. Melissa might be a Holt only by marriage, but she shared some of the family's impatience and restlessness, she mused. She was happiest when she was doing something, not just sitting and waiting. She was relieved when Pink declared the river safe for travel.

"We'll have to keep a close eye out, though," he warned them as they prepared to depart. "There might still be ice in the river. If there is, we'll have to get out of its way."

That might be difficult, Melissa thought, considering that the keelboat was not a particularly maneuverable vessel. Still, she deemed it worth the risk. Captain Tompkins always kept a steady hand on the tiller and a keen eye on the river ahead, and Melissa had full confidence in his abilities.

Early on a sunny morning, the crew poled the keelboat out into the current. Casebolt's concern about the ice proved to be groundless. To be sure, there were still places along the edges where the river had not completely thawed, but the main channel, which tended to weave from side to side, was open and clear.

The weather remained surprisingly mild. The temperature still dipped below freezing at night, but the sun was warm during the day.

On one such day, a couple of weeks after the party had left the Mandan village, Melissa was sitting by herself on the roof of the cabin, near the front of the boat. She was perched on a three-legged stool, taking in the countryside as it rolled past. There wasn't much to see: shallow bluffs bordering the river and beyond them a seemingly endlessly rolling prairie carpeted with new grass. Melissa was beginning to wonder if she was ever going to see a tree again.

"Not much to look at, is it?" a voice asked from beside her.

Pink Casebolt had come up to join her. She hadn't heard his approach. That was the mountain man in him, she thought; he moved quietly out of habit, even when there was no need.

"It's not the most scenic area I've ever visited," Melissa agreed. "But it has a certain appeal."

"I reckon. Some folks call this the Great American Desert. It's not really a desert, but I suppose it might look like that to somebody who was raised back east around all those forests."

"There are a lot of trees in Ohio, where I'm from."

Casebolt knelt beside the stool. "I thought you were from Carolina."

"Wilmington is my home now, but before that my parents and I lived near Marietta, Ohio, for many years. That's where I met my husband."

"Jefferson Holt."

"That's right. The Holt family had a farm near there."

Casebolt shook his head. "Hard to think of Clay Holt being a farmer, after all the stories I heard about him. I reckon he didn't take much to it, and that's why he came west."

"That might have been one of the reasons." Melissa knew the full story — that Josie Garwood had accused Clay of being little Matthew's father in order to conceal her incestuous relationship with her own brother, Zach — but she saw no point in dredging up the sordid details. Not for a relative stranger like Pink Casebolt.

"Once a fellow's seen the mountains, he hardly ever wants to go back to where he came from," Casebolt said. "Reckon you might even start to feel that way yourself, now that you can see them."

Melissa frowned in puzzlement, then looked to either side of the river. "What do you mean? I don't see any mountains."

"Not here." Casebolt pointed. "Up yonder."

Melissa looked, squinting as she tried to make out what he was pointing at. "I don't see anything," she said after a moment. "Just a little cloud bank low to the horizon."

Casebolt grinned. "Those aren't clouds, ma'am. That's the mountains."

Melissa sat up straighter. Could it really be? That low blue line along the horizon was their destination?

She turned her head to look behind her. Michael was back near the tiller, talking to Captain Tompkins, who was listening tolerantly to the boy's chatter. Terence O'Shay was there, too, sitting on a crate and puffing contentedly on a pipe. Melissa called to them. "Michael! Terence! Come up here, please."

O'Shay must have sensed the urgency in her voice, because he stood up quickly and said, "Come on, Whip. Your mama wants us."

Michael left the captain's side grudgingly. O'Shay grasped him under the arms and lifted him onto the roof of the cabin, then stepped up himself. As they came forward, Michael asked in a complaining tone, "What is it, Mama? I was talking to

Captain Tompkins."

Melissa put an arm around his shoulders and drew him close to her, then pointed toward the western horizon. "Look there."

"What is it?" Michael asked, still pouting.

O'Shay was standing behind them, looking over their heads. He took his pipe out of his mouth and said in a voice touched with wonder, "I do believe 'tis the mountains, laddie."

"The mountains!" Michael exclaimed. "The Rocky Mountains?"

"That's what most folks have taken to calling them," Casebolt said, "and they're sure enough rocky, all right. The Indians always called them the Shining Mountains, and I reckon that name fits, too. There's always snow up there, and when the sun hits them just right, they shine. They surely do."

Melissa's arm tightened around Michael's shoulders. "We'll be there soon," she told him.

"The mountains," Michael repeated, his voice hushed with awe.

As she looked at her son, Melissa remembered what Pink Casebolt had said a few moments earlier.

Once a fellow's seen the mountains, he

Will Brackett clutched his right hand, from which the torch he had been holding had been shot. Mouth open, he stared at the stranger, then spat a curse.

The stranger smiled. "I know what you're thinking. You're thinking you can tell your men to kill me and that they'll shoot me before I can kill you. But if you do that, you'll be wagering your life against the speed of my trigger finger. So it's up to you."

Along with everyone else in the clearing, Proud Wolf waited breathlessly while Brackett and the stranger locked eyes and waged a war of wills. Proud Wolf halfway expected Brackett to take the chance, but abruptly the young man said, "Do as he says. Put down your guns."

"And have those two louts release that young fellow, too," the stranger added, with a nod toward Proud Wolf.

Brackett turned his head and indicated with a jerk that the two men were to release their captive. As they did, Proud Wolf took a step forward and then moved to the side, being careful not to put himself between Brackett and the stranger. The pistol pointing at Brackett's head was the only thing keeping Proud Wolf and his friends alive.

Around the clearing, Frank Kirkland and Brackett's hired men were bending over and placing their guns on the ground. "Step back away from them," the stranger said sharply. As they obeyed, Ulysses Dowd, Oliver Johnson, and Frederick and Theodore Zachary quickly picked up the weapons. Proud Wolf began to breathe a little easier.

One of Brackett's men still held Audrey, however. He swung around suddenly, using one arm to hold Audrey in front of him as a shield, and jerked a gun from his belt. Proud Wolf saw him shove the barrel of the pistol under Audrey's arm and point it at the stranger. Audrey let out a frightened cry.

Proud Wolf flung himself toward the man, crashing into his side. At the same time, Audrey grabbed the barrel of the pistol and thrust it upward, so that as the weapon fired the ball went harmlessly into the upper branches of the trees. Proud Wolf looped an arm around the man's neck and threw him to the ground, forcing him to release Audrey.

The barrel of the stranger's gun never wavered. When Proud Wolf looked around, it was still lined on Brackett's head. Without looking away from Brackett, the stranger said, "Good work, lad. And you, too, young lady."

Through gritted teeth Brackett asked, "Who the devil are you?"

"My name is Quincy Reed," the stranger said. "This is my land, and I don't take kindly to having innocent people tortured and threatened with death on it."

"Innocent!" Brackett exploded. "This . . . this savage is no innocent! He tried to kill me, and he kidnapped this girl from her father's home in Cambridge!"

"That's a lie!" Audrey said. "I came with Proud Wolf of my own free will. I love him."

Proud Wolf put his arm around her and led her over to the other women. He was touched by what she had just said. She had told him in private that she loved him, but this was the first time she had declared her love in public.

Brackett, ignoring what she had said, railed at the man named Quincy Reed, "I have a legal document —"

"Legal where you come from, perhaps," Reed broke in. "This is the sovereign state of Virginia, and I don't give a damn what some Massachusetts magistrate has to say.

You probably bribed him anyway."

Brackett's face flushed a dark red. Proud Wolf wanted to smile at his discomfiture, but the danger of the moment had not passed. True, Brackett and his men were disarmed, but they were a rough lot, and the only thing holding them at bay was the pistol pointed at Brackett's head.

Dowd, Oliver, and the Zachary brothers moved to remedy the situation by herding Kirkland and the rest of Brackett's hirelings into a single group near one of the wagons. Now they could guard the men more easily. Quincy Reed nodded approvingly and finally lowered his gun.

"Now, as I was saying, this plantation belongs to me. I want you men off it. You're fouling the air."

"You can't force us to leave," Brackett blustered. "I'll come back with the local constable —"

"Go ahead," Quincy Reed broke in. "By that time these good folk will be my guests at my house, and I think if you try to visit uninvited, you'll find a rather hot welcome awaiting you. I wouldn't expect much help from the constable, either. His name is Fergus Buchanan." Reed hesitated, then added, "I fought the redcoats with his father Murdoch a few years back."

Reed was referring to the War of Independence, Proud Wolf realized. He had read about that war at the Stoddard Academy. He remembered thinking how odd it was that a battle of such magnitude had been fought in the eastern half of the continent and the people of his homeland knew nothing about it.

Quincy Reed was about the right age to have participated in that war, Proud Wolf estimated. He appeared to be in his early fifties. His face was tanned and weathered, with laugh lines around the eyes and mouth that bespoke a jovial nature. His thick chestnut hair was streaked with gray, but he was still tall and upright. He wore woodsman's clothes and an old-fashioned tricorn hat tilted to the back of his head. Proud Wolf would not have guessed from his garb that he was a rich man, a plantation owner, but that unpretentiousness only strengthened the instinctive liking Proud Wolf felt for him.

Brackett said stubbornly, "You can't get away with interfering with the law."

Reed laughed in contempt. "You're no more the law than a wild boar is. Take your lackeys and get off my land."

"You'll regret this, you bastard."

"What I'm already starting to regret is

not killing you outright," Reed said softly. He lifted the gun in his hand again. "Perhaps I will yet."

Brackett said quickly to his men, "Mount up. We're leaving."

"But Will," Frank Kirkland protested, "we can't just let the redskin go —"

"Hold your tongue, Frank!" Brackett snapped. "Didn't you hear me? I said mount up!"

Under the watchful eyes and ready guns of Quincy Reed, Ulysses Dowd, and the other men, Brackett and his followers went into the trees and mounted their horses. Brackett cruelly jerked his mount's head around and led the group back to the road. Not until they had thundered off into the distance did Proud Wolf relax.

Ulysses Dowd strode over to him. "Are you all right, lad?" he asked. "That rapscallion didn't burn you?"

"I am not injured," Proud Wolf replied. "Thanks to Mr. Reed."

Quincy Reed lowered the striker on his flintlock pistol and went to join them across the clearing. He held out his hand to Proud Wolf. "Glad I could be of assistance."

Proud Wolf shook his hand. "I am called Proud Wolf. I am a Teton Sioux, of the band led by Bear Tooth."

"I'm honored. A good ways off your usual hunting grounds, aren't you?"

"I came east to be educated as a white man would be." Proud Wolf smiled thinly and added, "I have learned much."

"It looks as if you have indeed," Reed grunted. He released Proud Wolf's hand and turned toward Dowd. "And you'd be the famous Professor Ulysses Xavier Dowd."

Visibly puffing up with pleasure, Dowd nodded. "That I am," he confirmed as he shook hands with Reed. "You've heard of me, then?"

"I saw your troupe perform when you passed through Richmond last year." Reed tipped his hat to Vanessa. "Mrs. Dowd. As lovely as ever. As are the rest of the ladies." He turned back to Dowd and Proud Wolf. "I never thought I'd meet you under circumstances such as these, though."

"It is my fault," Proud Wolf said without hesitation. "I have brought much trouble to my new friends."

"Balderdash," Walter Berryhill said. "You can't be blamed for anything that madman does. We've all seen for ourselves now that he's utterly insane."

Quincy Reed stroked his chin with one

343

hand. "I don't know about that," he mused. "The fellow struck me as just plain bad. You don't have to be crazy to be evil." He looked around at the group. "You'd better get ready to travel, good folk. You're all coming back to my house."

"We appreciate the offer of hospitality," Dowd said, "but we have performances to stage —"

Reed shook his head. "Perhaps, but you'll be safer at my house for a while. I wouldn't put it past that fellow to find some more guns and try to ambush you down the road."

"Brackett would do that," Proud Wolf said firmly. "I am sure of it."

"You're probably correct," Dowd conceded. "All right, then. So you're going to have some visitors, Mr. Reed. Can you find the space to put up all of us for a bit?"

Quincy Reed smiled. "I have plenty of room."

The mountains were indeed spectacular, Melissa discovered as the boat drew steadily closer, day by day. Their route took them to a point where the river forked, and Pink Casebolt directed them to the branch that flowed southwest.

"This is the Yellowstone," Casebolt told

them. "We'll follow it for a ways, then split off into the Bighorn. From what you've told me, that's where we'll find the settlement Clay Holt started."

As the boat was poled down the Yellowstone River, Melissa spent a great deal of time looking out at the rugged, snow-capped peaks in the distance. Michael, too, spent hours sitting cross-legged on the roof of the keelboat cabin, staring at the mountains. He told his mother raptly, "I'm going to climb every one of them."

"Perhaps you will someday," she said, bemused by his fascination. When she looked at him now, his resemblance to his father and his uncle Clay was stronger than ever.

Pink Casebolt seemed to be as entranced by the mountains as Michael was. This was a homecoming of sorts for the man. Melissa knew next to nothing about his background, but it was clear from watching him that he was glad to be back on the frontier. His bearded face was usually wreathed in a grin, and he spent as much time staring off silently into the distance as Michael did.

Melissa asked him about it one day, prefacing her question by saying, "Please, Mr. Casebolt, just tell me if I'm prying. I don't mean to be too personal."

"Go ahead," he told her. "I have no secrets."

"The mountains mean more to you than just a place to trap furs, don't they?"

"Yes, ma'am, I reckon they do," Casebolt answered. "You could say the only happy times I've had in my life were in those mountains. You see, I've been on my own since I was a little feller, not even ten years old. My pappy was a riverman on the Allegheny. Never knew my ma, since she died birthing me. Pap left me with a woman he knew whilst he was on the river, but she wasn't much account. Then he fell in the river and drowned." He shook his head. "Never did figure out why a feller who made his living on the river never learned how to swim. But that was my pa for you."

"How terrible," Melissa said. "And you weren't even ten?"

"No. I'm not sure exactly how old I am even now, because Pap said he'd be damned if he was going to celebrate the day my ma died. So I never knew my birthday."

Melissa felt a pang of sympathy. Pink Casebolt hadn't always been the rough-hewn mountain man he was now. Once he had been an orphaned little boy.

"I'm sorry, Mr. Casebolt," she said. "I'm sure that was a terrible time for you."

"I reckon. Don't recollect much about it. Don't want to."

"I assume you stayed with the woman who had been taking care of you?"

Casebolt shook his head. "No, ma'am. As I said, she wasn't much account, and I wanted to get away from her soon's I could. It wasn't a week after I got word about my pappy dying than I took off for the river myself. Worked my way down to Pittsburgh and got a job on a boat going up and down the Ohio."

"You did this at ten years of age?" Melissa asked in amazement. When she was ten, she had been nothing more than her father's pampered little darling.

"Well, thereabouts. But I was big for my years, and I did my best to give anybody who hired me an honest day's work. That'll take a feller a long way. Took me to New Orleans and back a heap of times."

"I'm sure it was a very difficult existence."

Casebolt chuckled. "I don't look back on those days fondly, that's for sure. I went hungry and slept out in the open many a time. But I stayed alive, and when I grew up some, I decided to head west one time when I was in St. Louis and heard some trappers talking about what it's like out here." He looked at the mountains again and sighed. "I have never regretted the decision, either."

Melissa reached over and patted the rough back of his hand. "I'm glad you came with us, Mr. Casebolt."

He ducked his head and looked faintly embarrassed. "I haven't even done anything to earn my keep yet. You could've come this far without a guide."

"I'm not at all certain of that," Melissa told him firmly. "None of us could have spoken to the Mandans when we were looking for a place to wait out the storm. And you've known every fork in the river, known which one we should take. I'd say you've earned your wages quite handily."

"Well, it's mighty kind of you to say so, ma'am."

Again she patted his hand. "Don't worry, Mr. Casebolt. It eases my mind considerably knowing that you're with us in case of trouble, and I consider peace of mind a very valuable commodity."

Before she could say anything else, Michael called to her from the rear of the boat, and she turned to see him pointing to the east. A herd of antelope, antlered heads raised, stood on the bank as still as statues. Melissa smiled. They looked like something out of a beautiful painting. "I see them, Michael," she called to her son as she stood up and went to join him.

What she didn't see was the way Pink Casebolt watched her go. There was longing in his eyes, longing mixed with despair. Melissa Holt was a married woman, a civilized woman, a lady. She wasn't for the likes of him, Casebolt told himself for the hundredth time since this journey had begun.

Or at least that would have been true back east. Out here on the frontier, things were different.

And just like that, Pink Casebolt allowed himself to hope. It was the worst mistake of his life.

CHAPTER SIXTEEN

Damn, but it felt good to have a horse under him again!

Even after three weeks in the saddle, Clay Holt was exhilarated by the feeling. He knew that Lieutenant Markham did not share the sentiment. For the first week after they left St. Louis, Markham rode gingerly, dismounted stiffly, and walked around their campsites awkwardly, trying manfully not to groan. His muscles had adapted a bit since then, but riding a horse would never be his favorite means of transportation.

Luckily, Shining Moon and Matthew were faring quite well. Shining Moon was as accustomed to riding as Clay was, and Matthew had been around horses since he was a little boy on the Garwood farm in Ohio. The mounts Clay had found for them were of fairly high quality — not particularly fast, but strong and tireless. By switching back and forth among them, Clay was able to keep the little group moving rapidly.

They followed the Missouri River most of the time, although Clay didn't hesitate to take out across country on occasion, eliminating some of the distance it would have cost them to follow the river when it made its great bends. Clay had covered all this ground in the past, and the terrain changed little on the plains. What appeared to an inexperienced eye to be a vast, featureless prairie was actually full of landmarks if a man knew where to look.

And not many knew where to look better than Clay Holt.

He called a halt each day about an hour before sunset, hating to lose that time but unwilling to build a fire after dark. "No need to tell the world we're out here," he explained. Caution was a habit, so each day he built a small, smokeless fire with dried buffalo chips, and Shining Moon heated their supper over the tiny flames before extinguishing them as darkness fell. The nights were still cold and the warmth of a fire would have felt good, but the travelers made do by rolling themselves in heavy blankets.

They bypassed the large Mandan village at which the Corps of Discovery had stopped six years earlier during their return from the Pacific. Clay remembered that visit vividly, and he figured that some of the Mandan might still remember him and welcome them, but the village was too far out of the way. And time was of the essence now.

La Carde was out there somewhere, ahead of them.

So was the second group of pilgrims, the ones in the keelboat, and Clay wondered about them more than once. The blizzard must have slowed them down, too, but they were probably still ahead of Clay and his companions. Clay hadn't seen them anywhere on the river.

One day, when they had stopped for a midday meal of hardtack and jerky, Shining Moon asked Clay, "We will go to the village of my people?"

Clay had given that matter considerable thought during the weeks they had been on the trail. "If La Carde came through the area, someone in your village or in New Hope likely will have heard about it," he said.

"It will be good to see my father. Perhaps my brother will be there as well."

"Didn't you tell me Proud Wolf went back east to go to school?"

Shining Moon nodded. "He wanted to

have a white man's education."

"Then he's probably sitting somewhere in a stuffy room, his nose buried in a book." Clay shook his head. "Poor fellow."

Markham came over and joined them. "He doesn't sound so unlucky to me. I've never met the lad, of course, but I wouldn't mind being back in the hallowed halls of ivy right now."

Clay stared blankly at him. "What in blazes are you talking about?"

"The university," Markham said. "Did I ever tell you I went to Harvard?"

"Not that I recollect."

"Well, I did. Family tradition. My cousins Thomas and Joseph went there, too, though a bit ahead of me. Wonderful days."

"I'll take your word for it." Clay looked over at Matthew, who sat not far away gnawing on a piece of jerky. "Maybe Matthew can go to a university."

Matthew stopped chewing and said, "The devil I will."

Clay frowned, and Matthew recovered quickly to go on, "I mean, I don't want to go to any kind of school. I want to stay out here on the frontier."

"I thought you wanted to sail a boat."

"Well . . . maybe I'll sail one across the

Pacific Ocean. All I know is I don't want to go back east."

Clay shook his head, stood up, and stretched. "Let's ride. No reason we can't chew jerky in the saddle."

"After all, it's made out of the same leather," Markham said with a grin.

The creek that ran through the valley in which New Hope and the Sioux village nestled was a tributary of the Bighorn River. The juncture of the two was some three miles north of the white settlement. Aaron Garwood had set a few beaver traps along the creek just south of where it ran into the river. It was not the best location for running a trapline; there were more beavers higher up in the mountains. But it was close to the settlement, and Malachi Fisher always gave Aaron a fair price for the pelts he brought in. Aaron didn't need much to live on: a few staples, a little pipe tobacco, a linsey-woolsey shirt or home-spun trousers.

These days he didn't feel that he had very much to live *for.*

Ever since his ill-fated visit to Bear Tooth's village a month earlier, he had been haunted by memories of Grass Song as she had looked when he first saw her —

slim, lovely, and shy — and the more recent images of her swollen with the child of her Sioux husband, whoever he might be. Aaron didn't know which of the warriors had claimed Grass Song as his bride, nor did he want to know. It didn't really matter. What was important was that she was denied to him forever.

Gripped by a black mood, he had gone about his daily routine in a daze. He fished, checked his traps, even talked to Malachi and Father Thomas, but at the end of the day, none of it meant anything.

Today, as he stumped along the bank of the creek to check his traps, he wondered if the time had come for him to move on. If this valley held only bad memories for him, it might be best to leave.

But where would he go? He could push on west, he supposed. Clay Holt had stood on the shores of the Pacific Ocean. If a Holt could do that, so could a Garwood.

Abruptly, Aaron stopped short and lifted his head. The oddest noise had just come to his ears. It almost sounded like . . . someone singing.

There it was again, drifting to him on the light breeze. And it *was* singing, damned if it wasn't! He walked faster, toward the sound.

He broke into an awkward run when he reached a small knoll. From the top of it he would have a good view of the valley where the creek and the Bighorn joined. As he gained the crest, he stopped and peered down the long, gentle, grass-covered slope on the other side.

A keelboat was being poled into the mouth of the creek, and the singing came from the men wielding the long, heavy poles. Aaron's eyes widened in amazement. This wasn't the first keelboat to come up the rivers and along the creek to New Hope, which was obviously where this one was bound. But it was the first one this year, and like all citizens of the frontier Aaron felt a keen excitement at the prospect of newcomers bearing goods and news from back east.

He put a hand to his mouth, tipped back his head, and let out the long, ululating cry of a loon. That caught the attention of the keelboat's crew, and they stopped singing — stopped poling, too, as they looked up the hill toward the lone figure standing atop it. Aaron raised his flintlock rifle and waved it back and forth over his head for a moment, then started down the slope toward the boat.

As he came closer, his astonishment grew. The boatmen looked like typical rivermen, including the lanky, red-bearded man at the tiller. But standing on top of the cabin were three figures the likes of whom Aaron had not seen in a long time. One was a small, towheaded boy, another a tall, broad-shouldered man with an unruly thatch of black hair. The third figure was the one who caught Aaron's eye and held it.

It was a woman. A slender, dark-haired woman who raised a hand and waved gracefully. There was something familiar about her . . .

"Sweet mother," Aaron breathed, and the words came out like a prayer. He hadn't seen Melissa Holt in years, but he would never forget her. He had been awed by her beauty ever since . . . ever since forever, he thought.

And now, wonder of wonders, here she was, standing on the roof of a keelboat in the middle of the wilderness.

Aaron started running again, the peg leg barely slowing him down now.

"Aaron!" Melissa called when he came closer. "Aaron Garwood, is that you?"

"Melissa!" he shouted back. Maybe Jeff was on the boat, too. Aaron looked closely at all the boatmen, but he saw no sign of Jeff.

The boat reached the creek bank. The big black-haired man hopped off first, then turned back to lift Melissa to the bank. As soon as her feet were on the ground, she ran to meet Aaron and threw her arms around him. He swallowed hard; it was almost painful having a beautiful woman in his arms. Melissa stepped back and rested her hands on his shoulders. Tall as she was, her eyes were almost on a level with his.

"Aaron, it's been years," she said.

"Since we all lived in Marietta," he agreed, hoping he didn't sound too awkward.

"That seems so long ago. It's so good to see you."

"Reckon I've changed a mite. But you haven't," Aaron said, searching for the right words. "You're still as pretty as ever, Melissa. Reckon I should call you Mrs. Holt, though."

For a second he thought he saw a shadow cross her face, but then it was gone. Maybe it hadn't been there at all, he told himself. She smiled and said, "We're old friends. You can certainly call me Melissa."

"All right," he said, fighting the impulse to duck his head and scuff the dirt with his foot.

They had not really been friends in those days, of course. The Garwoods had had little to do with the Merrivale family. Charles Merrivale had considered almost everyone in Marietta to be beneath him and his family, and the Garwoods were the lowest among the lowly. Aaron was honest enough to admit that. But he and Melissa had been acquainted with each other, and now they had Jeff in common, too, since Aaron still considered Jeff his best friend even though they hadn't seen each other in a long time. The adventures Aaron had shared on the frontier with Clay and Jeff had created a bond that would last all their lives.

"Where's Jeff?" Aaron asked, unable to restrain the question any longer.

This time there was definitely something wrong. The smile disappeared from Melissa's face, and he saw her body stiffen. Her hands tightened a little on his shoulders.

"Jeff isn't with me," she said. "He has business elsewhere. But there's someone here you haven't met before." She took her hands from his shoulders and turned toward the boat. "Michael! Come here."

The big, black-haired man had lifted the boy down from the keelboat. Now the boy ran eagerly to Melissa, followed at a slower pace by the man.

Aaron had no doubt the boy was Jeff and Melissa's son. The lad looked like both of them. Aaron expected him to turn shy when he reached his mother, the way most children would, and hide behind her skirts. Not this one. He regarded Aaron with an open, curious, straightforward gaze.

"Aaron, this is my son, Michael," Melissa said. "Michael, this is Mr. Garwood."

Aaron held out his hand to the boy and said, "Mighty pleased to meet you, Michael."

The boy shook Aaron's hand with a firm grip. "Call me Whip," he said. "What happened to your leg? You've got a stick there."

"Michael . . . ," Melissa started to scold, but Aaron shook his head to let her know it was all right. He was sure she had noticed the peg leg, too, but had been too polite to mention it.

"You can call me Aaron, Whip. A big rock fell on my leg and hurt it badly, so a fellow I know had to cut it off."

Michael's eyes widened. "You had your leg *cut off?*"

"That's right." Aaron leaned over and slapped the peg where it fitted onto his stump. "But I get around just fine with this peg leg."

"Bet it's good for making holes in the ground."

Aaron laughed, the first genuine laugh he'd experienced in a month. "Yes, it sure is."

Melissa still looked uncomfortable, so Aaron spared her any further embarrassment by distracting the boy. "Look over yonder and you'll see a beaver trap," he said, pointing toward some brush at the edge of the creek.

"Can I go look?" Michael asked, tugging at Melissa's skirt.

She hesitated, then nodded and said, "All right."

"But mind you don't get too close to it," Aaron warned him.

"I won't!" Michael turned and ran toward the creek.

The wide-shouldered, black-haired man was standing by silently. Aaron held out a hand to him. "Aaron Garwood," he said.

"Oh, I'm sorry," Melissa said quickly. "Aaron, this is my friend Terence O'Shay."

O'Shay's hamlike hand engulfed Aaron's. "Sure and it's pleased I am to meet you, Aaron," he said.

"I'm pleased to meet you, too," Aaron said.

"We're on our way to New Hope," Melissa said. "It's not far from here, is it?"

Aaron jerked a thumb over his shoulder to indicate the creek. "Just a few more miles downstream. You'll be there before you know it." He had been about to ask Melissa what she was doing here on the frontier, but she had answered part of the question. Another part remained, though — why were she and this big Irishman and the boy bound for New Hope?

"It's good to see you," he said, "but what brings you out here?"

"We've come to open a trading post," Melissa said with a big smile. "Terence and I are going into the fur trading business."

Jeff paced nervously back and forth outside the Tlingit bighouse. Today Vassily was meeting inside with the other *hitsaati,* the elders of the village, presenting Jeff's idea of establishing direct trade between the Tlingit and American ships.

Jeff was not sure Vassily himself was convinced the proposal had any merit, but he had agreed to bring it before the others and see what they thought. Many of the Tlingit leaders resented the Russians, and Jeff was counting on their hostility to sway them over to his side.

But there were others, such as Yuri, who believed the wisest course was to cooperate with the Russians. Jeff had seen Yuri enter the building a short time earlier. The glance Yuri had given him was as hostile as always. Yuri was not likely to forget or forgive the fact that Jeff had taken the woman he wanted.

Not that Jeff had had much choice in the matter; Vassily had forced him into the union. Still, Jeff could not bring himself to resent what Vassily had done. He had grown very fond of Nadia over the past months.

He was not in love with her, though, and as that thought went through his head while he paced in front of the meeting hall, a familiar surge of guilt racked him. While it was true that Melissa was far away and true that the two of them had parted on bad terms, he was still married to her. He had been raised to believe that a husband and wife should be faithful to each other.

He wondered suddenly if Melissa had

felt any such guilt when she found herself in the arms of Philip Rattigan that night in Wilmington.

Jeff shook his head fiercely. He was not going to descend into *that* morass again. He had other things with which to concern himself at the moment. And the door of the meeting hall was opening, which could mean that Vassily and the other men had reached a decision.

Jeff turned toward the door and watched the Tlingit elders filing out. His spirits sank as he noted their impassive faces. However, he reminded himself, Tlingit men often kept their expressions carefully neutral, at least around him.

That was not true of Yuri. Jeff had no difficulty reading *his* expression as he left the group and stalked down the path. Yuri was unhappy, and that bolstered Jeff's hopes. He stepped up to Vassily and said, "Well?"

Vassily nodded. "We will meet your boat when it returns," he said. "It must not sail to Sitka. We will have furs to trade with your people."

Jeff tried to contain his excitement, but he could not suppress the big grin spreading across his face. "You won't regret this, Vassily," he promised. "Your people will be much happier trading with us than being slaves for the Russians."

Vassily looked at him somberly. "Great care must be taken," he said. "The Russians must not know of this. If they find out, they will attack us."

A sudden worry occurred to Jeff. "What about Yuri?" he asked. "We both know he hates me. Do you think he might betray our plans to the Russians?"

Vassily shook his head. "Everyone agreed to keep this a secret, even Yuri. He will not betray his own people, no matter how he feels about you, Jeff Holt."

"I hope you're right. If Count Orlov were to find out what we're doing, he'd send soldiers out here."

"I know. That is why he must never find out."

Jeff's exhilaration overwhelmed him again. He threw his arms around Vassily and pounded him on the back. "You'll see," he promised. "This is going to work out fine for all of us."

Startled by Jeff's outburst, Vassily awkwardly patted his arms. But worry still lurked in his eyes.

Count Gregori Orlov sat at his desk in the sturdy log cabin that served as his headquarters in Sitka. He was trying to compose a report for his superiors in Moscow. He would send the report back with the first ship to arrive in Sitka from Vladivostok, probably sometime later in the month. The ice would have broken up enough by then for a ship to get through.

Orlov's fingers were almost numb with cold, and he handled the quill awkwardly. After yet another word deteriorated into an illegible scrawl, he cursed and gave up, tossing the pen aside. For a moment he considered knocking over the inkwell to vent his anger, but that would accomplish nothing other than to give his aide, Piotr, another mess to clean. And Piotr was sullen enough these days.

The count leaned back in his chair. He was a thick-bodied, hawk-faced man with a narrow mustache above thin lips. Even though a fire was crackling in the fireplace across the room, he was bundled in a heavy coat. He could never get warm these days. Spring would soon arrive in Russian Alaska, but that would not be enough to warm him either, he knew.

He missed Irina, his wife. Her loss was the cause of the chill that always gripped him now. He probably shouldn't have had his men cut off her head.

But, then, she never should have cuck-olded him with the American, Holt, either. Orlov had hoped to salve his wounded pride and restore some balance by luring Holt's wife into his bed, but that effort had been unsuccessful. Of course, he could have ordered his soldiers to take the Americans prisoner and forced himself on Mrs. Holt, but he would never have done such a thing. Count Gregori Orlov was capable of many things, but he was *not* a rapist.

Piotr entered the room from the outer office. "The ice on the bay is breaking up," he reported.

Orlov nodded. "I have heard it cracking all day."

The aide was a tall, slender man with sleek dark hair. He said, "It appears we have survived another Alaskan winter."

"Some of us," Orlov said.

Piotr's face darkened momentarily before he nodded curtly and left the room. He knew very well what the count meant.

And Orlov knew, or at least suspected, that Piotr had been carrying on an affair with Irina. Sometimes he wondered exactly how many men had been blessed with her favors, but it was not a question on which he liked to dwell. Only when he'd had too much vodka and the blackness descended . . .

With a sigh, Orlov blew on his fingers to warm them and then groped once more for the pen. Though he missed his late wife, he had no regrets about what had happened to Jefferson Holt. The meddling American had gotten precisely what he deserved. While Orlov had not given specific orders concerning how the Tlingit were to kill Jeff Holt, he hoped they had tortured him before allowing him to die slowly. The idea that they might have decapitated Holt and carried his head in the same sack as Irina's appealed to the count's sense of symmetry. Lingering on that image blunted his longing for Irina and brought a wry smile to his lips.

He sighed and went back to work on the report. Piotr appeared in the doorway again. "There is someone here to see you, Count," he said.

Orlov glanced up, irritated. Was he never going to finish this damned report? "Who is it?" he snapped.

"One of the Indians."

Orlov sat back, laid the pen down, and frowned. "One of the servants, you mean?" A number of Tlingit men and women remained in Sitka during the winter to work for the Russian officers; one woman kept house and cooked for Orlov, in fact, and also served as a vessel in which he slaked his lust when memories of Irina's flesh tormented him. Most of them returned to their villages for the winter, however, returning to the Russian settlement in the spring.

Piotr shook his head. "This man comes from one of the villages. He says that he must speak to you personally."

That puzzled Orlov, and angered him as well. These savages had no right to make demands of any kind on him. "Send the man in," he barked, "but he had best not be wasting my time."

"Yes, Count." Piotr disappeared into the outer office and returned a moment later, ushering in front of him a Tlingit man. The Indian's fur-lined hood was pushed back, revealing a dark, stolid face and black hair worn in two short braids. Orlov thought the man looked vaguely familiar but could not place him. Probably someone who had worked in the settlement before; it was difficult to tell these Indians apart.

The count came to his feet and strode across the room to stand in front of the fireplace. "What do you want?" he demanded in Russian, assuming that the

Tlingit spoke the language.

"I am called Yuri."

With an effort, Orlov controlled his impatience. "I did not ask your name," he said. "I asked what you want. Why did you come here to see me?"

"I am from the same village as Vassily." The Tlingit spoke slowly and precisely, as if he was not altogether fluent in Russian and had memorized what he wanted to say.

"Yes, yes —" Orlov suddenly remembered who Vassily was. He remembered as well the very important job he had entrusted to Vassily late the previous autumn. "Go on."

"I bring you news . . . of the one called Holt."

Orlov heard a sharp intake of breath from Piotr, who was standing just inside the door. The two Russians exchanged a glance. It was clear that Piotr did not know any more about this than the count himself did.

But suddenly Orlov wanted very much to know what this Tlingit had come to tell him. He smiled. "Sit down, my friend. Tell me all about Jefferson Holt."

CHAPTER SEVENTEEN

As Captain Canfield had predicted, the sighting of the other ship was the beginning of a deadly game on the high seas. The vessel dogged their trail, changing course every time the American ship did, and finally came close enough that Canfield could discern through the spyglass the Union Jack flying over the ship. The number of masts and the sheer size of the vessel made it clear that they were being pursued by a ship of the British navy, a warship veritably bristling with guns.

Under Canfield's command, the *Lydia Marie* sailed northeast, a course that would eventually take it to the coast of Chile. On the outbound voyage the ship had stopped at the Chilean city of Valparaiso, but Canfield had not intended to stop there on the return trip. It might be unavoidable, however, as he explained to Ned; as a neutral port, Valparaiso would provide a safe haven for the *Lydia Marie*. But the delay would mean that the ship would not make it around Cape Horn in time to avoid the winter storms. The crew might have to wait months for better weather.

After two days of dodging the British ship, Canfield called Ned into his cabin and brought out a bottle of brandy. "Have a drink with me," he invited.

Ned was surprised by this request from the normally rather dour captain, but he took the glass Canfield handed him. The captain filled his own glass and raised it in a toast. "To fair winds and better days."

"Fair winds and better days," Ned repeated, then clinked his glass against Canfield's.

The fiery liquor slid smoothly down Ned's throat. With a sigh, Canfield sank onto his bunk and motioned for Ned to sit as well. After another sip of brandy he said, "We must talk, Mr. Holt."

"Might as well call me Ned, Captain."

Canfield shook his head. "Not today. Today you are no longer a common sailor under my command. You are the representative of the men who own this ship and the cargo it carries."

"Lemuel March and Jeff Holt."

"Yes. It is their ship and their cargo that are at risk as long as we are being pursued by those damned Englishmen. What would you have me do?"

Ned blinked as he felt the awesome weight of responsibility settle on his shoulders. He wiped the back of his hand across his mouth and glanced down at the empty glass in his other hand. He wanted another drink . . . but the solution to this problem would not be found in a bottle of brandy, and he knew it.

Even more than the brandy, he wanted India. He had depended on her counsel and her experience at sea for a long time. If anyone on board the *Lydia Marie* knew what the best course of action was, it would be India St. Clair.

And yet, to call her in now would be to jeopardize all the work she had done insinuating herself with the crew. The looming presence of the British warship had only reduced — not eliminated — the possibility of a mutiny.

No, Ned told himself, like it or not, this was his problem to solve.

At moments like this, he almost wished he had never given up his life as a wastrel. In those easygoing days, his biggest worry had been whether his current mistress's husband would come home earlier than expected.

"What are our options?" he asked grimly.

"Only two, really," Canfield replied. "We can make a run for Valparaiso and seek sanctuary there. Or we can try to slip past them and make for the Strait of Magellan."

"If we reach Valparaiso?"

Canfield shrugged. "We'll be safe enough there. The Chileans can't afford to offend either the British or the Americans, so they'll stay out of it. The British won't force the issue because they can't risk pushing the Chileans out of their neutral stance."

"But we'd have to stay there," Ned said.

"For several months, probably," Canfield confirmed. "We've been cutting it close as it is. Any more delay and we'll have no chance of making it around Cape Horn before the winter storms begin and the southern seas become impassable."

"And if we head south and manage to slip past the British?"

"Then it's a race against the weather, still."

"What if they succeed in stopping us?"

"They will impress at least a quarter of our crew," Canfield said flatly. "Perhaps as many as half."

"Half our crew aren't British deserters!"

Ned exclaimed.

Canfield shook his head. "That doesn't matter. They'll claim everyone who was born in England, and if that's not enough to suit them, they'll impress Americans, too, and insist that they're English."

"What about the cargo?"

"It depends on the mood of their captain. It's entirely possible that they'll seize the cargo and claim that it's reparations for past grievances."

Ned thumped the empty glass down on the small table by his chair. "That's nothing but piracy!"

"Aye. But with only six cannons, we won't be able to stop them from doing whatever they want."

"We can fight, no matter how many cannons we have." Ned's hands clenched into fists.

"Certainly we can fight . . . but it's highly doubtful that we can win."

"Doubtful but not impossible," Ned said.

Canfield tossed back the last of his brandy. "No, not impossible. A lucky shot that brings down their mainmast, something like that — anything is possible."

Stroking a thumbnail along his jaw, Ned

considered everything that had been said. He grimaced. "I don't want to go to Valparaiso. If we're to have any claim on the trade routes we've established, we have to get back to Wilmington."

"True enough."

"What are the chances we can get past the British ship?"

"The *Lydia Marie* is smaller and perhaps a bit faster. In a straight race, I think this old girl could outrun the Britisher, even with its extra sails." A canny look came over the captain's face. "And as we've switched our course back and forth, I've tried to work us into position to make a run due south. The British ship is south-west of us now. There's room to slip between it and the coast."

"They'll move to cut us off," Ned warned.

"Aye, but if the night is dark enough, perhaps they won't see us until it's too late." Canfield smiled tautly. "And there's no moon tonight. The heavens themselves favor us, Mr. Holt."

Ned did not have to hear any more. He nodded and said, "That's it, then. We'll turn and make for the Strait of Magellan." He paused, then added, "But if they pursue us through the strait?"

"They'll never catch us," Canfield said confidently.

Quincy Reed had been right about having plenty of room for everyone in the acting troupe. The plantation house, at the end of a long, tree-lined lane, was enormous, rising two stories and sprawling over several wings. A deep porch ran along the front.

"Do you live here alone, sir?" Ulysses Dowd asked after Reed had ushered them all into a large parlor and insisted on having breakfast prepared for them.

"Except for the servants, yes," Reed replied. He nodded toward a painting that hung over the fireplace. It was a portrait of a stunningly beautiful blond woman. "My late wife, Jenny," Reed said. "A fever took her several years ago."

"We're so sorry," Vanessa murmured.

"The small portraits on either side are of our children, Thomas and Elizabeth," Reed went on. "Thomas is a lawyer in Richmond, with a wife and family of his own, and Elizabeth is married to a newspaper editor there. They have three children." He turned and pointed to a group portrait on the opposite wall. "My brother Daniel and his family. They're in Boston now. So that leaves me to keep this place going."

Elaine Yardley stepped a bit closer to him and said, "You must be very . . . lonely."

"Not at all," Quincy Reed said without hesitation, and if he saw the flicker of disappointment in Elaine's eyes, he made no sign. "Keeping a large plantation running smoothly and efficiently is no easy task. I'm quite busy most of the time." He smiled. "But I still enjoy a tramp through the woods every morning. It's lucky I was out there today, else I wouldn't have stumbled across your camp."

"We didn't mean to trespass —" Dowd began.

Reed stopped him with the casual wave of a hand. "Don't worry about that, Professor Dowd. Visitors are always welcome." His voice hardened as he added, "Unless they're like that fellow Brackett." He turned to Proud Wolf. "You're going to have to tell me why he hates you so."

"It is a long story," Proud Wolf said.

"I'm sure it is, but I'd like to hear it anyway. What say after we've eaten, you and Professor Dowd and I go in my study and discuss all this?"

Proud Wolf looked at Dowd, who

nodded emphatically. They all owed a great debt of gratitude to Quincy Reed, and the least the man deserved was an explanation. "All right," Proud Wolf said.

A black maid came into the parlor and announced in a soft voice, "Breakfast is ready for you and these folks, Master Reed."

"Thank you, Delia." Reed held out a hand and said to the others, "Please, if you'll all follow Delia . . . ?"

As they left the parlor, Oliver said quietly to Reed, "I imagine it takes a lot of slaves to run a plantation like this."

Reed shook his head. "I don't have any slaves. My people are all free and have been ever since my father Geoffrey was in charge."

The dining room was high-ceilinged and spacious. The long table in the center of the room was covered with a white linen cloth and platters heaped high with food. As soon as Quincy Reed had said grace, the members of the troupe dug in with a gusto born of long weeks on the road and meals cooked over a campfire. Proud Wolf sat next to Audrey and tried to hide a smile as he watched her tear into the ham, johnnycakes, and fried chicken. He ate ravenously himself.

When the meal was finished, Reed leaned back in his chair and said, "Delia will show you to rooms where you can rest for a time. Feel free to look around. You have the run of the house. I'd stay inside, though, if I were you, in case Brackett is lurking somewhere about." He looked at Proud Wolf and Dowd. "Gentlemen, if you'd join me . . ."

Proud Wolf squeezed Audrey's hand, stood up, and said to Reed, "I would like Oliver to join us."

Reed glanced at Oliver, who seemed taken aback by Proud Wolf's request. "Certainly," Reed said. "Mr. Johnson, if you'd come with us to the study . . ."

Oliver shrugged, then walked beside Proud Wolf as they followed Reed and Dowd along a richly paneled corridor into a room filled with books. Proud Wolf had never seen so many volumes outside of the library at the Stoddard Academy. There was also a polished hardwood cabinet on one wall in which were displayed several fowling pieces and an assortment of long-barreled flintlock rifles. The cabinet also held a brace of North & Cheney flintlock pistols identical to the ones favored by Clay and Jeff Holt, Proud Wolf noticed. They were fine weapons.

Reed brought out a small box of tobacco, and he and Dowd and Oliver packed their pipes and lit them. Reed went behind a large desk and sat down while his guests took the three comfortable chairs arranged in front of the desk. After puffing on his pipe for a moment, he said to Dowd, "In my younger days I had a good friend named Ulysses. Ulysses Gilworth. The best blacksmith I ever knew."

" 'Tis a noble name," Dowd said.

"Indeed." Reed turned his attention to Proud Wolf. "Now, tell me your story, my friend."

Proud Wolf hesitated, and Oliver urged him, "Go on. I think we can trust Mr. Reed."

"Yes." Proud Wolf looked at Reed and went on, "You saved my life, perhaps all of our lives. But you have made an enemy of Will Brackett."

Reed waved a dismissive hand. "I've seen his kind before. Hates you because you're an Indian, doesn't he?"

Proud Wolf nodded. He took a deep breath and launched into the story, telling it to Reed much as he had told it to the troupe a few weeks earlier, after their first encounter with Brackett. Reed listened attentively, smoking his pipe. Proud Wolf spoke of the beating he had received in Boston from Frank Kirkland and Brackett's other cronies, and of Brackett's later attack on Audrey.

When Proud Wolf was finished, Reed shook his head in disgust. "I should have put a pistol ball in the bastard's head, all right."

"That would have been murder," Dowd said. "You don't want to bring the law down on your head, Mr. Reed."

"Quincy," Reed said. "Call me Quincy. And you're right, Ulysses. If we want the law involved in this, they have to be on the right side. Proud Wolf's side."

"The law cannot help me," Proud Wolf said.

"Are you sure about that?"

Proud Wolf could not keep the bitterness out of his voice as he answered, "The law would not believe me."

"Well, *I* believe you," Reed declared. "I saw with my own eyes what sort of scoundrel Brackett is, and I know someone else who would believe your story if he heard it."

"Who?" Proud Wolf asked.

"My brother Daniel," Quincy Reed said, "who just happens to be a lawyer in Boston."

★ ★ ★

The British ship had cut the gap slightly between it and the *Lydia Marie*. Captain Canfield had sacrificed some distance for the chance to elude the warship completely. Now, in the late afternoon, Canfield and Ned stood on the bridge, and Ned lifted the captain's spyglass to his eye. In the western sky, the clouds that had hung over the sea for the past few days had begun to break. Ned was not particularly happy about that, but as Canfield had noted earlier, there would be no moon tonight. Still, Ned would have deprived the British of starlight if he could.

He peered through the glass and after a moment located the British vessel. He counted the sails, stopping when he reached five. Definitely a warship. He tried to count the gunports on the side of the ship, but it was still too far away. He lowered the glass with a sigh.

"They're bound to have seen by now that we're running south," Ned said to the captain.

"Aye," Canfield agreed. "But can they do anything about it? That's the question on which our fate depends, lad."

Ned glanced toward the east. "How far off the coast are we?"

"Far enough so that they can't pin us against the rocks, even if we have to angle in that direction." The captain turned and called down to the deck, "St. Clair!"

India lifted her head. "Aye, sir?"

"Check on the guns and make sure all the crews are ready to handle them."

"Aye, sir!"

Ned said quietly to Canfield, "The cannons would normally be Syme's job."

"I know that, but St. Clair's had more experience with them."

Ned frowned and looked back at India. He was unaware she knew anything about cannons. She had always been rather vague about her background: orphaned at an early age in London's slums; surviving any way she could until she was old enough to disguise herself as a male and sign on a ship as a cabin boy; sailing the seven seas in the years since. Ned knew she had learned to take care of herself; he had seen the bloody evidence with his own eyes. Obviously she had learned how to handle a cannon, too, somewhere along the way.

The wind shifted slightly as the sun went down, forcing the *Lydia Marie* to tack to port, then back to starboard. The maneuver brought the ship closer to the coast of Chile, but the land was still not in sight over the eastern horizon as the last of the light faded. Ned could no longer see the British ship. But the British couldn't see them either. Now the Americans would have to trust to luck, a fast ship, and a good captain.

Word was passed among the crew to remain as quiet as possible — no unnecessary talking, no moving around. No lights were to be struck. It was unavoidable that the ship itself would make some noise as it sailed south: the rustle of canvas, the creaking of lines, the groan of wood. But those were the only telltale sounds that would be coming from the *Lydia Marie* this night.

Full night had fallen. Stars peeked through the gaps in the clouds, tiny pinpoints of light that teased with their faint illumination. Ned stood on the bridge, his hands clenched on the railing, and peered out into the darkness. He didn't want to see the other ship, because that would mean the *Lydia Marie* was visible to the British, too, but sailing blindly through the night was hard on the nerves.

He heard a whisper of shoe leather on the planks of the deck and turned to see a small figure approaching Captain Canfield. India hissed, "All cannons loaded and ready to fire, Captain."

"Good job, St. Clair," Canfield breathed. "Pray we won't need them."

Ned was praying the same thing. He wished he could go to India, take her hand, draw her into his arms, and kiss her, perhaps for the last time.

He took a deep breath and told himself there was no need to be pessimistic. He and India would have plenty of time together in the future once this voyage was behind them.

As the ship continued tacking, a distant roar came faintly to his ears. That would be the surf against the rocky coast of Chile, he thought. Valparaiso was a good port, but they were well south of there now. The coast was lined with cliffs and rugged bays fanged with rocks that would rip out the hull of a ship with a careless helmsman. The waves were rougher now. The *Lydia Marie* was dangerously close to the shore.

Suddenly he stiffened as another sound came to his ears, this one from the west. It was the sound of canvas popping as the wind caught it, and that could mean only one thing — the British warship was closing in.

Canfield had heard the sound, too.

"Stand by," he ordered in a low voice.

Ned held his breath and strained to see what could not be seen.

Then, with a glare so bright it was blinding, flame geysered from the mouth of a cannon several hundred yards to the west. Instinctively, Ned flinched. The blast was loud, but not so loud that Ned could not hear the high-pitched whine of a cannonball cutting through the air.

With a huge splash, the ball plummeted into the ocean a short distance ahead of the *Lydia Marie*. A voice followed, shouting through a hailing cone. "Attention, American vessel! Heave to! Heave to by the order of His Royal Majesty!"

Canfield held out a hand, signaling to wait. Other than that, no one moved or spoke — or breathed — aboard the *Lydia Marie*.

"This is Captain Ramsdale of the *H.M.S. Rupert!*" the voice called. "I repeat, heave to and prepare to be boarded!"

Overhead, the clouds were shredded and blown away by the wind. Starlight washed over the sea. Ned could make out the dark bulk of the British ship now. It had turned so that it was no longer cutting directly toward them. Its port side now faced the American vessel; the British captain had an entire broadside of cannons at his command. And a fusillade from those cannons might well sink the *Lydia Marie*.

"Steady as she goes, helmsman," Canfield ordered calmly.

Ned felt the wind shift again. Above him, the sails popped as they filled. The wind was behind them again, out of the north.

Captain Ramsdale of the *Rupert* must have felt that, too, because there was a ragged note of impatience in his voice as he shouted, "Heave to! This is your last chance!"

"Mr. St. Clair," Canfield called softly, *"fire!"*

"Fire!" India barked in response, and at each of the three cannons lined up along the starboard side of the ship, gunners brought their smoldering punks out of the cans in which they had been concealed and touched them to fuses. The fuses caught with a sputter of sparks.

Ramsdale must have had a spyglass on the American ship, because a second later Ned heard him shouting, "Fire! Fire!" Not a heartbeat passed, though, before all three of the cannons on the *Lydia Marie*'s starboard side roared in unison.

Ned could not see the damage wrought by the cannonballs, but as the echo of the volley faded, he heard a loud crunching that he hoped was at least one of the balls smashing through the wood of the British ship. He held tightly to the railing as the *Lydia Marie* began to pick up speed.

"Riflemen!" India snapped from the deck. "Fire!"

A rattle of rifle shots sounded, only to be drowned out by the boom of the cannons on the *Rupert*. Again Ned heard the ugly whine of heavy lead balls cutting through the air. Several splashes sounded behind the ship, but there was also a loud crash as one of the balls swept away part of the railing around the afterdeck. It passed on over the ship, however, and did no further damage before falling into the water on the port side.

Ned saw flickers of light on the deck of the British vessel. Something sang past his ear, sounding for all the world like a giant insect. A rifle ball, he thought. He suddenly wished that Clay and Jeff were here with their long Kentucky rifles. The Holts would show those damned Britishers some real shooting!

Hard on the heels of that thought came an ugly thud, followed by a grunt of pain. Ned swung sharply away from the rail and saw Captain Canfield sagging toward the deck of the bridge. Ned sprang to the captain's side and caught his arm, steadying him. "Sir! Are you hit?"

"Ball . . . clipped me on the thigh," Canfield said raggedly.

"I can take you below —" Ned began.

"No! Just give me a hand . . ."

Ned slipped an arm around Canfield's waist to support him. He glanced down and saw a dark stain spreading on the light-colored leg of the captain's trousers.

Canfield turned his head toward midships. "Report!" he bellowed.

"Cannons reloaded," India's voice came back.

"Fire! Fire at will, Mr. St. Clair!"

India didn't have to relay the order this time. The gunners touched off their fuses, and a moment later the cannons blasted again. This time the volley was more ragged, and Ned could not tell if any of the shots struck their target. With a rumble like thunder, the *Rupert* returned fire, but with the freshening wind, the smaller, swifter American vessel had leaped ahead. Once again the cannonballs fell harmlessly into the sea.

"The wind is with us, Mr. Holt," Canfield said. "They can't catch us now." Worry edged into his voice as he added,

"But they still have a gun mounted on their bow."

"One cannon's not going to hurt us," Ned said.

Flame spiked again into the darkness, this time at the bow of the *Rupert*, even as Ned spoke. Something crashed on the afterdeck. A man screamed, and another shouted, "The mast! Mind the mast!"

Ned looked up and saw one of the sails collapsing. He groaned. A lost sail would cripple them, and the British ship could easily catch up to them and sink the boat.

Worse, he knew that India was back there somewhere.

Canfield grated, "Go see how bad the damage is, Mr. Holt."

"But, Captain, you're wounded —" Ned wanted to go, but he couldn't abandon Canfield.

"I'll hang on to the wheel. Helmsman, stand aside."

Ned wasn't sure that was wise, but Canfield was in command. He let go of the captain and hurried to the ladder leading down to midships. He slid down, his feet barely touching the steps, then broke into a run toward the stern. As he looked up, he saw that the mast had not collapsed completely. But it was leaning at a dangerous angle.

"Ned!"

That was India's voice. She was on the afterdeck, hauling desperately on a line with several other sailors, trying to keep the mast upright. It was a losing battle. Even as Ned raced to join them, he heard a grinding and splintering. He threw his head back and gazed up to see the mast toppling.

And it was falling right toward him.

"Ned!" India screamed again.

He flung himself aside, knowing that he would be crushed like a bug if the mast landed on him. The move was a desperate one, and he paid no attention to anything but getting out of the way. Lines snapped and popped all around him. Something struck the side of his leg, and he lost his balance. He had been close to the railing, and he realized now that in his haste to avoid the toppling mast, he had jumped the wrong way.

Ned felt himself falling. The side of his head struck the railing with stunning force as he plummeted past it. He threw out a hand, hoping to grab something, anything, and felt his fingers brush across the rough wood of the ship's hull. Then there was nothing under him but empty air . . .

And the sea below.

"Innndiiiaaa!" Ned shouted as he plunged toward the waves. The fall lasted an eternity, but when it ended, the heavy impact knocked all the breath from his lungs. The water closed around him, black and cold and remorseless, and he knew in that moment he was about to die.

His last thoughts were of India.

She saw him go over the side, though for a heart-rending instant she refused to believe what her own eyes were telling her. Ned had avoided the falling mast only to tumble over the railing and disappear into the sea. India let go of the line she was holding — no point in it now, anyway, since they'd lost the mast and the sail — and darted toward the spot where she had last seen Ned. She didn't know what she was going to do — leap over the side perhaps and try to rescue him?

But she had taken only a few steps when something slammed into the deck behind her, throwing her forward head over heels. Another cannonball from the British ship had crashed into the *Lydia Marie*.

India rolled over, dazed. She pushed herself up on her hands and knees and shook her head. For a moment she could not remember where she was or who she was. Then reality flooded over her. She staggered to her feet and looked around. Several men lay sprawled around her. One of them was mewling pitifully as blood spouted from the ragged stump below his right hip where his leg had been a few seconds earlier. No one could help that poor sailor now, India knew. He would bleed to death in minutes, but if he was fortunate he would lose consciousness from the shock first.

She didn't bother with the ladder but leaped down from the afterdeck to the midships. The gun crews were still manning the cannons. India raced over to the rearmost gun and shouted, "Cut it loose!"

"What the hell!" one of the gunners howled.

"Cut it loose!" she repeated. "We have to turn it so that we can fire back at the British!"

"We're beaten, damn it!" the man rasped back at her. "We lost one of the sails. We can't outrun that warship now!"

India's hand shot out, bunching the front of the man's shirt. She flung him aside with a strength that surprised her. Jerking her knife from its sheath, she slashed at the ropes holding the cannon in place. "Finish loading while I'm cutting it loose," she barked at the rest of the gun crew.

The men hesitated, then sprang to their work. The charge was rammed in place and the heavy lead ball seated atop it. India grabbed the cannon's carriage and lifted. She couldn't budge the weapon by herself, of course, but the other men leaped to help. The barrel of the cannon swung toward the stern.

"That's far enough," India snapped. Any farther and they would risk firing into their own afterdeck. She craned her neck and peered toward the *Rupert*. The British ship was closer now, threatening to pull even with the *Lydia Marie* again. If that happened, a British broadside would blow the American ship into kindling. India knew she had one shot, and one shot only.

"Stand clear!" she cried. Now that the cannon was no longer dogged into place, the recoil would throw it backward. She thrust out a hand, and the man with the punk seemed to know what she wanted. He gave it to her, and she held it to the fuse.

The men leaped away from the cannon as the fuse sputtered and flashed. India waited until the last second to make sure the cannon was going to fire. As the sparking fuse reached the touchhole, she flung herself to the side. The boom of the cannon assaulted her ears. The cannon was thrown backward on its wheeled carriage.

Before the echo of the blast died away, it was followed by an even larger explosion. India had landed prone on the deck. She lifted her head to see the blast that ripped through the center of the British ship. She gasped. The ball she had fired must have smashed through the hull and found the *Rupert*'s powder magazine. That was the only explanation for the destruction she saw unfolding before her eyes.

Sheets of flame leaped up from amidships on the British vessel. In the hellish glare, India saw the crewmen racing about madly. But there was nothing they could do — the explosion of the magazine was a death blow. Even crippled as the *Lydia Marie* was by the loss of a mast, she would get away from the British ship. As India groggily pushed herself to her feet, she heard the cheers of her fellow crewmen.

She cared nothing for that. She stumbled to the rail and looked out at the sea. The light from the burning ship lit up the waves. India searched for any sign of a man swimming or floating.

She saw nothing in the water but debris flung from the *Rupert*. A sob racked her as she clung to the rail.

Ned Holt was gone.

CHAPTER EIGHTEEN

Melissa was both amazed and gratified by the welcome she and her companions received in New Hope. Of course, as the wife of Jeff Holt and the sister-in-law of Clay Holt, she supposed the people of the settlement regarded her as one of their own. Even Malachi Fisher, whose trading post would be direct competition for the enterprise Melissa and Terence O'Shay hoped to establish, was more than gracious to them.

"Nothing like a little friendly rivalry to spice things up," Fisher said after Aaron had made the introductions. Pipe smoke wreathed the trader's head.

"Well, I hope that's true, Mr. Fisher," Melissa said, standing on the porch of the trading post. She thought back to the last time she had competed directly against someone in the business world, in Wilmington. That rivalry had led to piracy, arson, and murder as Jeremiah Corbett and Philip Rattigan had vied with Holt-Merrivale and the March Shipping

Line. Corbett, a merchant based in Wilmington, had instigated the violence, although Melissa had suspected at first that Philip Rattigan was part of it, too. Rattigan had proven her wrong by helping her expose his ruthless partner — and by saving her life along the way.

And then he had kissed her.

Melissa forced that memory from her mind and concentrated on the present. Aaron was introducing her to Father Thomas Brennan. The redheaded priest shook her hand warmly, but he seemed particularly glad to meet a fellow Irishman in Terence O'Shay. They pumped each other's hands and slapped each other on the back like long-lost brothers. Both men were soon reminiscing about places in Ireland that Melissa had never heard of, and within minutes they discovered that they might be distantly related.

"You and Michael can stay in my cabin if you like, Melissa," Aaron offered. "Until you get a house of your own, of course."

"You don't have to do that, Aaron," she said. "We don't want to put you out of your own home."

He shook his head. "It's no trouble," he assured her. "I can stay with Father Thomas for a while. I don't reckon he'll mind. Do you, Father?"

"Not at all," the priest said. "It's just good seeing a smile on your face again, lad."

"Well, then, thank you, Aaron," Melissa said. "Michael and I accept."

"What about you, Terence?" Father Thomas asked. "The quarters might be a bit cramped, but I venture to say there's room for one more."

"If you're certain," O'Shay said.

" 'Tis more than certain I am," Father Thomas replied, his Irish accent becoming more pronounced the longer he talked to O'Shay. "Come along now. I'll be showing you where the cabin is."

"And I'll take your things to my house, Melissa," Aaron said.

They all walked back to the keelboat, which was pulled up on the bank of the creek. Captain Tompkins and the rest of the crew would stay on board until they were ready to start back downriver with a load of beaver pelts. As long as the weather cooperated, it made a reasonable habitation.

Pink Casebolt stood on the creek bank, the butt of his flintlock rifle resting on the ground as he leaned on the barrel. "So this is New Hope," he said as he surveyed the cluster of cabins, no more than a dozen in all. "Reckon it must be the largest settlement 'tween St. Louis and the Pacific Ocean."

"The *only* settlement," Aaron said with a grin.

Melissa smiled at Pink. "Mr. Casebolt, you've been a sterling guide," she said.

"Shoot, I still say you could've got here just fine without me." Casebolt rubbed his bearded jaw. "I figured we'd run into more redskins than we did. Reckon we were lucky."

"Well, I can't thank you enough for your services." Melissa reached into the pocket of her dress, took out a small leather pouch, and held it out to Casebolt. "As we agreed."

Casebolt took the pouch and tucked it away inside his shirt. "Yes'm."

"You're not going to count it?"

"Don't reckon there's any need. I've been around you and Mr. O'Shay long enough to know you're honest folks."

O'Shay said, "I suppose you'll be heading for the mountains now, doing a little trapping."

Casebolt squinted toward the snow-capped peaks. "I don't know," he said slowly. "Thought I might stay around here for a few days, whilst I'm planning what to do next."

"You're welcome to stay as long as you want," Aaron told him. "We haven't run anybody out of New Hope yet, and we don't aim to start."

"Reckon it's settled, then," Casebolt said. "I'll find a place to pitch my bedroll. In the meantime, I'll give you a hand unloading the boat. No charge," he added hastily. "We're square already."

With everyone helping, it didn't take long to unload the keelboat. The bags belonging to Melissa and Michael were taken to Aaron's cabin. Melissa was already looking around the settlement, and her attention focused on a large, open piece of ground near the creek. She visualized the building that would rise there, a large, sturdy building of logs, the front section of which would serve as the trading post. In the rear would be the quarters she would share with Michael.

And someday, perhaps with Jeff. If he ever returned from Alaska . . .

Once the Tlingit elders had agreed to Jeff's proposal, the plan moved quickly. Jeff went with Vassily and two other men to scout out a suitable location for the rendezvous point. After a couple of days they settled on a small cove that was partially shielded from the view of the bay by a pine-covered jut of land. That suited his purposes perfectly, Jeff decided. The *Beaumont* was small enough to slip in, take on a cargo of furs, and slip out again with no one being the wiser, certainly not Count Gregori Orlov.

One evening after returning from the scouting trip, Jeff was sitting in the house he shared with Nadia and Vassily and the other members of their clan. Nadia was preparing a salmon for the evening meal while the men talked.

"We should have men watching for the *Beaumont*," Jeff said, "and canoes ready so that as soon as the ship is sighted, we can paddle out and meet it. That way there's no chance of it sailing on to Sitka."

"The Russians will wonder why the ship does not come back for you as promised," Vassily pointed out.

"That's right. Which is why Captain Vickery *will* go on to Sitka, but only after I've talked to him and explained the situation. Orlov will spin some story about me dying in an accident or some such. Captain Vickery will act properly incensed, but there won't be anything he can do. Orlov will tell him to leave and not come back, and Vickery will agree." Jeff grinned. "That's when the *Beaumont* will stop at the cove on the way south and pick up a load of furs."

A faint smile tugged at Vassily's mouth. "Your plan could work, my brother. But only if the Russians do not find out what we are doing."

"Keep an eye on Yuri," Jeff cautioned. "He's the only weak link, as I see it."

"He has not left the village alone except to go hunting. And he has always returned with fresh game."

Jeff turned that information over in his mind. Sitka was far enough away that a man could not go there and return in a single day. But hunting trips sometimes lasted several days. Vassily believed Yuri would not betray his people, and Jeff could only hope he was right. It was hard to predict what a man might do if his jealousy and hatred were powerful enough.

"I think from now on you should have someone watching Yuri all the time," Jeff suggested.

"That would be an insult to his honor," Vassily objected.

"I'd rather insult Yuri's honor than have a troop of Russian soldiers staring us in the face over their muskets."

For a moment Vassily said nothing. Then he shrugged expressively. "As you wish," he said.

"We eat now," Nadia announced.

Jeff smiled at her. The salmon, caught that morning, smelled delicious.

Over the next few weeks, as the weather grew steadily warmer, the Tlingit amply demonstrated their skills in woodworking. Cedar trees were felled near the cove Jeff had picked out — though none of the trees on the point of land that shielded the entrance were touched — and a crude warehouse began to take shape. Most of the men from the village took part in the construction, but Jeff insisted that none be forced into helping. He wanted only those who truly believed in the effort to be involved in it.

Not surprisingly, Yuri was not one of the men who joined in the labor. He and several of his friends did come down to the cove to jeer at the ones who had elected to work with Jeff.

"The Russians will burn your bighouse to the ground," Yuri said as he sat on a fallen log with his cronies. "If you are lucky, they will only flog the ones who have foolishly listened to this American."

Vassily and another man were carrying a log past Yuri. "If you do not wish to work, you should go away," Vassily said with a grunt.

"I have the right to be where I want to be," Yuri shot back.

Jeff had come up behind Yuri in time to hear the conversation. He said, "Unless your Russian masters tell you otherwise, isn't that right, Yuri?" He knew it was unwise to goad the man, but he was tired of Yuri's carping.

Yuri sprang to his feet and turned to face him. "No man is my master," he said angrily.

"What about Count Orlov? From what I've heard, you always do everything he tells you." Vassily vigorously shook his head, but Jeff ignored him. Maybe this would be a good day to settle things with Yuri once and for all, he thought.

A rapid spate of words in the Tlingit tongue flew from Yuri's mouth. Jeff spoke the language fairly well by now, but he could not keep up with what Yuri was saying. He caught enough of it, however, to know that he was being cursed all the way back to his ancestors.

Jeff waited for Yuri's tirade to run down, then said coldly, "Vassily is right. If you're not going to work, you should go away. You're useless."

Yuri's face twisted with hatred, and his hand went to the knife sheathed at his belt. With no more warning than that, he yanked the knife out and leaped over the log to lunge at Jeff.

Jeff was ready for the move. He stepped forward quickly to meet Yuri's charge instead of retreating from it. That surprised Yuri, who hesitated for a split second. In that pause Jeff brought his left arm up and blocked Yuri's right arm as the knife swept toward him. Stepping in closer, he threw a right-hand punch into Yuri's face. The blow didn't travel very far, but it landed with stunning impact on Yuri's nose. Jeff felt cartilage flatten under his fist and blood spurt across his knuckles.

Yuri went over backward, landing hard on the bare ground. Jeff came after him, his foot lashing out in a kick aimed at Yuri's knife hand. The kick connected and sent the knife spinning away into the brush nearby. Yuri clutched his wrist but did not utter a single sound of pain.

Jeff stepped back. "Try it without the knife, why don't you?" he said.

At the first sign of violence the workers had rushed to form a circle around Jeff and

Yuri. Yuri's friends surged forward, evidently to take up the cause of their fallen companion, but Yuri savagely motioned them back.

"I will deal with this outlander!" he rasped. "He is mine!"

Jeff stood calmly, fists loosely clenched. His demeanor said clearly, *I'm waiting.*

With a roar of anger, Yuri came up off the ground. He surprised Jeff with the speed of his attack. Jeff tried to dart aside, but Yuri managed to get a hand on him and jerked him into a bear hug. The momentum carried Jeff backward. Off balance and out of control, he felt himself falling when a small branch rolled under his stumbling feet.

Jeff went down with Yuri on top of him. The Tlingit's crushing weight knocked the wind out of Jeff, and now he could not catch his breath. Yuri wedged a hand under his chin and forced his head backward. Jeff felt a horrible, grinding strain in his neck.

He hooked a short punch into Yuri's midsection, but the man's coat absorbed most of the impact. Yuri only grunted, his sour breath gusting in Jeff's face. Jeff worked his other arm free and slapped at Yuri's ears with his cupped hands. That move succeeded in loosening Yuri's grip, and Jeff was able to arch his back and heave his opponent to one side. He rolled the other way and came to rest propped on his elbows. He dragged several lungfuls of air into his body and felt the dizziness that had threatened to overwhelm him a moment earlier begin to recede.

Yuri had not finished with him. He regained his feet first and attacked again, one leg lifted so that he could use his foot to drive Jeff's face down into the ground. Jeff twisted onto his back and raised his hands. He caught Yuri's foot and heaved. Yuri let out a surprised, angry yelp as he went over backward.

Jeff climbed to his feet, and this time he was upright a heartbeat before Yuri was. He bored in, slugging left and right before Yuri could raise his guard. Jeff's fists thudded into Yuri's face, rocking his head from side to side. Drops of blood from his pulped nose sprayed through the air with each punch and spattered the ground around him.

Yuri tried to lift his arms to ward off the blows, but he was tiring. Jeff pressed his advantage, driving him back toward the log on which he had been sitting earlier. Finally, with all his remaining strength, he launched a haymaker that crashed into Yuri's jaw. Yuri staggered backward, his knees hit the log, and he toppled over it, coming to rest on the other side. He lay motionless, legs draped over the log. A moan bubbled through his smashed, bloody nose. He would fight no more today.

Jeff stepped back and flexed his hands, feeling the soreness in the bones and joints. By tomorrow they would be so swollen he would not be able to work. But right now even the pain felt good. He had given Yuri what was coming to him.

Jeff glanced around at the other Tlingit. They all regarded him gravely, saying nothing. Vassily, however, was clearly upset. "Did you have to do that?" he asked.

"You saw him," Jeff said. "He pulled a knife on me. I was just defending myself."

Slowly Vassily shook his head. "This was more than that, my brother."

"Maybe so," Jeff admitted. "I don't reckon it's any secret that Yuri and I don't care for each other."

Yuri's friends had moved forward to check on him. They lifted him into a sitting position on the log. His face was smeared with blood.

"No good will come of this," Vassily predicted gloomily.

"No good was going to come of letting Yuri continue to poison what we're trying to do here," Jeff countered.

"We will see."

That was true enough, Jeff thought. Whatever happened as a result of this battle, they could only wait and see. One thing was certain: They would have to keep a closer eye than ever on Yuri.

With the help of Aaron Garwood, Father Thomas, the crew from the keelboat, and several men from New Hope, the trading post that Melissa had envisioned quickly became a reality. Even Malachi Fisher pitched in, making Melissa feel even guiltier about competing with him for the fur trade.

"Don't worry your head none," Fisher assured her as he hammered pegs into the puncheon floor. "I've been listening to trappers for years now talking about what it's like in the mountains, and I'm thinking that maybe the time's come for me to try my hand at that part of the business."

"You want to be a trapper?" Melissa asked in surprise.

Fisher shrugged. "It's a thought that's

been going through my head of late, even before you showed up, Mrs. Holt. But I wouldn't close down my store and leave, because folks depend on me. Maybe now I can do that without putting any hardship on anybody."

It seemed to Melissa that what Fisher was proposing was exceptionally generous, but the man seemed sincere. She could understand that he would have hesitated to close his trading post, even if he wanted to do something else with his life. Perhaps the new enterprise she and Terence O'Shay were launching would work out well for everyone, including Malachi Fisher. It certainly seemed that way.

Pink Casebolt helped out with the building of the new trading post, even though, by his own admission, he was not much of a carpenter. "Just never picked up the knack of it," he told Melissa one day as he struggled to cut a notch in the end of a log. "Reckon it was too much like real work."

"Work doesn't seem to bother you, Mr. Casebolt," Melissa commented.

"Not as long as it's work of my own choosing," Casebolt said. "But I purely hate working for wages, like when I was clerking in that hotel. And you said you'd call me Pink."

"That's right, I did. I certainly appreciate the help you've given us, Pink. I don't know how we'll pay you back."

"Don't you worry about that," he assured her. "I'm not doing this for pay."

Winter seemed to be truly over. All the snow in the valley had melted, although there was still plenty on the slopes of the mountains that loomed over the settlement. Most days the sky was clear and the weather pleasant, with only a slight chill remaining in the air. Malachi Fisher said that a late-season storm was still possible but unlikely.

After a little over a week, the roof of the new structure was in place, and Melissa and Michael moved into the quarters in the back. There was still some finish work to do on the rest of the trading post, but that could be completed while the two of them were living there.

"Are you sure you're ready to move, Melissa?" Aaron asked her as she was packing her things. "You and Whip can stay here in my cabin as long as you want."

Melissa was the only one in the settlement who still referred to her son by his real name. To everyone else the boy was Whip Holt, a name that seemed to please

Michael immensely. In the wide open spaces of the settlement he spent hours practicing with the long bullwhip his father had given him. Melissa still cringed sometimes when she heard the wicked crack of the whip as Michael wielded it, but she knew she would be wasting her breath if she warned him to be careful. And to be fair, he *was* amazingly competent for one so young.

"We don't want to put you out of your home any longer than we need to," Melissa assured Aaron. "You've been very kind to us, but now it's time we made our own home."

"Well, I reckon that makes sense," he admitted. "Let me give you a hand with those bags."

Since leaving Wilmington, Melissa had traveled lightly. It did not take long for her and Aaron, with helping hands from Terence and Father Thomas, to move everything into the trading post. The crates of trade goods they had brought from St. Louis had already been unloaded from the keelboat and stacked in the front room of the building, waiting for shelves and counters to be built. Melissa was confident they would be open for business by the time the trappers began bringing in the spring's first pelts.

That evening, after supper, Melissa stepped out onto the front porch, which ran the entire width of the building and was overhung by an awning made of the trunks of small saplings lashed together. Michael was inside in the living quarters, playing with the wooden toy soldiers he had brought with him from Wilmington. The porch faced east, so Melissa could not see the sun sinking behind the mountains behind her, but she could watch the last of the red rays as they slanted across the prairie on the other side of the creek. The tops of the thick new grass waved in the breeze. The air was cool, and Melissa was grateful for the shawl she clutched tightly around her shoulders. She leaned against a post, enjoying this peaceful moment.

Movement caught her eye, and she turned her head a little to see Pink Casebolt walking toward the trading post. "Good evening, Pink," she called.

Casebolt tugged on the wide brim of his hat as he came up to the porch. "Evening, ma'am," he said. "Enjoying your first night in your new home?"

"Very much so," Melissa replied. "This is a beautiful country. Isolated and frightening sometimes, but undeniably beautiful."

"Yes, it sure is."

Casebolt was looking intently at her, and Melissa felt the first faint stirrings of unease. She said, "What are your plans now, Pink? Are you going to run some traplines?" She smiled. "I can promise you, you'll receive a fair price for any furs you bring in."

"That was what I figured on doing when I came back out here. Going back to the mountains, I mean. I'm a pretty fair trapper." Casebolt rubbed his bearded jaw. "But here lately, I've been thinking that maybe that isn't what I want to do after all."

"I'm sure Captain Tompkins would consider hiring you on. I know you have experience with boats."

Casebolt shook his head. "Never cared overmuch for being a riverman, even though I was one for a long time." He stepped up onto the porch. He was not carrying his rifle, and he seemed to be having trouble figuring out what to do with his hands. Finally he hooked his thumbs in his belt and said, "I was thinking about staying here in New Hope."

"What would you do?" Melissa asked.

"I don't know," Casebolt said. "Maybe

you can give me an idea."

"Well . . . eventually Terence and I might need someone to help us run this business, but right now I'm certain we can handle everything ourselves —"

Casebolt stepped closer, startling her a little. His eyes bored into hers. "Give me a reason to stay, Melissa."

Before she could speak or move back, his hands reached out and closed around her upper arms. He pulled her toward him, and his mouth came down on hers in a hard, urgent kiss.

Melissa's eyes widened in shock. Casebolt had her pinned against the post and molded his body to hers.

Anger and fear surged through her in equal measure. Anger won out. She wedged her hands against his chest and shoved hard. He was too strong for her to move very far, but she gained enough room to pull her head away from his, breaking the unwanted kiss.

"How . . . how dare you!" she gasped.

"Damn it, gal, I been looking at you and wanting you for weeks now," Casebolt said, desperation in his voice. "Don't tell me you didn't know."

"I thought of you as a friend! Now let me go —"

"Melissa, I love you."

"Stop it! Stop it and let me go, Mr. Casebolt."

"Melissa —"

"Mrs. Holt! I'm a married woman."

Casebolt's mouth twisted. "Then where the hell's your husband? I ain't seen hide nor hair of him. All I've seen is that Irishman, and you can't tell me that you and him ain't bedding down together."

"Oh!" Melissa exclaimed furiously. "Terence and I are friends! Just as I thought you —"

"I want to be more than your friend." Casebolt leaned forward, trying once again to kiss her. Melissa squeezed her eyes shut and twisted her head away.

Suddenly he was gone, the painfully tight grip on her arms vanishing. She heard a yelp of surprise and then a loud thud and opened her eyes to see Casebolt stretched out on the porch with Terence O'Shay looming over him.

"Have ye lost yer mind, ye bloody spalpeen?" O'Shay demanded, his Irish temper boiling over. "Ye've no right to paw Mrs. Holt that way. Herself a married woman!"

Casebolt propped himself up on an elbow and with his other hand grasped his jaw and moved it back and forth. "That's what she said," he growled when he was satisfied that his jaw was not broken, "but I don't see any husband. I reckon you're the only one around here who gets to crawl into her bed, and I'm tired of it."

O'Shay trembled with rage. "Get on yer feet," he said. "Get up, damn you."

"Oh, I'll get up, all right." Casebolt started climbing to his feet. His hand went to the sheathed knife at his waist. "I'll get up and gut you, you whoreson!"

The mountain man uncoiled in a lunge, the knife whipping out of its sheath and slashing upward at O'Shay's midsection. O'Shay jerked back as Melissa screamed. Casebolt moved toward him, slashing back and forth with the blade.

Melissa heard running footsteps inside the building and turned toward the door in time to see Michael burst out, drawn by the commotion. She sprang toward him and grabbed him. "Mama! Let me go, Mama!" he yelled, but Melissa held him tightly.

She turned back toward the struggle between O'Shay and Casebolt. Casebolt feinted with the knife and then thrust it toward O'Shay's chest with blinding speed. The big Irishman was equal to the challenge, however. His hand shot out and locked around Casebolt's wrist. O'Shay pivoted, hauling Casebolt with him. Casebolt flew off the porch and landed in a rolling sprawl on the ground.

O'Shay leaped after him and landed with the heel of his boot on the blade of Casebolt's knife. Unable to free the weapon, Casebolt released it and scrambled away several yards, then sprang upright again. "I don't need a knife," he said as he glowered at O'Shay. "I'll kill you with my bare hands!"

"Ye're welcome to come and try," O'Shay responded.

His face contorted with rage, Casebolt leaped forward. He looked like a totally different man now. The friendly, colorful mountain man was gone, replaced by a ravening madman. Lust had driven him to that point, lust for a woman who could never be his.

O'Shay met him with a straight right that rocked him backward.

Men were coming from all over the settlement now, drawn by Melissa's scream. Aaron was hurrying toward the trading post as fast as his peg leg would allow. Not far behind him were Father Thomas and Malachi Fisher, as well as Captain Tompkins and the crew from the keelboat.

They formed a half-circle in front of the trading post and watched as O'Shay and Casebolt stood toe to toe and traded punches, slugging back and forth like primitive gods at war.

As a seasoned mountain man, Casebolt was probably a veteran of dozens of no-holds-barred, rough and tumble brawls. But Melissa knew Terence O'Shay's history. He had run the largest smuggling ring in North Carolina for many years, ruling a criminal empire through sheer strength and force of will. His big fists had dealt out justice and punishment to countless challengers. And he was taller and heavier than Casebolt, with a longer reach. The outcome of this battle was inevitable. O'Shay's fist crashed into Casebolt's jaw one final time and sent him careening backward to fall in a loose-limbed tangle.

"Get up," O'Shay urged him. "Get up, you!"

Father Thomas stepped forward and laid a hand on O'Shay's brawny shoulder. "I don't think he can, Terence," the priest said quietly. "I believe you've won."

"What in the world happened?" Aaron asked. "I thought you and Pink were friends, Terence."

"I thought so, too," O'Shay said. He

glanced at Melissa, and the message was plain to her. He wasn't sure whether she wanted him to say anything about what Casebolt had done to her. He made the decision himself. "He decided to pick a fight."

"I'd say that was quite a mistake," Father Thomas commented.

Casebolt rolled over onto his belly and groaned. A moment later he pushed himself to his hands and knees and groggily shook his head. O'Shay shouted to the other men, "Somebody give him a hand."

A couple of men from the keelboat crew stepped forward and hauled Casebolt to his feet. He shook his head again and regarded O'Shay and Melissa through bleary eyes.

"You'll be damned sorry for this," he rasped. "Both of you!"

"Get out of New Hope," O'Shay said coldly. "Don't show your puss here again."

"You can't do that!" Casebolt protested. "You ain't in charge here."

"I think it would be best if you went, Mr. Casebolt," Melissa said. Aaron moved up beside her, as did Malachi Fisher, Captain Tompkins, and several of the local men. It was obvious whose side they were on in this dispute. Slowly, all the men of New

Hope stepped up onto the porch of the new trading post, leaving Casebolt to stand alone in front of it, facing O'Shay.

Casebolt drew a deep breath and wiped the back of his hand across his bloodied, swollen mouth. "All right," he said. "I'm going. But you'll see me again one of these days. That's a damned promise."

He turned and stumbled away toward his makeshift camp.

"Mama," Michael said from his perch in Melissa's arms, "why is Pink so mad at everyone?"

"I don't know, Michael," Melissa said. But that was not strictly true. She did know. And although she was certain she had not encouraged him in any way and was not to blame for what he had done, she felt a pang of regret that the friendship they had forged on the long journey to New Hope had to end this way.

"Is he ever coming back?" Michael asked.

"He'd better not," O'Shay said, "if he knows what's good for him."

CHAPTER NINETEEN

It was all Clay could do not to whoop for joy as he rode beside the creek that meandered through the valley. A glance at Shining Moon told him that his wife felt the same way.

They were home.

The mountains that rose to the west were old friends to both of them. Shining Moon had grown to womanhood here, and Clay and his brother Jeff had arrived with the first fur trapping expedition to venture up the Missouri River to the high country. On that first trip they had been working for the Spanish entrepreneur Manuel Lisa, but since then Clay had roamed the mountains as a free trapper . . . until the Holt family reunion in Marietta had launched him into this adventure.

Now, although the pursuit of Comte Jacques de La Carde was still his primary concern, he had a chance to see the part of the world he considered his home. More importantly, Shining Moon would be reunited with her people. Though he had not said as much to her, Clay had decided that Shining Moon and Matthew would stay here while he and Markham pushed on, following the trail of La Carde.

"Nothing has changed," Shining Moon said as she rode alongside Clay. Matthew and Markham followed behind them.

Clay grinned. "Did you expect anything to change?" he asked. "I reckon those mountains have stayed about the same for a long, long time."

"I knew . . . but I was still afraid. We have been gone for so long."

Clay understood what she meant. He had felt the same concern, that when they finally returned to the mountains after months and months of delays, somehow everything would be different.

The log roofs of the settlement beside the creek came into view. "There it is," Clay said, turning his head to address Matthew and Markham. "New Hope."

"I've been there before," Matthew said dully. He had little reason to be pleased to see New Hope, Clay knew. For Matthew it was the place where his mother had been brutally murdered by a madman.

"It's not very large, is it?" Markham said.

"It's not New York or Philadelphia, that's for sure," Clay said.

"It's not even St. Louis."

"Still the biggest settlement you're going to find out here," Clay said cheerfully.

"Ah, well, one must take civilization where one finds it, I suppose."

As far as Clay was concerned, Markham could have his civilization. If Clay never ventured east of the Mississippi again, that would be just fine.

As they rode closer to the settlement, Clay spotted a large building near the creek that he didn't remember. He turned to Shining Moon. "That's new, isn't it?"

"It has been built since we left the mountains," Shining Moon confirmed. "What is it?"

"That big, it must be a new trading post." Clay swung his horse in that direction. "We'll stop there first, see if there's been any news of La Carde's party coming this way."

The four riders trotted up to the large log building and reined in. A tall, broad-shouldered man with a shock of black hair stepped out onto the porch and nodded pleasantly to them. "Good day to you folks. What can I do for you?"

Clay was about to introduce himself and

his companions when a small, towheaded boy burst out the door and yelled, "Uncle Clay!"

Clay stiffened in shock, as if he had been punched in the stomach. He recognized the boy immediately and said in disbelief, "Michael . . . ?"

A tall, attractive, dark-haired woman stepped out of the building, wiping her hands on her apron. "Hello, Clay," she said with a broad smile. "Hello, Shining Moon. It's wonderful to see you again." Then Melissa Holt lost the reserve she was obviously trying to maintain and ran forward, following her son.

Clay swung down from his saddle and found himself engulfed by the boy and his mother. Melissa kissed him on the cheek, then turned to embrace Shining Moon. Michael had his arms wrapped around Clay's thigh and was looking up at him with a gleeful grin. "Howdy, Uncle Clay," he said.

"Howdy yourself," Clay said, rumpling the boy's thick blond curls. He looked at Melissa and asked, "What in the world . . . Is Jeff here?"

She shook her head, and for an instant Clay saw a great sadness in her eyes. Thinking that something terrible must have happened to his brother, he exclaimed, "He hasn't gone under, has he?"

Melissa knew what a mountain man meant by that term. Quickly she shook her head again. "He was fine the last time I saw him," she said. "He's in Alaska."

"Alaska?" Clay repeated. "Where's that?"

"A long way north of where the Columbia River meets the Pacific, where you went with the Corps of Discovery. Farther north than even Canada," Melissa explained. "Russia owns it."

Clay vaguely recalled hearing of Alaska, now that he thought about it. He rubbed his bearded jaw. "What in blazes is my little brother doing way up there?"

"Trying to establish trade with the Russians."

That made sense, Clay thought. Jeff was about the tradingest fellow he'd ever met. He looked down at Michael, then back at Melissa. "What are you and the boy doing in New Hope?"

"The same thing Jeff is doing in Alaska, really." Proudly, Melissa waved a hand at the building behind her. "This is the Holt-Merrivale-O'Shay Trading Post and Fur Company."

428

"Are you sure you have room for all that on the sign?" Clay asked dryly.

"We'll put up a big sign if need be," the brawny, black-haired man replied. He stuck out a hand. "I'm Terence O'Shay."

As Clay shook hands with him, Melissa said, "Oh, I'm sorry. I should have introduced you. Clay, this is Terence. Terence, my brother-in-law Clay. Jeff's brother."

"Sure and I know that," O'Shay said with a grin. "I've heard aplenty about Clay Holt, from Jeff *and* from the folks here in New Hope."

"And I reckon Jeff mentioned you a time or two, Mr. O'Shay," Clay said. He turned and gestured to his companions. "This is my wife, Shining Moon, our friend John Markham, and the boy is Matthew Garwood. Melissa, you remember Matthew."

"Of course I do." Melissa smiled at the boy. "How are you, Matthew?"

"All right," Matthew responded.

"Your uncle Aaron is around here somewhere," Melissa told him. "I imagine word of your arrival will spread quickly, and Aaron will be here as soon as he can."

"How is Aaron?" Clay asked. The last time he had seen the young man, Aaron had been trying to adjust to having only one leg.

"He's doing tolerably well," Melissa said. "I don't believe he's really happy, though. But I'm sure just seeing all of you again will cheer him up."

O'Shay spoke up. "Why don't you folks go on inside and take a load off your feet? I'll tend to your horses."

"Mighty kind of you, Terence," Clay said. "I suppose we do have some catching up to do." *And some questions to ask about Jacques de La Carde,* he added to himself.

Melissa and Shining Moon were conversing as the group went into the trading post. The two women had become friends during the Holt reunion in Ohio, which gave Clay another reason to hope that Shining Moon would be willing to stay on in New Hope while he and Markham continued their pursuit of La Carde. Clay hoped to set a more demanding pace from here on, and although Shining Moon could ride faster and quite possibly fight harder than Markham, Clay knew he would worry about her if she was with them.

The trading post was well stocked. He saw barrels of salt and sugar and crackers, flasks of gunpowder, beaver traps, bullet molds, and just about anything else a trapper might need. "What happened to Malachi Fisher?" Clay asked. "He was running the trading post here when we left."

"Mr. Fisher decided to take advantage of the opportunity to close his business and become a trapper," Melissa said. "Terence and I brought a lot of goods upriver with us to start with, but Mr. Fisher was kind enough to sell us his stock."

"So Malachi's out of the fur trading business, is he?" Clay mused. "I didn't figure he'd ever give it up."

"The lure of the mountains got to him," O'Shay said. "To tell the truth, I feel it myself sometimes. I look up there at those peaks, and I think how fine it would be to be among them."

Clay understood the feeling completely — only he had always answered the siren call of the mountains.

Melissa led the way through the trading post to the living quarters in the rear. "Michael and I live here," she explained.

Clay was curious what had prompted Melissa to come to New Hope rather than stay at home in Wilmington. He suspected there was an interesting story behind the decision, and behind Jeff's presence in Alaska.

Michael seemed excited to see Matthew again. The two boys had never been close playmates — there was a difference in their ages for one thing — but they had spent a few weeks together in Ohio. Michael said to the older boy, "Want to see what I can do with a bullwhip?"

"You're still playing with that whip?" Matthew asked disdainfully. But after a moment he went on, "All right, I guess so."

"Come on!" Michael said. He grabbed Matthew's hand and tugged him out of the trading post. Clay waited for Melissa to call out a warning to Michael to be careful, but she didn't. Maybe she was finally accepting the fact that her son was no longer a baby.

Melissa gestured to the chairs around the table. "Please, sit down," she told the visitors. "I'll put some water on the fire for tea."

"That sounds mighty good," Clay said. "Don't go to too much trouble, though."

Melissa smiled. "For the two of you, there's no such thing as too much trouble. And for Mr. Markham, of course."

The young officer bowed slightly. "Thank you, Mrs. Holt. I heard a great deal about you from your husband when we were all together in Washington City."

"Oh?" Melissa turned back from the fireplace, where she had hung the kettle.

"You know Jeff, Mr. Markham?"

"Indeed I do. A fine man. But you know that."

"Yes," Melissa said. "A fine man."

Again Clay got the feeling that something was wrong. Waiting was against his nature, so he asked bluntly, "Melissa, what's Jeff doing up in Alaska? And how did you come to be here in New Hope? Is there some sort of trouble between the two of you?"

Shining Moon laid her fingers on Clay's hand, as if warning him not to be so direct. It was too late, though. The questions were out in the open, waiting to be answered.

After an uncomfortable moment, Melissa said, "Jeff and I went to Alaska together, Clay. He decided to stay, so Michael and I started back home. However, when the ship we were on reached New Orleans, I changed my mind about going back to Wilmington. I ran into Terence there, and we decided to form a partnership. This trading post is the result."

Clay tugged at his earlobe. "Why in the world would Jeff stay in Alaska?"

"There was . . . a woman involved."

Clay sat back in his chair, thunderstruck. Another woman had come between Jeff and Melissa? Clay couldn't believe it. He didn't *want* to believe it. He hadn't been around home a lot when he and Jeff were younger, but his little brother had been in love with Melissa Merrivale for as far back as Clay could remember. When Jeff and Melissa were married, Jeff was as happy as Clay had ever seen him. Later, when they were separated through no fault of their own, Jeff had vowed that he would never stop looking for Melissa until they were together again. To have gone through all that only to split up again, this time because of another woman . . .

"Maybe it's a good thing that my brother's not here after all," Clay said. "If he was, I might be tempted to beat some sense into that stubborn head of his."

Quickly Melissa said, "No, please, you mustn't be angry with Jeff. There was a lot more to it than what you're thinking —"

"I'm thinking he's a damned fool," Clay said, and again Shining Moon took his hand to rein him in.

Markham cleared his throat as if to speak, but they never knew what the young officer was going to say. They heard a clumping sound outside, and a second later Aaron Garwood appeared in the doorway. "Clay! Shining Moon!" he exclaimed. "They told me you were here, but

434

I didn't believe it. Then I saw Matthew outside. . . ."

Clay stood up and stretched out both hands to Aaron. Their clasp was firm, speaking silently of their strong friendship. Shining Moon came to her feet, too, and Aaron embraced her. When he stepped back, he looked somberly down at her.

Clay saw the look immediately and asked, "What's wrong, Aaron?"

"Well . . . I reckon you've got to know sooner or later, and since there's no way to soften the blow . . ." He faced Shining Moon. "I'm afraid that Bear Tooth passed on a while back. I'm sorry, Shining Moon, mightily sorry."

Shining Moon took a half-step back and flinched as if she had been struck. "My father . . . ," she whispered.

Clay put an arm around her shoulders. "I'm sorry," he told her. "Bear Tooth was a mighty good man." He asked Aaron, "Who leads the Teton Sioux now?"

"A warrior named Falling Sky."

Clay nodded. "I know him. A good man, but not the friend that Bear Tooth was."

Melissa moved up on Shining Moon's other side and embraced her. Shining Moon stood with her head down for a long moment. When she finally raised it, she said, "Where is Proud Wolf? He should be chief."

"Proud Wolf has never come back from the east," Aaron said. "I don't reckon anybody expects him back anytime soon. He went for an education, and that takes a while, I imagine."

"He should be here," Shining Moon said. "He must be told of our father's death."

"Father Thomas wrote him a letter and sent it downriver to St. Louis on a keelboat that left about a week ago," Aaron told her. "He addressed it in care of that professor who came out here and took Proud Wolf with him. I expect it will get to him sooner or later, but there's no telling when."

With the shock of this unexpected bad news, Clay had almost forgotten about Jacques de La Carde. The mission could wait a day or two, he decided. But Bear Tooth's death was one more reason it was best for Shining Moon and Matthew to remain in New Hope. As the daughter of the late chief and as a well-respected woman among the Sioux, Shining Moon might have an influence on the new chief. She might be able to temper any ill feelings toward the whites that might arise among her people. Clay would speak to her about that . . . but later.

For now, he tightened his arm around his wife's shoulders to let her know that he was there and that he shared her grief. That was enough.

"How long have you and your mother been here, Michael?"

"Call me Whip."

"Sure . . . Whip." He could go along with whatever the little brat wanted, Matthew thought. As long as he answered the questions Matthew wanted to ask.

"You mean here in New Hope?"

"Yes."

"About a month. Maybe a little longer." Michael moved the handle of the bullwhip back and forth, and the braided leather coiled and uncoiled at his feet with a faint hissing sound. Suddenly he drew his arm back, then snapped it forward. The whip licked out at the air like something alive and then cracked back loudly.

That *was* impressive for a little boy, Matthew thought. "Have you seen anyone else come through here?" he asked.

Michael idly flicked his whip. "What do you mean?"

"Another bunch of travelers," Matthew explained, holding on to his patience with an effort. "Foreigners, some of them. They'd talk peculiar."

Michael shook his head. "I haven't seen anyone like that. The only strangers who've come since we got here were some fur trappers. They brought in some pelts right after my mama and Mr. O'Shay opened the trading post. Mama traded for them and had them loaded on Captain Tompkins's keelboat."

Matthew felt a stab of disappointment. He would ask Uncle Aaron about La Carde's party, too, but Michael had sounded quite certain that the Frenchman hadn't passed through New Hope.

Matthew intended to find La Carde and pass along the news that his partner in the land grab, Senator Morgan Ralston, was dead. He would tell La Carde, too, that Clay Holt and Lieutenant Markham were his enemies and would try to put an end to his scheme. The Frenchman would be so grateful that he would reward Matthew and maybe someday give him a position of importance in the new French empire in the west. Admiral of the navy, maybe, Matthew mused. He had always liked boats.

"Do you want to try it?"

Matthew looked up. Michael was holding the handle of the bullwhip out to

438

him. With a shake of his head, Matthew said, "No thanks."

"I can show you how —"

"I said no," Matthew snapped. He turned and stalked off, saying over his shoulder, "I want to take a look around." He ignored the hurt in Michael's eyes. He didn't care what the Holt brat thought of him, never had.

New Hope . . . what a lie that name was. The place was as ugly as ever, just a scattering of crude cabins in the middle of the wilderness. He was meant for better than that, Matthew told himself.

But his mother had been meant for better, too, and yet she had died here. She was buried down by the creek, he recalled. He supposed he ought to visit her grave and pay his respects . . . but only if he had the time before he got on with the business of finding Comte Jacques de La Carde.

The large party of travelers paused on a wooded hilltop overlooking a valley between the towering mountains. The bottom of the valley was largely barren of growth, unlike the grassy swards they had tramped through earlier in the foothills. Here pools of mud roiled and bubbled, and steam rose from cracks that had been riven in the ground by some ancient catastrophe. A foul smell hung over the entire valley.

One of the men strode forward to look intently at the patch of ugly landscape in the midst of mountain beauty. He was tall and slender, and though his clothes bore the marks of a long, arduous journey, he wore them as if he were garbed in the most elegant attire in the middle of a Parisian ballroom. He took off a broad-brimmed black hat and ran his fingers through long, gray-streaked hair for a moment, then turned and demanded of one of the other men, "What is this place?"

"They call it Colter's Hell," the man replied. "Named after a fellow named John Colter, who was the first white man to see most of this country. When he came back to civilization and told folks about what he'd seen here, they thought he was crazy. Said he must have found the back door to Hell. That's how it got its name." The man chuckled. "Then more trappers came out here, and they discovered that Colter hadn't been making it up, after all."

The tall man surveyed the landscape again. "Can we get around it?"

"Sure. Won't be any problem."

"Let us go, then. We have already

wasted enough time."

And the passage of time was nagging at Comte Jacques de La Carde these days. The captain of the ship that would rendezvous with him on the Pacific coast would wait until the comte arrived, of course. He would not dare to disobey orders and leave. But each day the ship had to wait was one more day that something could go wrong. Hostile Indians could attack the ship and sink it and its precious cargo before La Carde had a chance to use his diplomatic skills to convince the red men that they should join forces with him. He was confident that, given the opportunity, he could make the savages his allies and mold them into a united fighting force with which he could resist all challenges to his new empire.

Challenges there would be. La Carde was certain of that. The United States would not simply surrender half the territory it claimed without a fight. But La Carde was convinced that once he had brought the Indians to his side and armed them with the most sophisticated weaponry Europe had to offer, he could repel any military invasion. It might never come to that. Already La Carde's associates were in Washington City, the American capital, preparing an aggressive legal strategy. The Comte de La Carde held legal title to millions of acres of land in the west, they would argue in court. The fact that those titles had been acquired in secret, by means of bribery, forgery, and outright theft, would never be revealed.

The comte had heard during his brief stay in New Orleans that Gideon Maxwell, one of the tools used by the traitorous Senator Ralston, had been killed in an accident, but that did not worry him. Maxwell had been a clever man; surely he had covered his trail adequately. And La Carde had complete confidence in Ralston. The senator from Georgia was clever, cunning, and completely unscrupulous, a combination that La Carde admired. Ralston would have done his job.

Of course, the senator was no doubt upset when he reached New Orleans and found that La Carde's party had already left. Ralston had intended to join them and be by La Carde's side as the new empire was carved out of the American west. A pity that was not to be. Perhaps, La Carde had thought when deciding to abandon Ralston, he would send for the man after the empire was established and offer him some minor functionary's job then. Or perhaps not.

The group of men, twenty in number, moved on, skirting the foul-smelling valley. Besides La Carde, there were four other Frenchmen in the party, nobles and military officers, as La Carde had once been, who had been easily persuaded to join him in this valiant effort to regain the glory that Bonaparte had foolishly bartered away. La Carde looked at them now: Sevarain, Bouchard, Martineau, and Baginot. Good men, but lacking the spark of genius that was his. Then there were the three Americans who had met him in New Orleans: Baker, Howell, and Pittman. They had all worked for various fur trading companies, and the exclusive arrangements Senator Ralston had promised them had been more than sufficient to draw them to La Carde's side. Pittman had been to the mountains several times and was serving as their chief guide, although he relied heavily on the men they had hired in St. Louis to round out the expedition. These were all Americans, crude, ignorant men who were simply working for wages and had no idea they were participating in a scheme so grand, so glorious, that its success would change the map of the world forever.

One of them was walking directly in

front of La Carde as the group followed a trail along a ridge overlooking Colter's Hell. He was a tall, gangly young man, probably not yet twenty years old, and he looked around him with an amazed, wondering expression that said plainly this was the first time he had been in this part of the world.

"Lordy, I never knew there were such things out here," he said. "If I had, I'd've come west before now."

La Carde tried to remember the boy's name. Recalling it, he said, "Esau, isn't it?"

The young man looked back at him in surprise. "Yes, sir, that's me."

"Well, Esau, look closely at these sights which have so impressed you. In years to come, everything about them will no doubt be changed."

Esau shook his head. "Begging your pardon, Mr. La Carde, but some things don't change, and I reckon the mountains are one of them."

La Carde smiled. "You are a very young man, with many things yet to learn."

"Maybe so, but I'll bet that five hundred years from now these mountains will still be here."

"Perhaps you're right," La Carde murmured.

*Of course the mountains will still be here,
you fool,* he thought. *But five hundred years
from now, they will be the backbone of a glorious and never-ending French empire.*

CHAPTER TWENTY

Proud Wolf awoke to the sound of hounds baying. He rolled over, unaccustomed to the feel of a soft mattress beneath him. He had slept in a bunk in the wagon, but it had not been remotely as comfortable as this bed in Quincy Reed's house. Throwing aside the quilt, he swung his legs out of the bed and stood up. Nude, he padded over to the window and pushed the curtains aside, blinking as sunlight poured into the room.

He spotted what had set the dogs barking. Several riders were coming down the long lane toward the house. From his bedroom at the front corner of the second floor, Proud Wolf had a good view of the newcomers. He recognized two of them instantly.

Will Brackett and Frank Kirkland.

The other three men were strangers. Proud Wolf could tell at a glance that they were not Brackett's hired ruffians. One of them, the man in the lead, was middle-aged and solidly built, with a florid face.

Brackett and Kirkland rode behind him, followed by the other two men.

Brackett's head lifted slightly, and Proud Wolf stepped back from the window. He turned and hurried over to the chair on which he had draped his trousers the night before. To his surprise he realized that they had been taken from the room and cleaned sometime during the night, without his knowledge. Once again he was struck by how dulled his senses had become since he had begun living in the white man's world. The idea that someone could have come and gone in his room at least twice without waking him was appalling.

He pulled on the clean trousers and looked around for his shirt. It had been cleaned, too, and hung up in an open wardrobe. Proud Wolf pulled it on, then left the room and started along a balcony toward a set of curving stairs that led down to the foyer. The door of another room opened as he neared it, and Audrey stepped out, fastening the top buttons of her dress. She stopped short and said, "Oh!"

Proud Wolf smiled at her. She looked well rested, her skin dewy and fresh.

"I saw Will and Frank coming," she said breathlessly.

"I know. I saw them, too."

"But who are those men with them?"

Footsteps sounded behind Proud Wolf, and Quincy Reed said, "The sheriff and a pair of deputies, no doubt. Come along, you two. Young Mr. Brackett will soon see the folly of bearding the lion in his den."

The three of them were not the only ones who had been roused from sleep by the barking of the dogs. The other members of the troupe came out of the rooms they had been given the night before. They all looked sleepy and rumpled.

Not Quincy, however. He was fully dressed and wide awake, and Proud Wolf got the impression that he had been up before the sun. Quincy was wearing a brown suit and a white linen shirt with an elegantly tied cravat. He led the way to the front doors with Proud Wolf, Audrey, and the others trailing behind him. When he reached the doors he threw them open and stepped out onto the porch.

"Good morning, Sheriff!" he said heartily. "What brings you out here on such a fine day?"

The five riders had reined in before the porch. The middle-aged man leaned forward in his saddle and regarded Quincy unhappily. "I think you know what brings me here, Senator," he said. "You're harboring a fugitive from justice."

Dowd moved closer to Quincy and whispered, "You're a senator?"

"Former senator," Quincy said from the side of his mouth. "Now I'm a simple farmer." He turned his attention back to his visitors. "That's a very serious charge, Sheriff Buchanan. Do you have any proof?"

The sheriff jerked a thumb at Brackett and Kirkland. "The word of these two fellows here — *and* the warrants they're carrying."

Quincy smiled. "Indeed. And how do you know you can trust these men?"

Kirkland could not stand it any longer. He lifted his arm and pointed a shaking finger at Quincy. "He threatened us with a gun. He was going to shoot Will!"

Sheriff Buchanan leaned over and spat. "I reckon if Quincy Reed really wanted to shoot your friend, he'd be dead now. The senator got plenty of practice shooting redcoats during the War of Independence."

Quincy waved a dismissive hand. "A long time ago," he said.

"Sheriff, I have a legal warrant for that savage's arrest," Brackett said between clenched teeth. "I demand that you serve it and take him into custody, by force if necessary."

Buchanan sighed, clearly caught in the middle and not liking it one bit. He said, "What are we going to do about this, Senator? You know I'm sworn to uphold the law."

"Certainly," Quincy replied. "But where was that warrant drawn and sworn out?"

Brackett snapped, "You know perfectly well it was drawn by a magistrate in Boston."

Quincy shrugged and spread his hands. "Well, there you are, Sheriff. A magistrate from Massachusetts has no jurisdiction in Virginia. That warrant is meaningless."

"Damn it, you can't —"

"Hold on a minute," Buchanan said, cutting into Brackett's angry protest. "We always try to cooperate with lawmen from other states, but come to think of it, I don't reckon we're bound to."

"That's correct," Quincy said.

"This is outrageous!" Kirkland exclaimed. "You can't mean that you're going to let him protect that red savage, Sheriff!"

"I mean what I mean," Buchanan said sharply, "and Senator Reed makes a good legal point."

"That Indian is wanted on charges of assault and attempted murder," Brackett said, "and the warrant I carry empowers me to take him into custody and return him to Massachusetts for trial."

Ulysses Dowd spoke up. "You mean you'll shoot him in the back as soon as you're out of earshot, don't you?"

Kirkland spurred his horse forward, rage contorting his face, but both Brackett and Sheriff Buchanan put out a hand to hold him back.

Proud Wolf had been listening to the conversation between the men, but he felt strangely removed from it. Now he stepped forward, his shirt still hanging open, and said, "I would speak."

"Look at him," Kirkland said with a sneer. "Nothing but a bare-chested savage."

Sheriff Buchanan shot a glare in Kirkland's direction, then said, "I want to hear what he has to say." Nodding to Proud Wolf, he continued, "Go ahead, son."

"I am Proud Wolf, son of Bear Tooth, warrior of the Teton Sioux. I came to the land of the white men in peace, and anything I have done, I did only to protect myself" — he glanced at Audrey — "and the woman I love."

Oliver Johnson was standing on Proud Wolf's other side. He cleared his throat loudly, as if in warning. Proud Wolf knew that even a man who appeared to be fair, such as Sheriff Buchanan, would not take kindly to the idea of an Indian being involved with a white woman. But that was the truth, and Proud Wolf would not deny it.

"He kidnapped her —" Kirkland began.

Audrey interrupted him. "That's a lie and you know it, Frank. I went with Proud Wolf because you and Will and the others attacked me."

Now Sheriff Buchanan and his deputies turned as one and cast hard looks at Brackett and Kirkland. Brackett ignored them and said, "We're wasting time here. Are you going to take the savage into custody or not, Sheriff?"

Before the lawman could reply, Quincy said, "That won't be necessary, Sheriff. We're prepared to honor the warrant for Proud Wolf's arrest."

"What!" Dowd burst out. "But you can't —"

Quincy continued, "I believe you swore me in as a deputy last month when you gathered up a posse to search for those thieves."

A smile tugged at Buchanan's mouth. "So I did."

"And I don't believe I was ever officially discharged from my duties. So . . ." Quincy turned to Proud Wolf, who had wondered for a moment what he had in mind. Now he thought he understood. "Proud Wolf, I hereby place you under arrest. You will remain in my custody until I have delivered you to Massachusetts for trial."

"No!" Audrey cried. "You can't take him back —"

Proud Wolf put a hand on her arm to silence her. "I will go," he said. "It is the only way to end this."

"Wait just a damned minute," Brackett sputtered. "What do you mean, you'll deliver him to Massachusetts? That's my job."

"Not necessarily," Sheriff Buchanan said. "We like to cooperate, but how we go about it is our business. That warrant you've got says the Indian has to go back for trial. Well, he's going to, but in the custody of my deputy here."

Kirkland snapped, "He's not a deputy!"

"Actually, he is." Buchanan smiled at Brackett, but his eyes glittered with contempt as he went on, "Now, if you don't like this arrangement, you can always go back empty-handed. But either way, your business in my county is over, and I expect you to be gone by this time tomorrow."

Brackett's mouth was drawn in a tight line, and his face was white except for two crimson patches on his cheeks. "You won't get away with this," he grated. "None of you."

Quincy took a step forward. "As the sheriff said, your business here is done, and you're not welcome on my land, Brackett. Get off now, or I'll swear out a warrant on *you*. I'll charge you with trespassing."

For a moment, Brackett did not say anything. Then he hissed, "You'll regret this," and pulled his horse's head around. He kicked the animal into a gallop. Frank Kirkland glowered at the people gathered on the porch, then turned and rode after Brackett.

"That was a good idea you had, Senator," Buchanan said. "Do you really intend to take the boy to Massachusetts?"

"Indeed I do," Quincy replied.

"Then watch your backs along the way. I wouldn't put anything past that fellow."

Quincy looked at Proud Wolf and nodded. "I intend to be careful, Sheriff," he said. "I very much intend to."

Dull-eyed and moving like a sleepwalker, India went about her duties on the *Lydia Marie* over the next few days. She could hardly believe that Ned was gone, that she would never see him again. Her grief was at odds with the image she had carefully cultivated among the rest of the crew over the past weeks, but she did not care. There was nothing she could do about it anyway.

In the aftermath of the battle with the British warship, India had found Captain Canfield's spyglass and searched the surface of the water for any sign of Ned. The sea was lit up by the burning hulk of the British vessel, and India was confident she would have seen him if he was there. But she saw only debris and the small lifeboats that had been cast off from the warship. She had no idea how many survivors had escaped the flaming wreck, nor did she care about their fate.

Later that night she had gone down to the captain's cabin. Canfield was propped up on his bunk, a bloody bandage wrapped tightly around his wounded leg. He had a flask of rum in his hand and took an occasional sip to keep the pain in his leg under control.

"What's the damage, St. Clair?" he asked.

"The mizzenmast is destroyed, sir, and the sail is down. We're working to get a temporary mast back up until we can put into port somewhere and make permanent repairs."

"Which won't be until after we've rounded Cape Horn." Canfield sipped his rum. "Casualties?"

India's throat swelled and threatened to close up entirely as she said, "One man killed, one man missing and presumed dead. Four wounded, none seriously."

"The dead man?"

"Carter, sir."

"And the missing one?"

India swallowed. "Ned Holt."

Canfield's eyes widened. "My God," he murmured. He was the only man on the ship who knew of the relationship between Ned and India. "What happened?"

"Ned was knocked overboard when the mast fell. I . . . I can only assume that he was unconscious and drowned without ever coming to."

"Did you carry out a search?"

"A brief one. I thought it best that we not remain in the area for too long, though. Mr. Harkin agreed."

Harkin was the first mate and had assumed command after Canfield's injury. The captain nodded slowly and sighed. "I'm sorry, St. Clair. Ned was a good man, a good sailor. Those damned British . . ." He shifted slightly and winced as pain shot through his leg.

"Yes, sir," India said. "But they paid for their attack on us."

Canfield smiled faintly. "Aye. It's not often that a warship is sunk by a trading vessel. The royal navy will want to keep this quiet, so that they don't look like fools." He sighed again. "Well, we shall proceed to the Strait of Magellan by the shortest possible course and continue our voyage back to Wilmington. Carry on."

"Aye, sir." India turned to leave.

"And St. Clair . . . good work back there. I'm truly sorry about Ned."

"Aye, sir," India said softly. As she went out of the cabin, she added under her breath, "So am I."

But not as sorry as the British were going to be, she had vowed. The sinking of the warship was just the beginning. No matter what it took, she would make them pay for Ned's death.

Since her conversation with the captain, the *Lydia Marie* had made good time, even with a replacement mast. The weather grew cold, and squalls raced over the sea. The ship dodged some and rode out the others.

Three days after the battle, the rugged tip of South America was sighted. India, bundled in a heavy jacket, was on duty and on deck as the ship negotiated the narrow passage between Cape Horn and Tierra del Fuego. Once through the strait, the *Lydia Marie* swung northward.

They were in the Atlantic now, India mused sadly, no longer in the same ocean in which Ned had perished. That lonely thought sharpened her sorrow.

That evening India sat belowdecks on a bench in the crew's quarters. She leaned back against the bulkhead behind her and heaved a weary sigh. She had been working hard since Ned's death, hoping that physical exhaustion would help to blunt her pain. Her eyes closed, and she sat that way for several minutes.

Someone sat down beside her. She opened her eyes and saw Yancy, the little Cockney sailor. " 'Ello, lad," he said. "Ain't 'ad a chance to say it yet, but I'm sorry about what 'appened to Ned 'olt."

India forced herself to shrug casually. "Yes, it's too bad," she said, as if Ned's loss had not affected her any more than had the death of Carter, the sailor who after his leg was blown off had bled to death.

"Y'know, I feel as if I'm somewhat to blame."

India frowned. "Why is that?"

"Well, I am British. If that warship 'ad stopped us, they'd 'ave put me down in their press gang."

"Did you desert from the royal navy?"

"I ain't saying I did . . . and I ain't saying I didn't," Yancy replied. "But that doesn't matter to those bastards. They take 'oever they want."

India nodded. "I've heard that conditions are bad on British vessels."

"Ah, they're bad everywhere," Yancy said with a wave of his hand. "Even 'ere. The crew gets fed up with taking orders from a bunch of toffs who don't know their arse from their elbow."

India's first impulse was to defend Captain Canfield and the other officers, but she remembered that she had led Yancy and the other sailors to believe that she was dissatisfied with their lot, too. She forced herself to agree. Ned might be gone, but there was still the threat of a mutiny to deal with. Now that the *Lydia Marie* had rounded the Cape and was on her way home, the possibility of trouble from the crew would once again rise to the fore.

"If you ask me," Yancy went on, "we should lower the American flag."

"What flag would you have us sail under?" India asked.

"Who says a ship 'as to sail under *any* flag? In my mind, she belongs to the men who sail 'er."

India looked at him intently, her eyes slitted. "That sounds like mutiny," she said boldly.

He patted her knee. "Just blatherin'," he said as he got to his feet. "But you'd do well to remember what ol' Yancy 'as to say."

She would remember, all right, India told herself as Yancy moved away. And when trouble came, as it seemed bound to do, she would be ready.

Once the decision had been made to return to Massachusetts, Proud Wolf wasted little time in getting ready to leave. He had few belongings, as did Audrey. They had fled from Cambridge with little more than the clothes on their backs, and they had accumulated little in their travels, primarily what they had been given by their friends in the acting troupe.

The most difficult part of the return would be leaving those friends, Proud Wolf realized that afternoon as everyone gathered in the dining room of Quincy Reed's plantation house. The troupe was planning to move on, and Proud Wolf, Audrey, and Quincy Reed would leave that afternoon.

"We'll miss you, lad," Ulysses Dowd said, pumping Proud Wolf's hand. He leaned closer and asked quietly, "Are you sure you're doing the wise thing?"

"I am certain," Proud Wolf assured Dowd. "I have run from trouble for too long. That is not the way of the warrior. I will face my enemy, and the spirits will decide who is right and who is wrong."

"You mean the Massachusetts law will, and I know how these matters end," Dowd said worriedly. "The fellow with the most money usually has the law on his side."

"Not in this case," Quincy said. "Proud Wolf will have the best representation possible: my brother Daniel."

"Well, I hope everything ends happily for you." Dowd threw his arms around Proud Wolf and slapped him on the back. "Good-bye, lad."

Dowd hugged Audrey and shook hands with Quincy. One by one, the other members of the troupe followed: Vanessa, Walter Berryhill, the Thurstons, Elaine and Portia, Frederick and Theodore Zachary.

Oliver was the last one to come up to Proud Wolf. The little man frowned darkly and said, "Blast it, I don't feel right about this. I know you have a good friend now in Mr. Reed, but I don't trust Brackett *or* the law in Massachusetts."

"I am sure everything will be all right," Proud Wolf told him. "When my name is cleared, I will return to my homeland. You should come and visit us, Oliver."

"Maybe I will, one of these days . . . or maybe . . . maybe I'll go with you now." The words came quickly, as if Oliver had reached a decision and wanted to voice it before he had time to reconsider.

"You mean . . . to the mountains?" Proud Wolf asked.

"Eventually. But why can't I come with you to Boston?"

Dowd overheard the question and boomed out, "Oliver, you cannot leave us. The crowds love you!"

Oliver turned to him and said, "I'm sorry, Ulysses, but my mind is made up. I'm going with Proud Wolf."

"Oliver, you do not have to do this,"

Proud Wolf told him. "I am sure every-thing will be fine —"

"No, I want to," Oliver insisted. "I've had my fill of touring for a while. I mean no offense, Ulysses. Your troupe is the best I've ever had the pleasure of traveling with."

Vanessa knelt and put her hands on his shoulders. "Are you sure about this, Oliver?"

"Yes," he said, "I am."

"Then that's what you should do." She leaned forward and kissed him on the cheek. "And we all wish you luck."

When everyone had said their farewells, the actors climbed aboard their wagons. With waves and shouted good-byes, they drove down the lane to the road that led toward Richmond. Proud Wolf felt a pang of regret as he watched them leave. They had been good friends to him and Audrey. They had taken the two of them in when he was wounded, had helped nurse him back to health, had shielded them even when Brackett had threatened them all.

When the wagons were out of sight, Quincy said, "I've had a coach prepared for our journey, but as for myself, I intend to ride horseback most of the way. What say you gentlemen? I have some of the finest horseflesh in Virginia in my stables."

The idea of feeling a good horse beneath him appealed to Proud Wolf. He said, "I will ride."

"I think I'd be better off in the coach," Oliver said with a chuckle. "I doubt you've got a saddle with stirrups short enough for me. Besides, Audrey will need someone to keep her company."

"Thank you, Oliver," Audrey said with a smile. "I knew I could count on you to be gallant."

"Ever the gentleman am I."

Quincy had the coach brought around and their bags loaded into the boot, then led Proud Wolf to the stable to select their mounts. The groom brought out a tall, sturdy chestnut gelding, which Quincy patted fondly on the flank. "This is my favorite saddle horse," he said "I've ridden his sire, his grandsire, and his great-grandsire."

"The blood runs fine," Proud Wolf said.

"Good blood usually wins out," Quincy agreed. "That's why I'm confident you'll prevail over Brackett in court."

"No matter what happens, I intend to return to my homeland."

Quincy regarded him gravely. "If it comes to that, I'll help you. You have my word on that, Proud Wolf. But I hope we can allow justice to run its course."

Proud Wolf selected a mouse-colored horse with a darker stripe down its back. He had ridden similar animals in the past and knew them to be good horses, despite their unremarkable appearance. The groom saddled the horses while Quincy and Proud Wolf returned to the house.

"There may be trouble along the way," Quincy commented as he led Proud Wolf into the study. "I wouldn't be surprised if Brackett and his bunch tried to ambush us. That's why we're going to be ready." He took a pair of flintlock rifles from the cabinet and extended one to Proud Wolf. "I assume you know how to use a gun."

Proud Wolf nodded. "I am more accustomed to bow and arrows, but I can shoot."

"Good, because I don't have a bow handy."

"I can make one," Proud Wolf offered.

"Take this instead." Quincy held out a North & Cheney pistol. "I plan to take along plenty of powder and shot, too. What about Oliver? Do you think he'd want a gun?"

Proud Wolf could not visualize Oliver

Johnson armed. "Perhaps a smaller pistol," he said.

"I have just the thing in my desk." Quincy opened a drawer and took out a pocket pistol with a grip small enough that Oliver could handle it. He tucked it behind his belt to give to Oliver later.

"Well," Quincy said with a grin as he cradled the long-barreled rifle in his left arm, "I'd say we're armed for bear, wouldn't you?"

"Our enemy is more dangerous than a bear," Proud Wolf said. "A bear does not hate."

"But a man does," Quincy said, patting the rifle.

CHAPTER TWENTY-ONE

When the Tlingit warehouse was ready, the hunters began bringing in pelts of all types: seal, otter, beaver, even bear. Each day, a group of women went from the village to work at the warehouse, Nadia among them. They stretched and dried the hides to preserve them, and the men bundled them into heavy bales that could be stacked in the hold of a ship.

All they needed now, Jeff thought, was the ship.

He spent much of his time supervising the activities at the warehouse, although he joined Vassily and some of the other men on a couple of hunting trips. He was inside the cavernous plank building one day when a young Tlingit hurried up to him.

"A ship comes!" the young man announced excitedly. He pointed toward the jutting shoulder of land between the cove and the bay outside. "The man standing watch saw it!"

Jeff felt his pulse race when he heard the

news. He cautioned himself that the ship might not be the *Beaumont*; it could easily be a Russian ship on patrol. Spring was far enough advanced now that most of the ice in the bay had melted.

"Do you know what flag it was flying?" Jeff asked before realizing that the Tlingit probably had no concept of flags.

Indeed, the man only looked confused. Jeff clapped him on the shoulder. "That's all right. I'll go see for myself. Ready the canoes." He broke into a run as he left the warehouse and circled the cove toward the little peninsula.

The few minutes it took to reach a spot where he could see out across the open water seemed longer than that to Jeff. He was breathing hard from the effort of running when he finally pushed through the underbrush and emerged at the edge of the trees. Staying in the shadows of the pines, he peered out to sea.

The ship was south of the point, sailing steadily northward. Jeff recognized the lines of the vessel immediately. It was the *Beaumont*, all right, returning to Sitka as Jeff had ordered the previous autumn. Seldom in his life had he seen a prettier sight than the ship cutting across the waves, its sails billowing in the wind.

He turned and hurried across to the other side of the finger of land, the side that faced the cove. Cupping his hands around his mouth, he shouted, "Launch the canoes!"

The Tlingit were waiting for the order. Three long canoes were drawn up at the water's edge near the warehouse, with men standing at the ready beside them. They pushed off and hopped agilely into the craft, taking up the paddles lying at the bottom. The canoes shot across the cove, one of them veering toward the shore so that Jeff could wade out and climb into it. Vassily was in command of this particular canoe. Jeff grinned at his friend.

The canoes maneuvered easily through the narrow opening of the cove and into the open waters of the bay. The *Beaumont* had drawn even with the cove and was about to pass it. "Tell the men to paddle hard, Vassily," Jeff said. "We have to catch up to the ship before it leaves us behind."

Vassily bellowed orders in the Tlingit tongue, and the men wielding the paddles doubled their efforts. Jeff had a paddle and put his own back into the chase. Slowly the canoes cut down the distance between them and the *Beaumont*. Jeff saw sailors gathering at the stern rail of the ship, watching the native craft that were over-taking them.

Jeff hoped the crew would not think the ship was under attack. The *Beaumont* was armed with rifles and a couple of cannons and could easily blow the canoes out of the water. But he was prepared to forestall such a response. He reached into his coat, pulled out a large piece of white cloth, tied it to his paddle with a rawhide thong, and lifted it over his head, waving it back and forth. He was confident that everyone on the ship knew the meaning of a white flag.

The *Beaumont* heaved to, slowing down to allow the canoes to catch up. Jeff spotted a familiar figure at the rail: Captain Vickery himself, staring in surprise at the hollowed-out logs that made swift, agile watercraft.

Jeff stood up in the lead canoe, balancing himself carefully, and shouted, "Captain! Captain Vickery!" *Won't this shock the old sea dog?* he thought with a grin. As far as Vickery would be able to tell, he was being hailed by name and in English by a native.

Vickery's voice floated back across the water. "Who are you?"

"Jeff Holt!" Jeff bellowed.

The *Beaumont* slowed to a full stop as

Vickery ordered the sails struck. A crewman tossed a rope ladder over the side as the canoes drew up alongside the ship. Jeff grasped the ladder and said to Vassily, "I'll be back as soon as I can."

"We will wait for you, my brother," Vassily promised.

Jeff hauled himself easily up the rope ladder. Captain Vickery and the ship's officers were waiting for him at the top. Strong hands reached out to grasp his arms and help him over the gunwale.

Jeff grinned at the still-startled Vickery and said, "It's good to see you again, Captain."

"And it's a pleasure to see you, Mr. Holt," Vickery replied. He looked out at the Tlingit in their canoes and back at Jeff. "But if you don't mind my asking, sir . . . what are you doing with these savages?"

"Compared to our friends the Russians, the Tlingit aren't savages at all, Captain," Jeff told him. "Let's go to your cabin, and I'll tell you all about it."

"Aye. I'm thinking that it's probably quite a story!"

In the captain's cabin, Vickery broke out a bottle of brandy and splashed some into a couple of glasses. Jeff lifted his glass and inhaled the fragrant bouquet. He closed his eyes for a moment, the better to savor the aroma. Then he tilted the glass to his lips and took a long, slow swallow, enjoying the warmth of the brandy as it slid down his throat.

"Ah," he said. "Don't tell my Tlingit friends, Captain, but there are some things with which their native beer simply cannot compare."

"Sir," Vickery said, "you were going to tell me what's happened since the *Beaumont* sailed last autumn."

"A great deal," Jeff said. "To start with, Count Orlov tried to have me killed."

"What!"

"And he had his own wife murdered," Jeff added grimly.

Vickery lifted his glass and drained the brandy in one swallow, then reached for the bottle again.

Over the next quarter hour or so, Jeff filled the captain in on almost everything that had happened, beginning with his kidnapping by Vassily and the other Tlingit and concluding with the news that on the shore of a nearby cove, nearly invisible from the ship, stood a warehouse full of furs waiting to be taken back to the United States.

"We don't even have to sail on to Sitka.

That's welcome news, sir," Vickery said when Jeff was finished.

"Yes, you do," Jeff said. "Orlov will be expecting you, and he'll wonder what's happened if you don't appear. He'll fabricate a lie about how I was killed in an accident, and I expect you to be properly outraged, Captain."

"That I will be!" Vickery promised.

"Don't carry it too far, though," Jeff cautioned. "With me supposedly dead, you'll have no reason to stay in Sitka. Leave there as soon as you reasonably can. I don't think Orlov will have you followed. He believes I'm dead, so he'd have no reason to. When you get back here, you can sail into the cove — there's barely enough room for the ship — and take on the cargo of furs."

Vickery rubbed his hands together. "It sounds like a good plan, sir. It'll be all I can do, though, not to fire a few volleys into the headquarters of that murdering Russian!"

"If we had half a dozen warships, I'd agree, Captain. But we can't risk it with only the *Beaumont*. We have to defeat the Russians with guile, not force."

"Aye, sir, I expect you're right."

"I'm glad Melissa didn't insist on

coming back with you."

The sudden look of discomfort that came over Vickery's face alerted Jeff that something was wrong. He sat up abruptly and said, "What is it, Captain? Is something wrong? Has something happened to my wife?"

"Well, I . . . I don't rightly know, Mr. Holt," Vickery admitted uneasily.

"You don't know?" Jeff came to his feet. "Didn't you see her before the *Beaumont* sailed from Wilmington?"

"Well, sir . . . Mrs. Holt never went back to Wilmington. She and the boy left the ship when we docked in New Orleans last fall."

"Good Lord." Jeff felt as if he had been punched hard in the chest. He struggled to find his voice again and finally asked, "Why? Why would she stay in New Orleans?"

"I don't believe she intended to stay there, sir. She happened to meet Mr. O'Shay, and the two of them decided to set off up the Mississippi River to St. Louis." Vickery swallowed hard. "I believe she said they were going out to the frontier to start some sort of fur trading business in a place called New Hope."

Jeff's heart hammered in his chest as he

struggled to take in this news. New Hope? Melissa had gone to New Hope? And what was that Vickery had said about O'Shay?

"She was with Terence O'Shay? From Wilmington?"

"One and the same, sir." Vickery pursed his lips. "I've always heard that he was a criminal, but I know that you and he are friends."

"Terence is a good man," Jeff said absently. "He never held certain laws in too high regard, but he's still a good man." He ran his hand through his hair. "I just don't understand it. . . ."

And yet, deep down, he was afraid that he understood all too well. He and Melissa had parted on bad terms, and she had been unwilling to go home to Wilmington without him and answer questions about his absence. What could she have said? *"Jeff stayed in Alaska with his Russian mistress."* Irina Orlov had not been his mistress, of course, but how could Melissa have known for sure?

He rubbed a hand over his face, closing his eyes against the ache that had sprung up in his head. He thought about Melissa and Michael, striking out for the frontier accompanied by Terence O'Shay. Melissa and O'Shay . . . ?

No. Jeff was certain there was no romantic involvement between them. He had never been totally convinced that nothing had happened between Melissa and that Englishman, Rattigan, except a kiss, but he knew that he could trust Terence with his life — and his wife. Still, there were so many other dangers that would face them between New Orleans and the mountains.

"Thank you for telling me, Captain," he said into the awkward silence that had fallen. "Has anyone heard from Mrs. Holt since she left New Orleans? Her mother, perhaps?"

Vickery shook his head. "Mrs. Merrivale had not heard anything when we sailed, sir. I don't know what's happened since then."

"No, of course not." Jeff squared his shoulders. There was nothing he could do about Melissa now. He said, "We'll carry on with the plan. You should be back here from Sitka in a few days. I'll have men watching for you, and when you arrive I'll send out a canoe to guide you into the cove."

"Aye, sir. Is there anything I can do for you before we sail again?"

Jeff shook his head. "No. Just . . . carry on, Captain."

That was all any of them could do, Jeff thought. Carry on.

Melissa had not realized how much she missed civilization until she sat and listened to John Markham describe life in Washington City. The young man was a colorful storyteller, and as he told of the balls and the new fashions and the government intrigues and the gossip, Melissa felt a pang of longing. She was growing to love the frontier, but sooner or later she would have to go home.

Sooner or later she would have to deal with the problems between her and Jeff.

For now, however, it felt wonderful having family around her again. Clay and Shining Moon were obviously glad to be in New Hope, although Shining Moon had been saddened to learn of her father's death. She and Clay had visited the Sioux village and spoken to Falling Sky, the new chief. When they returned, Melissa sensed that Clay was not particularly pleased with the way the visit had gone.

That evening after supper, as they sat in the living quarters behind the trading post, Melissa asked, "What's wrong, Clay? Are the Sioux going to cause trouble over our being here?"

"I don't know," Clay said gloomily. "Falling Sky's not as hotheaded as some of the younger men, but he's not the same kind of man Bear Tooth was, either. The Sioux are unhappy about the fact that there are so many trappers in the area now."

Markham said, "But surely they can't be worried about the beaver. You told me there were still plenty of beaver for everyone, white and Indian alike."

"There are," Clay said. "But this was the land of the Sioux before the whites came, and I reckon they're having second thoughts about sharing it."

Shining Moon spoke up. "My people want to live their lives the way they see fit. They are afraid the white men will change everything."

"Well, we might try to bring a little civilization out here, if that's what you mean," Markham said.

"The Sioux know nothing of what your people call civilization. All they know is that they have everything they need for the life they lead. Wakan-Tanka provides for them."

"But that's just —"

"That's what they believe," Clay said, interrupting Markham, "and they have every right to feel that way."

"Of course. But perhaps they shouldn't be so concerned about what we're doing. I'd say they face a greater threat in the long run from the French."

"The French?" Melissa repeated. "What do you mean by that, Mr. Markham?"

Markham glanced at Clay, who inclined his head to indicate that Markham should continue, now that he had brought up the subject.

"I mean, Mrs. Holt, that if a certain group of French aristocrats have their way, the western half of the continent will soon belong to France again. They intend to establish a new empire here."

Melissa stared at him, barely able to comprehend what he was saying. A French empire in North America? That was absurd. "But if that's true, why did France sell the Louisiana Territory to the United States?" she asked.

"That was Napoleon Bonaparte's idea," Markham said. "He needed the money to finance his wars against everyone else in Europe. But not everyone agreed with him, and a man named Comte Jacques de La Carde has started a movement to reclaim the western half of the continent for France."

"For himself, you mean," Clay put in. "If La Carde succeeds, Bonaparte won't be the emperor here. La Carde will."

Markham nodded. "Yes, you're right, I suspect. La Carde must be a power-hungry madman to have dreamt up such a grandiose scheme."

"Too big for his britches, you mean."

"Exactly," Markham said with a smile.

"I don't understand how this La Carde can hope to take over any American territory," Melissa said.

"By stealth, at least at first," Markham replied. He explained the land grab scheme that had involved Gideon Maxwell and Senator Ralston. "We anticipate that La Carde will fight for his cause on two fronts: in the courts and by trying to physically control the frontier."

"How can he do that without an army?"

"There's one for the taking already out here," Clay said. "If La Carde were to promise someone like Falling Sky that the Sioux would be left alone, he'd listen."

"The Indians," Melissa said softly. "Of course. If they were united —"

"The tribal rivalries are old and strong," Shining Moon interrupted. "It would not be easy to convince the different bands to fight together. But it could be done, if this man La Carde promised them enough."

"Where is La Carde now?" Melissa asked. Then, before any of the others could reply, the answer came to her. "He's already out here, isn't he? That's why you and Mr. Markham are here, isn't it, Clay? You're on La Carde's trail."

"It's *Lieutenant* Markham, actually," the young officer said. "On detached duty from the army for this special assignment. But yes, Mrs. Holt. We're after La Carde."

"As best we can tell, his party was the first one to leave St. Louis and head up the river," Clay said. "They were ahead of you and Terence."

Melissa shook her head. "We saw no sign of them on our way here."

"That's what we've found out. They must have split off from the river and taken another route. There are other trails through the mountains."

Shining Moon said, "We have asked Falling Sky to tell us if any of my people hear something of these Frenchmen."

Clay leaned forward and clasped his hands together between his knees. "You can help out, too, Melissa," he said. "You'll be talking to trappers who've explored all over these mountains. If you could ask them if they've seen La Carde's bunch, or heard about any foreigners traveling through the mountains . . ."

"Of course I'd be glad to help. This whole thing is amazing" — Melissa smiled wryly — "and rather hard to believe. But I know you're telling the truth, Clay, and if La Carde were to succeed . . ."

"It would cripple the country to have a French empire out here," Clay said grimly. "I reckon there's a good chance that sooner or later we'd have to go to war against them. And who knows what could happen then?"

"La Carde must be stopped. Is it all right if I tell Terence about this?"

Clay and Markham exchanged a glance. Then Clay nodded. "Jeff always trusted O'Shay. I reckon he'd want us to trust him now. But don't tell anyone else. We don't want La Carde to get wind of the fact that somebody's on his trail." He paused. "Jeff was with us when we started this job. I wish he could be with us at the end of it."

Melissa kept her face carefully expressionless. She wished Jeff was here, too, but for different reasons.

She wished she could know whether or not she would ever have a real marriage again.

★ ★ ★

Jeff was lying on his side when he came awake, buried under a pile of warm robes. It was another kind of warmth that had roused him from slumber. Nadia was cuddled against him from behind, her ample breasts flattened against his back. Her hand slid lightly over his skin, exploring his flank and then his hip before moving around to caress him. Jeff felt himself responding to her touch. She grasped him tightly. Her lips played along his shoulder for a moment; then her mouth opened and he felt the playful nip of her teeth.

Jeff groaned deep his throat. He rolled over and put his arms around her, pulling her nude form against his. His mouth found hers in a long, hungry kiss. He was wide awake now, overcome by passion and need.

They had made love earlier, and Jeff had sensed a certain desperation in the way Nadia had clutched him and cried out. He had been swept up in the sensation then, as he was now. He moved over her welcoming body as her arms twined around his neck and held him to her.

Once again her lovemaking had a frantic quality to it. Jeff tried to pace himself but realized that was not what Nadia wanted.

In a matter of moments she cried out hoarsely, and her body trembled under him. Jeff gasped as he, too, spent himself.

His head dropped onto Nadia's bare shoulder. He pillowed it there while she stroked his hair and murmured endearments into his ear. When he finally rolled off, she made a small sound of loss and disappointment.

Jeff waited a moment longer to catch his breath and allow his racing pulse to slow, then lifted himself on an elbow so that he could look at her. The faint light from the embers cast a rosy glow over her face. She was crying.

"Nadia, what is it?" he asked. "What's wrong?"

For a long moment she did not reply. Then she said in a hushed voice, "The ship has come."

"The ship? What ship?" Suddenly he understood. "You mean the *Beaumont*?"

"The ship from your home," Nadia said. "The ship that will carry you away from me."

Vassily must have told her about the *Beaumont*, Jeff realized, because he had not mentioned anything about it yet. He had not decided what he was going to do. The easiest choice, of course, would be to board the ship when it returned from Sitka to take on the load of furs. Then he could sail back to Wilmington if he chose, or he could do as Melissa had done and disembark in New Orleans to make the journey up the Mississippi.

Or he could stay right here, he realized. *That* might well be the most logical course of action to follow.

More ships would come, and someone would have to be in charge of the fur trading operation in Alaska. The whole arrangement had been his idea, and who better to manage it than the man who had thought of it?

Nadia, however, had assumed that he was leaving, that the *Beaumont* would take him away. That explained why she had made love to him with such urgency. He might soon be gone forever.

There was another question to be considered, Jeff realized. Would Vassily *allow* him to leave? He had survived Orlov's attempt to have him killed only because Vassily wanted someone other than Yuri to marry his sister. And the Tlingit had permitted him to live in the village and now considered him one of them. He never would have survived the winter without them. So if Vassily insisted that he stay here, "married" to Nadia, would Jeff really have any choice? The Tlingit could keep him here as a prisoner if they wanted to.

Nadia was still crying. She rolled over, turning her face away from him. Jeff put a hand on her bare shoulder. He had never wanted to hurt this young woman; he supposed he even loved her, in a way. But now, as he listened to her weeping, a stifling wave of guilt washed over him. He loved Melissa. He wanted to be with her, wanted to be with his own people. He should have told that to Vassily at the very first. He'd had no right to hurt Nadia this way.

Jeff stood up, wrapping a fur robe tightly around himself, and stepped out of the hut. The night was cold, as always. His breath fogged and hung in the air. He tilted his head back and looked up at the glittering stars and the brilliant spectacle of the northern lights. There was much he would miss about this strange and wonderful land.

But he had to go home. He knew that now. He bitterly regretted the pain his leaving would cause, but there was no other way.

After standing there for a long moment, he turned and went back into the hut. Nadia had to be told that she had guessed correctly: Jeff was leaving.

But she had fallen asleep, and he could not bring himself to wake her with the bad news. He lay beside her and stared up into the darkness for a long, long time before slumber finally claimed him.

CHAPTER TWENTY-TWO

Contrary to Proud Wolf's expectations, the journey from Virginia to Massachusetts passed with no trouble. They saw no sign of Will Brackett and Frank Kirkland, and although everyone in the little group was on the lookout for an ambush, no one attempted to stop them.

One of Quincy's servants, a lanky, jovial black man named Henry, expertly handled the team of horses that pulled the well-appointed coach in which Audrey and Oliver rode. For most of the trip Proud Wolf and Quincy jogged alongside the coach on horseback; occasionally they rode inside to rest their mounts. The turnpike leading north from Richmond was broad and well kept, allowing the travelers to make good time. The only thing that slowed them down was the spring rains that turned the road slick and muddy.

Quincy Reed was an entertaining companion. He reminded Proud Wolf of Sioux warriors, who were fond of sitting around the fire at night and telling tales of their exploits. Quincy could easily be prompted to speak of his adventures in the early days of the War of Independence.

"I was one of a group known as the Sons of Liberty," he said one evening as he sat by the campfire, smoking a pipe. "We dressed as Indians one night and dumped a shipload of British tea into Boston Harbor. People started calling what we had done the Boston Tea Party, but I assure you, we were deadly serious. We wanted our freedom from the British."

"Your brother Daniel," Proud Wolf asked, "was he one of these Sons of Liberty?"

Quincy laughed. "No, Daniel loved freedom as much as any of us, but at first he thought our methods were a bit . . . rash, shall we say? He came to agree, however, that action had to be taken. He and our cousin Elliot were two of the first agents in the intelligence network set up by George Washington."

Proud Wolf cocked his head. "I do not know what that means."

"They were spies, secret operatives."

"Scouts, you mean."

"Well, I suppose you could call them scouts. War is not as straightforward as it once was. Part of the price of living in the modern world, I suppose."

From the other side of the fire, Audrey said, "It sounds as if you were involved in just about everything important that happened in the war."

Quincy laughed heartily. "Between Daniel and Elliot and me, I'd say we were. We were all on hand for the signing of the Declaration of Independence in Philadelphia, too."

"I wish I could have been there," Oliver said. "It must have been exciting, being a part of history like that."

Quincy puffed on his pipe. "We didn't think of it as history at the time. We were simply trying to lead our lives the best way we could. Something doesn't become history until you look back on it. I assure you, while we were living through it, we were more worried about having a roof over our heads and enough food in our bellies . . . and about loving and being loved by those we cared about."

Proud Wolf and Audrey exchanged a glance, and then Audrey looked down into the fire. Proud Wolf thought he understood what Quincy was talking about. He and Audrey loved each other, but would that love last? He had discovered that he could not go on living in the East. Was what she felt for him strong enough that she would choose to go with him when he returned to his homeland?

That question could not be answered until the time came, Proud Wolf realized. For now he and Audrey were together, and that would have to be enough.

The turnpike ran from Richmond to Philadelphia, and from there another road led northeast toward Boston. During the early part of their flight from Massachusetts, Proud Wolf and Audrey had kept to back roads and sometimes cut across country, so it had taken them many days to cover a relatively short distance. After they joined the acting troupe, their route remained rather haphazard, as Ulysses Dowd stopped in every small settlement in the region, even if it meant backtracking now and then. The return trip went much more quickly, and in only nine days the coach was rolling over the narrow neck of land that led to the Shawmut Peninsula, on which Boston was located. Proud Wolf could see the low, rounded humps of Bunker Hill and Breed's Hill across the Charles River to the north. Beyond them lay Cambridge, home to Harvard University and the Stoddard

Academy for Young Men.

Henry obviously had made this trip before, because without waiting for directions he drove straight to an impressive mansion of brown brick on Beacon Hill. Boston Common was not too far away, and Proud Wolf remembered how he had been lured there and attacked by Brackett's cronies. He had never dreamed at the time that a potential source of help was so close by.

Proud Wolf and Quincy dismounted, and Proud Wolf helped Audrey from the coach while Quincy tied the saddle horses behind it. "Take the coach and team around back to the coach house," Quincy told Henry.

Oliver hopped down from the coach and looked around at the stately homes lining the cobblestone street. "This is a fine neighborhood, Quincy," he said. "I feel a bit out of place, lowly actor that I am."

Quincy laughed and clapped Oliver on the shoulder. "The first time I came here," he said, "I was nothing but a farm boy from the backwoods of Virginia. We came to visit our cousins the Markhams, who lived down the street there."

"They are no longer here?" Proud Wolf asked.

Quincy shook his head. "No, Elliot lives in New York now. His parents, Benjamin and Polly, both passed on years ago." He stepped up to the door of the mansion and rapped sharply with a brass lion's-head knocker. "It's late enough in the day that perhaps Daniel is already home from his law office."

A moment later a stout, white-haired woman in the black dress and starched white apron of a servant opened the door. Her eyes widened in surprise, and she exclaimed, "Mr. Quincy! Saints above, what are you doing here?"

"Can't a man come to see his favorite girl, Mrs. Gallagher?" Quincy asked with a twinkle in his eye. He swept the elderly woman into an embrace, which elicited a shriek of laughter.

A handsome, gray-haired woman appeared in the doorway and smiled tolerantly. "Quincy Reed," she said, "put my maid down this instant — and come give your sister-in-law a hug."

"Roxanne!" Quincy said as he set the flustered Mrs. Gallagher back on her feet. "Still beautiful, as always." He hugged the woman, whose gray hair still had a few strands of red in it. Then he turned to his companions. "Allow me to present some new friends. This is Proud Wolf, Mr. Oliver Johnson, and Miss Audrey Stoddard."

Roxanne's eyebrows went up. "Stoddard?" she said as she smiled at Audrey. "I was once married briefly to an Englishman named Bramwell Stoddard. A relative of yours, perhaps, Miss Stoddard?"

"I don't believe so," Audrey replied. "My family has been in America for several generations."

"A coincidence, then." Roxanne took Audrey's hand for a second. "I'm very pleased to make your acquaintance. Any friends of Quincy's are more than welcome here." She turned to Oliver and said, "Mr. Johnson."

Oliver had already swept his hat off and was staring up at this patrician beauty. "Madam," he said. "It's an honor."

Roxanne turned to Proud Wolf. If she was startled by the unexpected sight of a Teton Sioux warrior on her doorstep, along with a man only three feet tall, she gave no sign of it. "Welcome to my home," she said.

"Thank you," he replied gravely. "As Oliver says, it is an honor."

"Well, come along inside, all of you," Roxanne said with a smile and an easy familiarity that suggested she had not always been the lady of a very impressive manor. "Quincy, you should have written to let us know that you were coming."

"I took my leave of Virginia rather suddenly," Quincy said. "I could have posted a letter, I suppose, but we might have arrived first."

Roxanne arched an eyebrow at him as she led them through an elegantly furnished foyer. "You're not in some sort of trouble again, are you?"

"Why, Roxanne, you make me sound like a ne'er-do-well," Quincy protested.

"I only know that inside that staid, sober former senator lives the same reckless young man you've always been."

Quincy threw back his head and laughed. "You know me too well."

Roxanne took them into a parlor. Proud Wolf and Audrey sat down on a divan with elaborately wrought, fragile-looking legs. Proud Wolf was a bit uncomfortable, worrying that the furniture would collapse under them, but it seemed sturdy enough. Quincy and Roxanne took armchairs on either side of the divan, and Oliver settled himself on a footstool near the massive fireplace. "This is fine for me," he assured Roxanne when she offered to find him a smaller chair.

"What brings you to Boston?" Roxanne asked when they were all settled.

"We need to consult with Daniel on a legal matter," Quincy said, growing serious. "Will he be home soon?"

"He should be," Roxanne replied. "He goes into the office less these days than he used to, but he was busy this afternoon with his clerk drawing up some papers for a client. You'll be staying with us while you're here, won't you?"

"If it won't be too much of an imposition."

"It's no imposition at all," Roxanne said. "With the children grown and gone off to raise families of their own, sometimes this old house seems much too large for just Daniel and me. I'm always glad to have visitors."

The front door opened and steps sounded in the foyer. A man appeared in the doorway of the parlor, taking off a beaver hat and shrugging out of a top-coat. He stopped short when he caught sight of the visitors. He was shorter, heavier, and older than Quincy, but there was a definite resemblance. "Quincy!" he exclaimed.

Mrs. Gallagher appeared behind the

newcomer, and he quickly handed her the hat and coat. Then he strode forward. Quincy got to his feet and moved to meet him. They embraced, slapping each other on the back in the way of warriors, Proud Wolf noted. In their earlier days, Proud Wolf thought, these men must indeed have been warriors.

When the brothers had done with their greetings, Quincy turned to the others and said, "Daniel, these are some friends of mine: Proud Wolf, Oliver Johnson, and Miss Audrey Stoddard."

"Stoddard?" Daniel Reed said, echoing his wife's earlier reaction.

"No relation to Bramwell, dear," Roxanne murmured.

Daniel took Audrey's hand and held it between both his own. "I'm very pleased to meet you, my dear," he said. Then he turned and shook hands with Oliver. "Mr. Johnson, welcome to my home."

"Thank you, sir. You have a lovely home."

Daniel turned to Proud Wolf, showing the same aplomb as his wife. "Welcome," he said as he exchanged a firm handshake with Proud Wolf.

"I am honored to be here," Proud Wolf said.

"Blast it, you two," Quincy drawled. "I come calling with a Sioux warrior and a little fellow and a beautiful young woman, and neither of you asks what in blazes is going on!"

"We're accustomed to your habit of associating yourself with colorful individuals and lost causes, Quincy," Daniel said.

"This is *not* a lost cause."

Daniel settled himself in another armchair and motioned for the rest of them to sit. "We have some time before dinner. Tell me about it."

"Proud Wolf and Miss Stoddard are having some legal problems with a man named William Brackett."

Daniel frowned. "Arthur Brackett's son? I know the boy. Always struck me as rather a bad sort, but his father's very wealthy. Perhaps it's *because* his father is very wealthy. Arthur's bought him out of more than one scrape, I believe. Last I heard, the boy had been sent off to school."

"The Stoddard Academy for Young Men," Audrey said. "My father is the headmaster there."

"Yes, of course. I recognize the name now. What sort of trouble has young Brackett caused now?"

Quincy and Proud Wolf exchanged a

look, and Quincy lifted a hand. "Go ahead. Tell him."

"Will Brackett attacked Audrey," Proud Wolf said, "and tried to have me killed. Now he wants to have me arrested and charged with attempted murder."

"Brackett has a warrant sworn out on Proud Wolf," Quincy put in.

Daniel's eyes had narrowed as he listened to the accusations against Brackett. A smile tugged at his lips. "Well, then," he said, "it appears that we have our work cut out for us, don't we?"

Proud Wolf had a feeling that Quincy was not the only Reed brother with a fondness for lost causes.

The storms in the southern Atlantic were fierce and unrelenting, and for several days after the *Lydia Marie* rounded Cape Horn, the crewmen were on deck day and night battling the elements. They took turns taking quick catnaps. At the height of one particularly violent storm India decided it was muscle power and sheer will, not rope and canvas and wood, that was holding the ship together.

As they sailed northward the storms eased, and India found that she almost missed them. Without the distraction of turbulent weather she felt Ned's loss keenly, like a knife twisting in her insides.

During the worst of the storms, Captain Canfield had been forced to stay below and rest so that his wounded leg could heal. Once the weather and the sea had calmed, he came up on deck and used a crutch to get around. The *Lydia Marie* was sailing off the coast of Argentina one day when Canfield found India on the bridge, relieving the regular helmsman.

"Unless we run into another British warship, we're safe," Canfield said with satisfaction. "Another month and we'll be home."

"A great deal can happen in a month," India pointed out.

"Indeed it can." The captain lowered his voice. "Have you heard any more mutinous rumblings?"

India shook her head. "I'm still convinced that Yancy is the ringleader, if indeed there really is a group of mutineers. But perhaps they've decided that it wouldn't be worth it to try to take over the ship."

"Not worth it?" Canfield snorted in disbelief. "The hold is full of silks and spices from China. That cargo would be worth a fortune in England."

"I'll keep my eyes peeled, sir," she promised. "I'll let you know at the first sign of trouble."

"Do that, St. Clair. Lives may depend on your alertness."

Later India would wish that Captain Canfield had not put it so bluntly, but by then it was too late to do anything about it.

She did not think that trouble would come so soon after that afternoon's conversation, but that evening, as darkness settled over the sea, India heard a commotion as she was dozing in her bunk. She was so tired that for a moment she was tempted to roll over with her face to the bulkhead, pull the blanket over her head, and shut out the rest of the world. But the voices were loud and angry. With a sigh, she sat up and looked around the fo'c'sle for the source of the argument.

Several men were standing at the far end of the big cabin, clustered near the door. One of them suddenly lunged toward the door, as if trying to get away from the others, but another man grabbed his arm to stop him. The first man let out a shout of alarm that was suddenly cut off as another of the group stepped up close to him. This man's arm moved swiftly, and

501

when he stepped back a moment later, India saw that he had left a knife buried in the first man's belly. His eyes bulged in pain and horror as he pawed feebly at the handle of the knife. His assailant clapped a hand over his mouth to stifle any further outcry. The stabbed man slowly sank toward the deck, a widening circle of blood staining his tunic around the blade.

Shocked and for a moment unable to believe she had just witnessed a murder, India hesitated. Then she came up off her bunk and quickly reached back for the pistol she had tucked away under her blanket.

A step sounded beside her before she found the pistol. A ring of cold metal was pressed against her temple as a familiar Cockney voice rasped, "Don't do it, St. Clair. I'd 'ate to 'ave to blow yer bloody brains out."

India stiffened. "Yancy. What's going on here?"

"I think ye know good an' well what's going on," Yancy replied. "Move away from that bunk." He kept the pistol pressed to India's head as she straightened and took a step back.

The man who had been stabbed was on his knees now. The owner of the knife jerked the blade free, and the wounded man pitched forward on his face. Blood pooled on the deck beneath him.

The scuffle had attracted attention from others besides India. All around the room, sailors were sitting up in their bunks, staring at the man dying — or already dead — on the floor. Yancy lifted his voice and called, "If any of ye want the same treatment, speak up now!"

A stunned silence settled over the fo'c'sle. Yancy waited a moment, then nodded. "Good," he went on. "Glad to see ye've all got good sense." He turned back to India. "Now —"

"Put that gun down, you fool," she snapped. "You talk about good sense, and yet you hold a pistol to my head."

"That's because I don't trust you, lad. Ye were friends with Ned 'olt before 'e was lost."

"I was Holt's friend at one time. Not lately, though — or haven't you been paying attention?" All she could do, India knew, was continue the lie that she and Ned had had a falling-out. If she could convince Yancy that she was no threat to his plans, she might have a chance to turn the tables on him.

" 'Ow big a bloody fool do you think I

am?" he asked. "I know ye were just trying to get in good with us, so's you could spy on us for 'olt and the captain." Yancy's voice shook, and India could feel the barrel of the pistol quiver against her temple. "I should put a ball through yer brain right now, that's what I should do."

For a moment India froze, certain he was going to pull the trigger. Then, abruptly, he seemed to get control of himself. He relaxed slightly and said, "But ye might come in 'andy if I keeps you alive. Just don't try anything dicey now, or I'll kill ye. An' that's a promise."

"A promise from a mutineer. I wonder what that's worth."

A snaggletoothed grin split Yancy's face. "I reckon ye'll find out, won't ye? Come on, lad."

He herded India at gunpoint over to the group of men near the door. India was careful not to step in the spreading puddle of blood.

Yancy spat on the corpse. "Too damned 'onest for 'is own good. 'E got wind of what we been planning and decided to go to the captain with it. Couldn't let 'im do that, now, could we?"

"What about it, Yancy?" Siros asked. "Are we ready to strike?"

Yancy rubbed his grizzled jaw. "I would've waited a mite longer if I'd 'ad me druthers, but now's as good a time as any, I suppose." He turned and scrutinized the other men in the room. "Any lad who wants to be rich, come with us! The rest of ye best stay down 'ere out of the way, 'less ye want to wind up resting in Davy Jones's locker."

Several men stood up from their bunks, and one of them asked, "You're taking the ship?"

"Aye. We're tired of taking orders. A ship belongs to the swabs what sail 'er. An' that goes for the cargo, too!"

"We're with you, Yancy," another man said. He raised a clenched fist. "It's about time somebody taught those damned officers a lesson." His fellows shouted their agreement.

India felt sick inside. These men could talk themselves into feeling oppressed if they wanted, but nothing more than sheer greed was at the heart of this mutiny. Sailors on ships of the March Line were well treated and well paid, with no valid reason to mutiny except the wealth a stolen cargo would bring them.

"We'll sail 'er to England," Yancy went on. "I know plenty of blokes there who'll pay a good price for those spices and silks, a mighty good price." He waved with the pistol. "Come on, lads!"

Caught in the middle of the group, India had no chance to break away and sound a warning. Even though Yancy was no longer holding the gun to her head and watching her like a hawk, she knew that if she tried anything one of the others would cut her down without compunction. Many of the men were holding knives now, and a couple besides Yancy had pistols.

India was prodded out the door and up a companionway ladder that led to the deck. She emerged into a moonlit night with the crowd of mutineers right behind her. It must have looked as if she were leading the mob, she thought.

Clearly it looked like that to the men standing watch on the bridge, too. They turned at the sound of the approaching group, and one of them shouted, "Here now! Who's that? What do you want?"

"This bloody ship!" India heard Yancy growl, and suddenly a pistol blasted beside her head. The noise was loud, so deafening that she staggered a little and clapped a hand to her ear. Tears sprang into her eyes. Through them she saw the officer who had challenged the mutineers collapse loose-

506

limbed to the deck.

Someone gave her a hard shove in the middle of the back, sending her sprawling headlong on the deck. As the other mutineers gave a full-throated shout and swarmed up the ladder onto the bridge, Yancy knelt beside her and dug the barrel of his pistol into the back of her neck.

"The lads'll do the rest of the dirty work," he said.

India thought frantically, trying to come up with a way out of this predicament, a way to stop the mutineers before they took over the ship. Yancy had fired the shot that had downed the officer on the bridge, she believed, but she could not be sure. Even if he had, he might have another pistol tucked away. She could not be certain that the gun he was holding against the back of her neck was empty.

She heard a couple of screams that were abruptly choked off and was almost glad that she could not see what was happening on the bridge. Looming above her, Yancy chuckled. "They'll make short work of those scuts, ye can be sure of that."

"Those aren't the only officers on board," India grated through clenched teeth.

"No, but we're ready for the others, we are."

For a long, horrible time — probably no more than five or ten minutes, but it seemed much longer — India lay on the deck with Yancy kneeling atop her, his bony knee pressed into the small of her back, the muzzle of his pistol gouging her neck. Gunshots and yells and angry curses and screams filled the air around them, coming from all over the ship. India closed her eyes and wished she could shut her ears as easily. This bloodshed was exactly what she had hoped to prevent.

But the mutineers had taken her by surprise. Being forced to move up their plans had actually worked to their advantage, because India had had no chance to warn anyone of what was about to happen.

First the loss of Ned, now this atrocity, she thought bitterly. She had nothing left to live for. Yancy might as well go ahead and kill her.

That despairing thought filled her head for a moment before anger welled up and replaced it. She had vowed that she would avenge Ned's death, no matter what it took; she had promised herself that she would make the British pay. The only way she could do that was by staying alive. By any means necessary.

"Yancy," she grated.

"What is it?"

"Think what you will, but I've no love for anyone on this ship. Let me up and I'll join you. I swear it."

"And I'm supposed to believe ye, just like that?"

"You were right. Ned Holt was my friend. But he's gone now. He was the only one on board to whom I owed any allegiance."

"I'd like to believe ye, lad, I really would. You're one of the best sailors I've ever known."

"Then let me up," India urged. "Give me a chance, damn it!"

"Maybe, maybe . . ." He took the gun from India's neck. "I want ye on your feet anyway. Someone 'ere I want ye to see."

She noticed now that the sounds of fighting had faded. The mutineers' takeover of the ship must be complete. Yancy grasped the collar of her shirt and hauled sharply upward. She stumbled to her feet as she heard the sound of ripping cloth.

That worried her, but she had no opportunity to check for damage to her clothing. Yancy grabbed her shoulder and roughly jerked her around. By the garish light of torches she saw a couple of men fling Captain Canfield to the deck in front of her. The captain was wearing only his uniform trousers and a bloodstained shirt. He lifted his head to look up at India. He had a long gash down the side of his face and a large swollen knot on his forehead where someone had clubbed him.

" 'Ere's the 'igh and mighty captain now," Yancy gloated. "Not so quick to spout orders now, are ye, Captain Canfield?"

"Go to hell," Canfield said through gritted teeth.

"Ye'll be there afore me." Yancy stepped up between Canfield and India and pointed his pistol down at the captain's head. Then he eased up on the trigger and turned to look at India. "So ye want to be one of us," he said musingly. "There's only one way I'll believe ye, lad." He held out the pistol to her. "Take this and kill the Captain 'ere. 'E's the only officer left alive. Once 'e's dead, the ship's ours, good an' proper."

India couldn't help but hesitate, even knowing that Yancy was watching her closely. But then she forced her muscles to work, willed herself to reach out and take the pistol from him. Canfield stared up at her, his eyes already dull and dead. No matter what she did, he had only moments to live and he knew it. If India didn't kill him, one of the mutineers would.

So why couldn't she do it? she asked herself. That act would save her life and allow her the chance to take her vengeance on the British for Ned's death. It would be the simplest thing in the world to point the pistol at Canfield's head and press the trigger.

She took a deep breath.

"Good Lord!" yelled one of the mutineers pressing up closely behind Canfield. "Look at St. Clair! He's a *woman!*"

In horror, India looked down where the man was pointing. The tunic Yancy had ripped pulling her to her feet gaped open in front, and her right breast was clearly revealed in the gap. She had always been slender and not particularly well endowed, so wearing blousy clothes had been sufficient to conceal her shape, but it was obvious now that the small, pear-shaped mound of flesh showing through the torn tunic could not have belonged to a man.

India took an involuntary step backward as Yancy gazed at her in astonishment. Her last hope of pretending to join the mutineers was gone. No matter what she did now, she would be raped for hours on end, probably by every man on board, and then her throat would likely be slit and her body tossed overboard.

While the men were still mesmerized by the sight of a female breast, she jerked the pistol up in a flash and fired at Yancy. At least *he* would be denied the satisfaction of abusing her.

The flintlock pistol clicked uselessly. As India had suspected earlier, it was empty.

Suddenly Captain Canfield found the strength to surge up off the deck. "Run!" he shouted to her. He lunged at Yancy and wrapped his hands around the murderous little Cockney's neck, then flung him into the path of the madly charging mutineers.

India whirled, operating entirely on instinct now. She dashed toward the nearest railing as, behind her, the howling mob bore Captain Canfield back to the deck and hacked him to pieces with their knives. She sprang to the top of the railing. Someone fired a pistol. The ball whipped past her ear as she launched herself out and away from the ship in a long, arching dive.

She struck the black water and sliced cleanly into it, vanishing into the depths.

CHAPTER TWENTY-THREE

There was nothing more glorious than a spring morning in the high country, Clay Holt had thought many times in his life, and the feeling was confirmed once again as he stood on a shoulder of land that jutted out from the side of a mountain. Below him the foothills fell away sharply, all the way to the valley in which New Hope and the Sioux village lay.

Clay rested the butt of his flintlock on the ground and leaned on the long barrel as he gazed into the distance. This was the country that spoke to him, that claimed him as its own. He had climbed up here to take a look around and perhaps do a little hunting, but he realized now that his true motivation had been simply to feel the peace that the mountains gave him. This beautiful, sprawling country calmed the restlessness that had dogged him all his life.

He was home, and he fervently hoped he would never have to leave again.

He heard a puffing sound behind him as Markham struggled up the last few yards of the slope. "My, the air is certainly . . . thinner up here . . . isn't it?" he wheezed as he came up alongside Clay.

"I never really noticed," Clay said. "To me, it always seems the air is heavier when I'm down on the flat land."

"Well, I must admit, the view is gorgeous."

With a grin, Clay surveyed the young officer. He was wearing buckskins and moccasins now, and a coonskin cap like Clay's. He carried a flintlock rifle and had tucked a tomahawk behind his belt. Markham's beard had grown out over the past weeks, and Clay had to admit that he looked like a mountain man. Almost.

"Might be hope for you yet, Lieutenant," Clay said. "Stay out here a while, and you won't ever want to go back east."

"I doubt that very seriously," Markham said. "What I'd give right now to be in a clean, freshly pressed uniform, dancing in a Washington ballroom with a beautiful young woman."

Clay laughed. "I reckon you'll get over that."

"Who's that?" Markham suddenly asked, pointing down the winding trail they had followed up the mountain.

Chagrined that Markham had spotted someone following them before he had, Clay studied the distant figure's awkward gait. "Looks like Aaron. Let's go down and meet him."

Trotting down the trail, Clay raised a hand in greeting, and Aaron stopped to wait for them.

"Looking for us?" Clay called when Aaron was in earshot.

Aaron nodded and waved them on. "Shining Moon sent me!" he shouted back.

Clay shot a glance at Markham and broke into a run. Still weary from the climb, Markham followed at a slower pace.

"What is it?" Clay asked as he came up to Aaron. "Is something wrong?"

Aaron shook his head. "Shining Moon went over to the Sioux village this morning. When she came back, she said she had some news of La Carde."

Clay stiffened. "Did she tell you what it was?" he asked.

"No. Just asked me to fetch you as fast as I could. She would've come herself, but she said she had to talk to Melissa."

Clay wondered briefly what Shining Moon would have to discuss with Melissa, but he had no time to ponder the matter. He had to talk to her as soon as possible.

Clay's impatience made the trek back to New Hope seem to take longer this time. When they reached the settlement, he strode to the trading post. Shining Moon was there with Melissa and Terence O'Shay.

"What have you heard about La Carde?" Clay asked without preamble.

"Two warriors from a band of Sioux that lives southwest of here came to our village to trade," Shining Moon said. "They told of a group of white men they saw passing near the place you call Colter's Hell."

Clay was well acquainted with the strange place named after his old friend, John Colter. He had been there several times during his journeys through the mountains.

"How many men?" he asked.

"Twenty. They were going west."

It had to be La Carde's bunch, Clay thought excitedly. None of the fur companies had any organized expeditions in the area, and free trappers wouldn't have traveled in a group that large. But a party of renegade French nobles and their American henchmen would. It *had* to be La Carde.

"Do you think it's him?" Markham asked.

"It couldn't be anyone else," Clay answered curtly. "Let's get ready to travel." He caught Shining Moon's eye then and knew he could no longer postpone the discussion he needed to have with her. "I want you to stay here."

"What?" Shining Moon said. Her normally impassive face rarely registered emotion, but Clay could see surprise in her eyes.

"I want you and Matthew to stay here," he said. "Markham and I will have to move fast to catch up to La Carde."

"I have never slowed you down," Shining Moon said stiffly.

"No, but the boy might. And I won't leave him here alone."

Now that he had put it into words, Clay realized that was the primary reason he wanted to leave Shining Moon in New Hope. He couldn't afford to be saddled any longer with a child, not while he was trying to track down a man who represented a threat to the entire nation. Clay remembered all too well the havoc Matthew had wreaked in Ohio while he and Shining Moon were living at the Holt family farm. He couldn't very well unload such a dangerous burden on Melissa and O'Shay. Shining Moon at least knew to watch her back anytime Matthew was around. The boy had behaved fairly well recently, but Clay still didn't trust him.

"You leave me behind again . . . because of your mission."

Shining Moon's words were spoken quietly and calmly, but Clay felt them like the lash of a whip. "I have to do what I think is best," he said. He glanced at Melissa and O'Shay. Both of them looked uncomfortable.

After a moment Melissa said, "Shining Moon, I'd be thrilled to have you stay here with us. You'll be near your people, and if there are any problems between the settlers and the Sioux, perhaps you'll be able to smooth them out."

That was yet another good reason for Shining Moon to stay behind, Clay thought. But whether or not she would agree he could not guess.

Shining Moon looked Clay full in the face. "I will stay," she said, but Clay caught a subtle undertone of resentment.

He reached out and took her hand, squeezing it briefly. "Thank you," he whispered. He would try later to do a better job of telling her how much he appreciated what she was doing. He turned to Markham. "Better get ready to travel again."

"Right away?"

"La Carde's not getting any closer to us."

"I suppose not," Markham said with a sigh. "I'll go gather our gear."

"I'll see to the horses." Clay walked quickly out of the trading post.

Aaron came after him, hurrying to keep up with Clay's long stride. "Clay, take me with you," he said.

Clay stopped and looked at the younger man in surprise. "You want to go after La Carde with us?"

"That's right. I'm just as much a patriot as the next fellow, Clay. I don't want him stealing half the country to set up his own private little empire."

Clay hated to hurt Aaron's feelings, but he looked pointedly at the peg leg attached to the bottom of Aaron's right thigh. "I don't know that I can take along a cripple," he said bluntly.

Aaron's chin lifted defiantly. "On horseback I can move as fast as anybody else. I won't slow you down, Clay, and you know it."

Clay knew Aaron was right. He had no

good excuse for not allowing the young man to accompany them.

And yet, Clay still felt a twinge of guilt every time he looked at Aaron's left arm, which had never been the same after Clay had broken it in a fight — a fight that had happened so long ago it might have been fought by two entirely different people. Nor did Clay completely absolve himself from blame in the avalanche that had taken Aaron's right leg. Clay had allowed Aaron to go along when he and Proud Wolf were hunting down a killer, and their quarry had started the rockslide that crushed Aaron's leg. If Aaron were to come on this mission, what was liable to happen to him next?

Clay couldn't worry about that, he decided. Aaron was a grown man, capable of making his own decisions, and if he wanted to come along, that was his business. Clay clapped a hand on his shoulder and nodded. "All right," he said. "We'll saddle a horse for you, too."

Aaron's face lit up in a grin. "Thank you, Clay," he said. "You won't be sorry, I swear. You'll be glad you brought me along."

Clay hoped Aaron was right. For now, though, what really mattered was catching up to La Carde and finding a way to put a stop to the renegade Frenchman's plans before they took root.

"Let's see to those horses," Clay said.

Matthew was seething. After all this time, after traveling hundreds of miles, he was being left behind. Now he would never find La Carde! He would not have the chance to warn the Frenchman that Clay and Markham were intent on stopping him.

Nor would he have the chance to ingratiate himself with La Carde.

Perhaps he could wait until Holt and Markham had left New Hope, then secretly follow them. He pondered that idea as he went out on the porch of the trading post after Shining Moon had told him of Clay's decision.

It would never work, he realized. He was confident in his own abilities, but he knew that he could not hope to survive for long on his own in this wilderness.

No, they had him boxed in. He would have to stay here with Holt's redskin slut and the brat with the bullwhip. All his grand plans were ruined.

Somebody would pay for that someday, Matthew vowed.

And he *always* settled his scores.

The warehouse was stacked nearly to the ceiling with furs brought in by the Tlingit hunters. The women had been busy for days stretching and tanning the hides. Jeff surveyed the bales of pelts with great satisfaction. What was here would fill the cargo hold of the *Beaumont*, that was certain. There might even be more than the vessel could carry.

Nearly a week had passed since the *Beaumont* had sailed on to Sitka. Jeff expected Captain Vickery to be back any day now. He was eager for the ship to return; now that he had made up his mind what he had to do, he was chafing to get under way.

Vassily came up beside him. "I can tell from your look, my brother, that you have not changed your mind." His voice was sorrowful.

"I am sorry, Vassily, truly sorry," Jeff told him. "But I must go back to my home. Surely you can see that."

"I see that you have a home here now. And a wife."

Jeff sighed. Nadia had taken his news as well as could be expected, probably because she had prepared herself emotionally as soon as word reached the village of the *Beaumont*'s arrival the first time. In fact, Nadia seemed to be adjusting to the impending change more easily than Vassily was.

"I could have killed you, my brother," Vassily went on. "It would have been easy to do as Count Orlov commanded. And safer, too."

"I know. I can never repay you for what you did for me."

"Yes, you can."

Anger flared inside Jeff. He suppressed it with an effort and said, "I'm not going to have this argument with you, Vassily."

The Tlingit gestured at the warehouse. "We risk much for you," he said. "If the Russians were to find out . . ."

"You risk much, but your people will profit, too," Jeff pointed out. "The time will come when the Tlingit will be powerful enough to defeat the Russians. I can have the next ship bring you guns, so that you'll be as well armed as they."

Vassily rubbed his jaw and considered. "Good rifles?"

"Good rifles." Jeff knew he was stirring up a revolution, and his activities might not be looked upon favorably by the United States government. But the Russians were ruling Alaska with an iron fist, and he was anxious to do what he could to help the Tlingit cast off their oppressors. With the Russians forced to leave, he could deal openly and fairly with the Tlingit and the other Alaskan tribes. They would rule over their own land again and not have to subsist as slaves to foreign conquerors.

"Perhaps you will come back to us someday." Vassily said with a sigh.

"I'd say it's likely." *But not to stay,* Jeff added to himself.

"Nadia will miss you," Vassily went on, "but since she will not be a widow, Yuri will not be able to court her. She will still be married to you."

"That's right," Jeff agreed. He was relieved that Vassily had decided to be reasonable.

"Besides, the child will be a reminder that she is a married woman."

For several seconds the significance of Vassily's words did not penetrate Jeff's brain. He turned sharply toward the Tlingit, eyes widened, mouth open in shock. "What did you say?"

"I speak of the child Nadia is carrying —"

Before Vassily could continue, a shout

sounded from the lookout across the cove who was watching the bay. "The ship!" he cried. "The ship comes!"

Jeff gripped Vassily's shoulder. "What do you mean?" he demanded. "She has said nothing to me of a child."

"How could she?" asked Vassily. "You are leaving."

Jeff's hand dropped away from Vassily's shoulder. He stood riveted to the spot as the Tlingit bustled around him, drawn by the shouts from the other side of the cove.

Finally he shook his head to clear it and looked around for Nadia. They had to talk. If she had his child growing within her, then he had a right to know about it.

Canoes were launched from the shore to guide the *Beaumont* into the cove. The passage was narrow and barely deep enough for the ship. Jeff had performed enough soundings before he had settled on this cove for his headquarters that he was confident the ship could make it.

He glanced around the warehouse but did not see Nadia. She had been nearby only minutes earlier, so he was certain she was in the vicinity. Perhaps she had seen Vassily talking to Jeff and realized what her brother was saying. If she had not wanted Jeff to know of the baby, she might have hurried off into the woods to hide. Jeff could not guess how she felt about her brother telling him. He had no idea of far too many things, he told himself bitterly.

For several minutes he searched for Nadia, to no avail. He stopped at the edge of the woods that came almost all the way down to the shore and peered through the dense cedar growth. Then he sighed and turned back toward the cove. He had to deal with the ship's arrival. Personal matters would have to wait.

As he returned to the shore, he watched the *Beaumont* sliding through the passage. The helmsman, a skillful and experienced pilot, followed perfectly the lead of the Tlingit canoes. The ship slowed and dropped anchor just inside the mouth of the cove. It was a wise decision, Jeff knew; to proceed further would risk scraping the hull. Better to ferry the pelts out in the canoes.

Jeff's eyes narrowed as he peered at the *Beaumont.* He was looking for Captain Vickery, but he didn't see the familiar stocky, white-haired figure anywhere on deck. Nor did he recognize, offhand, any of the sailors who were working the lines. They were all just brawny, black-bearded ciphers to him. His mind was still too full of the dilemma he faced with Nadia.

But, distracted as he was, Jeff suddenly understood that something was wrong. The *Beaumont* was carrying three heavy cannons on the starboard side, facing the warehouse. Jeff knew those guns had not been there the previous year, and he was fairly certain they had not been there when he had visited the ship a week earlier. Where could the captain have gotten three heavy cannons?

Sitka.

Jeff's eyes widened in sudden horror. The three canoes that had led the ship into the cove were still close to the *Beaumont*, with half a dozen Tlingit in each canoe. Jeff broke into a run toward the shore, cupping his hands around his mouth and shouting, "Look out! Get away from the ship! *Now!*"

The warning came too late. Men in red coats stood up all along the starboard side and leveled rifles at the canoes. The weapons roared at the same time in a precise volley. Rifle balls shredded the air around the canoes. The Tlingit screamed in shock and pain as the lead ripped into them. Several tumbled out of the canoes into the water, while others slumped where they sat.

The rattle of gunfire brought everyone running out of the warehouse. Jeff stopped short when he saw the muzzles of the cannons being elevated slightly. He turned and waved his arms at the confused Tlingit on shore. "Get away!" he yelled. "Get away from the warehouse!"

Some of them reacted quickly and sprang away, but most remained standing just outside the warehouse, baffled and staring. Suddenly, behind Jeff, the three cannons on the ship blasted. He flung himself forward, burying his face against the ground as the heavy balls shrieked overhead. He heard the crashes as they slammed into the warehouse.

Debris rained down for several seconds. Jeff slowly lifted his head and saw the gaping holes in the front wall of the warehouse. He saw, too, the bodies, scattered like a child's broken toys between him and the damaged building. Moans and sobs filled the air.

Jeff scrambled to his feet and turned to look at the ship. The gun crews already had the cannons reloaded. There was nothing he could do to stop them. Again the cannons roared as Jeff threw himself down. This time the entire front wall of the warehouse collapsed under the onslaught.

Flames licked upward amid the smoke and debris.

Orlov. Orlov was to blame for this atrocity, Jeff thought as he rolled over and got to his feet again. The only thing he could be thankful for was that Nadia had disappeared when she had. Perhaps she had survived the attack. Jeff hoped so. He ran over to the other Tlingit. Some of them were still alive; a few appeared to be relatively unhurt and were already trying to see to the wounded.

Jeff looked around for Vassily. He was almost certain that Vassily had not been among the men who went out in the canoes to greet the ship. After a moment he located his friend. Vassily was writhing on the ground, clutching a bloodstained leg.

Jeff cast a glance over his shoulder as he knelt beside Vassily. Small boats were being lowered from the *Beaumont*, full of Russian soldiers carrying rifles.

"We've got to get you out of here," Jeff said as he slid an arm around Vassily and lifted him. "Orlov's men are coming. Yuri must have sneaked off and told him what we were planning."

"I did not believe Yuri could do such a thing," Vassily said. His normally florid face was ashen. "But he must have. No one else would have betrayed us."

Grunting, Jeff hauled Vassily upright. Vassily's injured right leg was useless, but he managed to balance on his left.

"We cannot escape," he said. "I cannot run. You must go, Jeff Holt."

Jeff shook his head. "I can't do that. I can't leave you here." Grief and regret washed over him. "This is all my fault."

"No. Not all. I, too, am to blame for saving you from Orlov the first time. And Yuri . . ." Vassily sighed. "My only regret now is that I cannot kill him before I die."

"You're not going to die," Jeff said. "Not if we get out of here."

Vassily pulled away from him. "I am staying," he declared. "I will fight the Russians. Never again will I bow to them."

Maybe it *was* time to fight the last fight, Jeff thought. Maybe today was as good a time to die as any.

Nadia suddenly appeared, on Vassily's other side. "Jeff!" she said. "You are hurt?"

He shook his head. "What about you?"

"No. I was in the woods when they attacked." She reached around Vassily to clutch his arm. "We must leave this place. We will take Vassily —"

Her brother lurched forward, forcing his

injured leg to work. "I will fight the Russians," he muttered.

Rifle shots cracked from the boats approaching the shore. A number of Tlingit men still on their feet fell, mortally wounded. A haze of acrid powder smoke hung over the cove now, floating above the shore. It stung Jeff's nose.

Nadia looked at him, her eyes pleading. She was carrying his child, he thought. He had to get her away from this chaos, this massacre. Within minutes the Russian soldiers would be on shore, and they would use their sabers to hack down anyone they found alive.

"Go!" Jeff said, grabbing Nadia's arm and thrusting her toward the forest. "Run and hide!"

She clutched at him. "Not without you!"

Jeff glanced around. Vassily had limped several yards away. He bent down awkwardly, picked up a length of wood, and hefted it like a club. He raised it over his head and stumbled toward the beach, where the boats were landing. Russian soldiers swarmed out of them, sabers flashing in the cold sunlight. Vassily waded into the soldiers, striking out left and right with his club. Two of them went down, their skulls crushed.

But then the sabers flickered up and down, up and down, and Vassily disappeared behind the steel curtain.

Jeff shoved Nadia toward the trees and ran alongside her. Flight was their only option.

Rifles cracked behind them. Branches jumped and fell, clipped off by the shots. But the huge tree trunks closed quickly behind Jeff and Nadia, sheltering them from the hail of lead. They both knew this area well, and Jeff was confident they would escape their pursuers.

But the warehouse was destroyed, and along with it his dreams of trading directly with the Alaskan Indians. His friend Vassily, the man to whom he owed his life, was surely dead. So were many of the other Tlingit men. The villagers would no doubt be brought back under the brutal control of the Russians. Count Orlov would make their lives a living hell as punishment for aiding the American.

He should have left the Tlingit village as soon as he was able to travel, Jeff realized now. The Tlingit should have killed him when they had the chance, as Orlov had ordered. They would have been better off. But instead they had tried to help him, and he had repaid them with death and destruction brought about by his own ambition.

He stopped short. Nadia paused beside him, panting and looking back wildly. "What . . . what are you doing?" she asked.

Jeff turned back the way they had come. "I can't run away anymore," he said. "I have to confront Orlov."

She grabbed his arm. "You cannot! You would be killed before you could get near him. Our only chance is to flee."

Jeff shook his head. "Not anymore. I'm sorry, Nadia."

"A noble gesture," a new voice said mockingly. "I should have expected no less."

Jeff froze, then turned slowly. Stepping out of the trees ahead of them, followed by a small squad of soldiers, was Count Gregori Orlov. He held a pistol in his hand, pointed with studied nonchalance at Jeff.

CHAPTER TWENTY-FOUR

"This is a preliminary hearing," Daniel Reed said quietly to Proud Wolf. "The magistrate will decide whether there are sufficient grounds to hold a trial."

The two men were seated, along with Quincy, at a long table in the front of the Boston courtroom. At another table to their right were Will Brackett, Frank Kirkland, and a man Proud Wolf assumed was their lawyer. A large crowd sat on benches behind them, including Audrey, Oliver, Roxanne Reed, and Professor Abner Hilliard, who had come from Harvard for the hearing. Jeremiah Stoddard had made the journey across the Charles River from Cambridge, although he had failed so far to even speak to his daughter. Also among the spectators was a well-dressed, middle-aged man with iron-gray hair and a stern demeanor. Audrey had told Proud Wolf earlier that he was Arthur Brackett, Will's father, one of the wealthiest and most influential men in New England.

Less than a week had passed since Proud Wolf and his companions had arrived in Boston. Proud Wolf had spent that time going over his story again and again with Daniel, omitting no details — except for the fact that he and Audrey were lovers. That was between the two of them alone. Proud Wolf would not dishonor the woman he loved by revealing the intimate nature of their relationship.

Daniel had also used the time to give Proud Wolf an intensive course of instruction in the way the law worked. Although Proud Wolf thought he was beginning to understand the white man's legal system, he much preferred the way the Sioux handled disputes. A chief and a council of elders could always be counted upon to be honorable and to make fair judgments. From what Proud Wolf had seen of it, he did not believe the white man's system was as reliable.

Still, he had trusted his fate to it — at least for the moment — and to the man sitting beside him.

"How can the magistrate not agree with Brackett?" Proud Wolf asked in a low voice. "Is he not the man who signed the warrant for my arrest?"

"Yes, he is," Daniel conceded. "But if I can demonstrate that Brackett lied and that the warrant never should have been issued, then he'll have no choice but to dismiss the charges."

"And issue some against Brackett," Quincy added from Daniel's other side.

Daniel cleared his throat. "Let's not get ahead of ourselves," he cautioned. "We'll deal with the charges against Proud Wolf first."

At that moment the magistrate came into the courtroom. Everyone stood up at the bailiff's order, then sat again as the magistrate settled himself in the chair behind the high bench at the front of the room. He rapped his gavel sharply as he looked out at those gathered before him. He was a rather small man, with wispy fair hair and a mild expression, but his eyes were sharp and alert. "Counselor Reed," he said, "why have you come before me today?"

Daniel got to his feet. "To surrender a person charged with a warrant of arrest, Your Honor." He turned to Proud Wolf and motioned for him to stand.

The magistrate frowned. "Why is he not in the custody of the constable?"

"Because I place a motion before you for

536

an immediate hearing on the charges, Your Honor," Daniel said.

According to Daniel, the magistrate was well aware of what was going on, Proud Wolf recalled. These questions and answers were a matter of formality. Daniel had visited the magistrate's chambers the day before to arrange this hearing.

The magistrate looked at Proud Wolf, a faint sneer curling his lips. "Does this . . . savage . . . understand these proceedings, Counselor?"

"He does, Your Honor," Daniel replied.

"Then how does he plead?"

"Not guilty to all charges."

The magistrate turned to the bailiff. "Read the charges."

The man did so. Proud Wolf listened impassively as the bailiff intoned the charges against him: assault, attempted murder, kidnapping. All lies, of course, but the magistrate had believed them once, or at least pretended to. Was there any reason to think that he might not agree with them again now?

"Well," the magistrate said when the bailiff was finished, "that's quite a list of charges. Are you sure your client would not like to change his plea?"

"Positive, Your Honor," Daniel said,

"because my client is innocent of all of them."

The lawyer for Brackett and Kirkland stood up rather lazily and said in a bored tone, "That has yet to be proven, Your Honor, and we are certain that it never shall be."

The magistrate waved his hand. "Yes, yes. Sit down." He picked up his gavel. "I order that the prisoner be held for trial —"

"Your Honor!" Daniel shouted before the gavel could fall. "My client is entitled to a hearing!" Behind him, Proud Wolf's friends were in an uproar.

"I've heard the charges, Counselor," the magistrate said. "They are serious enough to warrant a trial. Therefore the defendant is bound over and will be held in jail."

Proud Wolf's eyes widened, and his heart began to pound heavily. He felt like a deer caught in a snare. He wondered if he could flee the courthouse before anyone stopped him. Or perhaps he should just kill Will Brackett now with his bare hands and let them hang him.

"Your Honor," Quincy Reed said as he got to his feet, "may I be heard?"

The magistrate hesitated. He clearly knew who Quincy was and was reluctant to incur the wrath of a former senator. At the same time, Arthur Brackett was glaring at him, obviously expecting the magistrate to do as he had been told.

Finally the magistrate swallowed. "Speak your piece, Senator Reed," he said.

"Very well, Your Honor." Quincy came out from behind the table. "I'm not an attorney, as you may know. But I *do* have some knowledge of the Constitution — *my brother and I fought for the right for that precious document to be written in the first place!*"

"I say!" burst out the opposing counsel. "The . . . the senator's credentials as a patriot are not in question here! All that matters is the law."

"And according to the law, a person charged with a crime has a right to a speedy trial," Quincy snapped.

Daniel was quick to follow his brother's lead. "Your Honor, I request that the trial be held now."

"Now?" the magistrate sputtered. "Here?"

Daniel glanced at Proud Wolf, then nodded. "Here and now, Your Honor. We will dispense with the need for a jury and put our faith in your wise judgment."

The magistrate looked stricken. He looked at the bailiff and said, "We . . . we don't have time now, do we?"

"There are no other proceedings on the docket for today, Your Honor," the man replied.

The magistrate narrowed his eyes and glared at the bailiff. Among the spectators, Arthur Brackett was slowly shaking his head. But after toying with the gavel for a moment, the judge sighed and said, "Your request is granted, Counselor. Trial in this matter is hereby convened."

Proud Wolf was not sure what was going on, but Daniel grunted in what seemed to be satisfaction. "Thank you, Your Honor," he said.

The opposing attorney said peevishly, "As the injured parties, my clients demand the right to proceed first."

"Of course," the magistrate said. "We shall follow the rule of law. Call your first witness."

"We call William Brackett, Your Honor."

Brackett stood up and went to the witness chair beside the magistrate's bench, glowering at Proud Wolf along the way. He sat down, swore to tell the truth, and proceeded to tell nothing but lies for the next half hour.

Proud Wolf listened, his anger growing with each falsehood that came from

Brackett's mouth. Brackett described how Proud Wolf had come to the Stoddard Academy from the frontier and terrorized the other students with his savage ways. He claimed that Proud Wolf had provoked every confrontation and had attacked him with no warning on numerous occasions. He said that Proud Wolf had attacked Audrey Stoddard and tried to force himself on her, and that Brackett had tried to stop him, only to nearly lose his life in the process.

When Brackett had finished his story, Daniel was allowed to question him. Daniel's voice lashed out, accusing him of the very things of which he had accused Proud Wolf, but Brackett clung stubbornly to his story.

Proud Wolf sat in silence, trying not to clench his hands into fists. A council of Sioux elders would have smoked a pipe and consulted the signs and the spirits and would have concluded without doubt that Brackett was lying. The American magistrate, however, seemed willing, even eager, to believe everything Brackett said.

Frank Kirkland followed his friend to the witness chair and repeated everything Brackett had said. He stuck to his story as firmly as Brackett had when Daniel questioned him. The next witness was Jeremiah Stoddard, who, under intense questioning from Daniel, finally admitted that he had not personally witnessed any of the incidents Brackett and Kirkland had described.

"But I saw the results of that savage's behavior," Stoddard spat. "Someone like that has no place in civilized society."

"You may be right, Headmaster Stoddard," Daniel said. Proud Wolf glanced at him, unsure of what he meant by that. Daniel winked at him where the magistrate could not see, as if to tell him to be patient.

After those three witnesses, it was Daniel's turn to present Proud Wolf's case. He called Professor Abner Hilliard, who testified how Proud Wolf had come to be enrolled at the Stoddard Academy in the first place.

"The fault is mine, you see," Hilliard said. "I was certain that an intelligent young man like Proud Wolf could succeed no matter what the environment in which he was placed. That was a theory shared by my late colleague, Professor Donald Franklin, who was also well acquainted with Proud Wolf. I know him, as Professor Franklin did, to be a courageous, honorable young man who would never do any of the things of which he is accused. Why, Proud Wolf saved my life several times during our journey here from the western mountains."

Brackett's attorney could not dispute any of the facts of Professor Hilliard's story, so he did not even attempt to. Hilliard was followed to the witness chair by Oliver Johnson, who told of how the acting troupe led by Ulysses Xavier Dowd — "that world-renowned thespian" — had become involved in Brackett's pursuit of Proud Wolf and Audrey. When Oliver testified that Brackett had threatened to kill all of them, Brackett's lawyer was on his feet instantly, objecting to "provocative, unproven testimony!"

"If you'd like to delay the trial, Your Honor," Daniel said, "we can attempt to locate the rest of the Dowd troupe to corroborate Mr. Johnson's testimony."

"There will be no delays," the magistrate ruled. "You wanted a speedy trial for your client, Counselor, and that is what you shall get."

"Very well, Your Honor," Daniel said. "In that case, I should like to call Miss Audrey Stoddard to the witness chair."

Audrey's father, who was still in the

courtroom, sprang to his feet and bellowed, "No! I'll not have my daughter subjected to such an indignity!"

"Your Honor, Miss Stoddard wishes to testify," Daniel said.

"Miss Stoddard," the magistrate said tentatively, "is such your wish?"

Audrey got to her feet. "It is, Your Honor," she said, casting a defiant glance at her father.

The magistrate sighed. "Very well, then. Call your witness and proceed, Counselor."

As he watched Audrey step to the witness chair and sit down, Proud Wolf wished, not for the first time, that he had not allowed Quincy Reed to convince him to go along with this plan. Brackett was going to win, and Audrey would be humiliated in the process. This was more than he could bear.

"Miss Stoddard," Daniel said, "tell us about your relationship with Proud Wolf."

"He is my friend," Audrey said. "My great and good friend."

"Did he kidnap you from the Stoddard Academy?"

"That claim is insane," Audrey said, looking directly at Brackett. "I went with him willingly, because I knew he would protect me from the advances of Mr. William Brackett."

"Mr. Brackett and Proud Wolf had had trouble between them in the past, had they not?"

"Yes. Will lured Proud Wolf here to Boston and then had his ruffians hand him a terrible thrashing."

Proud Wolf waited for Brackett's attorney to object to that statement, but the man remained seated. Brackett lounged in his chair, a confident smirk on his face. It did not matter what testimony was given at this trial, Proud Wolf realized. The truth was meaningless. In the end, Brackett would win because he was the son of a rich, powerful man, and Proud Wolf would go to jail, would be caged like an animal, because he was nothing but an Indian.

Daniel asked Audrey a few more questions about Brackett, and then she was allowed to return to her seat when Brackett's lawyer had no questions for her. Daniel said, "Your Honor, that concludes our case." He started to go back to the table, then stopped and turned to face the magistrate again. "Oh, yes, one more thing. I move that all charges against my client, the Sioux youth known as Proud

Wolf, be immediately dismissed."

The magistrate frowned. "On what grounds, Counselor? Do you feel that your opposition failed to prove their case?"

"I *know* they failed to prove their case, Your Honor." Daniel looked around the courtroom, and his voice boomed out. "Everyone here knows what really happened and knows that my client is the victim, not the aggressor!"

"But there is a matter of proof," the magistrate reminded him. "All I can do is weigh the charges and the evidence and rule on what I believe to be the prevailing wisdom —"

"Your Honor," Daniel interrupted, "you cannot even do that."

The magistrate's eyebrows lifted. "I cannot?" he asked, his voice growing soft with menace.

"Daniel, what are you doing?" Quincy asked in a loud whisper.

Daniel forged ahead. "Your Honor, the only thing you can do is dismiss the charges, because that is the only thing you have the *authority* to do. You must declare that these charges never should have been brought in the first place, because this court has no jurisdiction in the matter!"

"No jurisdiction?" the magistrate blustered. "The offenses *occurred* in my jurisdiction."

"Alleged offenses, Your Honor," Daniel reminded him. "But the charges cannot be applied to Proud Wolf."

"And why not?" the magistrate demanded.

"Because he is not a citizen of the United States."

That brought an uproar from the crowd assembled in the courtroom. The magistrate struck his gavel sharply several times on the bench, and when a semblance of silence finally fell, he demanded, "What do you mean by that, Counselor?"

"Exactly what I said, Your Honor," Daniel replied calmly. "Proud Wolf is a member of a band of Teton Sioux residing in what is commonly referred to as the Louisiana Territory. The only governing body with any authority over his actions is the council of elders of his people. He has no legal status whatsoever in an American court of law. Unless and until the United States government sees fit to confer citizenship on the Sioux, you might as well charge this table or this chair with a crime."

Proud Wolf blinked. He wasn't sure he liked the idea of being thought of as less than a human being.

The opposing counsel was on his feet. "This is mad, Your Honor," he protested. "Slaves have been put on trial in this country, and *they* are certainly not citizens."

Daniel pointed at Proud Wolf. "This is not a slave!" he said loudly. "This is a Sioux warrior! A member of a different people, a people we have no right to judge!"

Again the courtroom was filled with noise, and again the magistrate had to gavel it back to order. When he could be heard again, he said, "Indians have been tried in court before, Mr. Reed."

"Yes, they have, Your Honor . . . illegally."

The magistrate's expression grew grim as he stared from Daniel to Proud Wolf and back again. Finally he said, "You may have a point, Counselor. If there were a treaty between our government and the Sioux —"

"No such treaty exists, Your Honor," Daniel said.

The magistrate grimaced. "In that case, I am forced to rule that an American court of law has no jurisdiction over the actions of this man, and I also rule that the charges against him are dismissed!" The gavel came down with a sharp crack.

"No!" Will Brackett was on his feet, shouting. "You can't do that, you fuzzy-headed old idiot!"

"Will!" Arthur Brackett caught at his son's arm. "Be quiet —"

Brackett threw off his father and strode forward. He leveled an arm at Proud Wolf. "Legally, this savage doesn't even exist, is that what you're saying?"

The magistrate nodded reluctantly. "That seems to be the only way I can rule, lad."

"Well, then," Brackett said as he pivoted on his heel, "I can't be prosecuted for killing him, can I?"

And with those words he jerked a pistol from inside his coat, leveled it at Proud Wolf, and pulled the trigger.

The Comte de La Carde sat beside the campfire and stared into the blaze, seeing his empire reflected there amid the leaping, dancing flames. In time it would expand beyond the boundaries of this mountain country, he told himself. It would spread all the way across the continent — beyond the continent, perhaps, into an empire that girdled the world, the

549

likes of which had not been seen since the days of ancient Rome.

A scream suddenly ripped the air.

Baker, Howell, and Pittman were all in the camp. They leaped up, cocking their flintlock rifles. So did the other Americans. Like La Carde, the other Frenchmen carried sabers, and as they scrambled to their feet, they drew the blades and looked around as if searching for someone with whom to fight a duel.

La Carde stood more leisurely. "What is it?" he asked.

Baker glanced at him. "I don't know. That sounded a little like Richards, one of the men I sent out to stand watch."

"It sounded to me like a man being killed," Howell said.

"Are there hostile Indians in this area?" La Carde asked.

Baker rubbed his chin. "This is Nez Perce country. They're like most of the other tribes. Sometimes they're friendly and sometimes they aren't. You just never —"

A thud interrupted him. Baker's mouth dropped open, and he stumbled forward a step or two before slowly pitching forward on his face. He landed in the fire, and the stench of burning hair and flesh filled the air. An arrow, its shaft still quivering, stood a good foot out of his back.

Bouchard let out a cry of horror, a cry that ended in a terrible gurgle as an arrow ripped into his throat. Blood gouted into the air as he went down, kicking and thrashing in his death throes. The other men leaped for whatever cover they could find as more arrows whipped through the air.

Damn those Americans! La Carde thought as he rolled behind a fallen log and pressed his face to the ground. They had promised him safe passage across the frontier. He could have stayed on the boat and rendezvoused with the others on the Pacific Coast, but he had wanted to see for himself the wondrous new land that was going to be his empire.

Now it appeared that he might die here, before he ever got a chance to see the realization of his glorious plans. Without him the dream would die, too. None of the others had his vision. Even if some of them should survive, they would never be able to unite the savages.

Those same savages he had planned to mold into his army might now be his executioners, La Carde thought bitterly. He fumbled for the pistol in his belt. If he died tonight, he would take at least one of the enemy with him.

Shrill, terrible cries split the night. The Indians were all around them, La Carde realized. The Americans were fighting back, their rifles cracking wickedly, but the night was full of shadows that made it difficult to see. La Carde lifted himself and risked a glance over the deadfall. He saw a buckskin-clad figure running toward him. He lifted the pistol and aimed . . .

The man in buckskins dropped to a knee and raised a long-barreled rifle to his shoulder in one smooth motion. Without seeming to pause long enough to aim, the man fired. Smoke and flame geysered from the muzzle of the rifle, the glare almost blinding La Carde. He had hesitated too long in firing, he thought, and he expected to feel the rifle ball slam into him. That would be the last thing he would ever feel.

Instead, something hot and wet splashed over him from behind, and he twisted his head to see a hideously painted figure looming over him. The savage held a tomahawk in an upraised hand, poised for a blow that would split La Carde's skull. But now that blow would never fall, because a rifle ball had punched through the man's throat, killing him where he stood. The savage simply had not realized yet that he was dead.

Then he flopped grotesquely backward, and La Carde looked back at the man who had saved his life. The man was not an Indian after all, but a white man with a short, dark beard. He sprang up from his kneeling position and wheeled around, driving the butt of his rifle into the belly of another Indian who was leaping toward him. Then he plucked a tomahawk from behind his belt and slashed at the Indian's head. The Indian went down.

The man pivoted again to meet a new threat. Two of the Nez Perce closed in on him. He blocked one's tomahawk with his rifle and kicked the legs out from under the other. The tomahawk in his hand leaped out and danced back like a thing alive, and the Indian who was still upright was suddenly covered with blood from the deadly wound he had suffered. The tomahawk had driven into the point where his neck met his left shoulder, sinking almost to the spine before its wielder pulled it back out.

La Carde could barely follow the man's movements, so swift were they. But every time the man struck, a Nez Perce died. La Carde couldn't recall ever seeing the man before, but what would strangers — white strangers — be doing here in the valley of the Columbia River, not far from the Pacific Ocean?

The man La Carde was watching was not the only stranger who had jumped into the fight. Gradually, as he watched the struggle between the Americans and the savages, La Carde realized there were two more men here he did not recognize. One of them was crippled in some way, but his handicap did not prevent him from fighting effectively against the Indians. The other was a young man with a dark blond beard, and although he looked nervous, he fought well. He fired a pistol into the face of an onrushing savage, then used his rifle as a club to down another one. The cripple, who wore a peg leg in place of his right leg, was also an excellent shot.

Suddenly the fight was over. The silence that fell was so abrupt that it was unnerving. The Nez Perce had fled, leaving their dead behind. The three newcomers quickly reloaded their weapons while they had the chance, and the other members of La Carde's party followed suit. La Carde's pistol was still loaded, since he had never fired it. He stood up from behind the fallen log and looked around.

Considering the bloody chaos that had filled the clearing only seconds earlier, there were few bodies lying on the ground. Baker was dead, of course, and still filling the air with the stink of his smoldering corpse. And Bouchard was dead, too, as well as another of the Americans who had been hired in St. Louis. But those were the only dead among the comte's party, La Carde saw to his satisfaction.

The Nez Perce, on the other hand, had lost six of their warriors, most of them killed by the strangers. This battle would have turned out quite differently, La Carde sensed, if not for the timely arrival of the three men.

The tall one, the one with the dark beard, glanced at La Carde and nodded. "Howdy," he said. "Are you the leader of this group?"

"I am," La Carde acknowledged, speaking English. "And you have our deepest gratitude, *monsieur*. If not for your assistance, those savages might have massacred us."

"Seems likely," the man said. "I'm glad we came along when we did and heard the commotion."

"I am the Comte Jacques de La Carde." He tucked his pistol away and stepped forward to extend his hand to the American.

The tall man, who wore a coonskin cap, took La Carde's hand in a firm grip. "Call me Clay," he said. "I'm mighty pleased to meet you."

CHAPTER TWENTY-FIVE

Jeff stood very still as he stared at Orlov. The count's familiar sneer had not changed one whit since Jeff had seen him last, months earlier. Behind Orlov, his aide Piotr and the Tlingit called Yuri stood with the Russian soldiers.

"It is good I came this way to intercept any who tried to flee from our attack on your foolish warehouse, Holt," Orlov went on. "I knew there would be survivors, and I want to teach these savages a harsh lesson." His thin lips curved in a smile. "And so I find myself with you in my power once again, thanks to my friend Yuri."

Nadia had caught her breath. She spat out a torrent of words in the Tlingit language, all of them directed at Yuri. Jeff had learned enough to recognize most of the insults. Yuri's face went taut, and he stepped forward. His hand flashed up in a slap that cracked across Nadia's face and rocked her head to the side. He was about to backhand her when Jeff tackled him.

The rage that welled up inside Jeff obliterated from his mind the threat of the Russian soldiers with their rifles. As he and Yuri rolled over and over on the ground, grappling with each other, they moved too quickly for the soldiers to risk a shot. Orlov raised a hand to hold them back.

Jeff got a hand on Yuri's throat and clamped down hard, digging his fingers into the man's muscular neck. Even as his face turned purple, Yuri managed to reach inside his coat, and the sunlight that slanted down through the pines glinted off the blade of the knife he jerked from its sheath. He lifted the weapon, ready to plunge it into Jeff's back.

Instead, Jeff rolled sharply to the side, bashing Yuri's wrist against the ground. Yuri hung on to the knife, but Jeff gripped his wrist with his other hand and kept the blade at bay. They were deadlocked, Yuri on top and Jeff on the bottom, Jeff with his right hand locked around Yuri's throat and his left holding off Yuri's knife hand.

The impasse was suddenly broken by an unexpected source. Staggering out of the woods came what seemed at first glance a bloody ghost, saber upraised, growling a wordless challenge. Vassily lunged toward

Yuri, and the saber he had liberated from one of the Russian soldiers came swooping down. Yuri looked up in shock in time to see Vassily looming over him before the blade cleaved his skull with a solid *thock!*

"Kill him!" Orlov screamed. "Kill him!"

From his position flat on the ground, Jeff watched the grisly scene unfold. He saw Yuri slumping toward him, eyes wide in death, the saber still lodged in his head. Beyond Yuri, Jeff saw the Russian soldiers lift their rifles to fire at Vassily, saw Nadia leaping forward. Several rifle balls struck her in the back, throwing her forward into the arms of her brother. Vassily was hit, too, although undoubtedly he had been mortally wounded at the cove. How he had managed to get this far and what had led him to this spot were questions Jeff would never be able to answer.

But as he watched Vassily and Nadia stagger under the onslaught of lead, something snapped inside Jeff. With an incoherent cry of rage, he threw Yuri's body aside and surged up off the ground. Yuri's knife had somehow found its way into his hand. The Russian soldiers had emptied their weapons in the volley that had claimed the two Tlingit, and there was nothing they could do to stop Jeff as he lunged at Orlov.

At the last instant, the count flung himself behind Piotr. Jeff's rush carried him into the startled aide, who had no chance to get out of the way of the knife thrust. The blade buried itself in Piotr's chest. He opened his mouth and grunted, blood bubbling from his lips as he stumbled backward.

Orlov turned and plunged into the woods. Jeff ripped the knife from Piotr's chest as the aide fell, then started after Orlov. At this moment he and the count might have been the only two people in the world; the Russian soldiers were completely forgotten.

But when they had finished reloading their rifles and fired after Jeff, the lead balls whipping through the air around him reminded him of their presence. He zigzagged back and forth, using the trees for cover. Something plucked at the sleeve of his coat, but that was as close as any of the hurried shots came.

Orlov had seen the tables turning on him and had given in to a momentary burst of panic, Jeff knew. He was still holding a loaded pistol, and as soon as he remembered that, he might well stop and confront Jeff. Besides, the soldiers were coming after Jeff now, no doubt reloading as they thrashed their way through the forest.

Jeff ran swiftly and easily after Orlov. His body felt exceptionally powerful. But his mind and heart were numb. His friend and the woman who was carrying his child had both died before his eyes. The pain of that loss was so great he could barely comprehend it. But he kept the grief tamped down in his soul and allowed the need for revenge to rise and take its place. That was all he existed for now: to settle the score with Count Gregori Orlov.

Orlov was making his way up a steep slope, panting and gasping for air as he broke through the underbrush. Jeff could hear him up ahead and track him by the sounds. He heard the Russian soldiers, too, shouting to each other as they pursued him. But he was outdistancing them and closing the gap between him and Orlov. He would have time for a final showdown with the count before the soldiers caught up to them.

Orlov broke out of the trees onto the rocky peak of a hill. Jeff was only a few seconds behind him. "Orlov!" he shouted. "Turn and face me, you gutless bastard!"

The insult to Orlov's honor stopped him

as perhaps nothing else would have. Breathing heavily, he turned toward Jeff, who slowed to a stop some twenty feet down the slope. "You are . . . a lucky man . . . Holt," Orlov panted. "Others die . . . in your stead."

"No more," Jeff grated. "Now it's just you and me, Orlov, the way it should have been from the first."

"I think not." Orlov drew in one more deep breath and blew it out, then leveled the pistol at Jeff. "You will stand there until my men arrive, and then I will watch you die."

"Answer a question first," Jeff said. "What did you do to Captain Vickery and the crew of the *Beaumont*?"

Orlov smiled. Confidence was flowing back into him now that he thought he had the upper hand. "I am not a savage, Holt," he said. "Your captain and his men are being detained at Sitka. When the ship returns there, they will be put on it and told to leave, never to return to the waters of Russian Alaska. I merely . . . borrowed . . . the vessel so that I could take you and your pathetic Indian friends by surprise. I judged that the time was right to teach them a lesson."

"You probably butchered half of them,"

Jeff accused bitterly.

"Then the remaining half will be more cooperative in the future, will they not?"

Abruptly, a new sound came to Jeff's ears. Somewhere down the hill, steel was clashing against steel, shots rang out, and men were screaming. The Russian soldiers had run into opposition of some kind, and Jeff could think of only one place it could have come from.

The Tlingit who had not been killed in the initial raid were fighting back. A once-proud race of warriors was attempting to regain, at least for a moment, a measure of its former glory.

Jeff smiled thinly. "You may not be getting the help you think you are," he said to Orlov.

The count grew pale as the sounds of battle receded down the hill. His soldiers were clearly on the run now, trying to escape with their lives from the vengeful Tlingit.

"You're here alone, Orlov," Jeff said softly.

"Die!" Orlov screamed as he thrust the pistol toward Jeff and pulled the trigger.

At the same instant, Jeff's arm flashed back and then forward. The knife he had taken from Yuri turned over and over as it spun through the air. Jeff threw himself to the side as the pistol ball sang past his ear. As he hit the rocky ground, he kept his eyes on the count. Orlov was staggering backward, the knife buried in his chest. Jeff's aim had been perfect.

The pistol slipped from Orlov's fingers and clattered to the ground. He pawed feebly at the knife, looking up at Jeff once with pain and surprise in his eyes. He stumbled again and then fell, toppling off the crest of the hill and tumbling out of sight down the far slope.

Jeff got to his feet and hurried to the top of the hill. He saw Orlov's body sprawled against the trunk of a tree some fifty feet down the slope. The count's hands worked ineffectually, pushing at the ground, then went slack. Jeff heard the death rattle in Orlov's throat as his final breath was expelled.

Orlov was dead at last, a justice too long postponed. Jeff turned away. He felt no triumph, only a dull sense of relief mixed with a hollow bitterness. He looked toward the cove and saw black smoke rising into the air. The warehouse and all the furs within were being consumed by fire.

He had helped bring about the devastation, Jeff thought bleakly. Many good people were dead because of the hatred and vengefulness of two men — men who did not even belong in this land.

With a sour taste in his mouth, Jeff started down the hill, unsure where he was going or what he was doing next.

And at the moment, not caring, either . . .

Will Brackett's pistol cracked like thunder in the crowded courtroom. Daniel Reed grunted and stumbled back a step. His right hand went up to grip his left shoulder as he fell.

Proud Wolf would never have believed that the stocky, middle-aged attorney could move so quickly. Daniel had reacted with the swiftness of a hawk and the courage of a mountain lion, throwing himself between Brackett and Proud Wolf.

Daniel's sacrifice had given Proud Wolf the opportunity to strike back. He seized it now, leaping onto the table and throwing himself at Brackett in a long dive.

Proud Wolf's shoulder smashed into Brackett's midsection, spilling both of them on the floor in front of the magistrate's bench. The magistrate was pounding on the bench with his gavel and shouting for order, but no one was paying attention. Quincy knelt beside his wounded brother to check on his condition, while the spectators pressed forward to watch Proud Wolf and Brackett grapple.

Brackett slashed at Proud Wolf's head with the empty pistol. The barrel raked along his forehead, opening a gash and stunning him for a moment. With a heave, Brackett threw the dazed Proud Wolf off. Proud Wolf rolled to the side and came up on his hands and knees, shaking off a moment of grogginess. He launched himself at Brackett again as he tried to struggle to his feet.

"I'm all right, I'm all right," Daniel said impatiently to his brother. He pushed Quincy away. "Give Proud Wolf a hand."

Quincy glanced over his shoulder and saw that Proud Wolf was holding his own against Brackett. But Frank Kirkland was about to join the struggle; he had drawn back one leg and was aiming a kick at Proud Wolf's head.

Uncoiling from his crouching position with a lithe grace that belied his age, Quincy spun around. A long stride took him to Kirkland's side, where he grabbed the younger man's shoulder and roughly hauled him around. Kirkland yelped, "What —" but Quincy quieted him with a well-timed right cross to the jaw. The blow jerked Kirkland's head to the side. His eyes rolled up and his knees folded, dumping him in an ungraceful heap on the floor. Quincy stepped back, shaking his right hand. It would be sore tomorrow, he thought with a grim smile, but the pain would be well worth it.

Meanwhile, Proud Wolf was still grappling with Brackett. They rolled against the magistrate's bench, and Brackett grabbed Proud Wolf's throat and slammed his head against it. Proud Wolf hooked a punch into Brackett's belly. Although both young men were taking a terrible beating, neither was ready to give up. Their mutual hatred would allow nothing less than a fight to the death.

Proud Wolf's spirit was lifted and energized. For too long he had tried to live the white man's way, and always, even when he was in the right, circumstances came around to strike against him. Now he was fighting back as a Sioux warrior should. He wished he had a tomahawk in his hand.

The magistrate, leaning over the bench and scolding them, knocked his gavel off the bench and onto the floor. Brackett spotted it and pounced on it, then raised it over his head. Audrey screamed again as the gavel flashed downward.

But Proud Wolf's head was no longer where it had been a fraction of a second earlier. He had pulled his upper body aside, and the gavel struck the floor. Brackett cried out in pain as the impact of the blow shivered up his arm. Proud Wolf rolled and caught hold of Brackett's leg, jerked him over onto his back, and wrenched the gavel from his numb hand. Proud Wolf's knee came down on Brackett's chest, pinning him to the floor. The situation was reversed now as Proud Wolf lifted the gavel high above Brackett's head.

Proud Wolf froze, poised to strike. Silence fell over the courtroom, broken only by the harsh breathing of the two combatants. Brackett stared up at Proud Wolf, his eyes filled with fear, his arrogance vanished as he looked up into the face of his own death.

With a convulsive movement Proud Wolf flung the gavel aside.

For another heartbeat, he stayed where he was. Then he pushed himself to his feet and took a step back. Brackett remained on the floor, stunned and unmoving.

Audrey rushed to Proud Wolf's side and threw her arms around him. "Thank you," she whispered raggedly. "Thank you for not killing him."

"He deserved to die," Proud Wolf said. "But I am no longer a *savage*."

"You never were." Audrey embraced him, sobbing now. "You never were."

Quincy clapped a hand on Proud Wolf's shoulders. "I think we've all seen who the savage is in this courtroom," he said.

Arthur Brackett pointed a finger at Proud Wolf and exclaimed in a loud, angry voice, "That man tried to kill my son! I demand that something be done, Indian or no Indian! He tried to kill William! You all saw it!"

The magistrate swallowed hard and said, "We saw your son take a shot at an unarmed man."

"You can't prosecute him for that," the elder Brackett blustered. "That Indian isn't a citizen! You made that ruling yourself."

"But your son *didn't* shoot an Indian," Daniel said. He had been helped to his feet, still clutching his bloodstained shoulder. "He shot me."

"By accident!"

"Hand me my gavel," the magistrate snapped at the bailiff. When he had it firmly in his hand again, he cracked it down on the bench and continued, "I hereby order that William Brackett be arrested and charged with the crime of the attempted murder of Mr. Daniel Reed, as well as disturbing the peace and discharging a firearm in a public building. Bailiff, take Mr. Brackett into custody."

"You can't do this, you damned fool!" Arthur Brackett protested.

The magistrate pointed the gavel at him. "Another word from you and I'll hold you in contempt of court and have you thrown into jail along with that worthless whelp of yours!"

The elder Brackett gaped in amazement at this display of backbone. Then he narrowed his eyes and said, "You'll be sorry you crossed me, my good man."

"I'm sorry I didn't stand up to you a long time ago, Brackett. Now get out, all of you. Just get out."

Quincy and Roxanne flanked Daniel as they left the courtroom. "We have to get you to a doctor," Roxanne said worriedly to her husband.

Daniel waved off her concern with his good hand. "Don't worry about me," he assured her. "I suffered much worse at the hands of the redcoats, back in the days when we were all fighting for our freedom against them — do you remember? — at Breed's Hill and Ticonderoga and —"

"Yes, dear," Roxanne said patiently. "I suppose if you're well enough to start reminiscing about those times, you're not too badly hurt."

They went out of the courtroom, followed by Proud Wolf, Audrey, Oliver, and Professor Hilliard. The professor was saying, "I can't tell you how sorry I am about all this, Proud Wolf. I never meant for your sojourn in the east to be so fraught with unpleasantness and peril."

"Do not worry, Professor," Proud Wolf told him. "I have learned much during my time here." His arm tightened around Audrey's shoulders. "I have learned what it is to love and be loved, and to have good friends like Oliver. And I have learned that my place is in the mountains, among my own people. I will return there as soon as I can."

"Oh, no!" Hilliard exclaimed. "You can't do that."

Proud Wolf stopped and turned to face the professor. "I cannot go back to the academy."

"Of course not." Hilliard glanced at Audrey. "Not under the, ah, circumstances. That's why I've made arrangements to have you admitted directly to Harvard. You see, I was confident that you would emerge victorious from today's legal proceedings, just as I am confident that you are ready to undertake a course of university instruction. I assure you, things will be different this time."

"Harvard?" Proud Wolf repeated hollowly. "You wish me to attend the university where you instruct?"

"Absolutely! What do you say, dear boy? There is much still for you to learn, and I promise you, learn it you shall at Harvard."

Proud Wolf looked at Audrey, remembering the doubts she had had when he asked her to go with him to the mountains. She had been unsure that she could ever grow accustomed to frontier life, and he was not certain that he had any right to ask her to uproot herself. True, she had brought some trouble into his life, but no more than he had brought into hers. It was all part of two people being together; joy and trouble often went hand in hand.

Besides, if she stayed here, she might be able to rebuild her shattered relationship with her father.

Proud Wolf's mind had been made up, but now he found his world turned upside-down yet again.

"Harvard?" he said.

The *Beaumont* dropped anchor off the coastline near the passage to the cove. Captain Vickery studied the landmarks along the shore through his spyglass. When he was certain he was in the right place, he ordered a small boat lowered into the water and picked a crew to man it. He himself was going to be among them. Each of the men was armed with a pistol and a rifle.

The previous week and a half had been confusing and chaotic. First the ship had arrived at Sitka, expecting if not a friendly welcome at least a civil one. Instead, Russian troops had swarmed over the vessel. Vickery had ordered the crew not to put up a fight until he knew what was going on. He was then taken by the soldiers to Count Orlov's headquarters, where Orlov explained that Vickery and his crew were to be held as guests for the time being — *prisoners* was more like it, Vickery thought — but that their ship would be returned to them at a later date.

Count Orlov had not kept his promise. In fact, he had left the settlement with a detachment of men from the garrison, sailing away in the *Beaumont* after several cannons from the fort had been loaded on it. Vickery had watched the ship sail out of the harbor from the window of the cabin to which he was confined with his officers.

The days in captivity had dragged by, and finally the *Beaumont* had reappeared in the harbor. Orlov was not on board, however. That quickly became obvious when the young lieutenant who was in command — and clearly unaccustomed to it — came to the cabins and ordered the Americans freed and returned to their ship. Vickery had tried to find out what had happened, but his questions were ignored. None of the Russians spoke much English, anyway.

But Vickery didn't need to be fluent in Russian to recognize the signs of trouble. Several canvas-wrapped figures were carried off the ship, and many of the soldiers were sporting bloodstained bandages. They had been in a battle of some kind, that much was certain.

Puzzled though he was, Vickery wasted no time casting off once the Russians had removed their cannons. Something had happened to Orlov, and there was no telling when the Russians might change their minds about letting the *Beaumont* and its crew go.

Now, a couple of days later, the ship had reached the spot where it was supposed to rendezvous with Jeff Holt and take on the cargo of furs bound for America. But no one had come out in canoes to meet the *Beaumont* this time, and as the small boat was rowed ashore, Vickery had a premonition about what they would find there.

"Good Lord, Captain, look at that!" one of the sailors exclaimed as the boat slid through the narrow passage into the cove. The man pointed to the far shore, where a heap of burned rubble marked the spot where the warehouse had recently stood. There were no signs of life anywhere.

Vickery felt eyes on him, however. The sensation of being watched was unmistakable. "Stay alert, lads," he warned his men.

A few minutes later, the hull of the small boat scraped on the rocky shore near the fire-gutted warehouse. Small sections of wall were still standing, but everything inside the structure had been destroyed.

Vickery stepped ashore, followed by most of his men. He ordered a couple of the sailors to stay with the boat. Holding their weapons at the ready, the landing party quickly explored the area around the devastated warehouse.

"There's no one here, Captain," one of the men said.

Vickery could not shake the feeling he was being watched, but he saw no one. The woods were quiet and peaceful.

"Something must've happened to Mr. Holt," another sailor said. "He would've been here otherwise."

"Aye," Vickery said slowly. He cupped his hands to his mouth and shouted, "Mr. Holt! Jefferson Holt!"

The name echoed back from the nearby hills.

"What do we do now, sir?"

"Only one thing we *can* do," Vickery said. "We'll wait offshore for a day and see if Mr. Holt turns up. Perhaps we'll send up a rocket or two, so he'll know we're here." The captain sighed. "If we don't see him, we'll have to assume that something has happened to him, too, and sail back to Wilmington."

"Empty-handed?" one of the men asked.

Vickery shook his head regretfully. "We've no other choice, lads."

But as the small boat pulled away from the cove a few moments later, Vickery looked back. There *was* one other thing he could do, he realized.

He offered up a small prayer for Jefferson Holt.

The next day, a single figure watched from a hilltop as the white sails of the *Beaumont* receded into the distance. The ship was leaving.

The man on the hill looked at the small ravine nearby where he had placed the bodies of Vassily and Nadia. He had covered them with rocks, building the cairn high. It was the least he could do for them.

When the ship had vanished to the south, the man picked up the rifle and the bag of powder, shot, and supplies he had scavenged from the battlefield down the hill. He tilted the rifle over his shoulder and began walking toward the cove.

One of the Tlingit canoes was there, concealed behind some brush. The lone man moved the brush aside and pulled the canoe out into the water. He cached his gear in the bottom of the craft and stepped into it, then picked up the single paddle. The canoe was meant to be handled by several men, but now its lone occupant steered it toward the passage into the bay. The canoe slid through easily into deeper water.

Paddling skillfully, the man turned the

canoe until it was facing south. Canada was down there somewhere, and beyond it the western coast of the Louisiana Territory. All he had to do was keep the coastline to his left and keep going.

Jeff Holt took a deep breath and then dug the paddle into the water, sending the canoe skimming over the surface.

CHAPTER TWENTY-SIX

This was not the first time Clay Holt had stood at the broad mouth of the Columbia River and looked out over the Pacific Ocean. Several years earlier, as a member of the Corps of Discovery under Captains Meriwether Lewis and William Clark, Clay had visited this same place. The Pacific had been an awe-inspiring sight then, an endless expanse of deep gray-blue melting at the horizon into the pale blue of the sky. It was no less impressive now.

"Magnificent, is it not, eh, Clay?" the Comte Jacques de La Carde asked from beside him where the two men stood on a rocky promontory.

"A fine thing to see," Clay agreed. He only wished he wasn't seeing it in the company of a snake like La Carde.

On the other hand, Clay could not complain about how the past few weeks had gone. After he and Lieutenant Markham and Aaron Garwood had picked up the trail of La Carde's party not far from

Colter's Hell, they had followed the Frenchman all the way up the valley of the Snake River, gradually closing in on their quarry. The Snake eventually flowed into the Columbia. It was not the route the Lewis and Clark expedition had taken, but Clay had been over much of this ground during his travels since then. They had bartered for a canoe from some friendly Shoshone, and that had allowed them to make better time, although the trip through the rapids fanged with black rocks known as the Dalles had been harrowing.

The night following the running of the rapids, Clay had spotted the glow from a campfire. He was certain it had been built by La Carde's men; only whites would be so reckless as to build such a large blaze. He figured on catching up with them the next night.

That was when fate had stepped in and sent a band of quarrelsome Nez Perce stumbling across La Carde's party. Clay had figured to walk in and hail the camp, claiming that he and Markham and Aaron were trappers who wanted to travel with the party for a while, but the sounds of gunfire had altered that plan in a hurry. Clay and his two companions had joined in the battle, helping to drive off the attackers, and as a result they had been welcomed with open arms by La Carde and his men. La Carde had even asked if Clay and his friends would be willing to serve as guides, since the one American who knew the trails had been killed.

Of course, Clay had been happy to oblige. The three men now had a reason to remain with La Carde's group until they reached the Pacific.

And here they were now, Clay thought as he leaned on his long-barreled rifle. The long trail that had started at the Holt family farm in Ohio with a letter from a dead man, that had taken him to the dangerous back alleys and glittering ballrooms of Washington City, that had led him down the mighty Mississippi River on the historic voyage of the steamboat *New Orleans* — that trail had finally come to an end.

The simplest thing to do now would be to put a bullet through the madman's brain.

Clay hesitated. He was not a cold-blooded murderer. He had maintained the facade of a simple mountain man for this long to see if his theories about the Frenchman's plans were accurate. He could play out the hand a little longer.

"What will you folks do now?" Clay asked. "Turn around and go back the way you came?"

La Carde had told him that they were simply a group of French diplomats on a sightseeing tour, and Clay had pretended to accept that fiction. Foreigners had come before to visit the American wilderness.

La Carde shook his head. "No, we are meeting a ship here. In fact, I believe it has already arrived." He pointed out to sea.

Indeed, there *was* a ship out there, Clay saw. "How did the captain know to meet you here?" he asked in some wonder.

"I have studied diligently the findings of the American explorers Lewis and Clark," La Carde replied with an indulgent smile. "I knew of this river and that it emptied into the sea. Such a landmark would be difficult to miss. The ship's captain has his orders. He is to cruise up and down the coast until he sees our signal fire."

La Carde had no idea he was talking to a man who had been here before, with the very explorers he had mentioned. Clay kept his face carefully expressionless as he said, "And then you sail back to France?"

La Carde did not reply immediately. Doubtless he was weighing the question of how much he could trust this American frontiersman. Clay had saved his life and, with Markham and Aaron, had driven off the Nez Perce raiders. The comte seemed to have taken a liking to him during the time they had traveled together.

What complicated matters was that Clay rather liked La Carde, too. When you were with the man, it was easy to forget that he was a schemer on a grand scale, a man who was ultimately responsible for several murders, possibly including that of Meriwether Lewis, that he was a would-be emperor who threatened the safety and sovereignty of the United States. With his easy smile and quick wit, La Carde was a charmer. Clay had to remind himself frequently of what the man really represented.

Finally La Carde said, "No, I plan to remain in America for a time. I want to visit that Indian village." He nodded toward a cluster of longhouses about a quarter of a mile up the shore from where he and Clay stood. The Indians who lived there were probably Chinook, Clay recalled, a generally peaceful tribe who made their living by fishing in the Pacific.

La Carde was going to try to bring the Chinook in on his plan, Clay speculated. With that accomplished, he could approach the other tribes that lived up and down the coast and bring them into the fold as well. Then he would work his way to the inland tribes: the Shoshone, the Nez Perce, and others. As each tribe was won over, La Carde would arm them with the guns that were likely on the ship, which would impress the other tribes and persuade them to become part of La Carde's new empire. Once he had united all the tribes, he could move against the Americans, perhaps drive the scattered frontiersmen all the way back to the Mississippi River. The western half of the continent would be lost to the United States.

Even as Clay thought about it, he knew it was a far-fetched plan, the kind that only a man of inordinate ambition and ruthlessness would undertake. On the other hand, considering the fragile foothold that the Americans had on the frontier, it was remotely possible La Carde could succeed. The British government, working through the fur companies in Canada, had sought to extend its influence down into the Louisiana Territory; Clay had helped put a stop to that, but only at great cost. Now the French, led by La Carde, were trying to accomplish the same thing: taking away what rightfully belonged to the United States.

Clay wanted to make sure there were guns on the French ship as he expected. Once he had ascertained that, he would have all the proof he needed to make his move against La Carde. He nodded toward the Chinook village and said, "Sure, we can go pay them a visit. Now, if you like."

The group moved out, trooping down the promontory and along the coast with Clay and La Carde in the lead. Following them were Markham and Aaron, the three surviving Frenchmen, and the other Americans. Clay had listened to enough talk around the campfire at night to have concluded that Howell and Pittman had worked for an American fur company. They had allied themselves with La Carde. The other Americans had been hired for the duration of the trip, but they seemed the sort who would be loyal to whoever was paying them. They would probably take La Carde's side in a fight. The only one Clay was unsure of was a tall, brawny young fellow named Esau. He struck Clay as the kind of man who would try to do what was right. Clay decided to have a quiet talk with Esau, before he and Markham and Aaron made their move. Another ally would help even the lopsided odds.

The Indians spotted the party of white men approaching their village and came out to greet them. Their canoes were pulled up on the beach, as evening was not far off. These were not the first whites the Chinook had seen; the Corps of Discovery had visited this same village, Clay recalled. But years had passed since then, and he did not think any of the Indians would remember him.

La Carde looked at Clay. "Do you speak their language?"

"A little." Clay raised an empty hand, palm outward, in the universal sign of peace. One of the Chinook men returned the gesture. "I reckon they're friendly enough."

"Good. Ask them if we can make our camp here with them."

Clay put the question to the Chinook who seemed to be the spokesman for the Indians. He stumbled a little over the words — it had been a long time since he'd spoken their language — but the Chinook seemed to understand him. The man nodded and made a sweeping gesture.

"He says we're welcome to make ourselves at home," Clay told La Carde.

"Excellent," the Frenchman said. "We'll gather some wood and build a fire on the beach. That will be the signal for the ship to come in."

As the others began to set up camp on the broad, sandy beach, Clay caught the eye of Markham and Aaron and strolled off a short distance. The other two followed him, and when Clay judged they were out of easy earshot, he said, "As soon as we know for sure that there are guns on that French ship, we'll move to put a stop to La Carde's little plot."

"Just how do you plan for us to do that?" Markham asked. "In case you haven't noticed, we're a bit outnumbered."

"And the odds will be even worse if La Carde's got those Indians on his side by then," Aaron added.

Clay nodded. "I know. That's why I figure we have to get the Chinook to understand what we're doing."

"How will you do that?" Markham asked.

"I'm the only one who speaks their language," Clay reminded them. "La Carde's relying on me to translate for him. Maybe he won't be saying exactly what he thinks he's saying."

Markham nodded slowly. "That might work. Maybe."

"I'll take maybe for now." Clay turned to

Aaron. "You've talked to that fellow Esau quite a bit. Reckon you could get him to join us, or will he go along with La Carde?"

"I don't know. Let me talk to him."

"Remember, we don't have a lot of time," Clay said. "Once the captain of that ship sees the signal fire, he'll probably send in a smaller boat. We'll most likely have to make our move when it gets here."

Aaron nodded. "All right. I'll go talk to Esau right now."

While they had been conversing, La Carde's men had gathered wood and stacked it on the beach. Now one of them took flint and steel and struck sparks that ignited the small pile of tinder heaped inside the stack of wood. The flames caught and spread, and soon the fire was blazing brightly in the gathering twilight.

Within half an hour a small boat appeared. La Carde and his men gathered on the beach; Clay and Markham joined the group but remained on the edge of it. Clay looked around for Aaron and saw him approaching with Esau beside him.

"Mr. Holt," the young man said quietly as he came up to them, "Aaron's been telling me some things. I swear to you, I didn't know what that Frenchman had in mind."

"I believe you, Esau," Clay said. "Are you with us?"

"Yes, sir, I am."

"What about the others? Do you think any of them would desert La Carde?"

Esau rubbed his chin. "I don't rightly know about that," he said after a moment. "There're a few who might side with us, but not many."

"A few may be all we need," Clay said quietly.

He fell silent and watched with the others as the boat came ashore. A man in a blue coat and a plumed hat stepped onto the sand and saluted La Carde. He spoke in rapid French, but Clay caught the words *"mon empereur."* He assumed the man was the captain of the ship.

Half a dozen sailors had rowed the boat in. They pulled it up on the beach and then unloaded a long wooden crate that seemed to be quite heavy. Clay had a good idea what was inside it.

La Carde turned, spotted Clay, and gestured for him to come over. Clay did so, but not before giving a quiet order to his companions. "Spread out and follow my lead."

Clay strode up to La Carde, and the Frenchman said, "I need you to speak to the Indians again for me."

"All right." Clay glanced at the Chinook. They had been hanging back from the fire, but they were edging closer now, clearly curious about the boat.

"Tell them to gather round," La Carde ordered, and Clay translated.

When several dozen Chinook had congregated around the fire, La Carde ordered one of the sailors to open the crate. The man produced a large knife and proceeded to hack the top of the crate open.

La Carde reached in and pulled out a rifle wrapped in oilcloth. He stripped the cloth away, revealing the smooth, polished stock and the long, gleaming barrel. The rifle was brand-new, Clay noted. La Carde must have stolen it and the other weapons from a military armory in France.

"Tell them we have hundreds of rifles just like this," La Carde said.

Again, Clay translated — accurately — into the Chinook language.

"Tell them we will give them these rifles," La Carde went on, "if they will fight with us against the Americans and their government."

That command, spoken in English, created an instant hubbub of surprise among the American members of La Carde's party. Clay noticed that the other French noblemen, as well as the sailors from the boat, had shifted their positions so that they ringed the Americans.

"Wait just a damned minute," one of the men said to La Carde. "What do you mean by that? You sound as if you're planning to go to war against the United States!"

"That is exactly what I am doing," La Carde said calmly. "And the time has come for you gentlemen to make a choice. Either stand with me and become a part of my new empire, or die here on this beach!"

A babble of curses and questions arose from the Americans. La Carde watched tolerantly for a moment, then lifted a hand for silence. "Come, come, gentlemen," he said. "It is a simple matter. I am the future. I am life. Join with me . . . or face death."

One of the men called out, "I'm with you, La Carde!" The cry was taken up by others. Clay had judged most of the men correctly — loyal to La Carde, Americans or not.

La Carde turned to Clay. "What about you, Monsieur Holt? You know now what I intend. You were not part of our original group, but fate has brought you and your friends to us. Will you truly join us?"

Clay pretended to hesitate for a moment,

then grinned slyly and said, "What was it you wanted me to tell the Chinook?"

La Carde gave him a broad smile. "That we will arm them and train them and mold them into the army of the New French Empire. That together with us they will rule this land!"

Clay looked at the Chinook. They were an unimpressive lot, short, bandy-legged, and not much in the way of fighters.

But every revolution had to start somewhere, and once La Carde had the other tribes on his side, things would look very different. In the split second that he hesitated, a myriad of thoughts went through Clay's mind. He could see a unified army of Shoshone, Sioux, Arapaho, Blackfoot, and Crow warriors pouring out of the west, sweeping across the plains, driving the American settlers back and further back. They would be reinforced by more renegade Frenchmen, shiploads of them, armed with rifles and cannons. The end result would be a war that would rock the frontier from one end to the other and make the rivers run red with blood. Could it really happen?

It could, Clay thought grimly. Unless he stopped it here and now.

"The Frenchman will take these guns,"

Clay said in the Chinook tongue as he pointed at the crate of rifles, "and use them to destroy your people. He wants your land, your village, your boats. He says that if you do not leave right now, he and his men will kill all of you, down to the lowliest babe! This man says that!" He finished by pointing at the smugly smiling Comte Jacques de La Carde.

The smile vanished as the Indians suddenly bristled angrily. They pressed forward. They were unarmed, but they outnumbered the Frenchmen and the Americans who had joined La Carde's cause.

"*Mon Dieu!*" La Carde exclaimed. "What did you tell them, you fool?"

Clay's hands tightened on his rifle. "That you plan to use the guns to wipe them out and take their land."

"Traitor!" La Carde exclaimed. "How . . . how dare you?"

"I'm no traitor," Clay said softly, "not to *my* country. I'm here to stop you, La Carde . . . just as I stopped Maxwell and Ralston."

Hearing the names of his allies, La Carde was thunderstruck. He gaped at Clay. "How . . . who are you?"

"Just an American," Clay said.

Then he ducked to the side as La Carde

let out a howl of rage and struck at him with the rifle he was still holding.

"Now, boys!" Clay yelled.

Markham, Aaron, and Esau struck as one, lashing out at the men standing nearest them. At the same time, Clay flung himself forward and tackled La Carde, driving him off his feet. The brand-new rifle La Carde held slipped out of his hands.

Several of the Chinook also jumped La Carde's men, providing at least a momentary distraction. Markham drove the butt of his rifle into the face of one Frenchman, shattering the man's jaw and knocking him out of the fight. Aaron jabbed the muzzle of his rifle into the belly of another man, causing him to double over, then slamming the rifle stock across his face. Esau, with his long reach, grabbed a man by the neck and held him still for the powerful, looping punch he threw with his other hand. The man went down heavily, out cold.

A rifle blasted, then another, as La Carde's men recovered from their surprise and began to fight back. In a matter of seconds, the beach around the big fire was a battleground. Knives flashed in the firelight, clouds of powder smoke puffed from the barrels of guns, and men fought and died. Markham, Aaron, and Esau found new opponents. Several of the Americans who had been loyal to La Carde only a few moments earlier now threw down their weapons and backed away, holding their hands high in surrender. Some of the Chinook had fallen, but others had overwhelmed the French sailors, choking the life out of them.

Clay had no time to see how the battle was going. He had his hands full with La Carde. The renegade nobleman fought with surprising strength and ferocity, snarling as he tried to get his hands on Clay's throat. He finally succeeded, pinning Clay beneath him on the sand.

Clay was struggling to breathe. His pulse hammered in his head, and a red haze slowly spread over his vision. Desperately, he brought his knee up into La Carde's groin, but the Frenchman shifted in anticipation of the move. Clay's knee struck only La Carde's thigh.

But La Carde's move brought him within reach of Clay's fist, which pounded suddenly against the side of his head. La Carde grunted, and his grip on Clay's neck slipped a little. Clay got a hand on La Carde's shoulder and heaved.

La Carde went flying off to the side.

Clay rolled over onto his belly and gasped for air, then pushed himself onto hands and knees. He glanced around, looking for his rifle, which he had dropped when he tackled La Carde. He couldn't find it, and La Carde was getting to his feet again.

The Frenchman ripped his saber from the scabbard at his waist and lunged at Clay, swinging the blade. Clay jerked upright and slid his hunting knife from its sheath. Sparks flew as steel met steel.

La Carde stepped back, still brandishing the weapon. "Now we settle this!" he shouted at Clay. "Man to man, steel against steel!"

The saber was three times as long as the hunting knife, but Clay grinned wolfishly and lifted the knife. "Come on, you rabid dog!" he urged.

La Carde charged, slashing back and forth with the blade. Clay had to move with blinding speed to parry the strokes. He let La Carde get closer even while he was fending off the saber, then suddenly kicked out at La Carde's legs. The kick connected with La Carde's left knee and threw him off balance. Clay slashed with the knife as the tip of the saber dropped momentarily.

The Frenchman was fast. He ducked

back and caught only the tip of Clay's blade across his cheek. He put his fingers to the wound and glanced in surprise at the crimson that smeared them.

"First blood to you, Monsieur Holt," he said. He raised the saber in a mock salute.

As La Carde spoke, Clay became aware that the chaos that had surrounded them moments earlier had ceased. The fighting on the beach seemed to be over. He glanced around and saw Markham, Aaron, and Esau covering a few of La Carde's men with their rifles. The three were scratched and bruised but seemed all right otherwise. The bodies of a dozen or more men, either dead or unconscious, were scattered around the beach. Chinook men, armed with rifles and pistols they had taken from La Carde's men, stood guard over the rest of the renegades and French sailors, including the captain of the ship.

"Clay!" Markham called to him. "What do you want us to do?"

Clay looked back at La Carde, saw the defiance still etched on the fine, aristocratic features. "You've lost, La Carde," he said. "There's not going to be a French empire in America."

"No!" La Carde spat. "I will never be defeated! I will not rest until France has regained the glory that is rightfully hers!"

Clay had been right all along: charming or not, the man was insane.

"Keep an eye on the others, Lieutenant," Clay told Markham. "I reckon it's time La Carde and I settled this."

"Clay . . . ," Markham began dubiously.

"Do as I said! This is between him and me." Clay started to close in on La Carde, knife at the ready.

La Carde laughed harshly. "You Americans are such fools."

"Maybe . . . but so far we've managed to win. We've known about your scheme for a long time, La Carde. I dealt with Maxwell and Ralston, and now I've tracked you down. It ends here."

"*Oui*," La Carde said. "It ends."

He sprang at Clay, the saber moving almost too quickly to see.

Now there was no sound on the beach except the crackling of the fire, the ring of steel, and the panting of two men fighting for their lives — but for more than their lives, Clay realized. They were fighting for their dreams, and for the dreams of their countrymen.

Suddenly La Carde tried the same tactic Clay had used earlier: He struck with his feet, lashing out with a kick aimed at

Clay's groin. Clay dodged to the side, realizing too late that La Carde's move was only a feint. The saber swept down and struck his right shoulder, glancing off the bone but opening an ugly gash. Clay's arm went numb and the knife slipped from his fingers as blood welled out onto the sleeve of his buckskin shirt. Then the Frenchman came in closer, going for his throat this time.

Clay dropped beneath the sweep of the saber. The blade sliced through the air a bare inch above his head. He bent and plucked the fallen knife from the sand with his left hand, bringing it up as he half lunged, half fell toward La Carde. The Frenchman was out of position and could not defend himself as Clay brought the knife up into his lower belly.

La Carde's mouth and eyes opened wide in horror as Clay ripped upward with the blade. The two men were locked together, leaning on each other, scant inches separating their faces. As Clay felt the hot gush of blood on his hand, he saw the Frenchman's eyes glaze with impending death. But still La Carde was able to gasp, "You . . . American . . ."

"And don't you forget it," Clay grated as he jerked the knife free and stepped back.

La Carde fell at his feet. Clay swayed a little but remained upright.

"Clay! Clay, are you all right?"

Markham had hurried to his side. Clay dropped the knife again, this time deliberately, and wiped the back of his left hand across his mouth. "My shoulder hurts like hell," he said. He started to turn away from La Carde's body but made it only halfway before his knees buckled. He went down, pitching forward on his face and landing in a warm, embracing darkness.

CHAPTER TWENTY-SEVEN

The port city on the Caribbean island was a neutral one, but British and American ships tended to avoid sailing into it at the same time, just to make things simpler for all concerned. War might be inevitable, but no one wanted it to break out here. This was a place for rum, and warm breezes, and warmer women. . . .

Captain Philip Rattigan strolled into the tavern in the early evening after his ship had been loaded with a cargo of sugar and rum. One of the few Englishmen who still traded with the Americans, he would sail back to the Carolinas with it. Truth to tell, Rattigan, a tall, handsome man with a shock of sandy hair, no longer considered himself much of an Englishman. He was a citizen of the world, and his only real concern was any profit he might earn for himself.

Well, most of the time, anyway. Deep down, he supposed, he was not quite as ruthless as he liked to think he was.

Right now he wanted a drink, so he was tempted to ignore the man gesturing to him from a corner of the tavern. But then he sighed and went over to join the man, a fellow sea captain called Atkinson. Atkinson was only an acquaintance, not a friend, but he greeted Rattigan with a big grin.

"Hello, Philip," he said. "How fares it with you?"

"Well," Rattigan said shortly.

Atkinson was sitting in a booth, and someone else was on the opposite bench, slouched back in the shadows so that Rattigan could not see him clearly.

"Join us for a drink," Atkinson invited.

Rattigan was about to decline, but then, for some reason, he shrugged and hooked a chair from a nearby table, dragged it over, and sat down. "All right," he said. "As long as you're buying."

"Oh, you won't mind buying a round or two," Atkinson predicted. "I'm about to do you a great favor, Philip."

"What sort of favor would that be?" Rattigan asked idly.

"You're on your way back to America from here, aren't you?"

"That's right."

"Then I have a passenger for you."

Rattigan shook his head. "I don't carry passengers."

"You might want to think that over," Atkinson said with a chuckle.

Rattigan, never a particularly patient man, stood up to leave.

"Wait," the other person in the booth suddenly said. "I really need your help, Captain Rattigan." The figure leaned forward, and the light from a nearby lantern revealed fine-boned features surrounded by short, tousled dark hair.

A woman, Rattigan realized with a shock. A very beautiful woman. He sat down again.

"I picked her up at sea, believe it or not," Atkinson said. "Down off the coast of Argentina. A castaway, I suppose. She's so closemouthed I haven't been able to get much out of her."

Not as much as he probably wanted, Rattigan would have wagered. The woman's eyes burned with spirit and fire.

"I need to get to America, Captain," she said. "Will you help me?"

Rattigan's heart was pounding, he realized. "Of course," he heard himself saying. "I'm a gentleman. But I'd like to know who it is I'm helping."

"My name," the woman said, "is India St. Clair."

The survivors from the *H.M.S. Cavendish* were at sea for four days in small, open boats following the battle with — and unlikely sinking by — the American merchant vessel. Then they were spotted and picked up by another British warship, the *Whatlington*.

The *Whatlington* was on its way back to England, and it docked in Liverpool some seven weeks after picking up the survivors from the *Cavendish*. During that time the extra men from the destroyed ship had been made good use of, since the *Whatlington*, like most British vessels, had been hit hard by desertion at every port. There was also one prisoner who had been impressed into service, a man who had been pulled unconscious into one of the boats after the battle.

It was that prisoner, a tall, muscular man with thick blond hair and beard, who looked around vacantly as he was led off the ship onto the dock at Liverpool. His wrists were shackled, and he was in the charge of the *Whatlington*'s third mate, who had orders to deliver him to the office of the harbormaster.

"Where are we going?" the prisoner asked. His accent was not British.

"Goin' to put ye on another ship, matey," the third mate replied. "The *Whatlington*'s 'ere for refittin', she is, but that don't matter to you. Ye'll be shippin' out again soon's the 'arbormaster finds another crew for ye."

The prisoner grunted. "Might as well, I suppose."

The third mate looked at him. That attitude alone proved that the man wasn't right in the head. He already bore the scars and bruises of beatings he had received aboard the *Whatlington*, and here he was saying it was just as well he'd be shipping out again. One thing was certain: Life for this man on British ships was going to be pure hell.

The harbormaster looked up as the third mate led the prisoner into his office. "Who's this?" the official asked.

"More fodder for the press gang," the third mate of the *Whatlington* replied. "A deserter."

"Of British birth?" The harbormaster pulled out a ledger.

The third mate shook his head. "Don't know. You can put 'im down as British, though. 'E won't tell you no different."

The harbormaster frowned. "Name?"

The prisoner stared at him blankly.

The third mate laughed. "What'd I tell you, guv'nor? 'E can't tell ye 'is name, nor where 'e's from, nor nothin' about 'imself. 'Is memory's gone, it is!"

"Good Lord!" the harbormaster exclaimed. "Is that true, man?"

The prisoner stared straight ahead and said nothing. For a second he opened his mouth, as if about to speak. There was a name, somewhere far back in the recesses of his brain, a name that might have been his own. But he could not know for sure, and so he said nothing. Then the name slipped away again and was gone.

The harbormaster sighed. "Touched in the head, all right," he said. "But I suppose he'll do for the press gang." He picked up the pen next to the ledger. "I'll just put his name down as John Smith. That'll do as well as any."

"All right, then." The third mate clapped the prisoner on the shoulder. "Good-bye . . . John Smith."

That wasn't right and the prisoner knew it, but he licked his lips and repeated softly, "John. John Smith."

Right or wrong, from now on that was who he would be.

★ ★ ★

The captain of the French vessel was quite cooperative once he realized that La Carde and all the other noblemen had been killed in the fighting on the beach near the Chinook village. He was given a choice by Clay and Markham: dump all the crates of rifles into the ocean and sail away with his crew and his life — or have the ship burned and take his chances with his men here on the edge of the wilderness.

By morning, the rifles were on the bottom of the sea and the ship was sailing away.

Markham had bound up the wound on Clay's shoulder the night before and rigged a sling for his arm. The arm was stiff and sore by the next morning, but Clay had some use of it.

"What do we do now?" Markham asked when the French ship was gone.

Clay glanced at the hut where the surviving Americans who had sided with La Carde were being held prisoner. "I'll talk to the chief of the Chinook and ask him to keep those fellows here until we've had a chance to start back to New Hope. I doubt any of them will cause any more trouble, but I don't want them on our trail. Once we're gone, the Chinook can turn them loose."

"But they're criminals," Markham protested. "They were going to help La Carde."

"But La Carde didn't get very far," Clay pointed out. "Besides, you remember what Thomas Jefferson said when he gave us this job. The government wants this whole mess kept quiet. The last thing they'd want to do is bring those men back and put them on trial."

Markham nodded slowly. "I suppose you're right."

"What about me?" Esau asked.

Aaron spoke up. "I thought you might like to come back to New Hope with us. I've got some traplines I could use a hand with. A couple of free trappers can make a good living in the mountains."

Esau scratched his head in thought, then grinned. "I reckon I'd like that."

Markham looked around at the beach and the ashes of the signal fire and the longhouses of the Chinook village. "It's hard to believe it's over," he said. "We've come so far, done so much, seen so many things."

Clay chuckled. "Maybe you'd like to stay out here on the frontier, too."

"Oh, no," Markham said quickly. "I have to go back to Washington City and deliver our report to Mr. Jefferson. It'll be up to him to decide how much of this ever makes it into the history books."

"It doesn't really matter, does it?" Clay asked. "We know it happened, whether the books ever say it did or not."

"We saved the nation. It might be nice to get credit for it someday."

"We don't know that," Clay said. "La Carde might have failed. It was a pretty risky scheme." He hefted his rifle in his left hand and turned away from the sea. "One way or another, it's over. Let's go home."

Spring had turned to summer, and now summer was waning. It had been a good season, Melissa reflected as she leaned on the counter in her trading post. She was alone at the moment; Terence was out dickering with some trappers over a load of pelts. Their enterprise was flourishing. All summer long the keelboats had come up the river and returned to St. Louis laden with cargoes of furs. Melissa had also received word that the Holt-Merrivale businesses in Wilmington were thriving.

One of these days the business might well stretch all the way across the country, she thought — perhaps even around the world. She wondered how the voyage to China had gone and how Ned and India were faring. She'd had no word about them.

Just as she'd had no word concerning Jeff.

But she thought of him often, missing him with an urgency that was almost painful. No matter what he had done — and she was no longer convinced that he had been unfaithful to her — they should have stayed together. Problems could not be solved, rifts could not be mended, when two people were apart. And she knew that Michael missed his father, too, more so with every day that passed, even though he said little about it. Like many men on the frontier, Whip was becoming laconic.

Whip! she thought with a smile. Now he had her using that name. But regardless of what name he called himself by, he wanted to see Jeff again. Melissa was sure of that.

Which was why there was a letter in Wilmington for Jeff, awaiting his return from Alaska. For all she knew he had already gotten it. In it she asked him to come to New Hope so that they could start over and rebuild their marriage. All she could do now was wait for his answer.

She found herself watching the trail, hoping for the familiar sight of a tall, lean figure striding toward her . . .

A shape bulked in the doorway of the trading post, startling her.

"Howdy, Melissa," a voice said as she straightened, gasping a little. She recognized the voice, but it wasn't the one she longed to hear.

"Pink!" she exclaimed.

Pinkney Casebolt leaned against the side of the door and grinned at her. "Surprised to see me? Told you I'd be back."

"Threatened us, you mean," Melissa snapped. She was not happy to see Casebolt again. She had hoped that he had gone back to St. Louis. Or deeper into the mountains.

"Aw, now, you know I didn't mean nothing by that." Casebolt advanced a step into the trading post. "I was just a mite het up. But I'm over that now. I've got a new business."

"A . . . new business?"

"Yep." Casebolt's face split in a grin. "Me and some friends have decided to go into the fur trading business. Going to open up a trading post. We're going to be competition for you, Melissa. Friendly rivals, I reckon you could say."

Melissa felt a cold ripple of fear. Casebolt was smiling, but she did not believe for a second that his intentions were friendly. He had come back for his revenge on her and Terence, as he had promised, and this was only the first move in his game.

He reached up and tugged on the brim of his hat. "Well, I'd better go. I reckon you'll be seeing a lot of me."

He turned, stepped down off the porch, and vanished.

A few minutes later Terence O'Shay returned and found Melissa standing rigid, clenched fists on the counter. "What's wrong?" he asked immediately.

"Pink Casebolt is back. He's opening a trading post." She laughed humorlessly. "He's our business rival now."

O'Shay cursed. "I'll kill him."

"No!" Melissa said sharply. "We can't do that. He says he bears no grudges toward us."

"You don't believe him, do you?"

"Not at all." Melissa took a deep breath. "Go find Clay," she asked. "We'll talk to him about this."

Clay had been back in New Hope since the middle of the summer. He had returned with Lieutenant Markham, Aaron Garwood, and a young man he'd intro- duced to the settlers as Esau Sloane. His reunion with Shining Moon had been a joyful one, of course, although he was saddened to hear of the increasing friction between the Sioux of Falling Sky's band and the white settlers. Matthew had been on his best behavior since Clay had left New Hope to pursue La Carde. He even seemed to have become friends with Michael, who was teaching him how to use the bullwhip.

Markham had started back east on the first keelboat to head downriver. His farewell had been bittersweet.

"I've learned a great deal from you, Clay," he said as he shook hands with the frontiersman. "And . . . and I've never met a better man."

Clay smiled at him. "You go back to Washington City and tell Thomas Jefferson he doesn't have to worry anymore. The country's safe."

"For now," Markham said. "There are bound to be other challenges, other threats." He paused, then added slyly, "Can I tell Mr. Jefferson that the next time something like this arises, we can count on Clay Holt?"

Clay slapped Markham on the shoulder. "Only if I can handle it without leaving these mountains!"

There was much truth to that. He had no intention of leaving the mountains ever again. He was back where he belonged, with Shining Moon and Matthew and Aaron and Melissa and little Whip. If Jeff had been here, too, things would have been perfect.

Which was one reason he was frowning as he entered the trading post with Terence O'Shay. Something had upset Melissa, and Clay didn't like that. He gave her a curt nod and said, "Who's this fellow Casebolt?"

Melissa explained quickly, and Clay's mind eased a little. "I'm worried that he intends to cause trouble for us," Melissa concluded.

"If he does, he'll regret it," Clay declared. "You're family, and nobody messes with the Holts. You'd think folks would've figured that out by now."

Melissa smiled weakly. "You'd think so," she said. Then she stiffened suddenly and peered past Clay's shoulder toward the open door.

He turned quickly, feeling a twinge in his right shoulder as he did. The saber wound had healed cleanly, but when the weather was right, or when he moved in a certain way, he still felt it.

That was life for you, constantly reminding a fellow of past troubles.

Right now he was worried that Casebolt might have returned already to harass Melissa. If he had, he would be sorry.

Melissa was staring out the door at a man who stood on the porch, but he wasn't Pink Casebolt, Clay realized with a shock. The man was tall, thin to the point of gauntness, and he had a long beard and long, matted hair. But both Clay and Melissa recognized him instantly, and the realization took their breath away.

"Melissa?" the newcomer said, his voice the croak of a man who hadn't used it much lately.

"Oh, my God," she whispered. "Jeff . . . ?"

Then she was flying out from behind the counter and racing across the room and throwing herself into the arms of the man who stood on the porch waiting for her.

"Melissa," Jeff said as he lifted a trembling hand and stroked her hair. "Melissa, I've come home."

"Don't ever leave me again," she said through the tears streaming down her cheeks. She lifted her head, and Jeff's mouth came down on hers with a hunger that neither of them could ever deny.

Clay grinned, then laughed out loud. He didn't know where his little brother had been or what he had been up to, but it looked as if he'd have one hell of a story to tell. And this was a good excuse for a celebration, too: the Holt brothers, together again. As they were supposed to be. If Pink Casebolt or anyone else wanted to cause trouble now, then God help them, because they would have both Clay and Jeff Holt to deal with.

Clay strode forward, hand outstretched, to welcome his brother home.